MAUREEN REYNOLDS

INDIAN SUMMER

BLACK & WHITE PUBLISHING

First published 2012
by Black & White Publishing Ltd
29 Ocean Drive, Edinburgh EH6 6JL

1 3 5 7 9 10 8 6 4 2   12 13 14 15

ISBN   978 1 84502 448 2

Typeset by RefineCatch Limited, Bungay, Suffolk
Printed and bound by MPG Books Ltd, Bodmin

ACKNOWLEDGEMENTS

Special thanks to A.K. Bell Mobile Library for all their help with the tea gardens of India and the Pitlochry Theatre for their help with research about theatre in the 1950s. Also to Jill and Hannah Sangster for their information on the theatre, and to the staff at Black & White Publishing for their help and support over the years. Last but not least, my thanks to my family for all their support and helpful suggestions and for always being there when I need them.

To Milly

PROLOGUE

The path was narrow and rutted with tree roots. He had lost his sandals at some point and his bare feet were cracked and bleeding. The rain was remorseless and sliced through the vegetation and trees like a knife, sending thick green leaves into his path and threatening to trip him up. One sharp branch caught him across his shins and he felt fresh, warm blood running down his legs and oozing between his toes. He thought his chest would explode as his heart thumped painfully with each step, and he wasn't sure if the wetness on his face was the result of the rain or his tears.

He stopped momentarily with his back to the rough bark of a tree. Was that another two gunshots he heard or just the initial two echoing around his befuddled brain?

Galvanised, he shot forward so quickly that he missed his step and rolled headlong down the hillside, catapulting like some acrobat at the circus before landing with a loud splash in the river.

When the cold water covered his head, he prayed for death but his final wish wasn't to be granted. A group of women were washing their clothes at the river and one brave young girl swam out and pulled him to the bank.

Before he passed out, his last memory was the large, dark, concerned eyes of his rescuer and the worried voices of the women as they bathed his wounds.

I

Looking back, Molly realised the year of change began the third week of April with the arrival of the letter and the heavy snowfall. It was Monday morning, and she had spent the weekend at her parents' house in Newport.

Her mother had said when she opened the curtains that morning, 'Oh no, there's been a heavy fall of snow through the night.' Molly went over to look and was dismayed to see a large drift of snow piled up beside the front gate.

'I hope I can get to work all right,' she said. 'It looks like I won't be able to open the gate, never mind get down to the pier to catch the ferry.'

At that moment the back door was opened and Marigold from next door appeared, looking like a refugee from the Himalayas. She was carrying Sabby the cat who looked most displeased to have snow on her coat. Their neighbour stood at the door, stamping the snow from her Wellington boots while Sabby shot into the warm kitchen, shaking large white snowflakes onto the rug.

Marigold looked annoyed. 'I know some bad weather was forecast but not this snowstorm.' The three women stood looking out of the window as the cold wind whipped up the snow into a mini whirlwind.

Molly voiced her concerns again. 'I really have to get into the office as we have a busy schedule today.' She stopped. 'I hope it's not as bad as this in Dundee. Maybe the rest of the staff won't manage to come to work.' She looked worried.

Nancy, her mother, went to put on the kettle for breakfast. 'Well your clients will just have to accept that these things happen and they'll make allowances for it.'

Molly wasn't so sure. McQueen's Agency was almost two years old and her client base was looking very healthy, but Molly knew that things could change very quickly. Then there was Edna's wedding on the following Saturday morning. She hoped this weather wouldn't spoil the day.

Edna, along with Mary, were Molly's first two workers at the agency and she held a special affection for them both. In fact, she was to be a witness at Edna's wedding to John Knox.

As if voicing Molly's thoughts, Marigold said, 'I hope the weather gets better for the weekend. Edna won't want to trudge through wet snow on her wedding day.' She walked to the back door but before she opened it she said, 'Never mind. My grandfather was a farmer and he always called this weather the "Lambing Storm". We sometimes get heavy snow when the lambs are here and it usually doesn't last for long.'

On that cheerful note, she departed back into her own garden and Molly watched with a sinking heart as she plunged almost up to her knees in a white drift.

By now, her father had come downstairs and her mother had bacon, sausages and eggs in the heavy iron frying pan.

'You can make the toast and tea, Molly, while I dish this up.' She turned to her husband. 'Have you seen the snow, Archie?'

He put the newspaper down and nodded. 'Well the paperboy has managed to do his round.'

Molly ate her breakfast quickly as she was anxious to get down to the pier to catch the early sailing. She was finishing her second cup of tea when Nancy said, 'Oh look, the postman is trudging up the path. He looks really fed up.'

Archie just grunted and finished the last slice of toast while Molly hurried upstairs to get her coat and boots. She had to pass the front door and the postman did look disgruntled. His heavy bag had a white coating of snow, as did his hat and jacket.

'What are the roads like?' asked Nancy, taking the small pile of letters from his gloved hand.

'Pretty bad, Mrs McQueen, but I think I'll manage to get through my round.'

Nancy moved back to the warmth of the kitchen, glancing at the letters as she did so. Placing the three brown envelopes which looked like bills onto the table she held the airmail letter in her hand with a small cry of pleasure. 'Archie, it's a letter from Nell in Australia! I wonder what news she has. It doesn't seem that long since we were out seeing her.'

By this time Molly was sitting down to put her wellies on. Although she didn't say anything, it was barely two months since her parents had come back from their visit to Nell, Terry and their daughter Molly, so, yes, it hadn't been a long time.

'Listen to this,' said Nancy, reading aloud from the letter. '*The weather is very hot and things are getting a bit dried up on the farm but rain is expected.*' She looked at Molly. 'I'm glad they're no longer at that sheep farm in the outback and have now moved to another farm nearer civilisation.' Terry had been offered a job as farm manager on a large farm in New South Wales, near the great Murray River and, according to Nancy, they were now living in a better house in a nicer climate.

Molly picked up her bag and was almost at the door when her mother cried out with joy, 'Nell's having another baby in December! She says they are both pleased and so is wee Molly. She says she wants a sister to play with.' Nancy turned to her husband and daughter. 'Isn't that the most wonderful news?'

Molly walked back and gave her mother a hug. 'Yes, it's lovely news. I'll drop Nell a line this week with my congratulations. Now I'll have to run if I'm to catch that ferry.' Before leaving, she noticed the sadness in Nancy's eyes and she suddenly felt so sorry for her parents, living so far away from their grandchildren.

Outside, the wind whipped up the snow as she made her way down the road to the pier, taking her time as the pavement was slippery with hard packed snow. She made it to the pier just in time, as the ferry was waiting to make its crossing. She decided to sit in the salon, away from the wind and the flurry of snowflakes. The river was choppy and the colour of steel. Everything looked bleak in this colourless world of black, white and grey. The passengers were even less colourful in their thick woollen coats and dark knitted hats and gloves with their faces pinched and white on this cold morning. Some of them stamped their feet in an effort to get warm, but it was a futile exercise as the wind rose from the water and eddied around the deserted decks.

Sitting in the salon with her hands tucked into her coat pockets, Molly experienced another yearning for the warmth and sunshine of Australia. The feeling was so strong that it was almost an ache in the pit of her stomach, and she had felt like this since her parents had arrived back from their holiday in February. Even though she longed to see her sister again, Molly knew her life and work was here in Dundee but she was thrilled by the news of another baby.

She tried looking out of the window but it was all misted up with condensation and it wasn't until she was almost to Dundee when she saw the landscape was as white and snowy as Newport. Still, by the time she reached Union Street she found the pavements were covered in a dirty grey slush. She was glad she had put on her Wellington boots, as deep pools of sluggish water lay in wait for the unwary or the feet of anyone unsuitably shod.

When she reached the Wellgate, Jean had already opened up the agency and she was pleased to see Edna and Mary collecting their assignments for the day. Edna was going to work until the Thursday and, much to Molly's delight, was planning on returning after her short honeymoon.

Jean was handing out the work sheets. 'Albert's Stores has asked for you again, Edna. His niece Nancy has another dose of Asian flu, and Mary, you have a job with Nicolls & Nicolls, a solicitor's office in Commercial Street. Two of the office typists are off ill and won't be back till next week.'

Molly had just a minute to say good morning to everyone before heading upstairs to hang up her coat. When she reappeared, Alice, Maisie and Deanna were receiving their job sheets for the day. Maisie and Deanna were going to their regular clients, Mrs Jankowski in Constitution Road and Professor Lyon in Windsor Street, while Alice had a job in Victoria Road.

As she watched the three women depart for their cleaning jobs she felt a glow of pride in her workforce and her agency. Turning the business into a secretarial and domestic agency last year had paid off handsomely and Molly was more than pleased with the way things were turning out.

Molly had a heavy schedule ahead as she was holding down a very demanding post in the wages department of the Dundee Council office. She had been working there the previous week and she expected it to be another week before the regular clerkess recovered from her badly twisted ankle – the result of a slip on an icy pavement. Although she was sorry about these accidents and illnesses of the various workers, she was grateful for the temporary work that came to her agency. Another bonus was the great demand for the domestic side of the business and she reckoned she would have to hire another woman soon.

Edna's forthcoming wedding was on her mind and she hoped all would go well on the day. Then the spectre of Nell's letter intruded on the happy wedding thoughts and she suddenly felt her world could quite easily crumble away.

As she walked along the Murraygate towards the council office, she gave herself a mental talking to. 'That's nonsense,' she mouthed silently. How could Nell's news make any difference to her hard-won business independence?

Feeling better, she quickened her steps, walking as best she could because the slush had melted into large pools of brown muddy water and she was careful not to step into them and soak her shoes or worse still, get huge dirty splashes on her nylon-clad legs. Professional secretaries didn't arrive at work looking like they had come straight from a walk along a rain-soaked country lane.

Before entering the council building, she inspected her legs and smoothed down her dark woollen coat, which covered her crisp blue blouse and grey pencil-line skirt. As everything looked fine, she put her worried thoughts out of her mind and pushed open the door.

2

Edna was glad to be back at Albert's Stores. She was almost a permanent worker by now as Albert's niece, Nancy, who worked in the office, was one of the world's worst hypochondriacs. As he often said, he would have sacked her ages ago but she was family and he didn't want to cause trouble.

He greeted her with one of his biggest smiles. 'Won't be long now till the wedding, Edna. Is everything going smoothly?'

'Yes, Albert, and we hope to see you both at the reception.'

'Oh the missus is looking forward to it, and she's bought a new dress.'

Edna smiled and put on her white overall.

A few minutes later, her friend Dolly Pirie came in, along with Mrs Little, or 'Snappy Sal' as she was better known in the shop.

'I thought you would be in today, Edna,' said Dolly. 'We've had two days last week with Nancy groaning like a strangled cat about her Asian "flu".' She turned to her neighbour, Sal. 'Isn't that right, Mrs Little?'

Edna was amused that Dolly always referred to her friend as 'Mrs', at least when she was in the shop.

'She was a right pain in the neck last week, coughing and moaning how she was dying. She could have won one of them Hollywood Oscars that we always see at the pictures,' said Sal, little realising how much she moaned in the shop.

She went up to the counter. 'Albert, that jam I bought last month tasted a wee bit mouldy. I was thinking about bringing it back but Dolly said there was nothing wrong with it, but I don't believe it.'

Albert rolled his eyes in annoyance. 'Well, Mrs Little, nobody else has complained and it was Robertson's Jam and they only make the very best.'

Mrs Little wasn't going to let him have the last word. 'Well I should have brought it back but I've finished it now, so I can't.'

Albert turned to serve another customer while Mrs Little mooched around the shop, no doubt looking for some more mouldy jam or cheese or something else to complain about.

Dolly said, 'I've got a pot of soup on the stove if you want to come up at lunchtime, Edna.'

Edna said she would and Dolly said, 'Thanks for the invite to your wedding reception and Mrs Little is over the moon that she's been invited as well. It was very good of you to think about us.'

'Well I wanted you to be there on my big day, Dolly, and I thought maybe Mrs Little might want to come. John and I will be so pleased to see you as you've been a great friend to me. If it hadn't been for you last year then there might not have been a wedding, so thanks for everything.'

'Will Eddie be there?'

'Yes and he's bringing his fiancée. He's another person I have to thank very much as you know he saved my life.'

Dolly nodded. She remembered that horrible time in Edna's life a couple of years ago when Edna's late husband's pal had threatened to kill her. But that was all over now and Edna now looked forward to a happy married life with John Knox, who had been her very first client at the agency.

Meanwhile, Deanna Dunn was with her favourite client, Professor Lyon. He had a pot of coffee waiting as she went through the front door, and some good news.

'Sit down, sit down,' he said as he poured out two cups of coffee.

Although she was an actress, Deanna was there to clean his house but as usual he helped her and there was never much work to do. To start with, the house had been really untidy but because she went there twice a week it was soon looking bright and clean.

'Now, Deanna, I have some good news for you. I have this friend who works at Pitlochry Theatre, which was the brain-child of an old colleague of mine, John Stewart. Have you heard of it?'

'Oh yes I have,' she said. 'It's called "the theatre in the hills" and it's been up and running now for about four years.'

He nodded. 'Yes, it has. It opened in 1951 in a tent in a garden and it's gone from strength to strength. Well, to cut a long story short, one of the young actresses for this year's productions has had to drop out and they're looking for a replacement. I hope you don't mind but I suggested you could be a replacement. It will mean a summer season in Pitlochry where you will stay, and the theatre puts on six plays every week, from the seventh of May until the first of October.'

Deanna almost dropped her cup in surprise. 'Will he take me on do you think, Professor Lyon?'

'Well you will have to do an audition, but I took the liberty of setting a date on Saturday morning and he is looking forward to meeting you. Can you manage to go?'

Deanna suddenly remembered that was Edna's wedding day, but all of the agency staff were going to the evening reception at Mathers Hotel so she would be back in time to be there.

She was so excited, until she remembered she would have to tell Molly. It would mean leaving the agency for the entire summer and she wasn't sure how Molly could cope with one less pair of hands. But this was too big an opportunity to miss and she nodded. 'That's fine. I'll go to Pitlochry on Saturday and hope I'm accepted.'

Professor Lyon beamed at his favourite domestic help. Well that wasn't quite true, because she was his first and only home help. 'You can catch the train at Dundee for Perth and then another train will stop at Pitlochry,' he said, pouring out another two cups of coffee.

At lunchtime when Deanna left Windsor Street to go to her afternoon assignment, she felt she was walking on air. An entire summer season in a theatre was something she had always dreamed of doing and it now looked as if it would happen. Provided, of course, that she passed the audition. Again she wondered what Molly's reaction would be, but then, full of confidence in her acting abilities, she gave in to the sheer pleasure of the future.

At five-thirty she was back at the agency. She saw that most of the staff were there but Molly was missing. For a moment her well rehearsed speech failed her and she knew she couldn't wait until the morning before passing on her good news. Then, with a feeling of relief, she saw Molly heading up the Wellgate and she hurried down to meet her.

Molly was taken by surprise, but before she could speak Deanna blurted out, 'I've got some wonderful news.' She paused. 'Well, it's wonderful for me but I'm not sure how you will take it, Molly. Professor Lyon has managed to get me an audition at the theatre in Pitlochry for a chance to perform with them for the whole of the summer.'

Molly, who had had a very busy day, seemed speechless.

Deanna said excitedly, 'I know it's bad news for you and the agency but it's a dream come true for me.'

Getting over the surprise, Molly asked, 'When will you be leaving?'

Deanna told her but then added, 'Of course I may not pass the audition on Saturday morning but I hope I do.'

'Is it this Saturday morning?'

Deanna nodded.

'Well I do hope you do get it, Deanna. It will mean I'll have to try and work around the schedules, but you have your future to think of. Now come into the office and we'll pass on your good news.'

'Oh, thank you! Thank you so much, Molly. You're such a good boss and I really appreciate your understanding.'

They both went into the office and everyone turned around.

'Deanna has got some great news,' said Molly.

With her face alight, Deanna told them of the wonderful opportunity that had been handed to her. She looked at Edna.

'I'll still manage to come to the reception on Saturday evening, Edna.'

Maisie, Alice, Mary and Edna then congratulated her and said they hoped the audition would go well, while Jean gave Molly a questioning look.

Then it was time for everyone to go home. Jean said. 'How will you manage with one member less if Deanna leaves? We have a heavy workload in the next few weeks.'

Molly shook her head. 'Oh something will turn up. It always does.' But when she went upstairs to the flat she sat down on the sofa, her mind in a whirl.

It did go through her mind that maybe Deanna wouldn't pass the audition but in her heart she hoped she would. For a brief moment she felt as if everything she had worked for was slipping away then she pulled herself together. That was just self-pity and she didn't want to fall into that trap. Of course she would find a replacement and she made up her mind to advertise the next day. And if Deanna's dream did fall apart then she still needed another domestic worker. In fact, she also needed someone else for the secretarial side and she made up her mind to make that two adverts.

3

After the snow and wintry weather of the previous few days, Saturday dawned cold but dry. The weather forecast said the sun would come out later in the day, and it did, just before Edna and John's wedding at 11.30.

Molly and Edna had spent most of the morning at the hairdresser and they were now sitting having a cup of tea before getting dressed.

Irene and Billy were already dressed for the big occasion and Molly couldn't help noticing how big Billy was. He obviously took his height from his late father, Will, because his mother was barely five feet, although she gained a few inches with her high-heeled shoes.

Molly had put the advert in for more staff and she had received a letter from Maggie Flynn, a girl she had met the previous year. Young Maggie was leaving school in June and was looking for a job on the secretarial side, which was good, though so far no one had been interested in the domestic cleaning position. Still Molly was determined not to allow her worries to overshadow Edna's wedding day.

As it was to be a small ceremony at the registrar's office, Edna had chosen a lovely blue dress and jacket while Molly had bought a lavender jersey wool suit with a white-and-lavender-checked collar. As they both sat in the bedroom at Paradise Road, Edna was so nervous.

'It won't be long now till you're Mrs Knox,' said Molly. 'John is a great man.'

'I know. I'm lucky I met him and he's so good with Billy. Almost like a father to him.'

Irene popped her head around the door. 'The taxi will be here in twenty minutes.'

'We're almost ready, Mum, just got to put on our hats and our flower buttonholes.'

Edna placed a pale blue hat on her head and pinned a corsage of carnations on her lapel. Molly's hat was pale lilac but her flowers were identical.

Fifteen minutes later, Irene's next-door neighbour knocked at the door. 'Just wanted to wish you all the best, Edna,' she said. 'And we'll see you tonight at the reception.'

Then Irene hurried in again. 'That's the taxi at the foot of the close, Edna.'

Edna took one last look around the familiar bedroom. 'Well there's no backing out now, is there?' but she was laughing when she said it.

All the neighbours from the close, plus a few from the other houses in the street, were standing on the pavement as Billy, followed by his mother, grandmother and Molly, got into the car. Billy was fascinated with all the onlookers and he waved at them while most of the women smiled and waved back.

By the time the taxi reached the City Square the sun had come out. Inside the registrar's John was waiting along with his brother James. Sonia, John's sister-in-law, was also there and she gave Edna an insincere smile while mentally looking her up and down. Almost as if she had arrived in sackcloth and ashes.

John was looking handsome in his dark blue suit while James, forever the artist, was more casually dressed in a cream linen jacket and trousers, but it was Sonia who almost stole the show. She had a fabulous fur coat casually slung over her shoulders. Under this was a silver-grey dress with a sparkling necklace and a gorgeous diamond ring, which Edna knew had originally belonged to her sister Kathleen, John's late wife. Molly was annoyed at her for trying to upstage Edna but when she saw the look that John gave his future wife, Sonia's tricks counted for nothing.

Molly found the wedding service moving and she felt tears at the back of her eyes when she thought of Tom, who had been very dear friend from her days in Australia until he was killed in a road accident. In fact, this accident had led to Molly coming home and starting her agency.

Then the service was over and Edna and John emerged into the sunshine as man and wife. Molly had bought some confetti and Billy showered it over his mum and his new stepfather.

Because it was a simple wedding, the couple had opted for a family meal in the Mathers Hotel in Whitehall Street, where a larger reception was planned for the evening, with fifty or sixty guests having been invited. The hotel had given them a lovely private room that overlooked the river and when the meal was served, Molly was surprised to discover how hungry she was. She had a small sherry and planned to have no more because she always felt sleepy after a couple of drinks. She knew it would be a long day and she would have to be on her feet for most of it.

When the meal was over, James stood up and made a great speech about what the brothers had got up to in their younger days.

John laughed and said to Edna, 'Don't believe all he said.'

James said, 'That's right, Edna. I'm talking about when we were boys and all the apples we pinched from our neighbours' trees.'

While Billy was wide-eyed at all these naughty revelations, Sonia had latched onto Irene. 'When John was married to my sister he was never at home. Always working abroad at his engineering projects. No wonder she was lonely.'

Irene was furious but she didn't want to show it. Instead she said, 'I've got to go and see to Billy.' And she hurried off.

Molly had overheard Sonia and she followed Irene. Edna's mum was in the cloakroom and she was dabbing her eyes with a small handkerchief. 'Don't let that awful woman annoy you, Irene. Look at the mischief she tried to do last year, but it's all backfired on her. She's really pathetic.'

'I know, Molly, but I do hope Edna will be happy. She lost her first husband in that bombing outrage in Palestine when Billy was a baby and then she had that terrible time two years ago with his pal Reg.'

Molly said she was sure it was going to be a happy marriage. 'John told Edna about his job when he was married to Kathleen and that he always regretted working away from home so much, but now he is keen to be a fiction writer after the success of his two engineering books. Just think what a great team they will be, and he adores Billy.'

Irene gave a huge sigh. 'I know. John has asked me to go and live with them, but I want to keep my own place, though I'll miss Billy. I've looked after him since he was a baby and he's been a big part of my life. I suddenly feel redundant.'

Molly understood Irene's feelings. Irene had been the most important person in both their lives, but now she wasn't. 'You'll still be a big influence on them, Irene, but you'll have your own life to live now.'

Irene smiled. 'You've been a great help to us, Molly, and Edna looks on you as her best friend.' She took a comb from her small bag and tried to tame the mass of curls. 'What about you? Are you still seeing Charlie?'

Now it was time for Molly to give a big sigh. 'Yes, we go out to the pictures and sometimes for a meal, but his job is very important to him. He's on shifts this week and will be working tonight but he said he'll try and get here for an hour or two after he finishes.'

Molly had met DS Charlie Johns when she opened her agency in 1953 and then last year when she had been involved with the missing girl, Etta. That had been when Charlie and she had become friendly but things were pretty much the same. They were still friends but nothing more. Molly realised it was her fault because she was ambitious and wanted to make her agency a success, but she often wondered if that was the true reason and not because she was frightened of having a relationship. Frightened of becoming too close to anybody in case they also died. When she had met Kenneth in 1953 there had been an attraction but he died, just as Tom had. She felt like some sort of jinx.

Irene smoothed the skirt of her floral patterned dress and said, 'We better get back into the company before Sonia hogs the whole show.'

Now that the meal was over, the wedding party had moved into the lovely comfortable lounge. Sonia had put her fur coat over the back of a chair as she sat beside James, John and Edna. When Irene and Molly appeared, Edna called them over and made room for them beside her and her new husband.

Irene said, 'When your guests arrive I'll wait an hour or so then I'll take Billy home and put him to bed. You can pick him up tomorrow.' She knew the couple weren't planning on going away as they had decided to have a family holiday later in the summer.

John smiled. 'That will be great, Irene, but make sure you stay for a couple of dances before you leave.'

Irene laughed. 'Oh my dancing days are over, John.'

John said, 'Oh I bet you are a wonderful dancer, Irene. What do you think, Molly?'

She looked at Irene's trim figure and her face that, in spite of a few lines around her eyes, was still attractive, and agreed with him.

As Irene went to fetch Billy, Molly moved over to speak to James. After his hilarious speech he had become quiet. She thought he looked morose but then so would any man who was lumbered with Sonia. 'Are you still painting, James?' she asked him.

His face lit up. 'Yes, I'm hoping to have another exhibition of my paintings this summer. They are selling well.'

'That's probably because you sell them too cheap, James,' said Sonia, suddenly butting in. 'I've told you time and again to raise your prices to Edinburgh's standards but you prefer to sell them to the people who don't know a painting from a photograph.'

James said nothing but he looked angry. Molly felt sorry for him, as she had seen his paintings and he was very talented. However he knew people who came to his small studio in Arbroath couldn't pay the same high prices as people in the big cities and he was grateful to make a good living from his work, but obviously not enough for Sonia. Molly was furious at her and she wished the woman had stayed in Edinburgh where she lived before landing at John's door last year when she was almost penniless.

Molly suddenly felt so tired. The waitress arrived with tea and coffee and small pieces of the wedding cake and she took a cup of tea from the woman. Maybe that would revive her. She wondered how Deanna was getting on with her audition then she firmly put this thought from her mind. In a short time the guests would be arriving for the evening and she had to be alert and sociable. The truth was she hadn't been sleeping very well this week but she knew she would have tomorrow off to relax.

At seven o'clock the first guests started to arrive. First to appear were Mrs Little and Dolly. Edna and John had organised a taxi for the two women and they seemed overawed with the splendour of the hotel, especially Mrs Little, who confessed that she had never been inside a hotel in her life. Dolly said she had, though. 'I got married in a wee hotel years and years ago but it was nothing as grand as this.'

Then Albert and his wife Mabel appeared. Edna was amused to see Albert in a black pinstriped suit with a white starched shirt, while Mabel had opted for comfort with a plain navy dress and sensible-looking navy shoes.

Molly and James stood beside the newlyweds to greet the guests and by quarter-past seven they began to arrive in large groups. Jean and her husband Bob, Mary and Stan and Alice, Sandy and Maisie.

When Eddie appeared with his fiancée Margaret, Edna gave him a hug while John shook his hand, both of them sincere with their thanks that the couple had managed to come to the reception.

Edna asked Margaret, 'Have you set the date for your own wedding?'

Margaret blushed and said nothing was settled yet but hopefully later in the year.

'I've a lot to thank Eddie for,' Edna told the girl. 'He saved my life two years ago.' It was now Eddie's turn to blush and his face went as red as his hair and Margaret laughed.

'He mentioned something but not the whole story.'

'Well you get him to tell you what happened,' said Edna. 'He's a real hero.'

A buffet was laid out and John announced that the guests should eat and drink and be merry, which brought a laugh from everyone.

Molly went over to see her colleagues. Mary was looking lovely in a white dress with blue polka dots, while Stan stood with his arm around her waist. Molly liked Stan and she was sure he would always be there for Mary.

'Have you heard how Deanna got on?' Mary asked.

Molly shook her head. 'She said she would come here later so we'll find out then.'

Molly was amused to see Billy doing the rounds with his grandmother. Billy was shaking hands with people and thanking them for coming.

'What a well-mannered boy,' said one woman, a comment that was overheard by John, who beamed with pride at his new step-son while Molly almost burst into tears at the joy and love in the air.

Alice and Sandy came over to talk and Molly couldn't get over the change in Alice. She remembered the plain-looking woman who had come to the agency last year. Married to a brute and a bully, she had at last managed to get her divorce and although she would never be a beauty, she had managed to make herself attractive and her plum-patterned dress was set off with a new sleek hairdo. Obviously Sandy had a lot to do with this trans-formation, and it looked as if Alice had found true happiness at last.

A feeling of desolation swept over Molly. Apart from Maisie, she was the only single woman in the company of couples. Even Dolly and Mrs Little had been married before, though they were now widowed. She wondered if Charlie would manage to appear, then once again she put the thought firmly to one side.

By now the three-piece band had arrived and they shuffled in with their musical instruments. There was a piano on the small stage for one, another musician carried his accordion while the third manoeuvred a small drum kit to the back of the stage. When the band started, Molly was whisked onto the floor and at the end of the dance she was hot and flushed but had thoroughly enjoyed herself. She went and sat beside Dolly and Mrs Little. Both women had small glasses of sherry and Sal was thrilled by the whole evening.

'What a good meal we had, didn't we Dolly, and now our sherries. Edna has also ordered another taxi to take us back home afterwards. What a lovely woman she is.'

Dolly was dumfounded by this praise from her friend. She later confided to Molly that she had never heard her say a good word about anyone until now. Then, to make Mrs Little's night complete, John came over and asked her for a dance. Albert then asked Dolly and the two women were waltzing like they were on *Come Dancing*. They arrived back at the table with shining eyes.

'Dolly, do you mind how much we loved the dancing in our young days?' asked Mrs Little.

Dolly said she did.

'I met my man at the dancing and we used to go every week to the Locarno ballroom. In those days I could dance all night but now one dance is enough.' Mrs Little said. A few moments later, however, she confessed, 'Oh, I think I could maybe have another go,' which was just as well because Albert appeared at her side.

'Fancy a trip around the dance floor?' he said.

Before anyone could blink, Mrs Little was up on her feet and on the floor. It was a foxtrot and it was clear she was a good dancer.

'Oh aye,' said Dolly. 'She was always light on her feet.' She laughed. 'What a pity she's such a complaining grump.'

Halfway through the evening, the hotel staff announced that there was still loads of food on the buffet and the band would be taking a break so that the guests could have tea or coffee along with what was left.

Mrs Little appeared with a plate heaped up and sat down with a sigh.

Dolly said, 'Are you stoking up for the whole of next week?'

'No I'm not. It's just that I'm having such a great time and I'll never get another chance like this again and neither will you, Dolly.'

A waitress appeared at the table and placed a teapot with three cups and saucers, sugar and milk.

Mrs Little beamed at the girl. 'Oh, thank you very much. It's just what I need after all my dancing.'

Dolly laughed but Molly suddenly felt sorry for the woman. No doubt her life revolved around her little world in Arbroath Road and her only bit of pleasure was her daily moan in Albert's Shop.

Then Molly saw James heading towards her and she thought she hadn't seen Sonia for some time. James had a glass of whisky in his hand.

'Is Sonia all right?' asked Molly.

James frowned into his glass. 'No, she's gone home. She took the car because she didn't have anything to drink and I've booked a room in the hotel. I'll get the train back to Arbroath tomorrow.'

Molly didn't say anything but she thought he was too good for Sonia. Poor James.

By now it was after ten o'clock and Irene and Billy were on the verge of leaving. Edna and John were saying cheerio to them.

'We'll see you tomorrow, Billy,' his mother said and they both went to the front door to see them into the taxi.

The same taxi was coming back for Dolly and Mrs Little and the evening would soon be over. It looked as if Charlie wasn't going to make it, but Molly hadn't really expected him to. There had been a series of robberies from large empty houses where the owners had been away either on holiday or on business, which meant extra work for the police officers on the case, and Charlie in particular.

Edna came over and spoke to Molly. 'Have you heard about the row between James and Sonia?'

Edna looked distraught. 'She's cleared off and left him.'

'Yes I know. James told me.'

'I wish she would just go away back to Edinburgh and leave us all alone,' said Edna, who looked as if she was on the verge of tears.

She then went to say goodbye to some of the guests who were leaving. There were still a lot of people on the dance floor and she had to skirt the fringes of the floor to see Albert and his wife, plus Dolly and Mrs Little.

Dolly gave her a hug while Mrs Little said what a wonderful night it had been. 'I haven't enjoyed myself like this in a long time,' she said. 'Thank you for inviting me, Edna.'

Edna, John, Molly and James stood at the front door of the hotel, waving as the guests departed. A cold wind blew in from the street then they turned and went back to the warmth and the dance.

4

Deanna couldn't sleep on the Friday night and by six the next morning she was sitting with a cup of tea. She had laid out three outfits on the bed, unsure what to wear to her big opportunity, while her mother fussed around saying she had to eat something substantial before she set off. Deanna's stomach was turning cartwheels at the thought of a cooked breakfast, but to please her mother she had a tiny bowl of cornflakes and a banana.

Back in her bedroom she tried on all the outfits then decided to reject them all and try something else from her wardrobe. She wondered about the theatre director. Was he young or old, or maybe middle-aged? She didn't want to appear too young but on the other hand she wanted to look like she had loads of theatre experience.

Her father appeared at the door. 'I think you should just be yourself, Deanna. Wear something that makes you feel good and then be natural. I'm sure you'll give a good impression as you always do.'

Deanna went over to give her dad a big hug. As usual, he was right with his fatherly advice and during her life he had never been wrong.

There was a tantalising smell wafting from the kitchen. 'That's the bacon and eggs cooked,' he said. He walked away and left his daughter alone with her choice of garments.

Deanna made up her mind. Because it was still quite cold outside she decided to wear her russet-and-gold-checked woollen dress with the brown-velvet collar and a short brown jacket. When she appeared in the kitchen her father nodded in an approving way. 'That's a great choice, Deanna. You'll knock that director off his feet.'

Her mother said, 'Well she might be knocked off her feet with hunger by then.' She turned to her husband. 'She won't eat anything cooked and it will be a long day.'

'Nonsense,' he said. 'I'm sure there's lots of cafés between here and Pitlochry. She can easily stop for a snack after the audition.' He gave his daughter a big wink and she laughed.

By ten o'clock she was standing on the platform at the railway station. The train for Perth was due at twenty past ten and she would catch a connection to Pitlochry at half-past eleven. She was due at the theatre at one o'clock so there was ample time to get there.

During the long wakeful hours last night she had the terrible thought that she would be late and miss the audition. Perhaps the trains would break down or worse, not run due to some catastrophe. But standing on the platform she had the comforting sight of other trains chugging into the station and belching huge amounts of steam into the vaulted roof.

Then at quarter-past ten she was relieved to see her train pull in and stop with a loud series of metallic noises. She managed to get a window seat and the carriage soon filled up with three women and two men. There was a great deal of stowing small suitcases away on the overhead luggage rack and as the train steamed out of the station, the two men opened their newspapers while the women, who seemed to be together, chattered most of the way to Perth.

Deanna soon deduced that they all worked in the same office and were going away for a short holiday as one of them, a woman called Miriam, explained. 'Although the cottage is on its own, it's still near to the town but there's lots of hills to climb and some lovely walks.'

'Oh Miriam, what a lovely place to stay. Your mum and dad are lucky to live away from the busy town,' said one of Miriam's companions.

Deanna was quite pleased to listen to this animated conversation as it took her mind away from the audition and very soon the train was pulling into Perth and they all disembarked. The two men made their way out of the station but Deanna was surprised when the three women stood beside her on the Inverness platform.

How strange it would be if they were all going to Pitlochry, she thought. When the train arrived the women headed for another carriage and Deanna found an empty compartment and spent the next thirty minutes looking at the scenery.

That was why she was surprised to find the women alighting along with her upon its arrival in Pitlochry. A man was waiting on the platform and Miriam ran forward. 'Hullo, Dad, thanks for picking us up.' They all went towards a black, battered station wagon and the suitcases were stowed into the boot as they all squeezed in the car. It set off with a belch of black smoke, no doubt on its way to the cottage in the country.

Deanna realised she was smiling and that she hadn't given much thought to the afternoon ahead as she set off for the main street. She had never been to this town before but was suitably impressed by its lovely shops, houses and what seemed like lots of hotels and guest houses.

There was a small café attached to a baker's shop and she went in and sat at a table by the window where she could see all the activity on the street. After a cheese roll and a pot of tea she had a wander around the shops then went to find the theatre. Professor Lyon was right when he said it was no longer situated in a tent. The theatre was now a proper building with a lovely bow-window frontage with the name 'Festival Theatre' above it. As she stood gazing at it, she felt nervous and her stomach was churning. She wished she hadn't had the cheese roll but of course it was too late now for regrets. She glanced at her wristlet watch. There was half an hour to wait so she made her way down the hill and sat on a bench beside an imposing-looking church, trying to compose herself.

At five minutes to two she set off back to the theatre with her head held high but her legs feeling quite wobbly with nerves. She made her way through the reception and a woman at the box office directed her to a small room where Mr John Stewart was waiting for her. He introduced himself and made her very welcome, so much so that some of her initial nervousness went.

He explained the reason for the audition. 'One of the young actresses has broken her leg and we need a replacement. She wasn't one of the main stars, but if you get the job you will have a part in all the six plays, which can be very demanding. How do you feel about that, Miss Dunn?'

Deanna took a deep breath before answering, as she didn't want her voice to sound weak and breathless, 'Yes I can do that, Mr Stewart.'

He said, 'I see you know Professor Lyon and he gives you a good reference.'

Deanna said she did know him and she was grateful to him for getting this wonderful chance.

John Stewart continued, 'The summer season lasts from May seventh until October first and the six plays this year are *Dandy Dick*, *Lady from Edinburgh*, *A Hundred Years Old*, *The Dashing White Sergeant*, *Arms and the Man* and *The Lass Wi' the Muckle Mou'*.

He then asked Deanna to walk across the room and read passages from a couple of the plays. Once she had done that, he stood up. 'I'll show you around the theatre,' he said.

Deanna followed him out and she was entranced by everything. It wasn't a huge auditorium but she could well imagine herself on the stage.

Then they went back to the room and he excused himself. 'I'll just be a moment, Miss Dunn. Would you like a cup of tea or coffee?'

Deanna said no because she doubted she would be able to swallow it as her mouth was so dry.

Within a few minutes he was back with a dark-haired, handsome man. 'This is Mr Maxwell Jackson, who will be directing the plays.'

Deanna stood and shook his hand.

Mr Jackson said, 'You don't have very long to study the parts, Deanna, before we open for the season. Do you think you can learn your lines by then?'

Suddenly Deanna felt really bold. She looked straight at him and said, 'Yes I can, Mr Jackson.'

Then the two men left. Deanna was so wound up that she was certain she had failed but John Stewart came back in and said, 'We've decided to give you a trial, Deanna. If you can move to Pitlochry next week we can find you lodgings in the town and you can read the parts and walk through them.'

For one brief moment Deanna thought she would burst into tears but that wouldn't have been very professional. Instead she said, 'Thank you very much, Mr Stewart. I'll do my very best!'

The main street was busier when Deanna left the theatre and made her way back to the railway station. She looked at her watch. It was four o'clock and she knew the next train left at five-thirty. Now that the ordeal was over she suddenly felt hungry. Walking down Station Road she noticed a sign for the Tower Restaurant. It advertised high teas and she decided to treat herself to a meal.

The restaurant was quiet, with only two tables occupied by two elderly-looking couples. A young waitress, who looked like she was still at school, appeared and Deanna ordered the cold ham salad with bread and butter, and tea.

While she was waiting, a large St Bernard dog ambled into the room and the two couples made a big fuss over it. One of the women gave it a leftover crust of bread which it wolfed down before plumping down on the carpet and promptly nodding off to sleep. When the girl appeared with Deanna's meal she spoke to the dog and made it go back into the inner sanctum that was obviously where its owners lived.

The girl apologised. 'It always comes out to see who is in.' She placed an appetising plate of ham on the table. 'Are you on holiday, Miss?'

Deanna shook her head. 'I've just had an audition at the theatre and I start on Monday.'

The girl looked overawed. 'I've never met an actress before. Are you famous and on television?'

Deanna said no but she still felt thrilled by the girl's reaction and she made up her mind there and then that one day she would be able to say yes to both questions.

When she was pouring out her tea she saw a woman's face peering at her from the kitchen door. The waitress came out with the milk jug and explained, 'I told the cook about you working in the theatre and she wanted to see you.'

Deanna smiled and thanked her for all the kind words, and after her meal she left a shilling as a tip.

She enjoyed the journey back because she was able to relax and when she reached home her parents were delighted by her news, although her mother was a bit worried by the fact she would be living away from home for the entire summer.

'I hope your accommodation is well run, Deanna, and Dad and I will come to see you often just to make sure. Another thing, how will you manage to wash your clothes?'

Her dad said, 'Oh stop fussing, Evie. Deanna will manage to look after herself. The theatre is hardly likely to accommodate their actors in a hovel, now is it?' But Evie wasn't listening.

'I know what we'll do,' she said. 'You can come back here on your days off and I'll do the washing and the ironing in time for you going back.'

Bob Dunn shook his head while Deanna gave him a lopsided smile.

'I better get changed and show face at Edna and John's wedding reception.' said Deanna and hurried from the room. An hour later she was on her way. The dance was still in full swing when she arrived, although some of the guests had left.

Molly spotted her and went over. 'How did it go, Deanna?'

'I've got the job, Molly, but I have to be back in Pitlochry for Monday morning. The theatre opens on the seventh of May so I don't have much time to learn my lines.' She gave her boss a worried look. 'I know it's short notice and I'm sorry.'

Molly was worried by the loss of one of her staff but she didn't show it. She didn't have the heart to spoil Deanna's big chance in life. Then Edna and the rest of her colleagues saw her and they all wanted to hear the news.

Before the next dance started Edna went up to the stage and announced, 'We've all had good news tonight as Deanna, our workmate, has just passed an audition for Pitlochry Theatre.'

There was a round of applause as some of the guests came over and congratulated her. For the second time that day Deanna almost burst into tears, as she was so overcome with emotion.

As the night drew to a close, Edna took Molly aside. 'I just want to thank you for being here for me today.'

Molly said it had been a pleasure and something she wouldn't have missed for anything.

Catching a change in Molly's demeanour, Edna said, 'How will you cope with Deanna's absence on Monday? I know how busy the schedule is.'

'Well it'll take some shuffling around but I'm not going to worry about it tonight. I'll spend tomorrow working everything out.'

'Come and sit down for a minute, Molly.' Edna went over to a small alcove which held a couple of chairs. For one moment Molly thought Edna was also going to hand in her notice and she suddenly felt if that happened then she wouldn't be able to cope. Edna had said John and she weren't going away for a honeymoon because they planned to have a fortnight's holiday in the summer with Billy and Irene if she wanted to come.

'My mum said she wouldn't mind working in Deanna's place if she got the job,' said Edna. 'Now that Billy will be living with John and me, Mum will have some time for herself.' She looked anxiously at Molly. 'What do you think?'

Molly was relieved. 'I think that's a great idea, as long as the work wouldn't be too much for her, Edna.'

'Mum will manage fine. She's younger than Maisie and look how well she does, especially with Mrs Jankowski.'

'I'll go and see your mum tomorrow and we'll talk about it and

I have to say, it's a big worry solved.' Molly laughed. 'Irene will have to go to Professor Lyon on Monday morning. We better watch out that he doesn't get a part for your mum in the theatre as well as Deanna.'

Both women laughed out loud. Then John arrived and, hearing their laughter, he said, 'Nice to see you both enjoying yourselves.'

Edna stood up and took his hand. 'We're just discussing Mum and her new job.'

John looked confused but his new wife said, 'I'll tell you all about it later when we go home.'

He put his arm around her waist and looked as if he would burst with pride.

It was half-past eleven and the last dance was announced. All the couples took to the floor. James asked Molly to dance, and Molly happily accepted.

She was a bit upset Charlie hadn't made it but she knew he was on duty. Still, she had hoped that the robberies would have been solved by now, but obviously they hadn't. She concentrated on her dancing partner. 'It's been a lovely day, hasn't it James?'

His face lit up. 'Oh yes it has. I'm so pleased that John met Edna. They will be very happy together.'

'Is there any word of Sonia, has she phoned the hotel or left a message?'

'No she hasn't but I'm just as pleased. I'll stay here tonight and get a train back tomorrow morning.' She glanced at his face and there was a steely look in his eyes that she hadn't seen before.

Then the band finished with a musical flourish and they wished all goodnight.

Some taxis had been ordered and the last remaining guests stood on the pavement in the cold night air. Alice, Sandy, Maisie and Deanna got into one taxi while Mary, Stan, Jean and Bob travelled together. Eddie, Margaret and another couple took the third taxi. Molly said she would walk back to the Wellgate but Edna wouldn't hear of it.

'We can drop you off on our way home to Constitution Street, Molly.'

Molly started to protest, saying the newly married couple might want to be alone but John insisted. 'We've all our lives to be alone, Molly, so hop in.'

They said goodbye to James, who looked so forlorn on the pavement, and as soon as they moved off, he went back inside the hotel.

John was really annoyed. 'I could wring Sonia's neck the way she's mucking him about. Do you know he had to buy her that fur coat just to come today because she said she wasn't keen on weddings? Then she clears off halfway through and she never spoke to you, Edna, did she?'

'I didn't mind, John.'

'Well I did. She's such a selfish woman and James is too good for her.'

Although Edna and Molly stayed silent, they both quietly said Amen to that.

When Molly reached the agency she decided to go straight to bed but there was a note pushed through the letterbox. It was from Charlie. He must have had it delivered by the policeman on the beat. He said he was sorry not to see her at the reception but the robbery case hadn't come to a dramatic end and he couldn't get away. He would try and see her tomorrow or Monday. She should have been disappoited, but actually, Molly was so tired all she wanted to do was go to sleep.

5

Molly woke up with a headache on Sunday morning. *I shouldn't have had the champagne yesterday*, she thought ruefully, going in search of a couple of aspirin tablets. But by the time she had some tea and toast she felt slightly better. Still, it had been a wonderful day.

She wondered what was the best time to go and see Irene. She knew that Billy was being collected during the morning and was now going to live in the house on Constitution Road. She didn't want to intrude until Billy was settled.

The clock was striking eleven when she put on her coat and hurried to Paradise Road. The wind was still cold but there was the sun trying its hardest to shine through the thin cloud cover.

The Hilltown was quite busy with people hurrying for their newspapers or perhaps a bag of morning rolls and maybe cigarettes. Everyone would no doubt have different Sunday morning essentials that they couldn't live without. She also met a small crowd of people, who, judging by their smart coats and hats, were obviously heading for St Andrew's Church at the bottom of the Wellgate.

When she reached Paradise Road she met Irene going down at the bin recess in the back green with her bucket. 'The door's open, Molly. Just go in and I'll put the kettle on when I've finished emptying the ashes.'

Molly was pleased to see a bright fire burning in the grate and she stood warming her hands until Irene reappeared. There was no sign of Billy.

'You've just missed Edna and John. They've collected all Billy's things and John will take him to school every morning and meet him at night.'

Although she sounded cheery enough, Molly could see that she was a bit upset. 'You'll find the house much quieter, Irene, now that Billy is away.'

Irene suddenly looked sad and said, 'Yes it's a big wrench. I've looked after him since he was born but it's only right that he's with his mum and his new dad.' She put two cups of tea on the table along with a plate of biscuits. 'And it's not that I won't see him as he plans to come down some evenings.'

Although Molly's headache had subsided slightly, there was still a pain between her eyes and she made a mental note never to drink champagne again, no matter what the occasion.

'Edna said you wanted to talk about coming to work in Deanna's place. Is that right?'

'Yes, if you want me,' said Irene. 'I feel I need something to do with my spare time and Edna was telling me that Deanna leaving suddenly has left you with a bit of a problem.'

Molly agreed that it had. 'I've placed a couple of adverts in the paper, but I'd love you to come and work in the agency. There's an opening for both the domestic and secretarial side. Which one would you like?'

Irene laughed. 'Oh thank you for your confidence in my office skills, which is zero, but I was thinking about Deanna's cleaning job.'

'When would you like to start, Irene?'

Irene didn't need to think about it. 'Oh, as soon as possible if that's all right with you, Molly.'

'Deanna has Professor Lyon tomorrow morning and a Mrs White in the afternoon, so if you could start tomorrow that would be great.' She laughed. 'I just hope Professor Lyon doesn't get you a stage part like Deanna or I'll be having another vacancy.'

Irene laughed as well. 'Oh you've no worries there, Molly. Can you imagine me on the stage?' She gave this some thought. 'Well, maybe if it needed a good clean.'

They sat together for another hour, discussing the wedding.

'It was a lovely day, Irene, and I'm so pleased to see Edna happily married. I'm also pleased that she will still be working because I can't imagine the agency without her.'

'They got some lovely wedding presents,' said Irene. 'Edna and John said they didn't want any presents because they have everything they need but they were both thrilled by everyone's kindnesses.'

Molly hoped that they liked the eighteen-piece china tea set she had given them and she knew James's present was a matching dinner set, plus a beautiful painting of the River Tay at Broughty Ferry.

Thinking of James, she wondered how he was this morning and if he was looking forward to being reunited with Sonia. Somehow she doubted that and it made her feel sad.

She stood up to go. 'Well I'll see you tomorrow morning at nine o'clock, Irene.' Irene said she was looking forward to it and Molly hurried out into the cold windy day.

When she opened the office door she saw the envelope on the mat. It was a letter from Charlie.

Hullo Molly,

I've missed you again. I'm off to work but hopefully see you sometime this week. Hope the wedding went well and once again, sorry I couldn't make it.

Charlie.

He signed it with two large kisses.

Molly sighed as she went upstairs to her flat. *We're like ships that pass in the night*, she thought. Or those little weather houses where either the man appeared or the woman, but never together. Still she had loads of work to do and her headache had finally gone, which was a blessing.

The next morning everyone was talking about the wedding, saying what a great time they had. Irene appeared, eager to start work and went off happily to Professor Lyon's flat. And Maisie hurried up the Hilltown to Mrs Jankowski.

Molly breathed a sigh of relief that Deanna's job had been filled and although she hadn't had any replies to her adverts other than Maggie's, she wasn't worried. She had spoken to Maggie Flynn about a job already, and it was agreed she would start work as a Saturday girl at the beginning of May then, just like Mary before her, she would become a full-time member of the team when she left school at the end of June.

Maggie was a regular visitor to the office, ever since Molly had met her during the search for Etta Barton the previous year and she had promised the girl a job when she finished school. This regular visit always amused Jean who said, 'I think Maggie is frightened you forget about her unless she keeps popping in to remind you what she looks like.'

Molly laughed at this character reference but she knew Jean was right. 'She's a bright girl and I have great hopes for her doing the job well.'

After the staff all left for their assignments, Molly went off to the council offices to work her final week. The staff member was recovering and due back at her desk the following Monday.

As Molly made her way along the High Street she felt a warm thrill of achievement with her agency. Everything was going well but what she didn't know then was how easily everything could unravel.

6

Maisie was also feeling quite pleased with life as she headed for Mrs Jankowski's flat. This was to be one of her bridge afternoons and Maisie enjoyed working at the house until Mrs Jankowski's friends arrived for their afternoon's entertainment.

She rang the bell and waited. Mrs Jankowski suffered from arthritis and it usually took her a few moments to open the door. This was usually accompanied by a series of explanations as the woman walked down the lobby. Today, however, there was no sign of her coming to open the door. Maisie looked through the highly polished brass letterbox and called out, 'It's just me, Mrs Jankowski.'

There was no sign of her but Maisie thought she heard a muffled cry. 'Mrs Jankowski, are you all right?'

Still no sign but by now Maisie was alarmed. She knew the woman never went out of the house because she couldn't manage the stairs. She called through the letterbox, 'I'm going to get help.'

Maisie's first thought was to go back to the office but then she remembered the couple from the next close who were two of Mrs Jankowski's bridge partners. There was no answer at their door either but then Maisie remembered the couple both had jobs. In a quandary, she had no option but to hurry down to the ice cream shop that was situated at the end of the close.

The owners, Mr and Mrs Iannetta, were Italian and it was the wife who was behind the counter.

'It's Mrs Jankowski upstairs,' explained Maisie. 'I think she's hurt herself and she's not answering the door.'

Mrs Iannetta called to her husband to look after the shop and the two women hurried upstairs.

Mrs Iannetta called through the letterbox and she said she definitely heard a cry of distress. 'I will get my husband to call the police as they will have to break down the door.' Maisie looked at the solid wooden door and didn't fancy their job.

The police came quite quickly and they brought a locksmith with them. He soon had the door open and the two women hurried inside along with the policemen.

Mrs Jankowski was lying in the living room with her arm in an unnatural-looking angle. Maisie knelt beside her. 'What happened, Mrs Jankowski?'

'I fall and not get up, Maisie. I lie here for hours.'

One of the policemen went and telephoned for an ambulance while Mrs Iannetta brought a pillow from the bedroom and put it behind her head. Maisie tried to soothe the woman. 'The ambulance will soon be here and the hospital will see to your arm.'

But Mrs Jankowski was very upset. 'I not want to go to the hospital. And how will I cope with one arm less?'

'Don't worry about that now. Everything will be fine, you'll see,' said Maisie, not believing for a minute that all would be fine.

Then the ambulance arrived and Mrs Jankowski was carried on a stretcher to the infirmary, which fortunately wasn't far, just further along the road. Maisie went with her but before she left she was worried about the door. The locksmith assured her he would put another lock on it and leave the new keys with Mrs Iannetta.

At the hospital, Maisie sat in the waiting room until a young-looking doctor came out and explained that it was Mrs Jankowski's wrist that was broken but that she would get home after a plaster cast was put on.

'Fortunately it's her left wrist and a clean break so she can still use her right hand,' he said.

Maisie thought to herself that she wouldn't have used the word 'fortunately' but she knew what the doctor meant.

It was after lunch when they got back to the flat. Mrs Jankowski was worried about her bridge afternoon.

'Do you want me to go and tell them what's happened?'

'Yes please, Maisie. Go to see Anita Armstrong, she lives on Hill Street. She mention to the rest not to come.'

Maisie climbed the hill and was soon knocking at Anita's door. When she explained what had happened, the woman said she would go and tell the other two people the news.

'Tell Mrs Jankowski that I'll come down to see her afterwards,' she said.

Maisie hurried back and when she went into the house, Mrs Jankowski was sitting in the chair. The room was very cold so she quickly got a bright fire going and went to make some sweet tea.

Mrs Jankowski seemed a bit sleepy and Maisie suggested she went to bed.

'I not know how I manage,' she said, sounding distressed.

'I'll come in every day and help,' said Maisie, wondering how she would manage to fit it in with her other work. Then Anita arrived and she went over to her friend. 'Now you're not to worry about managing, Gina. I'll come down every day and stay with you until late afternoon. Maybe we can get someone else to come in the evening.'

Maisie said she could come after work and make sure she had her tea and got ready for bed.

Gina Jankowski was overwhelmed by all the kindness and she had tears in her eyes.

Maisie put her arm around her shoulders. 'Now you're not to worry as we'll be here to help.'

Then Gina went to bed and was soon fast asleep. Maisie said, 'She fell early this morning and couldn't get up.'

Anita was methodical. 'I'll come down after my husband goes to work and I'll put the fire on and stay till late afternoon then if you can come then until nearly bedtime.'

Maisie said, 'I have to report to the office but I'll come back afterwards and have my tea with Mrs Jankowski then make sure she's comfortable for the night.'

Anita agreed, saying that would be fine. Ending their

conversation, Maisie then left her and Mrs Jankowski and headed toward the agency.

Maisie walked quickly down the Hill. Jean was in the office when she arrived. She told her the story and what had been planned.

Jean was sympathetic. 'I only hope you're not taking on too much. Has she got any family near at hand?'

Maisie said she hadn't mentioned anyone except her late husband. 'She has lots of friends so I expect she'll be well looked after. The doctor did say he didn't expect any complications.'

But when Maisie arrived back at the flat at five o'clock, Anita said she had become distressed at the thought of being on her own all night.

Anita came up with a suggestion. 'I can take you back with me and look after you in my house if that's a help'

Gina didn't want that. 'You have your husband to look after. I just be in the way.'

Anita said that was nonsense but Gina had made up her mind. 'I just stay in my home and try to settle.' But her face betrayed that bold statement.

Then Maisie decided to say what had been on her mind for some moments. 'I can stay overnight and when you come here in the morning I'll go off to my work.'

Gina looked relieved. 'You have a nice, comfortable bed here, Maisie, so you get a good night's sleep.'

So that was settled. At ten o'clock Maisie made two cups of cocoa. Gina was looking through a photograph album and showing her friend her life in Poland before the war. Gina and her husband had been a handsome couple and they looked really prosperous, with a large house in the background.

One photo, which featured a family in the garden, showed Gina, her husband and a young dark-haired child who looked about two years old. Maisie asked who she was.

Gina looked sad when she said, 'That is our niece, Maria. She die after we come here.'

Maisie looked stricken but Gina reassured her, 'It all happened such a long time ago.'

Later, when she lay in the bed, which was indeed comfortable, Maisie thought of the sadness of losing a young child but was so tired she fell asleep immediately.

7

Charlie appeared before eight o'clock the following morning. Molly was surprised to see him. He looked exhausted and she suspected that he was wearing the same shirt as yesterday.

He confirmed it, saying, 'We've had a tough night. We pulled in two suspects but we reckon someone with brains has master-minded all these robberies and the suspects aren't talking.'

Molly said, 'Have you had any breakfast, Charlie?'

He shook his head. 'I'm away home to get a few hours' sleep then it's back to work.'

'Well sit down and I'll make some bacon and eggs.'

Charlie said a cup of tea and some toast would be fine, but Molly had the frying pan on so she went ahead with the cooking.

When the meal was cooked, he made short work of it. 'I didn't realise I was so hungry, but thanks.' He drained his cup and added, 'When this case is finished I'll have more time to see you, Molly, and I'm sorry about missing Edna's wedding.'

'That's all right, Charlie. I'm the same about my work and I think we're both ambitious.'

He grinned. 'At the moment I would settle for a name and a conviction but the two crooks we've got are old hands and they wouldn't be able to organise a big crime such as this. No, maybe they're innocent or just minor players and they know it so all they've got to do is play dumb.'

After he left, Molly remembered she hadn't mentioned Deanna or Irene but by the look of him all he wanted was a good sleep. She would tell him all her news when he had caught 'Mr Big'.

She went downstairs just as Jean was opening up. 'Maisie will be in to see you later.' She mentioned the drama with Mrs Jankowski.

Molly said, 'Oh, I'm sorry to hear that! Though Mrs Jankowski seems to depend on Maisie a lot and I just hope Maisie isn't taking on too much responsibility. Still, I know she would offer her help because she is such a caring person.'

However, as Molly walked to work she had a sudden thought that all the carefully planned assignments at the agency were being slowly eroded. How would Maisie cope with looking after Mrs Jankowski every night and be able to come to work during the day? Molly would have to spend the evening juggling the work between Alice and Irene. Thankfully Edna was back, and Molly was grateful that the honeymoon was postponed until the summer. By then she should have some replies to her adverts.

She was also worried about Charlie. He had looked so worn out this morning and she hoped here would be an early solution to the robberies. At least he didn't have any worries with her getting involved with any more mysteries. Her work now was all just making the best use of the staff and the perpetual shuffling of rotas.

She was glad when she entered the brightly-lit council office and was soon immersed in her daily routine of typing and filing.

Deanna had arrived at Pitlochry on the Monday and she was now staying at a small guest house on the wonderfully named Lower Oakfield. The landlady was a bit like her mother but older, and she had made her very welcome. She had a tiny attic bedroom with a small bathroom along the corridor.

Although her stomach was churning when she turned up at the theatre, her worry was unfounded because the cast and staff had been very welcoming. Deanna felt like an established actress and she was determined to do her very best. She had been handed the scripts and she spent every day and well into the evenings learning her lines.

There was a feeling of expectation at the rehearsals, which she found exciting. Now and again during a quiet moment she wondered how Molly was coping at the agency and a small part of her was sorry that she had left so suddenly but then the next moment she felt as if her world was opening into a bright new future.

She wondered if any of her former colleagues would maybe manage to come and see her and she hoped that some of them would be able to pay a visit over the summer.

It was now the beginning of May and the first night was looming. Deanna lived with a strange mixture of fear and exhilaration. One good thing was the improvement in the weather. After the cold spell in April, the sun had come out and the temperature was rising. Deanna loved wakening up to the dawn chorus of birds and it was such a pleasure to walk along the streets of this lovely town with the gardens filled with daffodils and tulips and the trees with their new lime-green leaves.

According to her landlady, Mrs Walters, the town would soon be full of visitors who came to stay for their holidays or were one of the many people who came on bus tours. Mrs Smith had said that Pitlochry was casting off its winter coat and was looking forward to the summer season. Deanna knew what she meant because she felt she was shedding her old skin and was slowly emerging from her chrysalis into a butterfly that would soon fly away.

8

On Wednesday night Molly was surprised when Marigold turned up at her flat. 'I've been shopping in the town,' she said. 'I thought I would pop in and see you.'

Molly was delighted to see her. 'I'm planning on going to see Mum and Dad this weekend. I know Mum will be dying to hear all about Edna's wedding. It's a pity you couldn't come to the reception.' She knew they had all been invited.

'We didn't want to travel back over the river at night,' said Marigold.

'I could have put you all up here or you could have stayed at the hotel.' Molly understood that it would be a long journey just for a few hours and she couldn't have really accommodated the three of them in her small flat. But at least she had offered.

Marigold pulled a letter from her bag. 'That's why I'm here, Molly. I've ordered two tickets for the first night at the Festival Theatre in Pitlochry. I thought you would like to see Deanna in her first play of the season. I did ask Nancy and Archie but they don't like the theatre very much so I thought we could go and stay overnight. I have an old friend who runs a small guest house there and she can put us up for the Saturday night. What do you think?'

Molly was surprised but she had secretly thought of going to see Deanna at some point. The only thing was she wasn't sure of the work load on that Saturday. 'I would love to go, Marigold, but I must check if I'm needed here.'

Marigold was organised. 'Well you can check and let me know. I've booked the tickets and I'll phone my friend this week. I hope you can get away and have a break. It'll do you good.'

Molly said, 'Wait a minute while I run downstairs and check next week's work sheets. Sometimes Jean has work lined up well in advance and I should be able to check for a week on Saturday.'

She left Marigold with a cup of tea and a plate of biscuits and hurried down to the office. A few minutes later she was back with a clutch of work sheets in her hand.

She laughed. 'This is one of the advantages of living over the office.' She looked through them then smiled. 'Jean has me down for a day in the office doing the invoices so I can easily work round that and get off. Do you remember Maggie Flynn, the young girl from last year? She is coming in this Saturday to answer the telephone and get settled in before starting at the end of June. I can ask if she can also work next Saturday and we can have our weekend away.'

Marigold put on her coat and picked up her large bag with her purchases from her shopping. 'I've bought two pairs of towels from Smith Brothers as they were on a special offer.'

Molly went to put her coat on. 'I'll walk with you to Craig Pier.'

Marigold said it wasn't necessary. 'It's still light outside.'

'Nonsense. Anyway, I would like the walk. I've been shut in a warm office all day and a bit of fresh air will do me good.'

It was still daylight when they emerged into the Wellgate and it was a pleasant walk through the town to Union Street and the Pier. They had a quarter of an hour to wait until the ferry sailed but when it docked Marigold strode forward and boarded it.

Before she went she said, 'We can go by train or the bus. What do you think, Molly?'

Molly gave it some thought. 'If Dad doesn't need the car I could drive there. I'll speak to him this weekend.'

When she arrived home, she realised she was looking forward to going away.

The next morning Maisie arrived in the office, bright and early. Molly was concerned for all the extra work she had taken on looking after Mrs Jankowski every night, but Maisie had some good news.

'Vera Barton came to see her yesterday and she said that she could stay every night with her while Anita looks after her during the day. Then her bridge partners from the next close will help out at the weekends.'

Molly, impressed by all the good friends who were willing to help the elderly woman, said she was glad that she was being looked after.

Maisie nodded. 'Mrs Jankowski told me that her bridge partners are like a little club and they all look out for one another. That's smashing, isn't it?'

Molly said it was but she couldn't get over the fact that so many people from last year's drama were now coming back into her life. Well, back into Maisie's life, but it made her feel strange.

Then she mentally chided herself for that stupid thought. They all stayed in the same houses as last year and Mrs Jankowski's bridge club was obviously still meeting twice a week.

'How is Vera keeping?'

Maisie said she hadn't been speaking to her but Mrs Jankowski said she was fine and definitely getting better.

Before Molly could reply the rest of the staff hurried through the door and that was the end of the conversation.

Molly was relieved that Irene seemed to be enjoying her work, a fact that pleased Edna, and she said in the passing, 'I'm glad to see Mum looking so happy and busy.'

Jean said that there was a lot of work coming in and Molly said she would sort it out with her later in the afternoon.

As she walked to work, she wondered if she could possibly still get off next Saturday for the trip with Marigold to Pitlochry but she hoped so. It was just the restful kind of break she needed.

9

Charlie was on his way to the police station. There had been no new leads in the three robbery cases and he had released the two suspects in custody because of lack of evidence. PC Williamson met him at the office door.

'There's been another robbery, sir.'

Charlie, who had a headache, almost groaned out loud.

'Where and when?'

'Either last night or early this morning. A man called Bergmann, who has a house in Monifieth.'

'Well we better get there.'

PC Williamson drove the car and they were soon heading out of Dundee. When they arrived, they found that the house wasn't in the village but was situated on a side road. It was an imposing-looking house surrounded by a large garden with a gravel drive leading up from the road.

The house had a grey, gloomy façade and large windows with thick wooden shutters screening the rooms from prying eyes. Inside, the fingerprint man was dusting for prints and a young constable stood at the front door.

Charlie asked, 'Who discovered the break-in?'

The policeman came forward and said it was the housekeeper, Mrs French. The woman who came to the door was quite tall with short black hair and very attractive. When asked her name she said she was Laura French. She said she was thirty-five years old and a widow, which surprised Charlie because she looked like she was in her middle twenties and much too young to be widowed.

When they were seated in the dining room, she explained that she didn't live in but came every day to cook for the owners and clean the house and generally see that all was well. Charlie asked her where she stayed.

'I have a cottage in the village.'

'Who owns the house?' Charlie asked.

'Mr Bergmann. He has a jewellery business in Dundee. He's in Edinburgh at the moment but I phoned him as soon as I saw the broken door . . .'

'Do you know what was stolen?' he asked her.

The woman frowned. 'I'm not sure but when I arrived a pane of glass in the back door was broken and drawers had been pulled out in one of the bedrooms.'

Charlie had noticed some dark patches on the wall in the hall when he arrived. He mentioned this to Mrs French.

'Yes, there were some nice paintings there and also quite a few in the drawing room. They've also gone.'

'When is Mr Bergmann coming to Dundee?'

'He said he would be here by lunchtime,' she said.

Charlie said, 'Get him to make an inventory of what's been stolen and we'll be back later in the afternoon to speak to him. Now we'll have to look around the rest of the house.'

She went ahead and showed them the various rooms. It was certainly a grand house but apart from a few drawers lying on the thick carpets in one of the bedrooms and the broken pane in the door, the house looked untouched.

Later, out in the car, Charlie said to PC Williamson, 'The thieves must have had a van to be able to carry the paintings.'

Williamson wasn't sure if he should comment on this but, deciding he would take a chance, he said, 'Either that or a large car.'

Charlie nodded. 'Let's see if anyone saw a car or van coming from the house.' He looked out of the window at the Bergmann house. 'There's one thing that's puzzling me: If it's the same criminals who committed the latest robberies, why steal some paintings? It doesn't make sense.'

'Perhaps they thought there was something more valuable to

steal,' said Williamson. 'After all, the housekeeper did say that the owner has a jewellery business. Maybe the thief thought there was a hoard of expensive jewellery.'

Charlie said he was thinking the very same thing then added, 'But clearly this robbery was different. After all, they didn't go for the jewellery but for the paintings themselves. But why? A diversion to lead us on the wrong path? Still, I suppose paintings can be expensive and I've heard that some private art collectors spend quite a bit of money on works of art. Maybe the thieves thought they'd get more for the artwork in the Bergmann house than the jewellery.'

Williamson, who knew almost nothing about art, said, 'But would the art collectors not want to know who owned the paintings before buying them?'

Charlie said that most of them would but there were always some who would buy them without an ownership certificate. 'Criminals are very clever and someone could quite easily pass them off as family heirlooms from some old relative, and who would know any better?'

This was an eye-opener for Williamson, who was delighted to learn all about this criminal experience. He said, 'I didn't know that.'

Charlie just smiled. 'You'll soon learn, lad.'

They left the car and wandered down the drive. On the main road at the foot of the drive was a small hotel. PC Williamson said, 'It must be great to own a big house and grounds like this. I wonder if Mr Bergmann is related to the film star Ingrid.'

Charlie laughed but he was thinking to himself, *The last three burglaries had been in smaller houses than this, although they were still larger and grander than the average house.* He marched back to the car. 'Let's go. We'll come back this afternoon and speak to the owner.'

Back at the station, Charlie swallowed a couple of aspirin along with a cup of foul-tasting tea. Then at three o'clock they made their way back to the Bergmann house. The man was sitting in the drawing room with a list in front of him.

About seventy years old, tall with white hair swept back from an aristocratic-looking face, he introduced himself. 'Eric Lindstrom Bergmann.' His handshake was firm.

Charlie asked if he had made a list of stolen items.

'Yes I have, but I'm pleased to say the thieves didn't get a good haul. I would normally keep a lot of gems in my safe but I took them to my shop last week. I have a jewellery shop as well as a pawnbroker's business in the Hawkhill. I used to own two other shops, one in Glasgow and one in Edinburgh, but I sold these two years ago and now only have the Dundee ones. Apart from a few paintings by minor artists and some silver, there doesn't seem to be anything else missing.'

'Can I see your safe please?' asked Charlie

The man nodded and led the way to one of the bedrooms on the first floor, the one that had the drawers lying on the carpet. He opened a wooden cabinet that revealed a solid-looking safe. 'There is nothing in it at the moment except a few papers,' he explained. 'Anyway, the thieves would never have been able to open it.'

After another quick look around, they left with the list of missing items. When they were back in the car, Charlie said, 'The last three robberies managed to get a much bigger haul than this. Either this isn't related to them or the thief thought there was more in this house than there actually was.'

A couple of police constables were sent to check the neighbours nearest to the Bergmann house but they came back empty-handed. The nearest house was a small family-run hotel, but at this time of year it didn't have many guests and no one had seen or heard anything suspicious. They had also checked out the houses along the road but again no strangers with either a car or a van were seen and no one heard anything out of the ordinary.

10

On Friday evening Molly decided to visit her parents. She wanted to ask if she could borrow the car to go to Pitlochry. Her parents had just had their tea by the time Molly arrived, and Nancy jumped up, ready to make something for her.

'Please don't make anything for me, Mum. I'll get something later.'

'Nonsense,' said Nancy, taking a fish fillet from the cold store outside and coating it in fish dressing. 'It'll just take a few minutes to rustle up something.'

In spite of not wanting anything to eat, when Molly got a whiff of the frying fish she suddenly realised how hungry she was. She sat in the living room with her dad while Nancy bustled about in the kitchen.

Her father put down the evening paper. 'Your mum is glad to see you, Molly. She's been a bit down since getting Nell's letter, she says she wishes we weren't thousands of miles away from our granddaughter and now we won't see the new baby.' He stopped and warned her, 'Here she comes. Don't mention I've said anything.'

'Right then, that's your tea ready so come and get it.' She sounded cheerful but Molly wasn't fooled. It was a bright cheerfulness that masked a sorrow.

Molly also wished that Nell, Terry and wee Molly lived nearer but Australia was now their home and it hadn't been so very long since her parents had been on holiday there. However, Molly knew the news of the new baby and the fact that another holiday was out of the question had depressed her mum.

She mentioned her and Marigold's plans, then said, 'Come with us to Pitlochry tomorrow, Mum, and have a break.'

Nancy shook her head. 'No you go and enjoy yourself with Marigold and we'll hear all about it when you get back.'

Suddenly remembering why she came to visit them in the first place, Molly said, 'Can I borrow the car to go to Pitlochry, Mum? That's if you and Dad don't need it.'

Nancy called out to her husband, 'Molly would like to take the car this weekend, Archie. Is that all right?'

Archie said it was.

Molly then went to see Marigold to see if she wanted to drive back to Dundee with her and they could both leave together tomorrow. Marigold was packing a small suitcase but said she couldn't leave as an old friend was coming later in the evening.

'I'll catch the Fifie in the morning then we can set off when I get in,' she said.

Molly said she would park the car in Union Street and wait on her. 'It'll save me having to drive through the town twice. It will be easy to get to Perth Road then head north.'

With the plan in place, Molly went back next door and stayed with her parents until the last ferry back. She felt she had to be some company for them but she knew she was a poor substitute for her absent sister and her family.

It was eleven o'clock when she reached Baltic Street where she parked the car, and she was dying for her bed. Entering her flat, she saw that a note was through the letterbox. It was from Charlie.

Molly,
We're like a couple of pen pals these days. I'm still bogged down with work but have a great time with Deanna and Marigold. I'll try and see you sometime next week.
Charlie

For a brief moment Molly wondered how her life was turning out. She was worried about her parents and running the agency was quite stressful but she was proud of its success. As for Charlie, well, was the relationship going anywhere? She knew it was her fault but she felt powerless to make any changes.

As she slipped into bed she said aloud, 'Things will turn out OK.'

In spite of her worries, she slept soundly and she was pleased to see when she awoke that it was sunny outside. The thought of the drive into the country was so appealing and she always enjoyed Marigold's company.

She spent a couple of hours doing invoices then at ten-thirty she had parked the car and was standing outside Craig Pier. She had to smile when she saw Marigold walking up the ramp. She was dressed in a woollen dress with a warm cardigan, stout brown leather shoes and was carrying a waterproof jacket. A group of young girls got off at the same time and they were dressed for the warm sunny weather with cotton frocks and thin strappy sandals. They made straight for the car and Molly put Marigold's suitcase and jacket in the boot alongside her own canvas travel bag.

They made good time travelling along the busy Perth Road but once they were on the open road they both felt the break had begun. The Great North Road was quite busy with traffic and Marigold remarked that there were lots more cars nowadays.

They stopped at a café in Dunkeld for a light dinner then had a walk around the cathedral grounds. The sun and the river had a cathartic effect on Molly and she felt her worries slip away. She knew it was only temporary but she was determined to enjoy herself and she hoped Marigold felt the same way.

She parked in the Square and Marigold remarked on the neglected state of the quaint little houses that lined the street. 'It's a wonder nobody's thought of renovating these houses. Especially in such a lovely and historic place.' She pointed to the majestic bridge that spanned the river. 'Thomas Telford built that bridge, and do you know, a famous battle was fought over its tolls.'

Molly said she hadn't but was pleased to have had a guided tour.

They then headed northwards and arrived at the Bay Guest House in the early afternoon. It was situated almost across from the theatre and Molly was pleased that it had a small parking area for the car.

Mrs Smith greeted Marigold warmly. 'I haven't seen you for a few years,' she said. Marigold admitted it had been too long but said they were both glad to be here for the one night.

'I'll make the tea before you go to the theatre,' Mrs Smith said, showing them to their rooms which were small but cosy. The bathroom lay between the two doors, which was handy, said Marigold, who admitted she often had to get up during the night.

Molly was excited at the thought of seeing Deanna again but she hadn't told her she was coming. She was hoping to surprise her after the play.

Mrs Smith, who said to call her Bess, said that the theatre had been a great visitor attraction and her guest house was booked for most of the summer.

When Molly was in her room she asked Marigold how she knew the owner. 'We go back a long way,' said Marigold. 'Bess used to stay in Newport and we went to the same school. When her husband died she moved here and bought this place. We don't see one another very much but we still keep in touch by letter and at Christmastime.'

Later, Bess made a lovely high tea of fish and chips and Molly ate it all with relish. 'It must be the change of air,' she said to Marigold.

Molly had brought a new summer dress with a pair of red sandals to wear to the theatre, but as usual Marigold had on a woollen dress and another pair of sensible-looking shoes.

When they crossed the road and entered the foyer, Molly was entranced. Inside was a lovely auditorium but instead of being large and formal it was intimate and friendly. They reached their seats with a few minutes to spare. The play was called *Dandy*

Dick and Marigold said the writer was Arthur Pinero, a famous dramatist.

Deanna had said she would be playing minor roles but in this play she was on the stage a few times. Molly felt so proud of her as her presence lit up the stage. At the end of the play Molly sent a note backstage via one of the floor staff and within ten minutes Deanna appeared. She was delighted to see them.

'I can't believe you came all this way to see me. Thank you very much. Did you enjoy the play?'

'Yes we did and you looked wonderful in your role.'

Deanna grinned. 'Do you really think so?'

Marigold told her she knew a thing or two about the theatre and said she was great.

'I've had the most difficult two weeks trying to learn my lines but I think they like me here. I'm going to write a letter to Professor Lyon to thank him. How is he and who's looking after him now?'

'It's Edna's mother, Irene, and I'll pass on the message for her to tell him.'

Marigold laughed. 'Don't be surprised if he shows up some time to see you.'

Deanna asked how everyone was at the agency and the three women had a great gossip.

'We're staying at the guest house across the road. Come back with us and have a cup of tea,' said Molly. 'We can maybe also meet up tomorrow.'

Deanna's face fell. 'Oh I don't know. Brian, who works on the lighting team, has asked me to go for a drive tomorrow but I'll tell him I can't go.'

Molly said not to do that. 'We'll be back during the summer to see you in one of the other plays and we'll have a get-together then.'

Deanna was dubious. 'I can easily cancel it.'

Molly was adamant. 'No, Deanna, you go for a drive with Brian and enjoy yourself. Anyway we have to leave in the afternoon so we can easily fill in the time.'

Deanna thanked them again and headed towards the door, quickly followed by a handsome young man.

Marigold laughed. 'Brian, I presume.'

Bess was waiting up for them with tea and homemade scones with butter and jam. Marigold told her if she stayed here much longer she would be getting fat, a sentiment that was also uttered at breakfast when she placed huge plates of bacon, sausage and eggs in front of them.

Molly whispered that she didn't think she would need any food for a whole week when they returned home and Marigold said, 'Don't you believe it. We'll probably be hungry again by suppertime.'

Molly thought not but she smiled at her friend. 'It's great that the weather is still sunny and warm. I can hardly believe that we had all that snow a fortnight ago.'

Marigold nodded as she spread some marmalade on her last piece of toast. 'The joys of the Scottish weather never fail to amaze people.'

After so much food the two women decided to go for a walk before packing their suitcases and heading home. Marigold suggested a walk along the lovely Loch Faskally and up to the Soldier's Leap at Killicrankie.

The sun was warm as they set out. Molly, captivated by the scenery and the peaceful surroundings, was impressed. Before they reached the loch they passed the imposing hydroelectric dam that sat like a concrete sentinel across the river.

'When the Hydro Electric built the dam, they turned the river upstream into the loch and I think it's the only man-made one in the country,' said Marigold.

'Well it's beautiful, and what a great asset for the town.' Molly saw quite a crowd of people all walking down the opposite path.

'That leads to the salmon ladder. Let's go down and have a look.' Marigold didn't wait for an answer.

They walked down the steep path that led to the series of small pools, each enclosed in concrete walls with a wide pipe connecting each one. To Molly's surprise, a couple of salmon jumped out of the river before popping back in again.

She was delighted. 'I've never seen anything like it,' she said.

'The wonderful thing about the dam is it generates our electricity, all by the power of water,' said Marigold, who seemed to be an expert on all things hydroelectric.

They resumed their walk along the path that ran by the side of the loch. A couple of small boats were out on the water, each one propelled by the efforts of a young man at the oars while their female companions gazed at the scenery.

Marigold said dryly, 'I wonder if the good Brian will bring the fair Deanna here?'

'No,' said Molly, 'didn't she say they were going for a drive? He must own a car.'

'Maybe he borrows his dad's, just like you.'

Molly laughed loudly and a couple of ducks rose with squacking sounds into the quiet air. 'Oh look what I've done. I've frightened the birds.'

They walked in silence until they reached the Soldier's Leap. Once again Marigold did her history lesson. 'This is where the English redcoat soldier from the Battle of Killicrankie leapt to freedom. He was being pursued by the Jacobites.'

Molly surveyed the wide chasm and the foaming water rushing through and thought, *He must have been desperate*. She said so.

'Well if you had an army of ferocious men chasing you, wouldn't you do the same?' Molly admitted it would have been a toss up what she did, but then conceded that she would also have jumped.

They set off back along the wooded track. The trees made it seem gloomy but Marigold looked at the sky and said, 'I think the rain is going to come on. We better get a move on because you haven't brought a jacket, Molly.'

'You don't have one as well.'

'Oh yes I do.' She pulled a small waterproof pack from her handbag. 'This is a rainproof cape. I always carry one.'

Molly was amused. Marigold was armed for every occasion.

Then they both stopped. Angry voices sounded above their heads but because of the dense foliage they couldn't see anyone.

Then they heard the loud clap of thunder, followed by heavy rain.

Molly looked in dismay at her flimsy summer dress and the red sandals.

Marigold took her arm, 'If we hurry we'll get back and get changed.'

They only got a dozen steps along the path when there was a crashing sound on the left and they both stopped in amazement when it turned out to be a body tumbling through the trees and the bracken. As he fell on to the edge of the path his head struck a large boulder. They both ran forward. It was an elderly man and he was lying quite still, with blood pouring from a nasty gash on the side of his head.

Marigold reached him first but he seemed to have been knocked out.

'He needs a doctor and an ambulance.' She looked at Molly's shoes. 'I'll go and find a telephone box.'

Molly said she would go, as she was younger.

'You'll never be able to climb up with those sandals. No, I've got on better shoes so I'll go. I'll be as quick as I can and you can stay here with him.' With that statement, she hurried back along the way they had come. 'There will probably be a telephone box in Killicrankie.'

Molly watched her go with a great deal of trepidation. What if she fell as well?

The man muttered something so she went and knelt beside him. She felt helpless because she had nothing to put behind his head and she wished she had brought her coat. The man had light blue eyes and a ruddy complexion and she thought he looked to be in his sixties. He was also better prepared for the weather because he had on a thick woollen jacket.

When he saw her, he tried to speak.

Molly tried to reassure him. 'My friend has gone for the ambulance.'

He tried to shake his head but a spasm of pain crossed his face. He pointed to his pocket. Molly asked him if he wanted something from it. He made a slight nodding movement and she pulled a waterproof bag out and placed it in his hand. He pushed it back to her.

'Do you want me to take this?' Molly asked.

Again he made a slight nod and gripped her hand. Then he tried to speak, though his voice was laboured. 'You've got to warn them, you've got to warn them.'

Molly was worried by the amount of blood oozing from his wound, and she tried to stem it with a clean hankie.

'The ambulance will soon be here and it will take you to the hospital,' she repeated.

The man made a waving motion with his hand. 'Warn them about digging.'

Molly said she didn't understand, that he must lie still and not get anxious.

There was a plea in his eyes. 'Keep that bag and warn them about digging.'

Molly nodded and promised she would.

There was the sound of someone coming and Molly hoped it was Marigold. Instead it was a tall man with a waterproof jacket and hood and a scarf round the lower half of his face. He had his head down and looked surprised to see Molly kneeling by a body. She explained, 'This man has had an accident but my friend has gone to get help, she won't be long.'

'I've done a first-aid course, let me have a look at him.' Molly moved away and let the stranger kneel down. He tried to lift him up which Molly thought was stupid but he inspected the back of his head and placed him back down.

'Has he been able to talk?'

Molly said not much and it was all garbled, that she hadn't understood anything.

The man put his hand in the injured man's jacket pockets. 'Has he got any identification on him or anything else?'

She was on the verge of telling him about the pouch when

Marigold returned, sounding out of breath but saying that the ambulance was on its way.

On hearing this, the stranger stood up and said, 'Well I won't stay to be in the way.' He walked along the path that Marigold had just hurried down from.

The two women knelt beside the man and Marigold removed her jacket to place behind his head.

'That's odd,' she said. She felt for a pulse then said sadly, 'I think he's dead.'

Molly was upset. 'I thought he would get some stitches in his wound and be fine.'

Before Marigold could answer the ambulance men arrived and quickly took over. While they lifted him onto a stretcher one man asked them, 'On the phone you gave your address as Bay Guest House. Is that your permanent address?'

Molly said no and gave him her home address while Marigold did the same. In the quietness of the wood their voices were amplified but they were too upset to notice.

After the men left with their patient, Molly and Marigold hurried as quickly as they could back to Pitlochry. Bess was appalled when they appeared like two drowned rats and she quickly ordered them to have hot baths and to get out of their wet clothes, which she hung over the chairs in front of the kitchen fire. She then made some strong, hot tea and an hour later they were warmly dressed and ready to go home. The lovely weekend break had ended tragically and they made no stops on the way back.

It wasn't until Molly was halfway home that she remembered the man's waterproof pouch and his warning words. She had put it in the large pocket of her dress and with the arrival of the ambulance she had forgotten to mention it.

II

Betty Holden was surprised when she got back from church to find her brother wasn't in. *Bill hadn't said he was going out but as it is such a lovely day he must have gone for a walk*, she thought. By two o'clock she started to worry and when she saw the policeman coming towards the front door she knew something was very wrong.

The young man was a local policeman and although she knew his face she couldn't remember his name. Then it came to her, he was PC White. He sat on the chintz-covered sofa and tried his best to break the bad news to her gently. 'I'm so very sorry to have to tell you that your brother, William Reid, has had an accident.'

Betty let out a cry of distress and he stood up and went over to her. She said she was all right and he resumed his seat. 'Is he in the hospital? I must go and see him,' she said.

The man shook his head. 'I'm sorry to have to tell you that he died before the ambulance got him to hospital. He had no identification on him but one of the nurses who came on duty this afternoon recognised him.'

She began to cry – huge, noisy sobs that made PC White powerless to help. 'Can I go and get someone to come and stay with you? Your family or a friend . . . ?'

She made a movement with her hand. 'No, I'll be fine in a minute. It's just the shock and suddenness. Was it a heart attack?'

'No, he fell from the top path at the Soldier's Leap and his head struck a rock. He died of a fractured skull.' The man looked anxious. 'I have to ask if you or any of your family can go and identify him. I'll run you or them up to the hospital.'

Betty said she didn't have any family. 'I'll come with you and do that,' she said through her tears.

'You don't have to go right now if you would rather wait till later,' he said, feeling terrible that he was the bearer of bad news.

Suddenly the back door opened and her neighbour Ina came in. 'I saw the police . . .' She stopped when she saw the constable.

Betty turned her tear-stained face. 'It's Bill. He's had an accident and he's dead.'

Ina was shocked. 'That's awful, is there anything I can do?'

'This young man is driving me up to the hospital.'

'Would you like me to come with you?'

Betty wasn't sure if the policeman could take them both up but PC White said he could. Ina ran back to her house to get a coat and the two women got into the police car. Some of the other neighbours in the street who were in their gardens looked at the car as it passed but Betty didn't acknowledge them. She was still suffering from shock at the thought of Bill dying alone. She began to cry again and Ina put her arm around her shoulder.

They were taken to a side room in the cottage hospital where Bill lay. He looked quite peaceful. A white bandage covered his head wound, but apart from that he looked as if he was sleeping.

The hospital staff were sympathetic and kind. Betty said to the doctor that she was upset that he had died without anybody being there but he said it would have been a quick death and he wouldn't have known much about it.

As they were leaving, PC White said, 'If it's any comfort to you, Mrs Holden, the two women who found him stayed with him until the ambulance arrived so he wasn't alone.'

Betty gave a huge sigh. 'I would like to thank them. Do you know their names?'

The policeman pulled his notebook from his pocket. 'They were on holiday from Dundee and stayed at the Bay Guest House in Atholl Road.'

Betty said, 'That's Bess Smith's place.'

When they got back home, some of the neighbours who had heard the news came in to see her with their condolences. Ina stayed until the evening, making Betty eat some scrambled eggs, which she didn't really want but she ate up because she didn't want to hurt her friend's feelings.

Ina said, 'I can stay the night with you,' but Betty said she was all right so Ina left. She said to her husband when she returned next door, 'Betty is still in shock but she'll be more devastated tomorrow when it all sinks in.'

Later, Betty put on her coat and headed to see Bess Smith at the guest house. Bess was surprised to see her and she made her sit down with a cup of tea and some homemade shortbread.

'I'm so very, very sorry for your brother's accidental death, Mrs Holden, and my two guests were also shocked and deeply sorry.'

Betty said she wanted to write and thank them but she didn't have their address.

'Of course,' said Bess. 'Marigold is an old friend. Her name is Mitchell and she lives at Riverside, Newport on Tay. And her friend is Molly McQueen and her address is The Agency, Wellgate, Dundee. Let me write it down for you.'

Betty thanked her and returned to a lonely house with the scrap of paper.

12

When Molly arrived home it was almost eight o'clock and she threw herself down on the sofa. She had driven Marigold back to Newport and left the car with her parents before catching the ferry back to Dundee.

All the way back they discussed the tragic accident but got nowhere.

'What I can't understand,' said Marigold, 'is how he managed to stumble from the top path. I know the ground is a bit rough but loads of people go to see that attraction every day.'

'Maybe he had a heart attack or felt faint,' Molly suggested. 'And don't forget the angry voices we heard. Then there's the garbled message he gave me about warning someone not to go digging. It doesn't make any sense. And I've still got his pouch. I wonder what I can do about that?'

Marigold suggested she should give it to DS Charlie Johns.

'I feel sorry for his wife and family. What a shock they will get when they're told,' said Molly. 'Also, I wonder why that man didn't stay and talk to the ambulance crew. You would think he might have had something to say about it.'

'Maybe it's professional courtesy,' Marigold suggested.

By the time they had reached Perth both women had exhausted all the possible questions but one thing they did agree on was the fact that it had taken the shine off the weekend. That was why Molly was ready for bed by nine o'clock but she wanted to see what was in the waterproof pouch. It looked like one of those carriers that people who are into serious walking carry their Ordnance Survey maps in.

Although this was smaller it held two or three items. The first thing she pulled from it was a sheet torn from a newspaper, followed by a small diary and an empty envelope with the name *Mr W. Reid, Atholl Road, Pitlochry*. Molly put her hand in the pouch and found a single sheet of paper with names written on it. She couldn't understand what was so important about this trivial collection or why the dead man had been so anxious for her to take it and warn people? However, she was so tired that she decided to leave the puzzle until the next day and if Charlie turned up, she would hand it over to him and he could deal with it. She placed it under her pillow and was soon asleep.

The next day there was no sign of Charlie so Molly took everything out of the pouch again and studied the photo from the paper. The date was four months ago and it showed a group of eight men round a table at what looked like some sort of function. It must have been taken abroad because they were all dressed in short-sleeved shirts and shorts. It was an innocuous-looking picture and she couldn't understand the dying man's urgency with it. When she looked at the sheet of names, she wondered which ones matched up to the faces in the photograph.

She glanced at the diary, which was dated from 1947, most of it was written with a pencil, with the small handwriting filling the pages. Quite a lot of it was cryptic with initials, but on reading it Molly got the sense that the writer was living through difficult circumstances somewhere abroad.

She heard voices downstairs and knew there was no more time to ponder over things so she reluctantly put the pouch back under her pillow. By the time she got downstairs everyone had left. Jean was typing out some invoices. She said, 'There is a one-day assignment for you at the council office, Molly, and hopefully it will lead to more work as some of the staff are off sick.'

Molly picked up her bag and set off. This temporary council work was proving to be a boon for the agency, especially if it lasted for another week or two. She thought about Charlie and wondered how he was getting on with his robbery cases. She knew he wouldn't rest till he solved them but he had more or less said it was proving to be difficult.

By the time she finished at five-thirty, she was annoyed at herself for counting her chickens about the job. Seemingly the employees were coming back tomorrow so that was the end of that job for the time being.

She was considering cooking scrambled eggs or a cheese omelette for her tea when the phone rang. Not for the first time she was thankful that the office phone switched through to the flat in the evening and on Sundays.

'McQueen's Agency,' she said in her most professional manner, as she hoped it was more work coming in.

A woman's hesitant voice asked to speak with Miss McQueen.

'This is Molly McQueen,' she answered crisply.

There was a small silence then the quiet voice identified itself as Mrs Betty Holden. Molly racked her brain but couldn't remember anyone of that name.

Mrs Holden, her voice now firmer, said she had to see Molly as a matter of urgency. 'You were there when my brother died on Sunday.'

Molly felt terrible and told the woman how sorry she was that the man had died. 'He gave me a waterproof pouch, Mrs Holden, and I was going to post it back to the address which is inside.'

The woman continued, 'I must come and see you. Will you be at home sometime this week?'

Molly didn't know what the rest of the week would be work-wise so she didn't know how to answer. 'I'm not really sure, Mrs Holden. It all depends how much work comes in.'

Mrs Holden sounded anxious. 'I really need to speak to you about my brother.'

Molly wondered why the police hadn't kept his sister informed but she realised the woman was distressed.

She made up her mind. There was no work for her tomorrow so she could quite easily go and see Mrs Holden in Pitlochry and she would return the dead man's belongings. When she mentioned this the woman seemed relieved but she said, 'It's a long way to come.' Molly told the woman that it was the same for her and she didn't mind so it was all arranged.

Molly left a note for Jean on her desk and by eight-thirty she was on her way to the railway station. It had been raining during the night and there were deep puddles on the pavements. It was a totally different day from Saturday when the sun had shone. Everything was grey and damp but the gardens of the Old Steeple were showing colourful clumps of tulips and daffodils.

The station was also damp and musty as passengers hurried on and off the trains but Molly hardly noticed. Her mind was full of the dead man's final words, but she hoped his sister would know about the mystery of the news cutting. She had a cup of tea and a stale scone at the buffet in Perth then she caught the next train to Pitlochry.

Mrs Holden was waiting for her when she arrived at the address on the envelope, which was a lovely cottage on the street. It had a small, tidy garden with a wall around it. A watery sun had come out, making the street seem as if it had been washed clean. Molly was ushered into a small, cosy living room with a chintz-covered sofa and chairs and well-polished dark wooden furniture. Although it wasn't too cold outside there was a cheery fire burning in the grate and a small table with a tray holding cups, saucers and a plate of buttered pancakes.

After a very welcome cup of tea and three of the pancakes, Betty apologised for urgently phoning Molly. 'First of all, I want to thank you and your friend for getting help for Bill so quickly.'

Molly said she was sorry that it hadn't been quickly enough.

'The hospital told me he wouldn't have lived because he had two fractures of the skull which were fatal injuries but I'm so grateful that he wasn't alone at the end.'

Molly was surprised about the second injury and said so.

Betty gave a sigh and dabbed her eyes with a tiny hankie. 'Yes he must have hit his head twice against the rocks, one on the back of his head and another on his temple.' She sat up straight and looked at Molly. 'No, the reason I phoned was I suspected he had something on his mind. For the last couple of weeks he has had this worried expression on his face and when I asked him if anything was wrong, he said there was but he was going to sort it out.'

'Did he say what was worrying him?'

'No, he said he didn't want to say too much in case he was wrong about something.'

Molly took the pouch from her handbag. 'Your brother gave me his just before the ambulance arrived and he said I had to warn people. Have you any idea what he meant?'

Betty shook her head. 'I wish I did but as I've said he wanted to sort something out on his own and now he's dead.'

Molly took the newspaper cutting, the diary and the envelope out of the bag and handed them to Betty, who went in search of her glasses so she could read them. She sounded surprised when she saw the cutting. 'This is the same photo that was in the paper a few months ago. This was taken when Bill was working as a tea plantation manager in India and all these men with him also worked on the plantations at the same time.'

Molly asked if Bill had put the photo in the paper for any reason.

Betty shook her head. 'No, it was this man.' She pointed to a young, thin, gaunt-faced man who was sitting on the left. 'His name is Phillip Thorne and he wanted to organise a reunion but had lost touch with the group in 1947.'

'Did everyone in the photo go to this reunion?'

Betty shook her head again. 'No, that was the strange thing. When Bill wrote to him at the address he gave in the paper, he wrote back saying how pleased he was to hear from Bill. Later when he wrote to him again, his wife said he had been in an accident and had been killed.'

Molly scrutinised the paper but there was no name or address beside the photo.

Betty explained, 'Bill cut it off and put it in the drawer. In fact, it must still be there.' She went and rummaged through the sideboard drawer then returned to her seat. She handed it to Molly. It said to contact Mr P Thorne at 400 Strathmartine Road, Dundee.

While Molly was looking at the address, Betty was looking through the diary. 'This must have been his last diary in India because he came home that year. He loved the life over there and so did his wife Annie, but she died in 1945 and I don't think he ever got over it. She was cremated over there and Bill brought her ashes back with him and they were interred at Balgay cemetery. Then, of course, when he returned there was all the mayhem and upheaval when India gained independence in 1947. That's when Bill decided to come back.'

'What about the others in the photo, did they come back as well?'

'I've no idea. Bill hardly mentioned his time over there, although he did say they were all from Dundee and the surrounding district. That's why they ran the Dundee Club. They met every month I believe. When he came back, he lived on his own for some time in Dundee but my late husband and I asked him to come and stay with us.' She went over to the sideboard and returned with a photo in a frame. 'This is Michael, my husband. We moved here when he got a job with the hydroelectric dam until he retired five years ago. Sadly he died last year.'

Molly expressed her condolences. And although she was enjoying her visit, she still didn't know why Betty had been so insistent on seeing her.

As if reading her mind, she said, 'You'll be wondering why I wanted to see you urgently. Apart from wanting to thank you for all your kindness, I also wanted to know if Bill said anything other than what you've said.'

Molly said he hadn't. 'All he said was to warn them and something about "digging".'

Betty was puzzled. ' "Digging"? What did he mean by that?'

Molly shook her head. 'I don't know.'

'Why I've been so worried is because I came home early one afternoon after the paper printed that photo. I had gone shopping and Bill didn't hear me coming in. He was on the telephone and I heard him say that something had to be sorted out, something that should have been dealt with years ago. When I came in he slammed the phone down and he looked flustered. When I asked him if anything was wrong he said no, he had just had a bit of a row with an old friend. Then on Sunday evening I had two telephone calls but no one spoke. I can't think what it all means.'

Molly said, 'The only advice I can give you is to go to the police, Betty.'

'What would I say to them? My brother had a row with a friend and I've had two silent phone calls. They would think I was mad.'

'What are you going to do?'

'I was hoping that you could get in touch with the men in the photo. Bill has put their names and addresses on this piece of paper, and maybe they have the answer to all this mystery.'

Molly was unsure but Betty said, 'Bill did ask you to warn them and I'm wondering if you said you would.'

Molly tried to remember the exact words exchanged at the tragic scene and for the life of her she couldn't recall if she had promised or not.

'I don't have a lot of time to go round everyone as I have my agency to run.'

'Well, even if you can speak to a couple of the men then they will be able to clear everything up.'

Molly glanced at the clock on the mantelpiece. It was time to leave if she wanted to catch the train. Betty stood up and walked with her to the door. 'I'm sorry I asked, Molly. I know you are a busy woman. I'll just have to forget about it. Maybe some of Bill's colleagues will come to the funeral but I don't want to make a fuss then.'

'When is the funeral?'

'It's on Friday at 11am in the local church here in Pitlochry, but Bill will be buried in Balgay cemetery at 2pm. That's where Annie's ashes are buried and I know this was what he wanted.'

Molly turned at the gate. 'I'll do my best to contact some of them and I'll be in touch. Give me your telephone number and I'll phone you with any news.'

Betty thanked her and handed over the pouch with everything

inside. Molly couldn't help feeling it was an albatross around her neck as she walked to the station.

When she arrived home she scrutinised the photo and tried once again to match up the faces with the names Bill Reid had written on his scrap of paper, but it was useless. She would have to wait until she had contacted them all to put names to the men.

Studying the photo, they all looked so healthy and happy that Molly could hardly believe there was anything sinister behind Bill's accident. Then she remembered the sound of angry voices that they had both heard above their heads but that could have been something quite innocent. After all, people did have arguments and it could have been two walkers like herself and Marigold who had fallen out over something trivial. She tried to recall if any words had stood out but the men, because she was sure it was two men, hadn't been shouting, their deep voices had drifted down to the women below.

She picked up the diary again but because of the tiny, cramped writing she decided to put everything away and if she had the time she would go and visit the men, as they all had addresses in Dundee. That is, if they or their wives and family still lived there.

13

Charlie was frustrated with having no new leads in the robberies. Although a few known villains had been questioned he felt these cases had the mark of someone who was very clever. He didn't like the word 'mastermind' but that was what it looked like. Most of the people he knew who specialised in burglaries were mainly petty criminals who, when the opportunity arose, were able to break in and steal whatever they could but these cases had the hallmarks of meticulous planning behind them.

He looked at the case notes. The first robbery had been in a detached house in Broughty Ferry, followed a week later by another one in the same area, while the third one was a large bungalow half a mile from Ninewells. All three were either in isolated spots or stood on their own with not many houses near them.

Then there were the stolen items, which were considerable. The first house had lost four hundred pounds in cash, plus five hundred pounds worth of jewellery. The second one's haul was even more, with three hundred pounds of valuable silver, three hundred pounds of jewellery and four hundred and fifty pounds in cash, while the third one had mostly money and some jewellery, plus a collection of gold sovereigns stolen.

That was why Charlie was puzzled by this last robbery, which had a few minor paintings and a few items of silver taken. Either this case wasn't linked with the other three or else the thieves thought there was more to steal than there actually was.

He called PC Williamson. 'Bring the car around. We're going back to see Mrs French, the housekeeper.'

They set off in the rain but by the time they reached Monifieth the rain had stopped. The sea and sky still looked grey, with large black clouds gathering on the horizon, and it looked as if more rain wasn't far off.

PC Williamson said, 'Will Mrs French be at her own house or at her work?' Charlie told him he didn't know but they would try her work first and, failing that, then they would go to her cottage.

As it turned out, she was at her work. She looked surprised when she saw the two policemen on the doorstep but she politely asked them in. She walked towards the back of the house.

'I'm in the kitchen. I've just made a pot of coffee if you would like some.'

Charlie said they would, much to PC Williamson's relief, as he had missed his lunch break due to writing up reports.

The kitchen was large with a wooden table and chairs beside an old-fashioned dresser with blue and white plates on its shelves. A pot of coffee stood on the stove and she went to the cupboard and took out another two cups and saucers, along with a tin which held a delicious-looking Victoria sponge cake. Two large windows faced the back garden, and to the left Charlie saw washing hanging out on a line.

Mrs French noticed his look and laughed. 'I've just hung the washing out and I hope the rain stays off.'

Charlie said, 'Do you do all the work here on your own, Mrs French?'

He noticed she had lovely teeth when she smiled. 'Yes I do. There isn't a lot of work because Mr Bergmann is very easy to look after. This house belongs to his wife who's gone off on a cruise. Of course, there's more work to do even when she's here.' She looked at PC Williamson. 'Do have a bit of sponge. It'll go stale otherwise.' He didn't need another telling and was soon enjoying a huge wedge which had jam oozing from the sides.

'It's a lovely sponge, Mrs French. Did you bake it yourself?'

She smiled again, showing her teeth. 'Yes I did. I sometimes think I would like to have someone to be here to enjoy all my baking but I don't, so please eat up.'

Charlie gave him a warning glance and his face went as red as the jam.

'Mrs French, have you remembered anything else from the day of the robbery?'

'Oh, please call me Laura. No I haven't. I've told you all that I recalled at the time.'

Charlie stood up. 'Well thank you for your time, Laura, and if you do remember anything give me a call.' He handed her a card with his telephone number at the station.

Meanwhile PC Williamson was trying to brush the crumbs from his tunic onto the plate in case he had dropped any onto the tiled floor. At the door she gave them both a ravishing smile before closing it.

'She's a great-looking woman, isn't she, sir?'

Charlie nodded. 'Yes she is.'

14

Molly decided, if it was possible, to go to Bill Reid's funeral at Balgay cemetery on Friday afternoon. She was hoping to meet some of his colleagues and make an appointment to see them at a later date.

Luckily, as it turned out, she was free that afternoon. There was an assignment in the morning but she worked out she would have time to be there after her work. She had phoned Betty to tell her and was told that Betty would meet her at the main gate. It was raining again and Molly wondered if summer would ever come.

Molly stood by the gate with a black umbrella until Betty appeared in a car behind the hearse, then they were both driven to the graveside. Betty, dressed in a black coat, hat and gloves, looked terrible and her eyes were red-rimmed from crying. Sitting beside her was the minister from the church in Pitlochry.

'How did the service go?' Molly asked.

'Quite a few of our neighbours and friends were there but no one from the photo.' Betty sounded disappointed.

When they reached the plot, Molly saw a few people standing on the grass. Betty got out and went over to speak to them then the minister conducted the service. Molly stood a few yards from the small gathering and her spirits rose when she thought she recognised one familiar face. He looked to be about the same age as Bill but maybe a bit taller. He wore a dark suit with a black tie.

The rain didn't stop. It was a scene of dripping trees and wet gravestones. Molly suddenly felt depressed by the finality of someone's life and she longed to be away from all the sadness.

Then it was all over. As people left, Betty thanked them again then came over to stand beside Molly.

'I recognise that man. He's one of the men in the photo, isn't he?' Molly asked.

Betty nodded. "His name is Alex McGregor. He spoke to me a few minutes ago, although I couldn't bring myself to talk about all that's happened to Bill, his warning and all. Not today. Do you think you could go to him and have a chat?"

Molly said she could and hurriedly walked toward him to introduce herself. The man seemed surprised to be addressed so confidently by someone he had never met but he was polite all the same.

'I'm sorry to bother you at such a sad time, but can I ask you a few questions about your time in India with Bill?'

He gave her a startled glance but nodded.

'I don't want to ask here,' said Molly. 'Can I come and see you one night? Bill's sister Betty has asked me to try and find out more about his time in India. Do you still live at the same address as Bill had in his address book?' Actually the address was on a simple sheet of paper but the man wouldn't know that.

The man nodded. 'I'll be able to see you next Monday night, about seven o'clock, if that is all right?'

Molly said it was fine and he walked away. Betty asked if she wanted a lift and Molly said she would be grateful if the car could drop her off in the town somewhere if that was possible.

The minister, who seemed to be a friend of Betty's, chatted about the service on their way into town but within a few minutes Molly was out of the car and saying goodbye to the both of them. Betty said she would phone over the weekend.

After work, she was in the office when Edna appeared. Molly felt really guilty that she hadn't seen much of her since the wedding but Edna didn't seem to notice. She was carrying a shopping bag.

'We're getting James and Sonia tonight for a meal. It'll be great to see him but I'm not looking forward to Sonia's visit. John feels the same.'

'How is James? I wonder how he got on after the wedding when she walked out on him?'

'We don't know because we haven't seen them till now.'

'Your mum seems to be enjoying the job, Edna.' In fact, Molly was very pleased with Irene and she had received quite a few good reports about her work.

Edna's face lit up. 'Oh yes, she really enjoys meeting people and it's been a godsend to her after all the years of looking after Billy. Well, I better head home to start cooking the meal. John has done most of it but I wanted some fresh fish.'

Once Edna left, Molly was about to lock up when Charlie appeared. 'Do you fancy going out somewhere for a meal?' he asked.

Molly said if he didn't mind waiting until she changed, she would love to but she said she was going to see her parents afterwards so she would have to catch the ferry. Charlie said that was fine as he hoped to do some extra work tonight, looking through the files to see if he had missed something.

They walked down to Wilson's Restaurant in Union Street and Molly was glad to sit down and be waited on. When the waitress came she ordered gammon steak while Charlie wanted fish and chips.

'How's the case going, Charlie?' She noticed he still looked tired but by the look of him he had gone home and changed.

He shook his head. 'It's going nowhere. We had another robbery in Monifieth last week and we haven't managed to get any leads.' He looked so worn out and disappointed that Molly decided not to mention Bill Reid and his happy gang in India. There wasn't any mystery about his accident and Betty was probably making a drama out of nothing. She would go and see Alex McGregor on Monday and that would be the end of it.

Charlie asked her, 'How was the weekend with Marigold, and did you enjoy the play?'

Molly said they both loved it and Deanna was very good in it. 'We stayed in a great guest house. The owner, Bess, made us very welcome and we think we will go back later in the summer to see Deanna again.'

Charlie tried to look interested in the theatre but failed.

Molly said that was the plan but they hadn't made any firm commitment. She knew she should tell him about the accident but didn't want to mention that she might get involved. She knew how he was always telling her to stay away from trouble. She tried to be casual. 'While we were there we went for a walk to the Soldier's Leap at Killicrankie and we were involved in an accident.'

Charlie looked at her and put down his knife and fork. 'What kind of accident?'

'An elderly man fell from the path above and sadly he died. Marigold went to phone for an ambulance but it was too late.'

'Was he a visitor to the town?'

'No, he lived with his sister and she asked if I could go and see her.'

Charlie had stopped eating and he frowned at her.

'Why did she want to see you, Molly?'

Molly hated avoiding the truth but he would tell her to leave things alone. He would say that was why she had been in two situations in the past that had been dangerous. She thought, *He's got enough on his plate with his own work without being worried about me.*

'The sister, her name is Betty Holden, just wanted to thank us for helping her brother and because she phoned the agency, I didn't want to bother Marigold so I went on my own.'

'What, back to Pitlochry?'

'Yes, she was planning on coming to Dundee and I didn't want her to have to travel so I went there.'

'And what did she say?'

Molly was getting tired of this interrogation. 'She made me tea and buttered pancakes and thanked us for being with her brother before he died.' She cut up her gammon steak and didn't look at him.

'Look, Molly, please don't get caught up in any more mysteries.'

'Why would there be a mystery over an unfortunate accident, Charlie?'

He gave her an intense look then resumed eating his meal. 'I don't know, but I do know you.'

Molly wanted to change the subject. 'What about your cases? Have you met any interesting criminals?'

Charlie smiled. 'Oh I'm always meeting criminals but I'm a bit puzzled by the housekeeper in the last robbery.'

'Oh, don't tell me. She's elderly and had a heart attack or a shock.'

'No, she's certainly not elderly. She says she's thirty-five but she looks much younger, is very attractive and PC Williamson is fascinated by her.'

Molly said dryly, 'What does DS Johns think about her?'

This time Charlie laughed out loud. The people from the next table turned and looked then quickly returned to their meals. 'I think she's a puzzle. She says she's a widow so maybe that's why she's working as a housekeeper, but, like you, I always thought this kind of work-in service was usually done by older women. This woman looks as if she could run a successful company.'

Thankfully Molly's news from Pitlochry seemed to have been forgotten. They chatted while they lingered over cups of tea and Molly was surprised by the time. 'I'll have to run to catch the ferry, Charlie.'

He settled the bill and said, 'I'll walk down with you and then head for home.'

Molly said not to bother. 'You look really worn out and it means walking back to Shore Terrace for your bus. I'll see you later in the week, and thanks for the meal.'

They said goodbye at the foot of Union Street and she watched as he hurried to catch his bus. With a sigh she walked to Craig Pier just as the ferry was docking.

Her mother was waiting for her when she arrived at the house. 'Your dad's putting the heater in the greenhouse as it's been cold these last few nights.'

Molly said she didn't want anything to eat but her mother put the kettle on. 'I'll make some Ovaltine for us all.'

Her dad came back in and he was rubbing his hands. 'I wish it would get a bit warmer now that we're into May,' he said.

Nancy gave him a queer look and shook her head.

Molly asked if anything was wrong.

Her parents looked at one another again and Archie said, 'We weren't going to say anything just yet, Molly, but your mum and I have been seriously thinking of selling up here and moving to Australia.'

Molly was so shocked that she felt as if someone had punched her. 'What, sell this house and go and live permanently in Australia?'

They both nodded but Nancy said, 'We haven't made up our minds entirely but we're thinking about it. We would like to be near our grandchildren and Nell and Terry. Now, Molly, we want you to think about coming with us because we don't like leaving you here alone. You will get a good price if you sell the agency and there's nothing to stop you opening another one in Australia.' She made it sound as if moving to the other side of the world was simple.

'I don't know, Mum. It's a big decision.'

Her dad said, 'Of course it is, and as we've said, it's just a consideration at the moment.'

Molly stood up, not wanting to hear any more. 'I have to go and see Marigold.'

Marigold was also sitting with a warm drink but hers was cocoa. She was pleased to see her. 'Sit down and tell me all the news.'

Molly told her about going to see Betty and how the woman wanted her to see the men in the photo.

Marigold looked worried. 'Do you think that's wise, Molly?'

Molly didn't know but she said, 'That man, Bill, asked me to warn them and I know he trusted me to do it so I don't have a choice. Anyway, it's not going to be dangerous.' She felt her throat go dry. 'Have Mum and Dad mentioned their plans to leave here and go to live in Australia?'

Marigold said they had and she looked sad. 'I do hope you'll go with them.' She went to the sideboard and brought her a small glass of sherry. 'But still, remember that it's only an idea at the moment, Molly,' said Marigold comfortingly.

But rather than consoling her, Marigold's words only caused more worry in Molly's mind. If she had been much younger she would have been tempted to burst into tears, but instead she said, 'Yes, you're quite right, Marigold. I shouldn't really worry as it is only an idea.'

What she didn't say was that she hoped it remained an idea and not a foregone conclusion.

15

Edna wanted the meal to be special. She knew she shouldn't let Sonia intimidate her but the woman had the uncanny knack of making everyone feel inferior. Edna was cooking a fish dish that she had seen in her brand new cookbook, but between giving Billy his tea and then getting him off to bed, John had taken over and she hoped the dish would turn out all right.

At seven o'clock James and Sonia turned up and she waltzed in like she owned the house. 'Oh I see you've changed the furniture in here,' she said airily as she swept into the lounge.

John ignored her comment and went and stood beside his wife. 'Well, sit down,' he said.

Edna went into the little used dining room. A fire had been lit to warm it up and two lamps were also lit, making the place look cosy.

Edna was amused to see Sonia had dressed for the occasion. The only thing was, it was a meal with her relations and not a grand invitation to Buckingham Palace. Although Sonia's dress looked simple, Edna had the feeling that it had cost a lot of money. She was also wearing her late sister Kathleen's necklace and ring.

John had given Sonia a glass of sherry but James had asked for a small whisky. Sonia was holding centre stage when Edna reappeared. 'I keep telling James that we need to buy a bigger house. That poky flat of his isn't the proper place for a renowned artist.'

James muttered, 'Well I like it.'

Sonia gave him a pitying look. 'That's not the point. It's all to do with image. When customers come round to look at your paintings all they see are the small rooms and they go away with the image that you're an artist of no repute.'

James's face went red, and John and Edna were visibly annoyed.

John said, 'James's paintings have always sold extremely well.'

It was as if Sonia hadn't heard. 'And that's another thing. I'm always telling him to rent a nice shop in the town and convert it into an art gallery but he won't listen.'

Edna stood up, clearly wanting to change the subject and get on with the evening. 'Let's go in and eat.'

Sonia threw her a glance. 'Oh, we're eating in the dining room, are we? I thought we would be in the kitchen.'

Edna had had enough. She said sweetly, 'Well we knew you would dress up for the occasion, Sonia, so we decided to act graciously.'

John had to bite his lip to stop himself laughing but James didn't, bursting into laughter. 'That's you told off, Sonia.'

The two men turned to put their glasses on a side table so they missed the terrible look that Sonia gave Edna. Unfortunately Edna saw it.

Worse was to follow. The soup was delicious but when it came to the fish, Sonia got a small bone stuck in her throat and it took most of the evening to dislodge it. They tried everything from ice cream to loads of water until it was finally gone. She made such a fuss, saying she didn't feel like eating a pudding or coffee and she wanted to go home.

James went and turned the car around and within minutes they were away but not before he thanked them for a lovely evening.

Before he followed Sonia out to the car, John took him aside and said, 'You've got to get rid of her, James, or she'll ruin you.'

James said he realised that but she wouldn't budge from his so-called 'poky' flat.

After they'd gone, Edna was dismayed. She felt she had made a mess of the first family get-together. 'I'm so sorry, John. I really tried hard.'

'It's not your fault, Edna, or anyone's fault except Sonia's. She has always been like this and James has got to make her go.'

'But where will she go? You said she had lost her business and home in Edinburgh and that's why she landed back with you.'

John looked grim. 'I know, but something's got to be done.'

When Molly arrived back at the flat she couldn't settle. Her parents' news had floored her and even if it was just an idea she knew that her mother desperately wanted to be near her grandchildren.

To take her mind off her worries, she looked again at the newspaper cutting. Bill had put their names on the sheet, marked clockwise. Bill was at the top of the table with Douglas Kingsley, Alex McGregor, Pete Lindsay, J.P. Pritchard, Edmond Lamb, George Stevenson and Phillip Thorne, the man who had put the photo in the paper. There was no date, so Molly didn't know when it was taken but it was a social group and they all looked happy and relaxed. She scrutinised the addresses and they were all in the Dundee area. Alex McGregor lived in the Perth Road so he would be easy to see on Monday night.

She then looked at the diary and noted that Bill had started writing in it from the first of January 1947.

We've had a jolly new year's party. Had too much to drink but have to be back at work tomorrow. Worse luck. I miss Annie so much as she always loved the new year's celebrations.

The rest of that week had dealt with the day-to-day running of the plantation but because the writing was small and difficult to read she decided to leave it until she spoke with Alex.

She was putting it away when a small photograph fell out. It must have been between the pages. It was of a pretty young girl. She looked to be around sixteen and was wearing a thin floral dress, sandals and a straw hat. She was shielding her eyes from the sun and Molly wondered if it had been taken in India. At first she thought it was maybe Bill's daughter but then she remembered that Betty had said that neither of them had been blessed with children. She then wondered if it was an early photo of his wife Annie but the dress had a look of the post-war era.

By now she was tired so she slipped the photo back in the diary and got ready for bed.

16

Monday night was mild and pleasant so Molly decided to walk to Alex McGregor's house in Perth Road. She thought it would be one of the large houses but it turned out to be a flat above a ladies' dress shop.

She entered the close and looked at the nameplates as she climbed the stairs. The doors were solid-looking and the walls had the fresh shine of new paint. His flat was on the top floor and when she rang the bell it made a pleasant sound. After what seemed like ages, she heard Alex making his way to the door which he opened about two inches and peered out.

'It's me, Mr McGregor. I met you at Bill Reid's funeral and we arranged to meet tonight.' Molly felt she had to make this long introduction because he seemed to have forgotten about their arrangement.

He opened the door fractionally wider and said, 'Oh yes, I remember. Come in.' He led the way along a narrow hall and into the living room which overlooked the street. It had a comfortable feel about it with its old-fashioned furniture, a sturdy settee and chairs and a dining room suite that Molly thought was called 'Jacobean'. The window was almost hidden behind thick velvet curtains.

Molly sat down on one of the chairs and brought the pouch out of her bag. Alex said he would make some tea that she really didn't want but thought it was rude to refuse. Five minutes later he was back, carrying a tray with the cups and saucers. Once he was settled across from her, he said, 'I don't know what you're looking for and I'm not sure if I can help you.'

Molly handed him the contents of the pouch and said, 'Bill

Reid gave this to me just before he died and he asked me to warn you all.'

Alex's head shot up. 'Warn us? What about?'

Molly shook her head. 'I was hoping you might know the answer.' She felt at a disadvantage sitting opposite him, and as if reading her thoughts, he rose slowly to his feet and pulled over a small chair and sat beside her.

First of all, he looked at the cutting and the paper with the names. His eyes seemed to glaze over as if he was looking far back into the past. 'This photo was taken in March 1944. The Japanese armies were in Burma and we thought they would invade India but thankfully they didn't. The British army landed in Burma and surprised the invaders by forming an airstrip out of the jungle. It was a complete success. We were all managers of various tea plantations in Darjeeling, although Phillip Thorne,' he pointed to the young man, 'he had just arrived from Assam and was starting work on one of the plantations. The rest of us had been in the area for a few years and we all knew one another. Some of us who were married had wives living with us and they had their own Scottish club.'

Molly asked if his wife was one of them and he chuckled. 'No, I never married. I'm an old bachelor.'

Molly explained the background to Bill's death and his warning. 'I'm totally at a loss why he was so agitated.'

Alex stroked his chin. 'Maybe you misheard him.'

'Betty, his sister, said she was worried about him a week or two before this. She said he was having an argument on the phone with someone and he said it had to be sorted out, whatever that means.'

Alex looked at the cutting again but Molly realised he hadn't opened the diary. 'His diary is from nineteen forty-seven,' she said.

Alex said he had noticed that. 'Nineteen forty-six and nineteen forty-seven were terrible years in India. The Hindus and the Moslems were fighting for territory and the Moslem leader, Ali Jinnah, wanted a breakaway country. People who had lived together for years suddenly had to move, either to Moslem Pakistan in the north or the Hindu-controlled lands in India. Then the Sikhs' holy city of Amritsar was burnt to the ground, which meant more violence between the Moslems and the Hindus and Sikhs. Unfortunately, we were almost in the middle of it.' He shook his head slowly. 'Yes it was a terrible time. Not just for us but also for the thousands of people from both sides who were massacred.'

Molly said it was certainly a sad and terrible time but she still didn't understand why Bill had given his warning. 'Is that when you all came back?'

He shook his head again. 'No, most of us stayed until after independence but the place wasn't safe so we all left at various times. I think Phillip Thorne was first to go but I'm not sure in what order we left. J.P. left suddenly without telling anyone.' He pointed to the cutting again. 'Bill, Douglas Kingsley, Edmond Lamb, George Stevenson, Peter Lindsay and myself stayed for another couple of weeks.'

Molly was intrigued. 'Why do you think J.P. did that?'

'Well he had a big tragedy in his life.'

'What happened?'

Alex looked uncomfortable. 'I really don't want to talk about it as it's so sad.'

This statement surprised her. After all, whatever happened had happened years ago so why did he hesitate to elaborate now? 'If I have to carry out Bill's last wish then I need to know all I can.'

He sat in silence for a few moments. 'J.P. – we only ever called him that – and his wife lived in a bungalow on the edge of the plantation. It wasn't isolated but it was tucked away down a dirt track road. He had three children who were all at school in Edinburgh. About six weeks before independence, his daughter, aged sixteen, and his son, who was ten, came to visit. His oldest girl stayed behind with her grandparents. We were surrounded by violence but none of the plantation workers had been harmed which made it all the more tragic. It was during the monsoon

86

season when someone shot and killed his wife and daughter but the boy was lucky he wasn't there, otherwise he would have been killed as well.'

Molly felt sick at this news. 'Did they catch the killer?'

Alex shook his head. 'It was assumed at the time that it was rebel fighters. They were all over the place but whether they were from the Moslem or Hindu community, no one ever found out. Of course the police investigated it, but as I said the country was in turmoil.'

'What happened to the boy?'

'His father shipped him home to his grandparents and J.P. left not long after that. I certainly never heard from him again but maybe some of the others did.'

Molly opened the diary and took out the photo of the young girl. 'Do you recognise this girl?'

Alex took the photo and he began to cry. 'That's Naomi, J.P.'s daughter,' he said, wiping tears from his eyes with a large white handkerchief. 'She was a lovely girl.'

'When did the killings happen?'

Alex had to give this some more thought. 'Independence Day was on the stroke of midnight, the fourteenth of August, so it must have been late July or early August. It was the school holidays, that was why the two children were in India.'

'Can you remember anything else about that time, Alex? That Indian summer?'

'Oh I can remember a lot but nothing that would help you with Bill's warning.'

Molly realised there was nothing else to be gained and she thanked him for helping. 'There's just one more thing. What about the rest of the men in the photo, have you met up with any of them since you left India?'

'No I haven't. I thought something might come off about the reunion, but you know that Phillip is dead.'

Molly said she did. 'Bill had all the names and addresses written down. Do you think he kept in touch with them?'

'I don't know, he might have done but those addresses were

where they used to live in Dundee. They've probably all moved since then. I didn't know Bill had moved to Pitlochry until I saw the death in the paper. Even then I wasn't sure it was him.'

This time Molly stood up and Alex walked with her to the door.

'I'm sorry I couldn't help more but I wish you luck with your enquiries.' He paused. 'Can I say something?'

Molly nodded.

'Sometimes it's better to leave the past well alone. You never know what you'll find.'

Molly had a moment of déjà vu. How well she recalled Marigold saying the same thing in 1953 and how she had disregarded the advice.

As she walked away down the street she saw Alex standing at his window. He looked like a sad, lonely man with bad memories.

It was still light so Molly decided to go and visit Phillip Thorne's wife. She could catch a tramcar at Tay Street and it would take her to 400 Strathmartine Road.

As the tram trundled its way along the road, she looked out of the window to catch sight of the numbers on the shop doorways. That way she would have an idea where to get off. Mrs Thorne lived in a neat detached bungalow with a grass lawn and a gravel path edged with blue and white lobelia. The door was painted in a deep blue and the window frames were white. Molly had never seen a house that echoed the colours in the garden.

She rang the bell and hoped Mrs Thorne wouldn't mind her turning up out of the blue. She didn't know what to expect but when the woman opened the door it was a shock because she was in a wheelchair. Her right ankle was in plaster.

Molly explained her visit and said she was sorry for not calling or writing first. The woman said it didn't matter because she was always glad of company. She went ahead down the hall and into the front room that overlooked the colour co-ordinated garden. It was a light airy room with a three-piece settee suite with oatmeal-coloured covers. The modern sideboard held lots of photographs.

Molly got right to the point. 'Mrs Thorne, I've come about Bill Reid, who I believe was in India with your late husband. His sister has asked me to try and contact all the men in the photo your husband put in the paper.'

The woman pulled a packet of cigarettes from her pocket and offered one to Molly, who shook her head. 'I wish I didn't smoke but I can't give it up,' Mrs Thorne said ruefully. 'And call me Rhona.'

Molly pulled the cutting from her bag. 'I've just come from Alex McGregor's house and he gave me some background on his time in India. He said your husband tried to organise a reunion but he died before it could be arranged.'

Rhona nodded thoughtfully. 'Yes, that's right. We were both in the car when we had the accident. I ended up with this broken ankle but Phillip wasn't so lucky.' She took a hankie from her other pocket and dabbed her eyes.

Molly felt terrible, she shouldn't have come here to intrude on this poor woman's grief. 'Look, Rhona, I'll leave and not bother you, and I'm sorry if I've upset you.'

Rhona waved her hand. 'Please sit down. I see you're not up-to-date with the situation. Phillip and I split up during his time in India. When we were first married I went out to Assam with him but it was an awful place. Do you know it gets over two hundred days of rain a year and gets called the Scottish Highlands? Well, I stuck it for a couple of years then we moved to Darjeeling but my mother died and I came home.' She lit up another cigarette and blew the smoke towards the open window. 'To tell the truth, I never went back and I didn't see Phillip again until 1947 when he told me all hell had broken loose. He stayed here for a couple of weeks then got a flat in Ann Street then a year ago we met up and we had a reconciliation. Still it didn't last long, did it?'

'Rhona, did he ever mention the murder of Mrs Pritchard and her daughter Naomi?'

Rhona screwed up her face. 'Yes he did. Said it was a terrible time and that was one of the reasons he came home. That and the Indian independence.'

'Did he say what he thought had happened?'

'It was the warring sides, some rebel soldiers. Or least that's what he said. I never asked him much about his time there but when he came back here last year he had dreadful nightmares. That was why he wanted the reunion. To reassure himself that those days were over.'

'Alex said that J.P. Pritchard just left without any warning, did he say anything about that?'

'No, I don't think he knew that because he was the first manager to leave the plantations but I do know he hoped to meet up with the others and get all their news. But we'll never know now, will we?'

'I believe there was a son and another daughter of the murdered woman. Did your husband ever mention them?'

Rhona gave this some thought. 'He said the boy was sent back to the grandparents and the older girl was also there but I don't think he knew where.'

Molly was running out of questions and it was clear Rhona didn't know a lot except what her husband had told her.

'One last thing, did your husband ever mention anything about digging?'

Rhona looked puzzled. 'Digging. You mean in the garden? No he didn't but he did enjoy doing up the garden, as you can see, and he did a lot of digging in it before he got it looking the way it is now.

Molly didn't want to bother the woman any longer so she thanked her.

Rhona said, 'I'm sorry, I didn't offer you tea or coffee.'

'That's all right. I had some at Alex's house.' She said her goodbyes and hoped Rhona would soon be on her feet again.

It was still light outside when she caught the tram back to the Wellgate steps.

17

Alice Charles arrived at work the next morning at the agency. Today she would pay off the last instalment of her new dining room suite. That just left a fireside rug to buy and her house was now all newly furnished, so why did she feel apprehensive?

Her life had changed dramatically since her divorce from the abusive Victor and she valued her friendship with Sandy, who was one of Victor's workmates from the Caledon shipyard. Thinking back, she realised it was Sandy who was making her nervous. He was becoming very serious in their friendship, while she was content to live her own life without another commitment.

Last night while leaving her at the door he had said jokingly that it was a pity he couldn't stay, especially as it was pouring with rain at the time. They had both been to the Broadway Picture House and she was glad to be home as it had been a tiring day at work with two cleaning jobs, one of which was a spring clean with the client insisting every rug had to be lifted and every ornament removed and dusted.

She was almost away to her new assignment when Maisie, her friend and neighbour, appeared. Alice asked how Mrs Jankowski was keeping.

'She's a lot better,' said Maisie. 'She manages on her own now so her friends don't have to stay with her. I've got the removal of the dreaded curtains again today.'

Alice laughed. It was a well-known fact that Mrs Jankowski changed her thick chenille curtains every spring but this had been delayed due to her accident.

'I was hoping she had forgotten about them,' said Maisie, who remembered all too well last year when she had to balance on a stepladder to remove the heavy and very dusty items.

'How is Sandy these days, Alice? Did you enjoy the film last night?' she asked.

Alice nodded. 'He's fine.' She then added, 'Do you mind if I come in and see you tonight, Maisie?'

Maisie looked at her and said yes, she would be glad to see her.

They were on their way out when Mary hurried in. She was blowing her nose and her voice sounded hoarse.

'It sounds like you've got a bad cold, Mary,' said Maisie. 'You should have stayed in your bed.'

Mary said she had thought about it but she couldn't let Molly down because there was a lot of work to do for the next couple of days.

Then Molly appeared and she had dark circles under her eyes. She hadn't been sleeping very well due to her parents' planned move to Australia and also all the time she was spending on Bill Reid's case.

As Maisie and Alice hurried up the road to their respective jobs, Maisie said, 'Molly and Mary both look ill. I hope the agency is doing all right.'

Alice gave her a sharp, worried look but stayed silent.

Just before six o'clock that evening Alice was sitting with a cup of tea and an onion bridie in Maisie's house. She had been persuaded to stay and have her tea, and the truth was, she was enjoying not having to cook for herself. Afterwards they listened to the news on the wireless.

'Is Sandy coming round tonight, Alice?'

Alice shook her head. 'No.'

Maisie looked at her friend with a puzzled frown. 'You haven't fallen out with him?'

Alice said no, she hadn't. Suddenly she burst into tears.

Maisie was alarmed. 'Something has happened. What is it?'

Alice found the words were tumbling out of her mouth and

stopped to get a breath. 'I think he wants to move in with me, Maisie. He more or less said so last night and I don't want that. I've just got rid of one unhappy marriage and I couldn't face another one.'

Maisie sat quiet for a moment or two. 'What makes you think it would be unhappy? Sandy is a different man from Victor.'

'Yes, but don't you see? Victor was charming when I first met him and he didn't turn nasty until we were a few months married. By then it was too late.' She scrabbled in her message bag and pulled out a copy of *The People's Friend*. 'I read an article in here that said we always attract the same kind of man or woman in our lives and what do I do if that's the case?'

Maisie tried not to laugh. 'It's just a bit in the magazine to fill up space,' she said.

Alice shook her head. 'No, it was written by this woman who has studied this. She's an expert.'

Maisie said she hoped heaven would protect us from experts. However, she could see that Alice believed it.

'Well you're just going to have to be truthful with him and tell him you don't want a serious relationship.'

Then they heard the knock on Alice's door. Maisie peeped out from behind the curtain. 'It's Sandy. He's got a big bunch of flowers.'

'Oh no!' cried Alice. 'I can't see him.'

'He'll wonder where you are.'

Then the knock came to Maisie's door. Alice hurried into the bedroom. 'Tell him I'm not here.'

Alice stood with the door slightly ajar and heard Maisie sound surprised at Sandy's appearance. 'No I'm sorry, Sandy, I haven't seen Alice today. We were on different shifts. Was she expecting you?'

Sandy's voice was loud and clear. 'No she wasn't but I thought I would surprise her and maybe take her out for a meal.'

Maisie replied, 'Yes, I'll give her these lovely flowers and tell her you missed her.'

After he left, Alice looked at the flowers. 'Do you see what I mean, Maisie? Now I feel guilty and wish I'd never read that article.' She had a thought. 'You don't think he'll come back tonight, do you?'

Maisie said she didn't have a crystal ball in her dish cupboard.

'You're going to have to face him some time, Alice, and I think you should tell him how you feel.'

Alice nodded and went back to her own house. She didn't have a vase to put the flowers in so she settled for a large milk jug and she didn't turn the light on.

While all this romantic drama was going on, Molly was sitting with her half-eaten tea on the table and the diary in front of her. Alex McGregor had said the deaths of Naomi and her mother had happened just before independence day so she turned to July and August in the diary. The beginning of July was filled with all the mayhem and atrocities of the partition of India.

Terrible news today, twenty-six bodies found massacred in one of the fields. The Moslems are getting the blame. What is happening to this glorious country?

Then at the beginning of the second week was another massacre on a train with men, women and children murdered in cold blood. This time the dead were Moslems and the Hindus were said to be the culprits.

Molly felt a shiver in her spine. It was terrible reading the accounts of such horrible atrocities, and she could well imagine how the British managers felt being in the middle of it.

Then on the twenty-fourth of July she found the entry:

What a dreadful, dreadful day.

The word 'dreadful' had been underlined.

J.P.'s wife and poor Naomi have been found shot.

94

Everyone here is in total shock and the police are investigating.

The entry for the next day was just as harrowing.

The two bodies have been taken into the morgue in town. J.P. is inconsolable. Police think it was marauding bandits who carried out this terrible crime. They say they could be miles away by now. We are all still in shock.

Molly looked through the rest of that month and found out when J.P.'s son was shipped home. It was the twenty-seventh of July.

Michael still not any better. He is going back to Scotland tomorrow but he still hasn't said a word. The doctor says it is delayed shock at the dreadful news of his mother and sister's deaths.

Molly finished her cup of tea and wondered where Michael was now. He would be about seventeen or eighteen, she reckoned. He was no longer a child but a young man, and what about the older daughter who hadn't gone to India? Where was she?

On the twelfth of August there was an entry about J.P.'s disappearance.

No sign of J.P. He must have packed his bags and left. Douglas said he had talked about leaving but thought he meant along with the rest of us. We are all ready to go. I'll miss this place but thank goodness Annie isn't still here to see the country she loved like this. I can't think why J.P. didn't say goodbye, but he must still be in shock, which is understandable.

The last entry was on the eighteenth.

All packed up and ready to go, Alex left this morning and I'll be going this afternoon. Douglas will leave tomorrow. Edmond, Peter and George left yesterday.

Molly put the diary away. It was almost ten o'clock so she got ready for bed. She awoke at two o'clock after a vivid nightmare about marauding bandits with sharp bayonets and guns and ships going off to Australia without her. She didn't get back to sleep till five.

18

Charlie had another frustrating day with no new leads in the robbery cases. He had spent most of the day filling in his reports and decided to have an early night at home. Before catching the tram to his flat in Dens Road, he called in at the agency to see if Molly was in the office.

Jean said she was filling in for Mary, who was off with a very bad cold. Charlie asked her to tell Molly he had called but he would see her at the weekend.

While Charlie was at the agency, Molly was dealing with a difficult situation in the office of a large wholesale company. An important invoice had gone missing and seemingly Mary had been the last person to have it.

She had a good rake around the desk that, up till yesterday, Mary had occupied, but there was no sign of it. Feeling that the agency's reputation was at stake, she went to see the woman in charge.

Mrs Fielding was a stern-faced, grey-haired woman in her fifties. She wore a grey suit and blouse and Molly's first impression wasn't favourable. Mrs Fielding was very annoyed about the missing invoice and as she had a loud voice, most of the office staff heard the conversation. 'I think your girl isn't up to scratch here, Miss McQueen, and I have to say I'm not impressed with your agency.'

Molly tried not to be aggressive because she had no idea what Mary had done with the invoice so she tried to be reasonable. 'I have great faith in my staff, Mrs Fielding, and Mary is very conscientious.'

'Well if she's that good, where is the invoice?'

That, thought Molly, was the sixty-four-thousand dollar question.

'Did anyone else have it yesterday, Mrs Fielding?' she asked.

The woman snapped. 'No they did not. Your girl was working on that account and no one else.'

'Well I'll have another look for it.' That was all she could say.

The office got an hour's break for lunch so Molly decided she would have to go and see Mary. She wouldn't have too much time but hopefully the bus would get her there quickly, as the last thing she wanted to do was to be late in getting back to work.

Thankfully the wholesale office was near the centre of the town and when she hurried to Shore Terrace there was a bus standing at the stance. Mrs Watt opened the door when she hurried up the close at Moncur Crescent and she looked worried.

'The doctor has said Mary has bronchitis.'

Molly said she was sorry to intrude but if she could just have a quick word with Mary. Mrs Watt led the way to the back bedroom where Mary was lying in bed, propped up with two pillows. When she saw Molly she tried to sit up straighter.

'I'm really sorry to bother you, Mary, when you're ill but I need your help.' She went on to tell her about the missing invoice and the fuss Mrs Fielding was making about it. 'Can you remember where you put it as it's not in your desk?'

Mary had a bout of coughing but when she regained her breath she was indignant. 'Mrs Fielding came by my desk at finishing time last night and took it.'

Molly was furious but maintained a calm expression. 'Right, that's all I need to know. Now just you get better, Mary, and take your time in coming back to work.'

'I don't like that woman, Molly.'

Molly said neither did she.

At the door she apologised to Mrs Watt for bursting in. 'It's just that the supervisor was blaming Mary and I knew that wasn't true, but now I know what's happened I'll sort it out. I hope Mary feels better soon and make sure she doesn't come back to work until she is better, Mrs Watt.'

Mary's mum said she would.

On the way back in the bus, Molly felt tired. She was annoyed at herself for promising the dead man that she would honour his wishes but it all seemed a waste of time and didn't she have enough worries with her parents' plans of moving away? Not to mention the everyday worries of running the agency. Then there was her relationship with Charlie. Where was that going, she wondered.

She got back to the office with two minutes to spare. Mrs Fielding pointedly looked at her watch, but Molly went straight up to her.

'Do you have an office we can have a private talk?' Molly was conscious of six pairs of eyes and ears pretending not to listen or watch.

Mrs Fielding bristled. 'If you have any excuses for your staff then tell me here.'

This woman was annoying Molly by the minute. 'I think you would prefer to hear it in your office.'

The woman marched away to a small enclosure at the side of the room. When they were inside, Molly said, 'I've spoken to Mary and you stopped by her desk last night and took the invoice.'

'I did no such thing. The girl is—' She stopped and went to her desk. It was covered with papers and as she looked through them her face went red. 'I'm so sorry but I forgot I had it.'

Molly didn't want to rub her triumph in the woman's face. After all, there could be more work coming her way from this business, which incidentally she intended to take on herself. There was no way she would have any of her staff accused of inefficiency. 'It was an easy mistake to make, Mrs Fielding.'

When she left the enclosure six pairs of eyes watched as she went to her desk. At five-thirty, when it was time to leave, Molly was putting on her coat. Mrs Fielding came up to her.

'I just want to say thank you for keeping it all quiet from my staff.'

Molly said it was her pleasure.

Mrs Fielding hesitated for a moment then said, 'I often go for a cup of tea at this time. Would you like to join me?'

Molly had missed her lunch and she was hungry but the woman seemed to want some company so she said she would love to.

'I usually go to the Café Val D'Or in the City Square as it stays open till after six. Is that all right with you?'

Molly said it was fine and they walked the short distance to the café and climbed the stairs to the restaurant. When they were seated, Mrs Fielding asked Molly what she would like then ordered a pot of tea for two and scones with butter and jam.

Molly sat quietly in her chair, unsure why the supervisor had asked her to come. After the waitress brought the food Mrs Fielding said, 'I'm really grateful to you for dealing with my mistake so quietly.'

Molly said it was nothing but the woman went on. 'I'm having trouble coping with work just now as my husband is in Ashludie Hospital and is waiting for an operation on his lung. The mass x-ray mobile van discovered he has tuberculosis and it came as a shock to us both. In fact, I'll catch the bus to the hospital later to go and see him.'

'I'm so sorry to hear that, Mrs Fielding. I hope he gets better soon.'

'Call me Barbara, please. I'm afraid my work is getting worse and I'm frightened I'll be replaced soon if I can't keep up with the daily schedules.'

Molly sympathised with her. 'Is there anything I can do to help?'

Barbara said she could do with some help but felt Molly had enough with her hours at the office.

'Why don't we bring some sandwiches in at lunchtime and both of us can catch up with the backlog. I still have three days to go for my contract and we should be able to sort out quite a lot.'

'That would be a great help, Miss McQueen, and thank you.'

As they stood up to leave, Barbara insisted on paying and Molly said to call her by her first name.

Molly stood in the High Street and watched Barbara hurry up to the Lindsay Street bus station to catch the bus to the hospital. She had decided to have fish and chips on her way home but the scone had filled her up so she made a cheese omelette when she arrived home. The office was closed when she reached the Wellgate and the flat felt cold although it was a mild evening. She half wondered if Charlie would show up but he didn't so she studied the diary again, hoping that something would leap out at her but nothing did.

She didn't see the note that Charlie had left because Jean had left it on her desk.

The next day when the girls left for their midday meal Barbara and Molly started on the piles of invoices that were lying on the desk and in drawers. They worked hard for the hour and made some progress but Molly hadn't realised what a mess everything was in. She didn't want the rest of the staff to know about this arrangement so just before one o'clock she nipped into the toilet and appeared as the girls arrived back.

By the time Friday afternoon came round, both of them had sorted out everything. They filed the copies and got the invoices ready to be posted to the customers and suppliers. Barbara's desk was finally clear. As she got ready to leave that evening she said goodbye to the girls and went to say good luck to Barbara and to wish her husband a successful operation.

'Thank you again, Molly. I couldn't have done it without your help.' She pressed a small package in Molly's hand. 'It's just a wee token of my thanks.'

Molly said there was no need as she had been pleased to help out. 'If you need anything done again, give me a call, Barbara.'

Molly had decided to visit Mary and she hurried to catch the bus, saying goodbye to Barbara as she went to visit her husband. As she passed Imrie's Flower Shop in the Arcade she hurried in and bought a bunch of carnations.

Mrs Watt looked apprehensive when she saw her. 'There's nothing wrong with Mary's work?'

Molly smiled. 'No, Mrs Watt, I just wanted to bring her some flowers.'

Mary was sitting in the living room. She looked so much better.

'I just wanted to tell you that it wasn't your fault with the missing invoice, Mary. Mrs Fielding sends her apologies.'

Mary was pleased and Molly told her about the woman's problems. 'She just needed a little bit of help as we all do from time to time.'

When she finally arrived home, Molly opened the small parcel. Inside was a small box with three beautiful lace-trimmed handkerchiefs with the initial 'M' in each corner and she had to resist the urge to burst into tears.

Before she went to bed, she made her plans for the next couple of days. Tomorrow she would try and see more of the names from the photo then on Sunday she would go to see her parents. Before she went to sleep she was hoping that they had changed their minds about moving permanently to the other side of the world.

19

Molly caught the Blairgowrie bus from the bus station in St Andrews Street on Saturday morning. George Stevenson lived near Muirhead. She had looked his name up in the telephone directory and had rung him up yesterday to ask if he would see her. He sounded surprised by her request but when she mentioned Bill Reid he said he would be at home in the morning. He gave her directions to his house and as she stepped from the bus, the only building in sight was a large detached house surrounded by a large garden and fields.

A long drive led up to the gate and Molly was glad she had put on flat-heeled shoes. The door opened before she reached the house and a tall, slender and very elegant man stood on the threshold.

'Come in, Miss McQueen, I've made some coffee.'

Molly didn't drink coffee but didn't want to appear rude. The house was very large and inside looked like a museum. There was a suit of armour in the hall and a large statue of Bhudda welcomed any visitors.

He led her into a sitting room with lots of Indian artefacts. A large tapestry hung from one wall and a gigantic gong on a fancy carved base stood beside the door. For a brief moment Molly wondered if she had been transported to India.

After he poured out the coffee, he said, 'I should be offering tea because of my job with the tea plantation but I prefer coffee.' Although he smiled at her over the rim of his cup, he had an anxious frown. 'I can't think what this is all about but you mentioned Bill, and I hope he is well.'

Molly looked surprised. 'I thought you knew Bill was dead?'

It was now his turn to be taken aback. 'No I didn't. When did this happen?'

'It was three weeks ago and I've been asked by his sister Betty to see all his colleagues from this photo.' She produced the cutting from her bag and handed it to him.

He put on a pair of glasses and studied the photo. 'Goodness, this takes me back. It all seems such a long time ago and in another world. It says here that Phillip Thorne is hoping to contact all of us for a reunion. Is that why Bill's sister wants you to see us all?'

Molly hesitated. It looked like he hadn't seen the cutting or read the death notice in the paper. 'I'm sorry but that's not the reason, Mr Stevenson. Bill was killed in an accident and he had this cutting and all your names and addresses on him when he died.' She went on to explain her part in this. 'Before he died he asked me to warn you all.'

'Warn us against what?' he asked.

Molly said she didn't know but as she had promised the dying man she was only carrying out his last wish. 'Betty, his sister, also said he was very worried about something a few weeks before he died and she would like to know the reason why, if possible.'

George said. 'I'm sorry, but I'm puzzled. You said Bill died at the Soldier's Leap in Killicrankie. What was he doing there? Was he on holiday?'

'No, he went to stay with his sister and her late husband a few years ago. Did you not see this cutting in the paper?'

'No I didn't. I'm afraid I don't read many papers, but what does Phillip say about all this? He must have had word back from some of the men.'

Molly felt like the harbinger of doom. 'No, I'm afraid he is also dead. He was killed in a car accident after advertising the reunion in the paper.'

'This is terrible. What about the rest of them?'

'I've spoken to Phillip's widow and Alex McGregor but I've still to see the other three men. Have you had any contact with them?'

He shook his head. 'No, I'm ashamed to say that I haven't kept in touch with anyone. It was such a traumatic time in India at the end that I just wanted to forget all about my time there.'

Molly stayed silent but thought that this cutting himself off from his past didn't tally with the contents of the house.

'There was a murder there, I believe. Mrs Pritchard and her daughter Naomi?'

He turned his head towards the window and didn't speak for a moment or two. His voice was sad when he finally spoke.

'Yes they were killed. It was a terrible time and the police said it was bandits. The entire country was in an uproar with killings every day of the week. We used to see piles of bodies lying on the roads. It's a sight I don't want to remember.'

Molly couldn't blame him. There didn't seem to be any more he could add so she said, 'Thank you for seeing me, Mr Stevenson, and I'm sorry if I've brought back painful memories for you.' She handed him her card. 'If you remember anything else about that Indian summer, please give me a ring.'

Looking at the card, he said, 'Oh, you run an agency? That's interesting because sometimes we use some temporary secretaries, perhaps I'll give you a call.' He added, 'And please call me George.'

As she was going out the door she suddenly remembered. 'I almost forgot. I believe J.P. Pritchard left India very suddenly. Did you ever meet up with or hear from him when you arrived back in Scotland?'

He shook his head. 'No I didn't. Has Alex seen him or did Bill leave any word that he had met up with him?'

Molly responded, 'No.' She paused. 'George, does the word "digging" mean anything to you?'

He laughed. 'The only digging I know is what I do in the garden. Is it important?'

'I'm not sure but it was what Bill said before he died.'

He saw her to the door. 'I wish you luck with your task.'

As she walked down the drive, a car came slowly past her and stopped. A sturdy-looking woman, who was unfashionably dressed and wore no make-up, rolled down the window. Molly put her age about fifty.

She had a deep voice as if she smoked too many cigarettes. 'Can I help you?'

Molly said no. 'I've been visiting Mr Stevenson.'

'And what did my husband have to say for himself?' she replied quite sarcastically, which Molly thought was odd.

'Oh just some business from his time in India.'

The woman looked bored. 'I see. Is he looking for help with the book we're writing?'

Before Molly could answer, she drove up the rest of the drive and Molly heard the wheels squeal in protest on the gravel as it came to a stop.

He hadn't mentioned a wife, she thought, but then it was none of her business. Alex McGregor had said he was a widower when he lived in India so it looked as if he had remarried when he came home and she wasn't surprised because he was still a handsome man. She was beginning to tire of these jaunts to people from the past.

She was in luck when she reached the road because a bus came into view. As she sat down, she mentally went over the interviews she had done so far. With a bit of luck she could maybe see the other three men and that would be her job finished.

She took out her sheet with the names and addresses. Peter Lindsay lived along the Arbroath Road near Baxter Park, Edmond Lamb in the Hawkhill and Douglas Kingsley in Broughty Ferry.

Molly decided first of all to go to see Edmond Lamb and when the bus stopped at the bus station she quickly made her way along the Overgate, past West Port and up the Hawkhill. He lived in a tenement block a few yards past Kincardine Street. Although it wasn't a run-down building, it had certainly seen better days and Molly was struck by the difference in each man's living arrangements. George Stevenson seemed to be more affluent than his old colleagues, but maybe he had married money. She recalled the outfit worn by the woman in the car and it hadn't been a cheap, mass-produced model, even though it had been an unflattering tweed suit.

Edmond lived on the second floor. A small, cheap-looking plastic nameplate was screwed to the dark brown painted door and a mat saying 'Welcome' stood on the landing. Molly wondered if the man would make her welcome but she knocked anyway. There was no answer so she knocked again. She heard steps coming to the door but instead of opening it, a nervous voice asked, 'Who is it?'

'My name is Molly McQueen. Can I have a few words with Mr Lamb?'

'What do you want to know?'

Molly was getting exasperated. Did the man want to conduct a conversation through a closed door?

She kept her voice polite. 'It's about Bill Reid and your days in India, Mr Lamb.'

The door opened an inch and Molly saw a stout chain attached to the wood. A round face with thick grey eyebrows peered out at her. 'What does Bill want?'

'Can I come in, Mr Lamb? I don't like talking to you from the landing.'

The man grudgingly opened the door with a good deal of muttering and she was finally inside a small lobby that was painted in a hideous bottle green. It was like being in a cave under the sea.

When they moved to the living room it was so different. Light streamed in from the window that overlooked a grassy drying green.

'Well sit down and tell me what you want.'

The chair was very comfortable and Molly was able to view the man in a better light. About seventy years old, not very tall, he had put on a bit of weight since the photo had been taken but he was almost bald now. With the bushy eyebrows it looked as if his hair had stopped growing on his head and had transferred to them.

Molly pulled the cutting from her handbag and showed it to him. He put on a pair of glasses and studied it with great care.

'Yes I remember when this was taken. What does Bill Reid want with me?'

'Bill is dead, Mr Lamb, and he gave me this cutting just before he died. He asked me to warn you all.'

'Warn us, what about?'

Molly sighed. 'I wish I could tell you but I don't know. Could it have something to do with the deaths of J.P. Pritchard's wife and daughter during that summer in India?'

'So you know about that as well?'

'Yes I got the story from Alex McGregor and George Stevenson.'

'My, you have been busy. Yes it's true about the deaths but the police said it was bandits and no doubt you've been told about all the violence at that time in India. That's why we all left.'

'Did you speak to or see Mr Pritchard before he left suddenly?'

'No I didn't. That was another mystery. We all thought he would have said goodbye but I expect he was devastated by the deaths and there was his young son who was traumatised by them. He got shipped home then his father must have followed a day or so later.' Molly pointed to the cutting. 'Did you reply to Phillip Thorne about the proposed reunion?'

'No I didn't for the simple reason I didn't see it.'

'Did you see Bill's death notice in the paper?'

'No I didn't. I don't read many papers now.' Then the light struck his face and she saw why. His eyes had a milky look to them, a sure sign of cataracts.

'What did you think happened in India? You all must have had your own thoughts at the time.'

'We were shocked, but it was violent times we were living through. Splitting the country into two nations was diabolical. It was a wonderful country before, with the different faiths all living together.' He shook his head sadly. 'Yes it was a terrible time.'

Molly knew there wasn't anything else this old man could add to the story. 'Just one more thing, Mr Lamb. Does the word "digging" mean anything to you?'

He turned his head away so Molly missed the flicker of fear, but when he spoke, his voice was firm. 'No I don't. I never do any digging as I don't have a garden.'

When Molly was walking away, she didn't see the curtain of the window that overlooked the street get pulled back an inch or two.

She decided to leave the other two men till another day, as it was a fool's errand with the same blank looks and the same tragic tale.

20

When Molly arrived back at the agency, Maggie Flynn was on the telephone. The girl was due to start work full-time after she left school in a couple of weeks. Normally she would have kept her in the office until she had some more experience of agency work, just as Molly had done with Mary when she left school in 1953; however, she was short of secretaries and Maggie would be sent out on assignments as soon as the school holidays began.

'I'm going to make some tea, Maggie, would you like a cup?'

Maggie said she would. 'I've written down all the telephone messages for you and a young woman came in hoping to see you. She saw your advert for a secretary and she wants to apply for the job if it is still open.'

Molly was surprised. The advert had been put in the paper a few weeks ago, just after Deanna left to go to the theatre in Pitlochry.

'Did she leave her name and address, Maggie?'

The girl passed a card over and Molly saw it was all neatly written down: *Grace Carson, Commercial Street, Dundee.*

Molly then turned her attention to the telephone messages. One from her mother saying she would see Molly tomorrow and did she want to come for her dinner? The second one was from Charlie. He was going to call by this evening.

As it was only two o'clock, Molly decided to go against her decision to wait to contact the others another day and left to make a call on Peter Lindsay. She caught a bus and was dropped off at Baxter Park Terrace. This was another tenement building but Peter lived on the ground floor. When she rang the bell, the door was opened almost immediately. Standing on the threshold was a round-faced, plump man with a cheery expression. Molly had read Charles Dickens' *Pickwick Papers* at school and her mental picture of Samuel Pickwick matched Peter Lindsay exactly.

He had an impish look when he asked her, 'Now what does a young lady want to see an old man for?'

Molly introduced herself and was soon sitting in a very warm room that was full of furniture. There was a sofa and two chairs, two bookcases overflowing with books and magazines, a dining table with four upright and solid chairs. A large ginger cat was curled up on the rug in front of the fire, which in spite of the warm day was blazing in the hearth.

Molly declined a cup of tea and pulled the cutting out of her bag and handed it to him. He lost the cheery expression and looked at her carefully. 'This is a surprise from the past, I must say.' He read the caption. 'How is young Phillip these days?'

Molly said he was dead, as was Bill Reid.

'Oh that's too bad.'

'Mr Lindsay, Bill's sister has asked me to get in touch with you.' She explained how Bill had died. 'Before he died he asked me to warn you all but I've no idea what he meant. Do you know?'

'No I don't.' He pointed to the photo. 'This was taken years ago, in the early forties or thereabouts. It was a different world and a different life out in India. We were all colleagues back then. We called ourselves the Dundee Club, as most of us came from here.'

'Yes, I've been told that. Also, what do you remember about the deaths of Mrs Pritchard and Naomi?'

Peter's face went pale. 'What can I say? It was a dreadful time. I felt so sorry for J.P. but then he left suddenly, a couple of days after his boy. The police investigated the murders but no one was ever held responsible as it was assumed it was the result of the ongoing violence that surrounded us all.'

Molly felt she was hearing the same story over and over again. What had Bill meant by his warning? She certainly didn't have a clue.

'Bill mentioned the word "digging". Have you any idea what he meant?'

Peter shook his head. 'I haven't the foggiest.'

During these meetings with the various men, one thing was bugging Molly. 'Have you met up with any of your old colleagues since you all came back from India?'

She was surprised to see a guarded look in the man's eyes.

She continued. 'Did you read about the proposed reunion or Bill Reid's death in the papers? Alex McGregor was the only one of the group who attended the funeral. I would have thought most of you would have made the effort, seeing you all seemed to be such good friends at one time.'

'Yes I saw the photo in the paper but I didn't get in touch with Phillip. He was younger than us when he came to Darjeeling from Assam and he was having domestic problems with his wife. She hated her life in India and the very first opportunity she had she scampered off back to Blighty.'

Molly said she knew that, but they had got back together again before he died.

'I didn't see the notice about Bill's death because I didn't know he had moved to Pitlochry,' said Peter.

Molly was puzzled. 'Do you keep in touch with any of your old colleagues?'

He was silent for a minute then went and picked up the cat. 'I have to put him out into the drying green as I don't want him piddling on the floor.'

He was gone for only a few moments but Molly had the irrational notion that Peter might run away rather than face any more questions, but before long he reappeared and sat down again. 'You asked if we all kept in touch but the answer is no, we did not.'

'Why not, if you were friends in India?'

Instead of answering, he said, 'During all your investigating, Miss McQueen, have you managed to find and question J.P. Pritchard?'

Molly was flustered. 'No, I haven't. I don't have his address and don't know much about him except that his son went back to his grandparents in Edinburgh after the murders of his mother and sister. I've been calling this dreadful time "the Indian Summer".'

He sat back in his chair and wiped his face with a large white hankie. After a moment of silence he said, 'An appropriate title I think.' He scratched his chin with a fleshy index finger and looked at her. 'Then it's just as I thought. Haven't you asked yourself why he disappeared?'

'Oh I wouldn't say he's disappeared. He's probably changed his address. Maybe to protect his older daughter and son – he doesn't want any memories from that time.'

Peter wasn't convinced. 'And yet the rest of us all stay in the same places we came back to.

'I never married but India was a strange country for some wives. Some loved it and others hated it but I would say that J.P.'s wife was one of the former. She adored the life with an intensity I had never seen before. She was a lovely woman, full of life, and the Pritchards used to have the most glorious parties. We all looked forward to those evenings.'

'I don't see what their parties have to do with anything,' said Molly.

'Well, look at it his way: There were eight men, if you include her husband. Phillip's wife had left, Bill's wife Annie was dead, George was also a widower while myself, Edmond and Douglas weren't married. Amongst all the confusion and violence of the times, there was this lovely woman who was so full of life and laughter. It was a potent mix.'

Molly didn't know what to say.

'Maybe the rest won't tell you the truth but the reason none of us have kept in touch is that, at the back of our minds, the murders could have been committed by any one of us, even her husband.'

'Surely her husband wouldn't kill his sixteen-year-old daughter.'

He gave this some thought. 'No, maybe not. So that lets him off the hook, but at the time we all felt guilty. Looking at each other with the look that said, "did you do it?"'

'But why did Bill ask me to warn you all?'

'Maybe he knew who did it.'

'Then why didn't he tell you all, or go to the police?'

'What would the police have said about a crime that happened years ago in a foreign country? Moreover, a crime that the local police investigated and said was caused by bandits.'

By now Molly was confused. She understood that anyone could have been a suspect but no one else had said anything.

She thanked him for his time and escaped back to the bus stop. She knew she had to see Douglas Kingsley and get his version of events. After that it was out of her hands. She looked at her watch and decided she had time to catch another bus to Broughty Ferry.

Douglas's house was a neat detached, stone-built villa over-looking the sea. There was a huge brass knocker shaped like an elephant's head on the bright blue door. A middle-aged woman wearing a floral apron opened it and stood gazing at Molly like an inquisitive owl, an image heightened by the big round glasses on the edge of her nose.

Molly was expecting Douglas to answer but she said, 'Can I have a word with Mr Douglas Kingsley please?'

'I'm Mrs Kingsley, come in.'

Molly thought silently that he must have married after leaving India. The big window of the living room had a wonderful sea view and was very tastefully furnished. Mrs Kingsley shouted along the hall, 'Somebody to see you, Douglas.'

A tall, dapper man with a shock of grey hair appeared. He was dressed in brown corduroy trousers, a sleeveless jumper that had seen better days and a pair of gardening gloves. Molly saw a tattoo of a snake on his right arm, just below his shoulder. He looked inquisitevly at her.

Molly apologised for dropping in like this but he was charming and asked her to sit down. He called out, 'Can we have some tea please, Bunty?'

The woman replied it was just coming.

Molly once again produced the cutting and told the man the

story behind her visit. 'I hope your wife doesn't mind me dropping in like this?'

'My wife? Oh you mean Bunty? I stay here with my brother and she's his wife. I'm sorry to hear Bill's dead. We were good friends out in India and I liked his late wife Annie very much.'

'Did you see this cutting and the death notice in the paper?'

He looked sad. 'No I didn't. We've been away for a month. The three of us have been to a family wedding in Perth and we stayed on for a holiday. We just got back a week ago.'

Molly told him Peter Lindsay's theory about the murders and how she called it 'the Indian summer'. To her surprise, he burst out laughing. 'I'm not laughing about the murders because they were terrible. It's just good old Peter and his crime tales. He was forever reading magazines with true crimes. He used to get them posted out to him. He would spend hours trying to work out the murderers or solve the crimes. We used to call him Sherlock. Any little thing that happened on the plantations, he would spend hours trying to work out the conclusion, and more than often get it all wrong.'

'So you don't agree with his version of what happened? That you all suspected each other?'

He laughed again. 'No I don't. I mean we were all devastated but saying Susie Pritchard was a *femme fatale* was all in his imagination. The woman was always baking or gardening and although they did throw some parties they were always rather dull affairs. At least I thought so.'

Bunty appeared with the tea on a small trolley. Molly was amused to see sandwiches, cakes and biscuits but when she was handed her cup of tea she suddenly realised how hungry she was.

'So it's not true that you have all avoided each other since coming back from India?' she asked after placing her empty plate back on the trolley.

He gave this some thought. 'Some of us met up during that first year back. I went to see Bill when he still lived in Dundee and we both went to see Alex. I know we all exchanged cards that first Christmas but as time went on this was reduced to an occasional letter the following year.' He put his cup on the trolley and turned to give her a frank look. 'Then I suspect our lives all went in different directions and we lost touch. I know Bill tried his best to keep in touch but once we were all back here in the cold of a Scottish winter and away from the heat and work of the plantations, it all seemed like a different world.'

Molly could understand that attitude. 'Why do you think Phillip Thorne had to put the photo in the newspaper, asking you all to contact him?'

'Phillip left India before the rest of us and he went to work in Ceylon on another tea plantation but as the rest of us were either at retiring age or getting near it we just packed up and came back to Scotland. Because he was much younger than the rest of us when he came to Darjeeling, he would have had to get another job. J.P. was also a bit younger than us so we assumed he had moved onto another job as well.'

'Do you know if J.P. came back here as well?'

He rubbed his chin and sat back in his chair. 'No I don't and neither did the rest of us. It was a mystery why he left without saying goodbye to any of us but I do know that no one had any word from him that first year. Bill tried to get in touch with his family in Edinburgh but when he went to see them they had moved away and hadn't left a forwarding address.'

'What about the older daughter and the ten-year-old son, had they vanished as well?'

'Well in the November of 1947, Bill came to see me and he said there was no trace of any of them in Edinburgh so the trail grew cold and over the years I've certainly put it all behind me. We were good mates back then but I'm afraid we weren't that close when we came back.'

Bunty came in and wheeled the trolley through to the kitchen. Molly thanked her for the lovely tea and picked up her bag, ready to leave.

Douglas laughed and Molly looked at him. She thought she had done something comical. 'I'm remembering Peter and his sleuthing. One day Susie said she had lost a sentimental ring and couldn't find it. Peter said he would look for it as it was probably lost in the garden. He didn't have the deerstalker hat or pipe but he had this gigantic magnifying glass and he scoured every bit of the garden. Every tree, leaf and vegetable.'

Molly said, 'Did he find it?'

He burst into laughter again. 'No he didn't, but that's when we nicknamed him Sherlock. Mind you, Susie was upset because she loved that ring.'

'Was it valuable?'

'You bet it was. It had an unusual design. Twisted gold bands with a lovely Indian ruby in the centre. J.P. had given it to her as a wedding anniversary gift the year before.'

'Perhaps it turned up later,' said Molly.

'Not if she lost it in that garden. In India, cultivated gardens soon resembled the jungle, but maybe it'll turn up one day and make one impoverished farmer a good sum of money.'

Molly had enjoyed her afternoon and she thanked him for making her welcome.

'I'm so sorry to hear about Bill and Phillip and if you leave me Bill's sister's address I'll drop her a line,' he said.

She was almost out the door when she said, 'Oh I almost forgot. Bill mentioned the word "digging". Have you any idea what he meant?'

He laughed again. 'Just what I've been doing all afternoon, digging the garden.' He became serious and a deep frown appeared on his forehead. 'No, I'm sorry to say I haven't a clue, except it might refer to Peter's digging in the garden, looking for the ring. Maybe he found it and said nothing and has since sold it for lots of money.'

Molly recalled the slightly shabby, overcrowded flat and thought not.

She got back to the agency just as Maggie was leaving.

'Thank you, Maggie, for looking after the office and I'll see you next Saturday.'

'I'm really looking forward to starting work here after the school finishes for the summer holiday,' Maggie said.

'And we're looking forward to having you on the staff.'

This pleased the young girl and she hurried out. A few minutes later Charlie appeared. He looked tired as he sat down on the chair.

'How is the investigation going, Charlie?' Molly asked.

He gave a mirthless laugh. 'It's still going nowhere, but the pressure is on to find the culprit or culprits. There haven't been any more robberies so that's one blessing,' he said before changing the subject. 'Do you fancy going out for something to eat and maybe go to the pictures afterwards?'

Molly said she would love to do both but to give her a minute to freshen up and change her dress.

They had a lovely high tea in their usual eating place, Wilson's Restaurant in Union Street, and then went on to the Greens Playhouse to see *The Caine Mutiny* with Humphrey Bogart as Captain Queeg. Halfway through the picture, Charlie fell asleep.

21

He was nervous and couldn't sit still. After all this time why had the past suddenly sprung up and appeared? Then there was that young woman and all her questions. He had thought he had covered all his tracks but if he kept calm nothing could be proved. After all, it was years ago and thousands of miles away but every time he heard the term 'Indian summer' it all came back to him. The heat and the flies, the monsoon season with its incessant rain and that dull feeling of hopelessness and longing that wasn't reciprocated. He should have handled it better but he didn't and now he had to watch his step.

He was in dangerous waters but he thought his manner with that Molly McQueen had gone off rather well. She might think he was strange but what of it? Lots of people were strange.

22

Eric Bergmann was nervous. He had worked in the shop until late and had run into the thunderstorm a few miles from Monifieth. Although the night should still have been light, the storm and heavy rain made it feel more like autumn than midsummer. He glanced for the hundredth time at his briefcase, which lay beside him on the passenger seat, and felt that shiver of nervousness again. He thought to himself that the deal had to be a dodgy one. Common sense made him realise that the jewellery he had bought that week was far lower than the market price to make it legitimate, but that being said, he had still laid out a considerable sum of money. The quicker he had it in his safe in the Monifieth house and away from the shop the better. The road was quiet at this time of night and he glanced at his watch. Eleven forty-five. He would be home by midnight.

The sea on his right was invisible in the heavy rain but he could hear it surging onto the shore. Thankfully Mrs French was on holiday and he would have the house to himself. The turning to his drive loomed before him and he slowed down. The hotel on the seafront must have had visitors because the main rooms all had bright lights burning, plus a few of the bedrooms also showed a dull glow behind closed curtains. He had no fear that any guest would be wandering outside in a night like this and he drove slowly up towards the front door.

He decided to leave the car at the front and put it in the garage tomorrow. That way he wouldn't get soaked. Pulling his raincoat up around his neck and keeping his head down, he clutched the briefcase and made a quick dash for the front door.

There was a flash of lightning and for one brief moment he

thought he saw a dark figure, but thinking he was mistaken he inserted the key in the door. Which meant he didn't see the shadow come up behind him or the raised arm with the crowbar. The blow was quick and instantly brought him to his knees. He didn't feel any pain to start with, but it soon developed into an intense throb and, overwhelmed by the traumatic assault on his head, he passed out.

The figure dragged him from the wet doorstep back to his car.

Molly and Charlie emerged from the picture house into the storm and had made a dash for the bus home. When she reached the Wellgate steps she said, 'Just you stay on the bus, Charlie, and I'll hurry home. You really need your bed as you look so tired.'

'I'll be fine after I get a good night's sleep. I'm working tomorrow but I'll see you sometime next week.'

She hurried down the steps and into the agency. The office wasn't too dark because of the streetlights and she made her way up to the flat. She was also tired and looking forward to her bed. It had been a busy day with all her various visits to see the men from the photo.

Eric Bergmann raised his head. The sun was shining in his eyes and he felt sick and groggy. He couldn't remember where he was until he made out the interior of his car and it seemed to be at an odd angle.

He tried to raise his head but a sharp pain shot through his skull and he fell back on the seat. There was the sound of waves on the shore and the tangy smell of seaweed and he had the absurd thought that he must have parked on the beach.

Suddenly a face appeared at the window. An elderly woman tried to open the door but it was jammed. He heard her voice but it seemed to come from a distance, like he was hearing it in a dream.

'Are you all right? I'll go and get help,' said the voice, and he heard the barking of a dog.

Before he once again fell into unconciousness, he thought to himself that it was just a bad dream.

The woman tugged at the dog lead and hurried up the beach to the telephone kiosk in the village. She rang 999. 'The car has run off the road onto the beach and the driver is injured,' she reported to the voice on the end of the emergency line.

She then retraced her steps, much to the dog's delight, as this walk was longer than his normal morning stroll. She noticed the man was still unconscious.

Within a few minutes of returning to the scene, a man and a dog appeared and he also tried to open the car door. It wouldn't budge. 'There's no damage that I can see,' he said, giving the handle another pull. 'It looks like the doors are jammed. The driver's window is open but I don't think we can get him out through that.'

Then, much to their relief, the ambulance pulled up and two men got out and sprinted over to the car.

'The doors seem to be stuck,' the man said. They all peered in the window just as Eric raised his head.

'We're trying to open the door,' said one of the men from the ambulance.

Eric was confused because of the terrible pain in his head. He heard the metallic sound of the door being wrenched open.

One of the men reassured, 'We'll soon have you outside, sir.'

The men went back and brought the stretcher but before Eric allowed himself to be carried away, he asked where his briefcase was.

The men searched the car. 'There's nothing here, sir.'

Eric thought he was having hallucinations. Of course his briefcase was on the passenger seat! He tried to get off the stretcher, but one of the ambulance men restrained him and he was soon on his way to the infirmary.

One of the ambulance men took the names and addresses of the woman and man who stood and watched as the vehicle drove away. They chatted for a minute or two. The man said, 'It seems a funny place to go off the road but he was lucky. If he had gone off further up he would have had a six-foot drop.'

The woman nodded and they moved away in different directions. As she walked away with her spaniel, she wondered if the driver had been at some function and had drunk too much alcohol. If he had, then he had paid a high price for his folly as he had looked terrible when brought out onto the stretcher.

Back in her house, her husband had just got out of bed and as she cooked the breakfast, which they always had on a Sunday, she told him of her early morning discovery. Stopping in the middle of lifting a rasher of bacon from the frying pan, she turned to her husband and said, 'I do hope he's going to be fine. He looked like death heated up before being taken away.'

Her husband, who wasn't an unkind sort of person but was hungry and waiting for his ham and eggs, said, 'Will you be long cooking that bacon, Elsie?'

As she turned back to the stove, Elsie gave a slight shake of her head at her thoughtless husband and quickly shoved four bacon rashers and two fried eggs onto his plate. She then filled the dog's bowl with half a tin of dog food, which the dog quickly wolfed down, before finally sitting down with her toast which had gone cold.

23

Molly wasn't looking forward to going to see her parents today as she was afraid what the news would be about Australia, but it was a beautiful sunny morning and it would do her good to get out of the flat.

After a quick breakfast of cornflakes and milk, she made her way to catch the mid-morning Fifie. When she arrived at Craig Pier she was astonished to see a large queue waiting to buy tickets. There were a lot of families, with the mothers clutching bulging message bags, filled no doubt with food to sustain them during their day out. The river was calm and sparkled in the sunlight. She slowly let the problems of the last few weeks drop away as she stood on the top deck and watched the town slowly grow smaller as the green shores of Newport beckoned.

She decided to write to Betty Holden with the results of her talks with Bill's ex-colleagues and perhaps meet up some time soon and return his possessions, and having made up her mind on that, she let the sun's warmth relax her taut neck and shoulder muscles and clear her mind.

When the ferry docked at the pier she let the crowd of chattering people and excited children disembark first then slowly followed them onto the road. She was surprised to meet Marigold, who was dressed in a thin woollen suit, a summer hat and white gloves. 'I'm going to church and I have to meet my friend Peggy. Come in and see me before you leave,' she said.

Molly wanted to ask her what the situation was at home but Marigold was obviously running late and didn't want to keep Peggy waiting.

Her father was in the garden when she arrived at the gate and she knew her mother would be in the kitchen getting the dinner ready. He showed her the flowers he had planted earlier in the spring and said he was hoping to plant more lettuce in the small vegetable plot at the back of the house. For a moment this cheered Molly up and she wondered if these small everyday things meant they had abandoned the notion of going away.

'The meal will be about twelve o'clock,' her mother called from the steamy kitchen. 'Make us all a pot of tea if you like and take a cup out to Dad.'

Molly filled the kettle and placed it on a spare corner of the stove. As she set out the cups and saucers she suddenly realised how important it was to her life that her parents lived near her. She couldn't visualise them being away on the other side of the world for the rest of their lives. She carried out two cups of tea to the garden and sat down on the bench. She had offered to help her mum but Nancy liked to work alone in the kitchen. Molly smiled when she thought about this little quirk. Her mother had always been like that, even when she and Nell were both children.

It was when they were sitting down to steak pie and new potatoes that Australia was mentioned.

Nancy said, 'Dad and I have written to Australia House to make inquiries about emigrating.'

Molly could hardly bear to look up from her plate but when she did it was her dad's sympathetic gaze she saw.

'So you're going through with it?'

Her dad helped himself to more potatoes. 'We're only making enquiries at the moment, Molly, but if we do decide to go we want you to come with us.'

Suddenly all the sunshine of the day left her and she felt cold inside.

Nancy said, 'We're not going to sell the house right away. We thought we could maybe rent it out until we were a hundred percent sure we're happy and wanting to stay.' Well that was one small blessing, Molly thought, but the cold stab of uncertainty stayed with her.

'I don't know if I want to come with you both.' She knew she sounded like a five-year-old child again with the threat that if she withheld her favour then all would be right with her world.

Nancy didn't argue. 'Well there's time for you to change your mind, Molly. As Dad says, we have only made some enquiries. Now I've got fruit salad and ice cream for the pudding. Do you both want some?'

Actually, fruit salad and ice cream was the last thing on her mind but she smiled and said, 'I'd love some.'

After they had finished, Marigold appeared and all talk of leaving was over.

Nancy said, 'Marigold, go out into the garden with Molly and I'll bring you some lemonade.'

Marigold sat in a shady spot. 'How is the investigation going?'

Molly shook her head. 'I've seen all the men in the photo but it seems to be the unanimous verdict that it was bandits who killed the Pritchard women. It was a terrible time of upheaval and violence during the partition of India into two separate countries. None of the men knew what Bill was warning them against.'

Marigold looked serious. 'Well they would say that, wouldn't they?'

Molly had thought the same thing. 'Do you think they're lying?'

'Well maybe not them all, but if one of them has a dark secret he won't admit it or want anyone else to find out.'

'I've done what Bill wanted and seen them all, so that's the end of it. I'm going to write to Betty and tell her then I thought we could go up to see her some weekend to return the pouch. We could maybe see another play and meet up with Deanna.'

Marigold said that would be great. 'I'll have another look at the programme we bought and see what's on and we can book up with Bess at her guest house.' She stretched out on her seat. 'How is Charlie these days?'

Molly didn't answer right away because Nancy appeared with the lemonade. 'I'll leave this with you and I'll be out in a minute or two. Dad is having a wee nap inside,' Nancy said.

When she had gone back inside, Molly filled two glasses and handed one to Marigold. 'Charlie is fine. He has this difficult case just now and I don't think he's sleeping very well with the worry of it. He even fell asleep in the middle of the picture last night.'

Marigold laughed. 'A policeman's lot is a hard life.' As she sipped her drink, she looked at Molly. 'Archie and Nancy have told you about Australia?'

Molly said they had and how worried she was about it.

'Maybe once they've gone and seen the new baby when it comes, they'll decide the life out there isn't for them. Especially as they're not selling the house right away.'

Yes, that was one blessing, Molly thought again.

When it was time to go home later in the afternoon, she boarded the ferry for the crossing, along with the crowds all surging on board with the adults looking tired and the children still as excited as they were on the outgoing trip.

24

Charlie was out on a call when the report came into the police station about Eric Bergmann's car accident. When he came back, he sat down to read all the messages that had landed on his desk and he immediately noticed the name. The report said Bergmann had been taken to the Royal Infirmary with a head injury. Charlie quickly left the station and made his way to try and interview him.

The infirmary was busy when he arrived because it was Sunday afternoon visiting time but he made his way to the porter's cubicle and showed him his warrant card.

'If you sit down here, I'll get the doctor to come and speak to you,' the porter said, hurrying along the corridor.

Charlie waited fifteen minutes before a young doctor arrived and they both went along to the ward where the injured man was.

When they reached the doctor's office, he said, 'I can't let you speak to him as he has a bad concussion. He has had a serious blow to the back of his head but fortunately his coat collar was pulled up and because it was a thick, double-lined collar, it cushioned the blow slightly. He was found in his car early this morning by,' he looked at his notes, 'by a Mrs Elsie Grant who lives in Broughty Ferry.'

'What was the reason for the crash, do you know?'

'No, I don't. He hadn't been drinking but I haven't questioned him yet as he's been sleeping since he came in. If you come back tomorrow maybe he'll be able to tell you what happened.'

Charlie knew there wasn't going to be an interview with the victim until he was a bit better so he thanked the doctor and stood to go.

'There is something odd,' the doctor said. 'The two ambulance men said Mr Bergmann kept repeating he had a briefcase with him but nothing was found in the car.'

Charlie asked, 'Is it possible to speak to these men?'

'Ask Henry, the porter, when you go out and he'll find out if they are still on duty.'

'I'll do that and I'll come back tomorrow.'

Henry went to look for the men and twenty minutes later he came back with a tall man following him. 'This is Jack Miller. He was on duty this morning when the accident victim was admitted.'

Charlie asked the man to sit down. 'What time did you get the call to this accident, Mr Miller?'

'It was seven-thirty when we took the call from the emergency service and we drove straight there.'

'Did it look like a road accident? As if he collided with someone?'

Jack Miller rubbed his chin. 'No I don't think he hit something else as the car doesn't seem to be damaged except for the door which had to be wrenched open. Still, you would have to ask the mechanic at the local garage. He came and towed it away I believe. To my way of thinking, it looked as if he ran off the road and when the wheels hit the beach and the dunes it sank to one side. The driver's window was open but apart from that there's nothing else.'

'You had some difficulty getting the patient out?'

'Yes, the door was jammed and as I said, we had to break in.'

'Did he have the keys in his pocket?'

The man had to think about this. 'No, they were still in the ignition.'

'Did he mention a briefcase?'

'Yes he did, he kept coming in and out of consciousness and we were in a hurry to get him to hospital. As we were putting him on the stretcher he asked about the case. Well, I had a good look around the car and I couldn't see it so I told him it wasn't there. He got quite agitated and we were concerned about him. I asked the woman who found him if she could have a look under the car and in the boot but she said there wasn't anything. The car was empty.'

There was just more question. 'Have you any idea which direction the car was coming from?'

'Well it was slightly facing in the Monifieth direction – as if he had been driving away from Broughty Ferry – but I can't be sure. When he skidded off the road, the car could have turned before it hit the beach.'

Charlie thanked him and the man left to finish his shift. Hurrying back to the station, Charlie met PC Williamson who had just finished a late lunch.

'Get the car, Williamson, we're going to see Mrs French.'

The constable's face lit up at the thought of some more Victoria sponge, even though he had just eaten a pie, beans and chips.

However, before going on to see Mrs French, Charlie said to stop at Elsie Grant's house. She lived in a small cottage at the far end of the esplanade. And she was flustered when the two men arrived at her door and one was in a police uniform.

She put a hand to her chest as if she was about to hear some bad news. Charlie put her mind at ease when he said, 'I would like a quick word about the accident you reported this morning, Mrs Grant.'

She showed them in to a small room that was obviously kept for visitors. An old-fashioned parlour, as Charlie's parents would have called it.

'Oh, it was such a terrible shock when I saw the car. I was out walking with Sally, our dog, when I came across it. At first I was frightened to look inside.' She made a small movement with her hand. 'You know what I mean? I was frightened the driver was dead, but thankfully he raised his head for a moment before becoming unconscious again. Then another man appeared with his dog after I'd phoned 999 and we both waited until the ambulance arrived.'

'Do you think this man knew the victim?'

She shook her head. 'No I don't think he did as I often see him and his dog when I'm out and about with Sally. I didn't know the driver either.'

Charlie mentioned the briefcase but before he could finish the sentence, Elsie went on, 'Oh, he made a fuss about that I can tell you. When the ambulance man said there wasn't anything in the car the man tried to get off the stretcher. Then I had to have a look in the boot and under the car but I didn't see any case and I have the ambulance men and that man with his dog as witnesses.'

Charlie managed to calm her down. 'I'm not suggesting anything, Mrs Grant. I'm just trying to get a clear picture of the scene.'

But Mrs Grant hadn't anything new to add to what Jack Miller had said, so he thanked her for her time and they left, but not before adding, 'Your quick thinking has helped the man get help promptly and I expect he's grateful.'

This bit of praise made her cheeks go red but she was pleased that she had been a help at the driver's moment of trouble.

When she went back into the kitchen and told her husband the news about the interview, he said, 'It's a pity you got involved with that, Elsie. You wait and see, the police will always be at our door from now on.'

This frightened her but he added, 'Is the tea almost ready? I'm starving.'

She was annoyed by his uncaring manner. 'That's all you ever think of, your blasted stomach.'

Charlie asked PC Williamson to drive to Monifieth to see Mrs French. But when they arrived at the Bergmann house it was all closed up with the shutters hiding the interiors of the rooms.

'Maybe she's gone to see her employer at the shop,' suggested Williamson.

Charlie, who had gone round the back and found the doors all locked, said. 'Let's go and see if she's at home in the village.'

They found her house at the end of a row of terraced houses with large gardens facing the road. The door opened at his second knock and Laura French stood in the small hallway. She looked terrible but stood aside to let them enter. There was a small suitcase standing in the lobby but she moved it to let the two men pass.

The front room was tiny but well-furnished and comfortable. She sat down and faced them over a small coffee table that separated the two sofas.

Charlie was immediately aware how ill she looked and it was obvious that she had heard the news about Bergmann. 'Were you working in the house yesterday and this morning, Mrs French?' he asked.

She shook her head and wiped her red-rimmed eyes with a small handerkerchief. 'No, I've been on holiday for a few days and I just got back this morning. The hospital phoned to tell me about Mr Bergmann and I couldn't believe it.'

Charlie noticed her face was shiny with sweat and her hands were shaking. She saw him look at them and clutched them into fists before putting them in the pockets of her cardigan.

'He had his wallet in his jacket with his name and address in it but he's still unconscious with severe concussion,' she said. 'The doctor said to telephone tomorrow and maybe he'll have recovered a bit more.'

She looked intently at Charlie, as if he was a clairvoyant who could foretell the future.

'Yes, the doctor told me the same thing. You say you were on holiday?'

She nodded. 'Yes, that's right. I heard the car came off the road at the far end of Broughty Ferry. He must have been travelling home. I wonder if he swerved to miss a dog or a cat?'

Charlie said that was one possibility. 'It's said there was a briefcase in his car but there's no sign of it. Do you have any idea about this case or whether he mentioned it to you?'

'No he didn't but he sometimes carries his briefcase when he comes home but not always. Is it important?'

Charlie didn't answer. Instead he said, 'Maybe he's got mixed up about it. Perhaps it's still in his shop or office.'

There was nothing new to be learned from her but he said as they stood at the door, 'The doctor is sure he'll make a full recovery so don't worry, Mrs French. I'll be in touch with you again.'

When they were out in the car, Charlie laughed at the constable's disappointed face. There had been no cups of tea on this visit and certainly no Victoria sponge cake.

25

Molly waited at the office on Monday morning to see Grace Carson, who was coming for an interview. The rest of the staff had all been in and had left for their assignments.

Seeing them off, Molly thought Alice looked tired and she hoped the work wasn't proving too hard for her. Some of the jobs that came in were physically demanding, especially if it was a house with children. Alice always seemed to get the hard end of the domestic side because she was the youngest. It never occurred to Molly that the reason was Sandy.

Jean was busy filing when the new recruit arrived. Molly took her upstairs for her interview. The woman was taller than her with smooth black hair, an attractive face with a pale complexion and dark brown eyes. She was dressed in a navy skirt and jacket with an immaculate white blouse with pale blue stripes. Grace explained she was twenty-seven years old and she didn't have any references, which Molly thought was odd.

Grace explained. 'I lived in South Africa with my parents but when my father died at the beginning of this year, my mother and I came home to live in Scotland where we lived before going to Cape Town. My father worked there and I did a secretary training course before working in various office jobs.'

Molly explained that the agency, although busy, could have some times when there was little or no work and perhaps Miss Carson would prefer to look for a permanent office job.

She shook her head. 'My fiancé is still in Cape Town but he'll be coming here in a month or two. We're not sure where we'll live after we're married so working here would suit me fine, that is, if you think I'm suitable?'

'Would you wait here for a moment please while I speak to my receptionist?'

Molly went downstairs and spoke to Jean. 'What work do we have on the books, Jean?' she asked.

Jean went to the filing cabinet and brought out a folder. 'We're booked solidly for the next two months to cover holidays in various firms and, of course, we always have the emergency bookings when staff are off ill.'

Molly said, 'The woman upstairs is looking for a job. She's called Grace Carson and I'd like to hire her.'

Jean said she looked like an efficient type of person and was beautifully dressed, which was a big plus in this job.

Molly nodded and went back upstairs. 'Well, I'd like you to come and work for the agency, Miss Carson, when can you start?'

Miss Carson looked pleased. 'Thank you. I can start as soon as you would like.'

'I see your address is Commercial Street. Is that where you'll be living?'

'Yes it is. My mother and I have rented a flat there until we decide what we're going to do after my fiancé comes here.' As she was leaving, she said, 'I was worried that without references I would have difficulty in finding work so I'm really grateful to you.'

Molly said she would see her the next morning.

After Grace left, Molly went to telephone Betty to make arrangements about returning Bill's belongings but there was no answer so she got ready to go to her work, which was back in the council office. Hopefully this would turn out to be another week's job, or with a bit of luck, even longer.

Alice could hardly concentrate on the cleaning of Mrs Baird's kitchen, even though it was grubby after the three children had left for school. Sandy had tackled her last night about her reluctance to see him and instead of telling him the truth she had made some stupid excuse, saying she didn't want her ex-husband Victor to find out about them. He had said that she wasn't to worry about what Victor would say as there was a rumour that he was leaving the Caledon to go and work in one of the Govan shipyards. He had told some of his mates that the boxing scene on the west coast was the place to be if he wanted to make a name for himself. Everyone knew he wanted to be a boxer and enter in the championship games.

As she gathered together all the dirty breakfast dishes from the kitchen table, she decided to take Maisie's advice and tell him the truth. Feeling better now that she had made the decision, she put the dishes in the hot soapy water and began to turn the kitchen into a clean and sweet-smelling place. She knew Mrs Baird was grateful for all her hard work as it meant she could have time with the three-month-old baby.

Alice scoured the sink with Vim powder and wondered how she would cope with four children like Mrs Baird. The answer was 'with difficulty', but then she thought it would be fine to have a couple of little ones but she would never have children if she carried on like this, being frightened of commitment.

Thankfully she managed to finish early and she headed home, rehearsing her speech during the bus trip. Maisie met her on the stairs and she asked Alice to come in for a quick cup of tea.

'I'm going to tell Sandy the truth tonight,' Alice said as she sat at the wooden kitchen table.

Maisie said that was the best way. 'It's best to put him out of his misery so he can look for someone else who would love to marry him.'

Actually this wasn't what Alice had in mind. She loved going out to the pictures with him and having fish suppers together but it was the thought of getting married and history maybe repeating itself. Suddenly she was jealous at the thought of some unknown woman taking her place and she was so confused when Sandy turned up at seven o'clock.

Before he had a chance to speak, she blurted out. 'I do love being with you, Sandy, I really do, but I . . .' She stopped, unsure how to put it into words. It wasn't as if he had asked her to marry him, and she thought what a fool she would look if he didn't understand what she was going on about.

Turning to the easy chair, she pulled the magazine from under the cushion and thrust it in his hands.

He looked puzzled. 'How to knit a cardigan,' he said.

'What?' she took the magazine and saw to her annoyance that it wasn't at the correct page. She wet her finger and skimmed through the pages until she found the article. 'Read that, Sandy,' she said.

He sat down and quietly read the article then looked at her. 'Do you really believe all this rubbish, Alice?'

'It's written by a qualified expert and she should know about these things.'

'So what you're saying is that I'll start behaving like Victor?'

By this time she was full of misery. 'No I'm not, but I do worry about it. Victor was so charming when I first met him.'

Sandy said, 'And you think I'll be the same, Alice?'

'No I don't but I hope you understand how I feel?'

'Oh I understand all right. One man treats you badly and you think we're all the same.' He put the magazine down on the table. 'I'll just get away then and not bother you any more.'

He went out the door as she got to her feet but he was halfway down the stairs when she reached the door. She thought about calling after him but decided against it. Sitting down in the empty kitchen she thought that this was what she wanted so why was she full of misery?

The door opened and for a brief moment she thought it was Sandy coming back to reassure her but it was only Maisie.

Maisie took one look at her friend and asked. 'How did it go? Did he put your mind at rest?'

Alice burst into tears. 'He won't be back, Maisie. He didn't say it but I think I've insulted him by comparing him with Victor.'

Maisie said that was rubbish. 'He'll be back tomorrow night, just you wait and see.' But as she put the kettle on to make some tea, Maisie wasn't sure that he would. She knew him well and he was a quiet man with strong principles and he would have been very hurt to be compared to Victor. Even if at one time they were pals.

26

Charlie and PC Williamson were at the Royal Infirmary before lunchtime. Charlie hoped Mr Bergmann was now able to tell him what happened on Saturday night. They were met by the ward sister and told them to sit in the corridor until the doctor finished his rounds.

Charlie was impatient. He had a lot of work to catch up on as he was no nearer solving these robberies. Andrew Williamson, on the other hand, was quite enjoying his view of some of the pretty nurses passing back and forth, but he knew better than to stare so he pretended to study some of the various posters on the wall. One in particular which showed in gruesome detail the inner workings of the human body.

The clock on the wall said half-past eleven when the doctor hurried down the passage, his white coat flapping and his stethoscope hanging from the pocket. Charlie and Williamson stood up as the man approached them. 'Mr Bergmann is awake but I don't want you to question him for long, only for a few minutes as he is still concussed.'

Charlie said he wouldn't upset the patient and they followed the doctor into the ward. Two long rows of beds lined the walls but the bed nearest the door had screens around it. The doctor opened the screen and the three men went to the bed.

Mr Bergmann lay with a white bandage around his head which matched his pale complexion and contrasted with the bright blue-striped pyjama top. The doctor took his pulse and checked his eyes while the two policemen sat on uncomfortable wooden chairs. After he was satisfied with both tests he left, with another word of warning about tiring the man out.

Eric Bergmann closed his eyes but Charlie said, 'I'm DS Johns and this is PC Williamson. Can you tell us what happened to you on Saturday night?'

The patient opened his eyes but they seemed to be unfocussed then he turned his head with a small cry of pain. 'Have you found my briefcase?'

Charlie said there was no briefcase in the car and the man turned away with a loud groan. 'What happened to you, Mr Bergmann? Did your car run off the road?'

He shook his head slightly and whispered, 'No, I was at my house but I think someone hit me over the head. I can't really remember.'

Charlie was taken aback by this statement. 'But your car was found in Broughty Ferry and it looked like you were on your way home when you had the accident.'

'No, I didn't go off the road. I was on the point of opening my door when I was hit and I remember the time, it was eleven forty-five because I looked at my watch.' He turned and stared at Charlie. 'You have to find my briefcase, there is valuable jewellery in it.'

Charlie's heart sank. This looked like another robbery. 'How much is this jewellery worth?'

The man sighed. 'A lot of money, DS Johns.' He lay back on his pillow just as the doctor appeared.

'I think my patient has answered enough questions for now.'

Charlie thanked Mr Bergmann and said, 'I'll be back in tomorrow and I hope you get better soon.'

The man nodded but as soon as the two policemen were out of the room he turned to the doctor. 'Were my keys in my coat pocket when I was brought in, Doctor?'

The doctor said he would check. Half an hour later he was back. 'You had your car key, watch and wallet and this bunch of keys.'

The doctor watched as he looked at the keys, sorting through them as if looking to identify them. They were all there except the three which were the key for his shop and the keys for his two safes. The one at the shop and the one at the house.

When the doctor left the room, Eric Bergmann lay back again on the pillows and began to cry softly. He had lost everything and he didn't think his insurance policy would cover all his losses. He would have to sell his house and shop, plus tell his wife that her extravagant lifestyle was at an end. Mrs French would also be out of a job now that he was finished as a businessman. He would have to tell the police the grim news that, by now, all his valuable stock was gone.

Outside, as they got into the car, Charlie told Williamson to drive to Monifieth. He also said that when they got back to the police station he would get some of the policemen out on a door-to-door search for any witnesses. 'It looks like he came home and was attacked there then driven to the beach and dumped. Maybe someone saw something that night.' He honestly didn't believe anyone would have seen anything because of the thunderstorm but hopefully there would be people out walking dogs or coming back from the pub or the pictures.

When they reached the house, Charlie was surprised to see the housekeeper. 'I thought I should be here in case Mr Bergmann gets home. I've cooked some food for him.'

Charlie said he was staying in the infirmary and the woman looked stricken. 'On Saturday night your employer said he came to the front door and was attacked there. He has also had his briefcase stolen that contained a lot of jewellery. Do you mind if we have a look around the house and the grounds?'

She nodded and went ahead of them. 'As you know, the house isn't as big as it looks. You saw the bedrooms on your last visit when we had the robbery.'

As Charlie accompanied her around the rooms, Williamson went outside and had a good look around the garden. There were no tyre tracks because the drive was covered with gravel but at the back of the house it was possible to make out a few tracks on the hard packed earth. He noted this in his book.

Laura French kept up a conversation as they went around the house. 'I have a good job here and Mr Bergmann has been very decent to me. Mrs Bergmann is all right, I suppose, and she is away a lot of the time. He pays me a good wage and also pays the rent on my house so I owe him a lot.' She began to cry and tried to wipe the tears away with the back of her hand.

'So you don't come from the area?' Charlie asked.

She gave him a quick sharp glance, then said, 'No, I originally lived in Glasgow but my marriage was unhappy so when I saw this job advertised I applied and was lucky to get it.'

'I thought you said you were a widow, Mrs French?'

She gave a mirthless laugh. 'I know. I've told everyone here that I lost my husband but I suppose that is the truth because I did lose him, if not in death then certainly in divorce.'

When they were in the bedroom where the safe was kept, Charlie knelt down to take a look at it. There were no marks or scrapes on it and if it had been opened it must have been with the key.

'Does Mr Bergmann keep another key to the safe?'

She shook her head. 'I don't think so. I expect he keeps it on his key ring, along with the keys to the house, his shop and his office.'

There was nothing much to see in the house. It was all very neat and clean and well-polished but there was no sign of any break-in.

When they came downstairs, Williamson was waiting at the front door. 'I didn't see anything out of the ordinary in the garden but it is very large and I suppose there are lots of hiding places where a briefcase could be stashed.'

Charlie said to get the squad of men to search the garden thoroughly after they questioned the people in the houses nearest to this one. As Charlie looked around it was clear that the house was situated up from the road but he had noticed the hotel a few yards from the drive on his first visit.

He got the constable to stop there and they went into the reception area. It wasn't a large hotel and Charlie deduced it had at one time been a dwelling house like its neighbour up the drive. He rang the bell and a young girl came out of the little office behind the desk. She gave them a huge smile.

Charlie told her they were from the police station, investigating a robbery from her neighbour, and she said she was the daughter of the owners. Her name, she said, was Janet Davidson.

Charlie asked her, 'Did you see anyone near the house either walking or in a car, around eleven forty-five on Saturday night?'

'No I'm sorry I didn't. I wasn't here on Saturday as I went to stay with my pal in Dundee. My parents run the hotel and they were here as we had some guests staying. They came for a golf weekend and they left this morning.'

'When will your parents be back?' he asked.

She looked at the clock. 'They've just gone to Dundee to stock up the larder and the bar so they shouldn't be too long.'

'Please tell them I'll be back to see them tomorrow.'

27

Grace turned up for work on Tuesday morning fifteen minutes before she was meant to. Jean had just opened the office door and Molly had appeared from the flat. Grace was dressed in her navy suit with a bright blue blouse and she had a large satchel type bag slung over her shoulder.

Molly had worked in the council office the previous day but she decided to send her new recruit there for the rest of the week's contract. Grace met Edna, Mary, Maisie, Irene and Alice. She smiled brightly at them before walking briskly out of the door to her job.

Molly was alarmed by Alice's appearance. It seemed like she hadn't slept and her eyes had the red-rimmed look of recent of crying. Maisie had a protective arm linked through hers and they both set off, along with Edna's mum, Irene. Outside the door Maisie had a word with Alice before making her way to Mrs Jankowski's house while the other two women set off in a different direction.

Edna was looking radiant. Marriage certainly suited her and for one brief moment Molly envied her. She asked after John and Billy.

Edna said they were great. 'Billy is doing really well at school because John teaches him new things at home. He loves everything to do with cars and vehicles and John has loads of books on these subjects. The only snag is Sonia. We both think James is at the end of his patience and John wishes she would go back to Edinburgh. He hates the thought that his brother is being treated like that but there's not a lot we can do.'

Molly sympathised with her. 'No, I expect James won't listen to any criticism from anybody.'

After the staff had left, Molly said, 'I'll go upstairs and type out all my notes from the talks I had with the tea managers, Jean. If you need any help then let me know.'

Jean said she had invoices to type up and post but she would phone upstairs if she needed Molly.

Molly laid out her notebook with all the notes she had taken from the men. She wanted to give these to Betty so that she would have an idea about her brother. One thing that wasn't possible was the reason Bill was worried about something. As far as she could see, the retired tea managers were all leading quiet and simple lives after putting the horrors and nightmares of India behind them.

It was just before twelve o'clock when Jean phoned. 'I've had a Mrs Stevenson on the phone, Molly. She's looking for a temp to come and work two days this week.' When Jean mentioned the address, Molly realised it was George Stevenson's wife who had phoned.

Molly went downstairs and said she would go tomorrow and Thursday to the Stevenson house and Jean returned the call to tell the woman. As Jean was talking to the client, Molly placed her notes in a folder and put them in the filing cabinet. She planned to get in touch with Betty but she would do it sometime this week. When she handed over the pouch to Bill's sister, that would be the end of the matter.

As all the work was in hand, Molly suddenly decided to go to see her parents. It would save her going over at the weekend. However when she arrived at the door it was locked. Molly had a feeling of foreboding.

Marigold hurried out. 'They're away to Dundee, Molly. I think they were planning on coming to see you. Come in and have a cold drink.'

It was a lovely hot sunny day and Molly gladly followed Marigold into her garden. She didn't want to question her friend because she was frightened of the answer and Marigold kept away from the subject as well. When they were sitting in a shady corner of the garden with its colourful display of flowers, Marigold said, 'I was thinking of going to Pitlochry this weekend to see another play at the theatre. It's *A Hundred Years Old* and I would love to see it.' She put her glass down and looked at Molly. 'Would you like to come with me? We can stay at the Bay Guest House and come back on Sunday morning. We won't go for any walks this time but maybe Deanna can meet us for a morning coffee.'

Molly's stomach was still churning and she hadn't touched her lemonade. Marigold stayed silent and gazed around the garden. That rose bush was getting too straggly, she thought to herself, and the hedge needed trimmed. She would tackle these jobs later, or maybe tomorrow.

Molly suddenly said, 'I'd love to come to Pitlochry with you. It'll be a chance to return Bill Reid's things to Betty.'

Marigold said that was great and she looked forward to phoning Bess Smith to make the overnight booking. 'Will we take the train this time, Molly, or will you borrow the car?'

Molly wasn't sure. 'I'll think about it and let you know before Saturday.' She stood up. 'Well I better get back. We'll probably cross over the river in opposite directions and I'll miss my parents. Will you tell them I was here?'

Marigold promised she would.

Molly walked back through the town. The sun shone on the grey buildings and small shops and there was a festive air about the streets. People lingered in the warmth, wearing colourful summer dresses and the benches at the City Square were filled with people taking advantage of the sunny day. *This was what it must have been like in India*, she thought, *but of course it would be much hotter than this*. She recalled the lovely weather in Australia and she knew her parents would love the warmth instead of the cold Scottish winters and indifferent summers. Still, that didn't make it any easier for her to contemplate them going away for good. But did she want to go with them? She was proud of her agency and how successful it was, plus she enjoyed working with her staff.

When she reached the agency, Jean said her parents were up in the flat. 'I offered to make them some tea,' she told, 'but they said they would wait for you upstairs.'

Molly thanked her and climbed the stairs. Her dad was sitting on the studio couch and her mum was filling the kettle.

She turned when Molly came through the door. 'Ah, you're just in time for something to eat.' She opened the oven door and the succulent smell of onion bridies wafted out. 'Now where are the plates?' she said more to herself than to Archie and Molly. Molly scanned her mother's face for a sign of what lay ahead but she looked like she always did, very efficient and cheerful.

When they were all seated around the dining table, Nancy gave a nod to her husband and he put down his knife and fork. 'Molly—' He stopped and cleared his throat. 'We've just got back from our interview with the emigration officer and he has approved our move to Australia. We will be leaving some time this year. We said we wanted you to come with us but it's entirely up to you.'

Molly wanted to burst into tears but all she said was, 'So you've made up your mind to go?'

28

The next morning Charlie and Andrew Williamson, both dressed in plain clothes, were back in Monifieth. Charlie was hoping the owners would both be at home this time. When they entered the reception area, it was quiet. From somewhere upstairs they heard the sound of a vacuum cleaner and Charlie rang the bell that was placed on the reception desk.

The sound of the machine stopped and a woman hurried down the stairs. She wore a blue overall over a summer dress and Charlie noticed perspiration on her face and neck. She pulled a large white cloth from her pocket and wiped it away. She was about forty years old, with dull blonde hair tied up with a ribbon at the back and dark-shadowed blue eyes. Charlie thought she looked tired.

She moved around the desk with a smile. 'Good morning.'

Charlie showed her his card and the smile was replaced by a worried frown. 'We spoke to your daughter about the robbery in your neighbour's house on Saturday night.'

Her face grew serious. 'Come into the lounge. We can talk there,' she said, moving towards a door opposite them.

The room was small and cosy with a selection of chairs and small tables. A fire had been laid in the stone fireplace but it was obviously not needed during this hot spell.

'Would you like something to drink? I can make some tea or coffee if you want it. I'm here on my own this morning as my husband has gone for the shopping. He would rather do that than the cleaning,' she said, sitting down on the edge of one of the armchairs. Charlie sat across from her while Williamson took a chair by the door. She was finding it hard to look at Charlie and she kept rubbing her thin hands as if she was feeling cold. It was clear she was worried about this visit and that the two policemen weren't welcome.

Charlie said they didn't want any refreshments and he could well imagine the disappointment on the constable's face. He got straight to the point. 'Your neighbour, Mr Bergmann, was involved in a car accident late on Saturday night and his briefcase is missing. I wonder if anyone here in the hotel saw anything suspicious?'

Mrs Davidson said she had heard about the incident from her daughter Janet. 'Harry, my husband, and I were both here that night. We were very busy that weekend with all the rooms booked by a party of golfers. I hoped the terrible thunderstorm wouldn't spoil their game the next day but after the storm passed over it turned out a fine night.'

'Mr Bergmann says he came home about eleven forty-five, did you see him or his car?'

She shook her head. 'No, I didn't go outside during the storm.' She looked a bit sheepish. 'I'm afraid of thunder and lightning, you see, and even in the hotel I just wanted to hide under the bed. But of course I couldn't do that. Not with the hotel full.'

Charlie looked around the room. 'Do you have a bar here, Mrs Davidson?'

'Yes we do. It's for registered guests only. We don't cater for the outside trade.'

'So your guests were mainly in the bar?'

'Yes they were. They finished their evening meal about nine o'clock and they ended up with their drinks until they went to their rooms about midnight.'

Charlie had had a good look round the outside of the hotel on his last visit and four of the windows overlooked the Bergmann drive. 'I wonder if we can have a look at the rooms that face the back of the hotel?'

The woman looked a bit flustered. 'I haven't managed to clean all the rooms yet. We had more golfers in last night.'

Charlie said he wasn't there to inspect the cleanliness of the place. He wanted to see if anyone could have witnessed what happened that night.

Mrs Davidson got to her feet and they all moved up the carpeted staircase. There was a long lobby at the top with seven doors leading off from it. 'There's three bedrooms that face the back and also the bathroom,' she explained. She opened the first of the doors and Charlie and the constable went in while the woman stood at the door like some lookout at a bank raid.

The room was in the throes of being cleaned and the vacuum cleaner stood against the wardrobe. Charlie went over to the window and he could see the drive and the front door of the Bergmann house. The other two rooms had a view of the drive but not the door, while the bathroom had the bottom half of the window fitted with frosted glass. To get a view of the drive, the person would have to climb on the wooden stool with the cork seat. If a guest in this room had looked out the window at the right time on Saturday then they would have seen if the car did go up the drive like Mr Bergmann had said.

Charlie turned away from the window. 'Are you friendly with the Bergmanns?'

'Well, I wouldn't say we were friends but we do speak when we see them. He's lovely, but I think she's a bit snooty. I believe she's away on a cruise and by the look of her fashions I expect she costs her husband a pretty packet.' She looked down at her own cheap cotton dress and unflattering overall and sighed.

'What about Mrs French, do you know her well?'

Mrs Davidson looked at the far corner of the room. 'No I don't know her well. I know she lives in the village but she hasn't been here very long. She has a bike that she uses to come to work and she will nod to me in the passing but she never stops to have a chat. But there again, I'm usually busy too and I probably wouldn't have time to chat to her.'

'I've just one more question. Did you or your husband or any of the guests go outside between eleven o'clock and half-past midnight, or even later?'

She looked evasive. 'I don't think so. Harry went out to the courtyard with a crate of empty beer bottles, but that was around ten-thirty, and one of the guests went out to his car during the storm but I'm not sure what time it was. All I remember is he came back in soaking wet and we had to hang his raincoat up to dry.'

'Can I have a list of your guests that night, especially the one who was outside please?'

She didn't look happy at this request. 'Oh, I don't know. Harry will be annoyed at that as it is our livelihood here and we can't have any unpleasantness.'

Charlie said he could always copy them down from the hotel register so she went and came back a few minutes later with the list and handed it over. 'The man who went outside is at the top of the list.'

Charlie thanked her. 'I'll need to speak to your husband. When is the best time to come back?'

'He has lots of jobs he does and I'm never sure where he'll be at any given time. If you phone when you're coming he'll have to stay in and see you.'

When the two men left the hotel, Charlie saw the upstairs curtain move an inch or two. 'What did you make of that?' he asked Williamson.

'Well it's clear she's frightened of her husband and she doesn't care for Mrs French. It also looks like she does all the donkey work in the place.'

'Do you know what I think? I would say that Mr Davidson isn't at the shops but is hiding upstairs.'

Williamson was surprised. 'Will we go back in and see him?'

Charlie said no. 'We'll save him for another day. I want to go and see this golfer called Tom Chambers, who lives in Perth.'

29

Molly was back on the bus to the Stevensons' house but she was unsure what work Mrs Stevenson wanted her to do. The sunny days of the past couple of weeks had disappeared and the heavy black clouds and the weather forecast said heavy rain was expected later in the day.

She made her way up the drive but as she reached the door, it was suddenly opened and the woman stood waiting for her. 'I saw you coming, Miss McQueen.'

Mrs Stevenson led the way to the large room that Molly had visited earlier – the one with all the Indian artefacts – but today, with the gloomy weather outside, it looked so different from that first view.

Mrs Stevenson was talking as she led the way. 'Please, call me Anna,' she said, lifting a large pile of papers from the chair in front of the desk that held a typewriter and a small ornate urn full of pencils.

Molly studied the woman. She looked quite fearsome in this room that resembled a museum. Tall, with a square-shaped face that was bereft of any powder or lipstick, thick wiry grey hair and a heavy tweed-pleated skirt with a lovely blue cashmere jumper. The only personal adornments were a large diamond ring and a beautiful deep blue necklace. Molly wondered if they were sapphires but they had to be fake stones, she thought. If they had been real the necklace would have cost a fortune.

Anna said, 'The reason I've hired you Miss . . . Pardon me, but what is your first name?'

Molly told her.

'As I said, the reason I need help, Molly, is I need a typist to type out my book which I've written in longhand. I'm almost finished with it so I reckoned a couple of days this week and the same next week, and if I need any more help then we can come to an arrangement.'

Molly sat down at the desk and almost groaned out loud when she saw the transcript of the book. The handwriting was small and cramped and she reckoned a typist would need more than a month to type it out.

Molly picked up page one and saw there was no title. 'Have you got a title for it, Anna?'

Anna said no. 'I've been toying with a few titles but I haven't made up my mind yet. If you leave the first few lines blank then you can put in the name when I've thought of something suitable. It's all about growing up in India where my parents owned a tea plantation. I thought it would make an interesting story as people seem to like tales of the exotic golden East. My husband is helping me with some of his own experiences and he calls it "our book".'

Molly tried to think of any book she had seen about the exotic East but she couldn't think of any. Still, she wasn't here to pass any judgement but merely to do what the customer wanted.

Anna said, 'I have to go out. I've got a meeting to go to. I'm the chairman of the group so I have to be there. I'll leave you but I'll be back about midday.'

On that note she swept out and Molly saw the car pass the window and go down the drive, then she turned her attention back to the desk. First of all, she made sure all the pages of the book were in the right order then she made a start on this bestseller from the exotic East.

She was busy typing and trying to decipher the terrible handwriting when she became aware that George Stevenson had entered the room. He carried a tray with a teapot and two cups and a plate of biscuits.

'Trust my wife not to offer you anything to drink,' he said, pouring the tea into the fragile china cups. 'This is the best Darjeeling tea on the market.'

Molly would rather have kept working but she didn't want to

refuse so she took the cup and moved away from the desk. 'I'd better not spill tea on your wife's papers.'

He gave her a lopsided smile. 'My wife's a damn fool writing a book about growing up in India but as usual she knows best and I'm helping her.' He put down his cup. 'How did you get on with the other men? Did you give them the warning?'

Molly said she had but it all seemed so unnecessary as they didn't have a clue what Bill Reid meant.

'That's what I thought when you came here. Still, it's a great pity that Bill's dead. We were all so close when we were in India but when we all came back it wasn't the same. We all had our own interests by then and our paths never seemed to cross.'

Molly put her empty cup on the tray and went back behind the desk. 'I'd better get back to work. Your wife said she would be home by midday.'

She bent her head to pick up the next page so she missed the bitter look that crossed his face. When she started typing, he said, 'Well I have my own work to do so I'd better get moving as well.'

As the morning wore on, Molly became quite immersed in the story. It told of a privileged upbringing, with Anna being looked after by a series of nannies as her parents lived a very social life with parties, polo matches, horse racing and visiting the other Europeans in the area. Anna had been a very inquisitive child and had noticed all that went on around her, and by the time she arrived back home from her meeting, Molly could almost visualise the tastes and smells of life on the plantation.

On her arrival, Anna bustled into the kitchen and appeared with a plate of sandwiches and more tea. This time the tea tasted different and Molly deduced this wasn't the finest Darjeeling.

She called out, 'George, lunch is ready.'

He ambled in and almost threw himself down on the fireside chair. Molly said she would go into the kitchen or the garden and eat her packed meal but Anna wouldn't hear of it. 'I've made enough for the three of us, Molly. We usually have our main meal in the evening and just have a snack at this time.'

Molly noticed that George had already devoured four of the sandwiches and his wife gave him a baleful look which he chose to ignore.

Although Molly was hungry she didn't want to eat anything. Anna took the plate away from the side of the table nearest her husband and Molly lifted one small morsel of bread. She wasn't sure what the filling was but she didn't want to peer under the bread.

The snack was over in fifteen minutes and Molly felt sorry for George because he still looked hungry, but she thought he had been in the house all morning without his wife so he could easily have made himself something substantial. Surely a plate of bacon and eggs was well within his capabilities.

By four o'clock, Molly was finished for the day.

Anna said, 'I'll see you on Friday.'

Molly stood at the bottom of the drive until the bus arrived and within an hour she was back in the agency.

30

He had the same nightmare again. The one where he was struggling for breath in the monsoon. He heard the shots but it all seemed so unreal, almost as if he was a bystander instead of the perpetrator. Then he saw someone standing watching him from the dark green fronds of the trees. It was a woman's shape but she seemed to float in and out of his vision, like a ghost. Then suddenly the form became clear as he wiped the rain from his eyes. It was that woman with all her questions. The one who had arrived to torment his dreams and his life, just when he thought he was safe.

Safe, what a great word but would he ever know the feeling of being safe again? Should he do something about her? Or lie low and hope it would all pass over like it had done years ago?

The rain was still pouring from a leaden sky and he thought he would never be dry again. He started to throw off his shirt, to let the rain wash his hot body.

He woke up. For a moment he didn't know where he was. Then the familiar shapes of his bedroom became visible and he sighed. The blankets were on the floor and he was drenched in sweat.

31

Charlie and Williamson were in the car on their way to Perth. It was a beautiful morning after a night of heavy rain and the river looked calm and sluggish. It didn't resemble the same river at Dundee with its tides and currents. Small bands of salmon netters were busy at work as they passed but Charlie didn't seem to notice them as he was studying the list in his hand. 'Tom Chambers lives in Inchaffrey Street and I've asked the local police force to let him know we are coming.'

The man lived in a flat in a tenement halfway along the street. He answered the door with a worried frown on his face. 'Come in,' he said, stepping aside to let them pass. 'I've no idea what you want to question me about.'

Charlie said, 'It's just some routine questions about your golfing trip to Monifieth.'

Tom Chambers looked confused but showed them in to the living room where a small, dark-haired woman was sitting. He introduced her as his wife. There was also a brown-and-white spaniel lying in a basket.

'I hope you don't mind my wife staying here?'

Charlie said he didn't.

'Mr Chambers, on the Saturday night of your golfing weekend you went outside to your car during a thunderstorm around eleven forty-five. Is that correct?'

Tom gave his wife a quick glance and nodded.

'There was an accident that night and a suspected robbery and what I would like to know is, did you see anything or anyone on the drive leading to the house that lies above the hotel?'

Tom gave this some thought and looked at his wife again. 'I

had to go out in that awful storm to take Bob for a walk.' He pointed to the dog. 'Ella, my wife, was away that weekend as well and we didn't have anyone to look after the dog so I took him with me. The hotel owners don't allow animals in the hotel so I had to keep him in the car. I went out to feed him in the early evening and took him for a walk but I thought he would need another one before I went to bed.'

'And did you see anything suspicious?'

'No, I was walking along the side of the hotel grounds when a car passed and went up the drive. The car headlights were on and someone got out and the front door opened.'

Charlie was surprised but he didn't show it. 'How did you know it was the front door, Mr Chambers?'

'I saw the light from the hall or whatever, it spilled out onto the step. Then the car headlights went out and the car was driven around the back of the house. To be quite honest, I wasn't paying too much attention to it as I was desperate to get back inside and go to bed. We had a tiring game of golf on the Saturday.'

'So no one else came out or went in?'

'Well, normally I would have been back putting Bob into the car but he ran away around the back of the garden and I had to call him. I think he saw a rabbit and went after it.' He gave his wife a rueful grin and she smiled back.

'The little devil,' she said. 'He's always doing that.'

'As I said, I was standing waiting for Bob to come back when the car came down the drive, it was going quite fast, I thought. Then the front door opened again and a van followed the car. It was also going fast.'

'Did anything else happen to come down the drive?'

Tom shook his head. 'Not while I was there anyway. The car and the van went along the road towards Broughty Ferry and I put Bob back in the car and gave him a rub down with his towel. Then I went back inside and the owner kindly dried my raincoat by the side of the fire.'

'The van, Mr Chambers. Can you tell me if you saw what make it was, and the colour if possible?'

'I'm not sure. I did think it was a Ford van and it looked grey but I'm not sure, sorry.'

Charlie said that was fine. 'You've been a great help.' He glanced at the spaniel. 'Both you and Bob.'

Mrs Chambers was delighted. 'Do you hear that, Bob? You've been a very clever dog.'

Bob wagged his tail and took the praise in his stride.

Mrs Chambers said, 'Would you both like a drink of tea or coffee?'

Much to Williamson's annoyance, Charlie said they didn't.

Back in the car, Charlie said to drive to a small café he had spotted on their way in and soon both of them were sitting down to two breakfasts. They were the only customers so Charlie felt it was safe to discuss the case.

He said, 'Well, the question is, if Mrs French was on holiday, who opened the door?'

Andrew Williamson, who desperately wanted to be promoted to detective one day, was honoured at being asked for his opinion. 'Did Mr Bergmann get someone else to do the housekeeper's job when she was on holiday or off for any reason?'

Charlie shook his head. 'He didn't mention any other staff but we'll ask when we see him.' He poured another cup of tea, thinking. 'I wonder if he employs a cleaner, and if so, does she have a key to the house?'

Williamson was trying his best to come up with sensible suggestions. 'I know there was no sign of a break-in but could a burglar maybe have got in some way and was waiting for Mr Bergmann to arrive back home?'

Charlie looked doubtful but said that was one possibility to be investigated. 'That would take a lot of planning. The simplest thing would be to attack his victim and just steal his keys.'

Williamson's thoughts wandered to the large garden. 'Do you think he gets a gardener to cut his grass and look after the grounds? It could even be someone who comes to the house on a regular basis.'

Charlie said that was something else to be looked into. He

noticed more customers beginning to trickle in, and not wishing to continue their conversation in public, Charlie stood up, looking for the waitress to give him the bill.

When they left the café, Williamson asked, 'Are we going back to Dundee?'

Charlie said yes but first he wanted to see Mr Bergmann again at the infirmary.

It was the same doctor on duty when they arrived at the hospital. He didn't look particularly pleased to see them. 'I can't talk to you now as I'm just starting my ward rounds. I think Mr Bergmann will be able to go home this afternoon or tomorrow at the latest.'

'We just want a quick word with your patient. We won't be long.'

The doctor looked displeased but he walked with them into the ward and spoke to the sister who placed the screens around the bed.

Eric Bergmann was looking a bit better as he had some colour in his face but when he saw the policemen he became distressed. Misinterpreting this, Charlie said he had heard that he was maybe getting home later that day.

'It's not that. The doctor brought my belongings to me yesterday and my keyring has three keys missing from it. The key to my shop and the two keys to my safes. I had a great deal of valuable jewellery in my briefcase and my safes. The case has gone and I can only surmise that the safes have been emptied.'

Before he stood up, Charlie said, 'We have a witness who saw your car going up the drive late on Saturday night. Someone opened the house door then the car drove away, followed by a van. Was there someone else other than Mrs French in the house?'

The patient lay back with a deep sigh. 'No, the only ones with a key are myself, my wife and Mrs French.'

Charlie asked him. 'Do you employ a temporary housekeeper when Mrs French is on holiday?'

Mr Bergmann said he didn't.

'What about a cleaner? Do you have someone who comes in every day or once a week?'

Mr Bergmann shook his head. 'Or someone who does the garden?'

Again, the man shook his head. 'No I love gardening and I do all the grass cutting and my wife does the planting. It's her hobby while I get some exercise and fresh air after being shut up in the shop all day.'

Charlie checked the bunch of keys. 'We have checked the outside of your premises, Mr Bergmann, and everything was secure but we'll be back in touch as quickly as we can.'

The two men hurried from the ward and didn't hear the patient saying it was all too late.

32

Alice had never felt so alone in her life, which was saying something. She had spent long lonely days in the Carolina Port Orphanage but she was in the same position as all the other children and she had been reasonably happy there. Even when her mother had died when she was twelve, she hadn't felt as abandoned as she did now. Sandy had stayed away ever since her heartfelt talk with him and she cried most nights when she lay trying to get to sleep. She knew she had to pull herself together for the sake of her work. She had noticed Molly giving her a concerned look the other morning.

Maisie had tried to help her, even suggested going to see Sandy and explaining how her friend felt, but Alice was mortified by this. 'He'll think I'm begging him to come back and I don't want that,' she had said.

It was four-thirty in the morning before she had fallen asleep and now she had slept in. She was due at her work at eight-thirty and it was now eight o'clock. Jumping up, she quickly got washed and dressed, brushed her hair and jumped on the tramcar that dropped her off at the foot of the Wellgate. If she ran all the way up the street she would only be a few minutes late.

She was at the agency door when she felt faint and the last thing she saw was Molly looking at her.

Molly and Jean were busy with the invoices when Alice rushed in. At first the two women thought she had tripped but when they went to help her up they saw that she had fainted.

When Alice came to, Molly helped her upstairs and made her

lie down on the studio couch. Alice tried to stand up, saying, 'I'm sorry I slept in but I'll get to work right away.'

Molly said she should stay where she was and Jean arrived with a cup of sweet tea, which was, according to her, the panacea to cure all ills. Alice was grateful to be able to lie back because she didn't think her legs would be able to bear her weight in spite of it being so slight.

Molly sat beside her and asked her if anything was wrong, and to her consternation, she suddenly burst into tears. She told her she hadn't been sleeping or eating very much and how she had slept in and had to run up the street.

'I'll take you home, Alice, and I want you to stay off work till you're feeling better.'

Alice said she would be all right in a moment and be able to go to work but Molly was adamant, though first she had to arrange for someone to take over Alice's work. She thought she would do it herself once Alice was back at home, but then Irene appeared. She had arrived just after the incident and hearing what had happened, she had a suggestion. 'The young daughter of my neighbour is waiting to go to university and she is looking for work until September.'

Molly was unsure. 'It'll be on the domestic side, Irene. Do you think a young girl would want to do that?'

Irene said she would. 'I could go now and speak to her and see what she says.'

Molly left her to arrange that with Jean and she set of with Alice to catch the tramcar to Arthurstone Terrace.

When they reached the house Molly asked her, 'You will go and see the doctor today?'

Alice said she would. 'I'll wait till Maisie comes home and we'll go together.'

Molly asked her if the doctor did a morning or afternoon surgery but Alice said she would rather wait till the early evening as she just wanted to go back to bed. 'I'll be back at work tomorrow, Molly,' she said.

'I want you to take the rest of the week off, Alice. Don't worry about your wages as you'll be paid as normal but I'd rather you took some days off to have a good rest.'

Molly went to put the kettle on but Alice said she didn't feel like anything to eat or drink. 'I'll go and lie down,' she said.

Molly didn't like leaving her so she waited until Alice was tucked up in the big double bed in the small back room before she left.

Although Alice still felt dizzy, within a few minutes she was fast asleep.

Maisie arrived at five-thirty and before going into her own house she hurried in to see her friend. She had already left for her work before Alice came in this morning, which meant she only learned of her fainting turn after finishing work.

Alice was up and dressed when she knocked at the door. Maisie bustled in. 'Molly tells me you fainted, Alice, and that I've to take you to the doctor. How are you feeling now?'

Alice tried to put on a brave face but Maisie knew her too well. 'What's wrong?' she asked, sitting down beside her.

Alice sat quite still as the tears streaked down her face. 'I think I'm expecting a baby, Maisie.'

Her friend almost fell off her chair. 'What?'

Alice became embarrassed, a deep red flush spreading over her face and neck. 'It was after Edna's wedding. It was such a great night at the reception and the dance and I suddenly felt so carefree and happy when we all came back in the taxi.'

She turned her anguished face to her friend. 'I've been full of guilt ever since and that's why I said I didn't want a serious relationship with him. That I only wanted us to remain as friends.'

Maisie said, 'Well he'll need to be told right away.'

'No.' The word came out like a bullet. 'I'll just have to manage on my own and anyway, maybe I'm not.' She gestured with her hand. 'You know?'

'Well we better get ready to go and see the doctor and he'll be able to confirm it or not,' said Maisie. The two women walked down to Victoria Road where the doctor had his surgery and they entered the waiting room that was half-full with patients. They had to sit for almost an hour but when Alice came out, the look on her face said it all.

Maisie gave her an enquiring look while Alice just nodded. 'He confirmed it.'

'Let's get back home and I'll cook us both some supper. Have you had anything to eat today, Alice?'

She said she hadn't but added, 'I don't feel hungry.'

Maisie made scrambled eggs on toast and a pot of strong tea, but although Alice picked at it, when Maisie went to wash up the dishes, she had to throw half of it in the bucket.

33

Bergmann's Fine Jewellery & Pawnshop on the Hawkhill was a large, imposing shop with a big window that had a metal screen protecting the glass from being broken, either in a robbery or in an accident. Behind the glass was a wooden shelf unit that had held the various items of jewellery but was now bare. This was normal practice for jewellers' shops in case someone broke the window to steal the contents.

There was the three brass balls pawnbroker sign above the solid wooden door and a small dark alley ran alongside the shop. Charlie had walked down this alley that was merely a dead-end passageway with its wet, slimy cobbles and strewn litter. Another substantial wooden door was set into the wall stating the pawnbroker's opening hours.

Charlie had organised a locksmith to meet him at the jeweller's and pawnshop and he stood with PC Williamson and the fingerprint team waiting for the man to arrive. A small group of people stood across the street, anxious to know what was going on, and there was a ripple of excitement when the small van arrived and the man walked over to the shop.

A voice called from this small audience. 'When's the pawnshop going to be opened? My ma wants to pawn her wedding ring.'

This brought a ripple of laughter from the group, which the policemen ignored. Charlie and the team walked down the small alley while PC Williamson stood at the mouth of the passage. It was his job to see that no one came down who wasn't on official business.

Mr Whyte, the locksmith, who owned a business further up the street, brought out his tools and began to try and open the door. Because it was substantial he couldn't hurry. There had been heavy rain showers early that morning but it had dried up and a watery sun had come out. After a few moments, finally the door was open.

Charlie said, 'The shop door will also have to be done and new locks put on both doors right away, Mr Whyte.'

The man nodded and moved to the front of the shop where his movements were being eagerly watched by the spectators who had grown over the past half hour. Women on their way to the shops stopped and asked what was going on. One wee wag said, 'I think they've found a dead body in there.'

This was greeted with gasps of horror and PC Williamson was sent over to send them all home. They all moved away with reluctance and muttered complaints against the heavy hand of the law until one voice said, 'If there is a dead body in there, maybe the murderer is still inside.'

This statement was met with squeals of dismay from the women who pushed their message bags further up their arms and scurried off to the safety of the foot of the Hawkhill.

Inside the shop was all quiet and the fingerprint team were already working on the large safe in the back shop of the pawnbroker's side of the business. Meanwhile, Charlie was joined by Williamson and they inspected the front shop where all the display cabinets were empty. A layer of dust lay on the glass counter and where the sun shone through the front window tiny motes of dust danced in this golden ray.

'Mr Bergmann puts all his jewellery in the safe every night,' said Charlie. 'Let's hope it's still all there.'

The fingerprint team had dusted the locks before the locksmith came and they said it looked like the door and the safe door had all been thoroughly wiped clean. The safe, which couldn't be opened without its key, was presumed to be empty.

'This is a professional gang, Charlie,' said one of the men, and he agreed with him. Mr Bergmann's fingerprints should have been on the locks and the safe but the only prints were on both the shop and pawnbroker counters. The team took away lots of prints to compare should any culprits be apprehended, but it was more than likely to be members of the public who regularly used the shop.

The team left in their car while Charlie and Williamson waited until the locksmith had finished his work and had handed over four new keys, two for each door. Mr Bergmann would have to contact the safe maker to get another key made for that.

When the shop was safely locked up, Williamson said, 'Where do you want to go now, sir?'

Charlie wondered if the man had been released from the infirmary as he didn't relish meeting the formidable doctor again. He said, 'We'll try his house in Monifieth and if he's not there we can question Mrs French again. Maybe she saw something before going on holiday, like someone hanging around.'

The housekeeper opened the door when they arrived at the house. Once again, Charlie was struck by her white face and red-rimmed eyes.

'Mr Bergmann is in the lounge,' she said, walking quickly ahead of them. 'He's not long home from the hospital and he's still not fully recovered.'

The man was sitting in a large wing-backed chair by the window. He was dressed in a quilted dressing gown and he still had the bandage and padding around his head. He looked gaunt and even thinner than Charlie remembered him. The housekeeper had lit a fire in the stone fireplace and even though it wasn't that cold, it made the room feel cosier. A tray with a teapot and cups sat on the low table but the cup still had liquid in it, as if he hadn't drunk any. He turned his head when the men entered but there was no expression on his face.

Charlie and Williamson asked if they could sit down and the man nodded wearily. Mrs French had closed the door behind them and had obviously gone to the kitchen to keep out of the way.

Charlie handed over the four new keys. 'Did you put all the jewellery from the window and shelves in the safe every night?'

He nodded.

'We can't open the safe because there is no key but you will have to arrange to get someone qualified to open it, Mr Bergmann.'

Again, he nodded wearily.

'We think the safe is empty but can't prove it until it's opened. I want you to tell me what you had in your briefcase.'

Charlie produced a set of photos that showed the jewellery stolen during the three raids a few weeks ago.

'Did you buy any of these items?' he asked.

Eric took the photos and glanced at them but shook his head. 'I've seen these photos as the police brought them round after the robberies. I didn't buy or see any of these.'

'Well what did you buy?'

Eric pulled his dressing gown around him as if he was cold. 'A few weeks ago a young, well-dressed man came into the shop. He had some items for sale that he said belonged to his late grand-mother and he wanted to pawn them. There was a good quality emerald brooch, two diamond rings and a Rolex watch. A few days later he turned up with the brooch but this time with rubies, three diamond rings and another Rolex watch. I gave him a hundred pounds for them and he went away quite happy, saying he would redeem them shortly. Then last week he came in with some more smaller pieces of jewellery and said he had made up his mind to emigrate to Canada and would I consider buying everything. I said I would value his items and if he came back on Saturday I would offer him a price.' He stopped and took a sip from the cold tea.

'And did you buy it?'

He nodded. 'I valued everything to around a thousand pounds and I offered him five hundred pounds for the lot. He immediately agreed and I handed over the money and he went away. After he'd gone I started to worry. He hadn't said he wanted more and at first I thought he didn't know the value of the items but I decided to bring them home to my safe here in the house until I could sell them on.'

Charlie asked him, 'Did you suspect it was stolen?'

'No, I didn't. I just wanted to have them out of the shop in case he came back next week saying he hadn't been paid enough. I would have told him I had sold them on but would have given him some more money.' He turned and looked at the two men. 'I'm a fair and honest businessman and I wouldn't have cheated him if I could have made a fair profit.'

Charlie said the shop was now lockfast and the old keys were now obsolete.

Eric said it didn't matter, did it? There was nothing left to sell in the shop.

'The pawnbroking side is still intact. We don't think anything was stolen from there,' said Charlie and was taken aback when Mr Bergmann burst into loud laughter.

'Of course they didn't touch anything there as I would be lucky to get fifty pounds for the entire stock!'

Suddenly Mrs French knocked and came in. She lifted the tray and asked if there was anything else Mr Bergmann wanted.

He gave her a weary look. 'No nothing, my dear Mrs French. Not unless you find my missing stock and save me from ruin.'

Charlie and Williamson were shown out by her and at the door, she said, 'This has been a wicked, wicked thing to do to a lovely old man.'

As they drove away, Andrew said, 'Do you think there's any connection to the previous robberies?'

Charlie looked grim. 'Oh yes I do, and it's someone very clever behind them.'

34

Molly was back at the Stevensons' house on the Friday. George met her at the door; he was carrying a golf bag and clubs. 'Her ladyship is waiting for you to type out the latest chapters of her saga,' he said as he walked past and got into a small Ford car that was sitting on the gravel by the front door.

Molly met Anna in the hall. She was dressed in a similar tweed skirt and pale beige jumper with the blue necklace gleaming against its surface. 'I have to go out for an hour to a meeting, Molly. Can I leave you with the manuscript to type?'

Molly was surprised by this but she said she would get to work right away. After Anna left with a huge briefcase and got into her own car, the house seemed so quiet. The large statue of Bhudda with its gleaming surface and inscrutable face seemed to watch her every movement, which she knew was daft.

She sat down at the table and looked through the next batch of the story, quickly typing it. Once again she became engrossed in the tales of growing up among the tea gardens of India and of the luxurious lifestyle. Molly wondered when she had married George but no doubt it would all unfold as the story continued. They seemed so incompatible, she thought, but then she knew that opposites are often attracted to each other.

There was a large amount of photos sitting beside the pages and she knew Anna had mentioned using some of them in her book. Molly picked up a few and they showed a life far removed from her own. People dressed in the styles of the thirties and forties sitting on elephants and men with rifles and a dead tiger at their feet. Someone had written on the backs of the photos all the details and dates and Molly realised she was looking at history not so far removed from the present day but in the totally alien and magnificent world of the Raj.

Molly checked to see if any photos were dated from the early forties and she came across one with Bill Reid and a woman who must have been his wife Annie. They looked so happy together and she was suddenly sad at how he had ended up. Then she came across one with the Pritchard family, J.P. and Susie with Naomi and a thin, pale-faced little boy with a serious expression and spindly legs. Susie was a beautiful woman and in the photo she was holding up her left hand to the camera. The ring with its twisted gold bands was clear and although the intensity of the Indian ruby wasn't captured by the lens, one thing was certain: It was obviously a well-loved ring and it was a great pity it had been lost. Some of the other managers had been photographed and they all looked so healthy and happy, all except George, who sat with his arms folded and a serious expression as he was captured for posterity.

There was another photo of Susie Pritchard with J.P. and George. George was gazing at the woman with a smile on his face, which was a far cry from the previous pose. Molly checked the dates and they were all taken just before independence.

The last one showed Anna and George. It had been taken in a studio and looked like it could have been a wedding picture. Anna was dressed in a tweed suit with a plain blouse that was buttoned up to her neck and sturdy shoes, while George simply looked impassive. Molly put the photo beside the one with Susie and he looked to be a very different man.

She looked at the clock on the sideboard and saw that it was almost lunchtime. She hurried up with her typing and had finished the pages a few minutes before Anna came back.

She was no sooner in the door than her husband came in. He was lugging his golf bag out of the car when his wife announced that the sandwiches were ready. Once again they sat around the small gateleg table that Anna said had come from her parents' house in Darjeeling and Molly wished she could take her own sandwiches out into the garden to escape the sullen looks from George.

The rest of the afternoon passed quite quickly and as the hall clock struck three it was time for Molly to tidy the desk and make sure all the pages were in the right order. Anna appeared and said she would see Molly on the Tuesday. 'I have to go to another meeting but just close the door behind you and George will lock it,' she said as she hurried out to her car and drove down the drive.

'That's typical of the ruling classes,' said a voice from the doorway. Molly looked up and saw George standing in the hall. 'She's going to a meeting in Dundee and you would think she would have offered you a lift.'

Molly said she was happy to take the bus but he shook his head. 'Hop into my car and I'll run you home.' He walked ahead with the keys in his hand.

Molly would much rather have taken the bus but she didn't want to refuse his offer as he was paying her wages for the work done on the book.

He stayed silent until they were clear of the village and then he asked her, 'What do you think about my wife's book?'

Molly decided to be honest. 'I like it. She describes a life in India which will be foreign to people and I think they'll enjoy it.'

He drove in silence again before saying, 'Oh I suppose it'll be good. My wife had a privileged upbringing until the country gained its independence and then her folk were just like the rest of us. Out of a job after all the hard work in planting the tea gardens and trying to produce a decent yield of tea every season.'

'When did you both get married? Was it in India?'

He laughed. 'No, it was in London. We were passengers on the same boat coming home and we had a shipboard romance. It seemed like a good idea at the time. I was a widower and Anna had never married.'

'I saw the photos that she left with the manuscript. Were you good friends with Susie Pritchard and her husband?'

He gave her a sharp glance. 'I knew them, but then we all did. She was one of the managers' wives who loved the place. My late wife hated it and she didn't come to India with me. She said it was a dangerous place to live with all the snakes and the heat and the natives.' He smiled to himself. 'Then during the winter of 1944, she slipped on the ice and fell into a river and was drowned. So much for dangerous India.'

He was a good driver and Molly was soon at the Wellgate. She half-turned to thank him when he said, 'Now Susie was something different. She was like a breath of fresh air.'

Molly got out of the car and was surprised to see a dreamy expression on his face. It was as if he was no longer on the smoky streets of Dundee but back beside the tea gardens of Darjeeling.

When she walked into the agency, Grace was sitting at the desk. She stood up when Molly came in. 'I'm holding the fort until Jean comes back from posting letters. I finished at the council office ten minutes ago and they need me back next week.'

Molly said that was wonderful news and once Jean had returned, Grace left to go home.

35

James was so angry. His face was red and he could barely talk because of the anger.

Sonia, on the other hand, was cool and unruffled. 'I don't know why you're angry, James. I only suggested buying the gallery because it will help you with your paintings.'

'I don't need a gallery to show off my work. The house has always been where my customers come to buy.'

It was Sonia's turn to get riled. 'That's why you'll always be a second-rate artist. You think the people who come to buy a tourist painting of the seaside is enough? If you have a proper gallery, just think what kind of customers you will attract.'

'Sonia, a gallery costs money and I would have to increase my prices and that would be out of the reach of most of my customers. I find it's the tourists who buy from me, not the rich customer who probably goes to Edinburgh or London for his art.'

Sonia tried to keep her voice low. There was no need to act like a fishwife. 'But if you had the proper premises then they would come and buy from you.'

James had had enough of Sonia for one day. 'The answer is no.'

'But I've told Leonard that we'll buy his gallery.'

'Well, you'll just have to tell Leonard that we're not.' He picked up his painting gear and went down the stairs of his small house in Arbroath and set off down the street to the harbour.

Sonia picked up a small vase and threw it at the door where luckily it didn't smash but landed heavily on the carpet. She looked around the small but picturesque house and almost burst into tears. James could be a famous painter if he would let her take him in hand. Instead he liked to potter about with his paints and brushes and as long as he covered his costs, he was happy. She put on her coat and wound a lovely blue and green chiffon scarf around her head. It was just as well he didn't know how much she had paid for it.

Hurrying down the main street she soon arrived at the empty shop that she was hoping to turn into a world-famous gallery. Leonard Matthews was sitting on a folding chair in the empty interior with a cigarette in a holder, watching the smoke curl to the ceiling. When she entered, he said, 'As usual, Sonia, you look divine.'

She was flattered by this cosmopolitan man who had travelled the world. 'I'm sorry, Leonard, but James won't budge. He doesn't want to buy this place.'

Leonard's heart sank but he put on a 'man of the world' look. 'Do you know what I think? I think you are too good for him.'

She smiled at this compliment.

'You'll soon persuade him, Sonia. Just give him time to think about it and he'll buy the place if he knows you really want it.'

Sonia wasn't so sure.

James sat at his easel by the side of the harbour wall as the visitors milled around him. The sun was warm and small children were holding ice cream cones in their small sticky fingers. These were his customers and he had enjoyed painting the local scenes. He tried to calm his mind but the thought of Sonia intruded on it and he was angry again. He wondered, not for the first time, why he had ever thought he was in love with her.

36

Charlie had just left the police canteen when the telephone rang. It was Eric Bergmann. 'I'm at the shop and I've just received a very worrying letter, can you come and see me?' At that moment Charlie was busy but the man had sounded anxious so he left the office and headed towards the Hawkhill.

The window was still bare but the front shop door was open so Charlie went inside. Eric was sitting on a stool with a white envelope lying on the counter beside him.

'I didn't know you were planning on opening the shop, Mr Bergmann,' said Charlie.

Eric shrugged. 'I'm planning on selling the business but I have to be here for my customers who have pawned their goods.' He pointed to a notice on the wall. 'This shop will close in two weeks, so if you wish to redeem any goods they must be uplifted before the date.'

While he was speaking, an old woman approached with a small bundle which she placed on the counter. Eric said he was sorry but he wasn't taking any more goods and he showed her the notice. The woman looked disappointed but she left through the side entrance.

'You said on the phone that you have had a letter. Is this it?' Charlie pointed to the envelope.

Eric said yes and he handed it over. There was no letter inside. Instead two keys were lying wrapped in a soft piece of paper. He looked enquiringly at Eric.

'Yes, that's my safe keys. The thief has returned them.'

Charlie was confused. 'Why would he do that I wonder?'

Eric said it didn't matter what the reason was, he wouldn't be using the safe again, either here in the shop or in his house. 'I don't know if they are playing games with me. Have they made copies and are hoping I'll put more valuables inside?'

Charlie didn't think there would be any prints from the metal but he had to take them away to make sure. He scrutinised the envelope but it was a plain white one and the postmark was Dundee.

He said as much and Eric shrugged again. It was heartbreaking to see how the man had given up on his prosperous business, all because of criminals.

'I'll bring them back once the fingerprint guys have seen them,' he said.

As he was leaving another woman came in. 'I'm really sorry that you're giving the shop up, Mr Bergmann.' She handed over her pawn ticket. 'I'll just redeem this.'

Eric took the ticket and went to the back of the shop, returning with a man's suit. 'That's seven and six you owe me, Mrs Petrie.'

Charlie saw that he didn't use the cash till but had a small cash box lying beside him and he gave the woman change from a ten bob note from that.

Back at the station, he handed the keys over but he wasn't holding out any hope of a fingerprint discovery from the keys. This thief or gang were too professional to make a mistake like that.

After handing over the keys, Charlie decided to go to the house in Monifieth to see the housekeeper. He also wanted to speak to Mr Davidson, the hotel owner, as he hadn't had a chance to see him until now.

The sun was warm as he drove to Monifieth and when he arrived, the place was busy with visitors and locals all out enjoying the lovely day. There were a couple of cars in its courtyard but the hotel was quiet. There was no sound of anyone vacuuming today but he heard voices coming from the back so he made his way down the narrow corridor and arrived at the kitchen. The Davidsons were sitting at the table. He was eating a bacon roll and she was writing down accounts in a ledger.

She saw Charlie first and let out a small cry of surprise. The husband turned and choked on his roll. After his fit of coughing stopped he turned an angry face to him. 'Good God, man, what a fright! Do you never think of knocking? Creeping up on us like that.'

'Actually, I did knock but you didn't hear me,' said Charlie. 'But now I'm here I want to ask you some questions about the night your neighbour was assaulted and robbed.'

Mr Davidson was indignant. 'That had nothing to do with us and as my wife told you we didn't see anybody that night because we were too busy.'

'When you were out in the courtyard, did you see anyone, either walking or with a vehicle?'

The man rolled his eyes. 'I've just told you we didn't see a thing. There was a ruddy great thunderstorm that night so we didn't fancy going out into the torrential rain.'

'That's a pity,' said Charlie. 'Well I'll leave you to get on with your meal.'

He walked back down the corridor and out into the sun. He drove up the drive to the Bergmann house, hoping the house-keeper was there. She was. When she opened the door Charlie thought she looked dreadful. It was clear that she had been crying but she tried to pull herself together and she asked him to come in.

'Mr Bergmann isn't here. He decided to go to the shop today.'

Charlie said he knew that. 'I've just come from there. He got his safe keys back in the post from the thief or thieves.'

'Oh that's good news,' she said, trying to wipe her face with a tiny scrap of fabric that already looked soaked.

'Well it's not. He can't use the safes because they might have had copies made and it would be quite easy to come back and have another clear out.'

'Do you want a cup of tea?'

Charlie said no, he didn't and she looked relieved.

'How are you keeping?' he asked.

She turned away. 'Not very good. Mr Bergmann has given me

two weeks' notice as he can't afford to keep this house on. He's going to sell the house and the shop and when his wife gets back from her cruise they will look for somewhere smaller.'

'Will you get another post as a housekeeper?' he asked her.

She shrugged. 'I've no idea. I'll have to look for another job with accommodation as I'll be homeless as well. The cottage was being rented by Mr Bergmann and he was paying all the bills.' She had a defeated look to her face which was not unlike her employer. 'I certainly can't afford to keep the house on.'

'What about a job in the hotel at the foot of the drive?'

A look of distaste crossed her face. 'I don't think so. Not with that awful man who owns it. Every time I come to work he leers at me and I've seen him looking up here with binoculars. I think he spies on me.'

Oh he does, does he? thought Charlie. *That's very interesting.*

37

Molly wasn't looking forward to going to Pitlochry on the Saturday but she didn't want to disappoint Marigold who had booked two tickets for the theatre and the overnight accommodation at the Bay Guest House. The plan was to meet Marigold at the railway station and they would travel up together. Union Street was very busy with people as she waited at the entrance to the station and she saw her friend hurrying up the road from Craig Pier.

Then as she turned her head she suddenly saw Grace enter the station with a man. He had his back to her but Molly got the impression they were together. She called out and went after them but as she reached the entrance a large crowd was milling about. They had obviously got off a train and were hurrying onto the street.

When Molly did reach the concourse, a train was pulling out and there was no sign of Grace or her friend. She wondered if this was Grace's fiancé and he had arrived back from Cape Town.

She heard Marigold call her name and she forgot about Grace. Their train was due in at any minute so they bought their tickets and went to the platform. Molly had her folder with all the notes from interviewing Bill's former colleagues that she wanted to give to Betty. She had the copies back in her filing cabinet in case she would have to look at them again, which she thought unlikely.

Marigold handed Molly a letter. 'It's from your mother,' she said.

Molly put it in her bag along with the folder, planning to read it at the guest house.

'I'm really looking forward to this weekend,' said Marigold. 'Especially the play.'

Molly smiled and said she was also looking forward to seeing Deanna.

Molly brought the folder from her bag and opened it. The first few pages were fine but the rest of the document was upside down and some of the pages were mixed up. She knew she had put it away correctly before filing it and couldn't understand why it was like this. It looked as if it had been read and put together again, but who would want to read something that was no use to anyone but Bill's sister?

Marigold saw her puzzlement and asked her if there was something wrong.

'No, except his report is mixed up and it wasn't like this when I put it in the filing cabinet.'

'Maybe Jean has mixed it up with something else,' Marigold suggested.

Molly didn't think so but accepted that solution because no one in the office went near the cabinet except herself and Jean.

She took the letter from her pocket. 'I'd better read Mum's news and hope it's not bad news,' she said, smiling at her friend who was looking out of the train window as it sped northwards.

Marigold nodded but said nothing. She knew what Nancy had written because she had told her.

Molly read the letter in silence and her heart sank. 'Mum says that Dad has been offered a part-time job with a boat-building business near to where Nell and Terry live. Dad got friendly with the owner on their last holiday and he's offered to sponsor their application to live in Australia. Does that mean they will be moving quite quickly?'

Marigold replied, 'That's what Archie said. I'm sorry about that, Molly, but they have made up their minds to go. Have you thought any more about joining them?'

'No, I haven't.' Which was the truth. Molly had made a conscious effort to put the entire idea out of her mind in the hope that if she didn't think about it then it would go away, which she knew was stupid but she couldn't help it.

'That means the house will soon be put up for sale, Marigold?'

Her friend said she didn't know about that but hoped that it wouldn't.

They spent the rest of the journey in silence. Each with her own thoughts on the matter.

After they got their bags dropped off at the guest house, the two women made their way along to see Betty, who was expecting them. She had the kettle on when they arrived and they settled down to a welcome cup of tea and more homemade pancakes.

Molly handed her the report, which she had sorted out into the proper order. 'I've spoken to all the men but they all say the same thing. They haven't been in touch with Bill for some years now and they were all sorry to hear he had died.' She handed over the folder. 'You can read what they said for yourself, Betty.'

Betty moved over to the writing desk and came back with a small wooden box. 'I found these letters in Bill's suitcase under the bed and he was in contact with some of them.'

Molly looked at the papers in her hand and suddenly thought it was a red letter day for herself, what with the bad news from her parents and now this contradiction from the dead man's suitcase.

She opened the first one. Bill had kept the reply, along with the original letter. He had written to Phillip Thorne the day after the cutting had been in the paper.

Dear Phillip,

What a surprise when I saw the photo in yesterday's paper and what memories it brought back. I'm not sure if the rest of the chaps will want to meet up but I include a list of their last known addresses if you want to get in touch with them. I would love to meet up and you can let me know how things go as it will be great to hear all your news since we left India.

Regards,

Bill Reid

Dear Bill,

You are the first to get in touch and I will contact the rest of them, so thanks for the address list. I'm back living with my wife, Rhona. You remember we had split up prior to me leaving but we've since met up again and are very happy. I'll be in touch soon.
Yours sincerely,
Phillip

There was a second envelope but when Molly slipped the sheet of paper out it had no address on the letterhead, or a signature. There was a jagged tear that looked like it had been torn off. The letter also seemed incomplete, as if some of the pages were missing.

I'm hoping you can help me. I saw the newspaper cutting and Phillip Thorne gave me your address.

She looked at Betty. 'Was there anything else in the suitcase, Betty?'

Betty said there was but nothing that was connected to this.

'Do you mind if I take these with me? I'll make sure you get them back.'

Betty wanted to know what Molly would do now.

Actually she had wondered the same thing. 'When we get back I'll go and see Rhona Thorne to see if he also had letters from any of them. Also this mystery person.'

As they walked back along the busy pavement, Marigold said, 'Just give this up, Molly, as you have enough to cope with, the worry over your parents and trying to keep your business going. I'm sure Betty will understand that whatever happened in India was all long ago and her brother had an unfortunate accident.'

Molly had also made up her mind to finish with this after talking to Rhona. Then she would be able to cope with whatever lay ahead of her.

By the time they got back to the guest house, Molly had a

headache and the last thing she really wanted to do was sit in a theatre all evening but after swallowing a couple of aspirins she felt a bit better.

The theatre was full and Molly was pleased that they had seats near the stage. The play was called *A Hundred Years Old* and in spite of not wanting to come, as the play progressed she began to relax and enjoy the evening.

As usual, Deanna was great. Molly had written to her after deciding to come for another visit, and once the performance had finished, she and Marigold waited backstage, hoping Deanna could meet.

In the end, Deanna arrived and Molly and Marigold said how much they had enjoyed the play. As it was a lovely summer night, the three women went and sat on a bench in the Memorial Garden with its scent of roses.

Deanna said, 'I'm having a wonderful time, Molly, but tell me all about the agency.'

Molly mentioned the newcomers, like Grace, Maggie and Jane, but said everyone was doing well and the agency was going from strength to strength.

'How's Brian?' asked Marigold.

Deanna blushed. 'Oh, we still go out together and I like him a lot.'

'Well, as long as you're happy with what you're doing, Deanna, but have you thought what you'll do when the season finishes?' Marigold had obviously been thinking about later in the year.

'I've managed to get a few months at the Dundee Rep and there's word about doing a pantomime in Glasgow at Christmas,' she said excitedly. 'Now that I'm doing this season here in Pitlochry, I've been told by the stage manager that I may be asked back again next year. Which would be great news!'

It was just before midnight when they parted company and Deanna hurried back to her lodgings while Molly and Marigold walked back to the guest house. It was still light and although a breeze had sprung up, it remained mild.

★ ★ ★

After breakfast the next morning they arrived at the railway station to catch the morning train back to Perth and then on to Dundee. Molly said she would go over on the ferry with Marigold but she said she would be fine on her own so they parted at the railway entrance. Molly didn't feel up to seeing her parents after the bad news in the letter but she said, 'Tell Mum and Dad that I'll be over to see them some night this week.'

She wondered if she might run into Grace and her friend but there was no sight of them. The streets were busy as people wanted to be out in the warm sunshine and Molly had seen that the queue for the Fifie was quite long and stretched up to the bottom of Union Street. She hoped Marigold wouldn't have too long a wait to cross the river.

She let herself into the agency and locked the door behind her. The air inside was hot and slightly musty as she went straight to the filing cabinet. The copy of 'the Indian folder', as she had named it, was lying in the drawer. Taking it out she saw that the sheets were all the right way up and in numerical order.

She closed the drawer and went upstairs with a puzzled look on her face.

38

Mary was also puzzled. It was Friday night and for the past week Stan had been hinting at good news but said he didn't want to say what it was until it was finalised. On the Saturday night when he came to take her to the pictures, his face was wreathed in smiles. Sitting together on the tramcar, he couldn't contain himself any longer. 'Mary, do you remember I told you we have an office in Hong Kong?'

Mary nodded, not sure what that faraway office had to do with going to the pictures.

'Well my boss, Mr Traill, who is the chief accountant, has told me that they need a replacement chartered accountant in the Hong Kong branch and I've been offered the job there. It'll be a two-year commitment but all the fares and accommodation will be paid for and it's a chance of a lifetime.'

Mary said congratulations but her stomach was churning. 'You'll be away for two years, Stan?' She didn't mean to sound despondent but he turned a worried face in her direction.

'Yes, it's initially for two years but it could be for longer.'

Mary thought the news was getting worse. Stan was planning on leaving for two years or more and he seemed to be pleased with the idea.

'You know, Phil and Linda are planning to get married this August when he gets leave from the army and that I'm to be the best man?' When Mary nodded, he went on, 'Well this job will be from September so it'll all work out.'

Phil was his best pal and currently he was in Germany doing his two years' National Service and Linda was the girl who worked with him at Keiller's Sweet Factory. Mary had met them when she did an assignment there last year and that was when she had met Stan.

'So I won't be able to see you for two years, Stan. Is that what you're trying to tell me?'

He took her hand. 'No that's not what I meant. I want us to get engaged this week then get married before I leave and we can go out to Hong Kong together. Tomorrow we'll go and get the ring and we'll tell your mum and dad tomorrow night.'

Mary shifted in her seat. 'I don't think Mum and Dad will be pleased about me getting married at seventeen, Stan.'

He looked worried. 'You do want to marry me, Mary?'

'Oh I do, but not just yet.'

'Do you want us to get engaged?'

Mary wanted that very much. Being engaged wasn't such a big commitment as a wedding. 'Yes I do.'

He tucked her hand in his. 'Well let's go to the jeweller's tomorrow and choose your ring.'

All during the film, Mary couldn't concentrate on it and she didn't sleep very well that night. The next morning the two of them went to the city centre to look at rings. Mary saw lots that she liked but it was one from M.M. Henderson on the corner of Union Street that she chose. It was two diamonds on either side of a blue sapphire and the tall, gangly young man behind the counter said it was one of their best rings.

Stan suggested a meal out to celebrate but instead they went to the Washington Café for two coffees.

Mary kept looking at her gorgeous ring and watched as the sunlight glinted off the stones. Her eyes were shining as she looked at Stan, her fiancé, and she was so happy.

Then the spectre of telling her parents marred the happiness but she tried not to show this to Stan.

39

When Molly came downstairs on Monday morning most of the staff were standing around Mary, admiring her new engagement ring.

Edna said. 'You never mentioned you were getting engaged, Mary.'

Mary told them it had been a big surprise but she didn't mention Hong Kong as she wanted to see Molly alone and give her the news. She was still a bit shocked at how quick everything had gone and she remembered how her parents had reacted to the news.

Molly was taken aback at the engagement as she still considered Mary to be the schoolgirl who had been one of the two original members of her staff back in 1953.

'Congratulations, Mary,' she said. 'I can't believe you will soon be married.'

Actually neither could Mary, but she remained silent.

'Can I see you before I go to work, Molly?' she asked her and Molly looked surprised but said to go upstairs and she would join her after all the assignments were done.

Molly was very pleased with Jane, the young girl who was standing in for Alice. She had tackled a lot of hard work during the past week and she was very good-natured about it. Always wearing a smile, she had had good reports about her work.

Molly went up to see Mary just as Grace hurried in. Giving Molly a quick smile of apology, she said, 'Sorry I'm a bit late,' but she didn't give an excuse and Jean handed her the work card.

'It's another week at the council office, Grace.'

★ ★ ★

Mary was sitting on the couch when Molly entered and she looked unhappy. It wasn't the ecstatic look expected from a newly-engaged girl.

'What's wrong, Mary?'

Mary twisted the ring on her finger. 'Stan surprised me this weekend, Molly. First with the engagement but also with the news he is going to work in Hong Kong this September.'

Molly said, 'How long will he be away?'

'Two years and he wants us to get married before he goes and take me with him.'

Molly suddenly felt she was standing on shifting sands and that the earth was moving under her feet. She sat down beside Mary.

'But you're still only seventeen. What do your parents say about this?'

Mary frowned. 'They weren't very happy about it and said we should wait until he comes back to work here in Dundee then get married then. They like Stan very much but they said the same thing you've said, Molly. I'm too young.'

'I see. I quite understand their concern. I mean, when Stan returns from Hong Kong you'll still be under twenty-one and even that's young to be married.'

Mary said Stan had gone away and said if that's what they wanted then he would abide by it but he didn't look happy. 'I'm really dreading meeting him tonight because everything has suddenly become serious.' She stood up. 'Well, thanks for listening to me and I better get off to work.' She had her head down and looked to be on the verge of tears as she left.

Molly sat for a few moments longer. It seemed to her that everyone was on the move. Well, not everyone, but people she cared about. She was on the point of going back downstairs when Alice knocked at the door. Molly thought she still looked ill.

'Alice, come in. How are you feeling now?'

'I've come to start work, Molly and I'm sorry to let you down last week.'

Molly felt in the mood for a cup of tea and she said, 'Sit down and tell me how you are keeping. I think you still look very pale and tired, Alice, and do you think it's a good idea to come back to work so soon?'

Alice said she was still tired but she needed the work. 'I need my wages every week, Molly, especially now I'm having the baby.'

Molly was so surprised she almost fell of the edge of the couch.

'You're having a baby?' She sounded like a parrot repeating what its owner had just said.

Alice looked down at her lap and nodded. 'Sandy doesn't know and I don't want to tell him so I'll have to keep working for as long as I can.'

Molly made them both a cup of tea and some toast. 'Alice, I want you to take this week off.' When Alice looked worried, she said. 'Don't worry about this week's wages as I will pay you. I want you to get better. Have you seen a doctor?'

Alice said she had. 'Maisie went with me last week.'

'The work you do here is very hard, Alice. Some of the cleaning jobs are strenuous and I don't want you taking ill or harming the baby.'

'I told the doctor about my job and he said as long as I don't overdo it I'll be fine,' she said.

Molly thought about this and said, 'Well, still take this week off and build up your strength and I'll see you next Monday.'

Alice said thank you but added, 'I don't want it to get out just yet, Molly. As I said, Maisie knows but she won't say a word.'

Molly told her the secret was safe with her.

Once Alice had gone, Molly washed up the cups and went downstairs. Jean was on the phone and when she had finished the call, she said, 'I'm going out for a couple of hours, Jean, but I'll be back to do the afternoon rota in McKay's office.'

This was a job that had come in three weeks ago and Molly covered for the typist who had to go for a hospital appointment on Monday afternoon but this was her last visit. She quickly joined the queue on Victoria Road for the Downfield tramcar as she wanted to have another word with Rhona Thorne about the letter Bill had sent to her late husband.

Betty Holden had been surprised by this letter as she thought Bill hadn't replied to the request but she had been wrong. Bill had seemingly written the very next day after the cutting was published.

When Molly arrived at the bungalow she was surprised when the door was answered by Rhona, minus the wheelchair. She still had a thinner plaster on her ankle but was able to walk with the aid of a stick. She looked pleased to see Molly and ushered her in to the living room, which held a haze of blue cigarette smoke. Molly saw a half-smoked cigarette in the ashtray but Rhona quickly stubbed it out. 'I'm still trying to give it up and hopefully I'll succeed when I'm back at work,' she said with a little laugh. 'It's this hanging around the house all day that's driving me daft.'

She flopped down on the chair and put her foot up on a small footstool.

'How did the interviews go?' she asked and Molly said that was why she wanted to see her.

'Bill's sister Betty found a letter from your husband in reply to the one Bill sent him. She was under the impression that your husband had died before anyone had got in contact with him.'

Rhona said she didn't know who had been in contact with Phillip because she wasn't all that interested. 'I would have been out at work during the day and I presume the postman had delivered the letter in the morning. Phillip always left my mail for me to open but he didn't always say what had come for him. Phillip knew I hated my days in India so he was very careful about talking about this reunion. I did say at the start that I thought it was a bad idea.'

'Why did you think that?'

Rhona looked out of the window at the blue and white flowers that were starting to wither before answering. 'I remember those days and I always thought it was a claustrophobic kind of life out there. The men would meet up about once a month while the wives would see one another every now and again.' She reached for her packet of cigarettes and lit one. 'I hated that life and I think the men and their wives looked down on me for my attitude.'

'Did you know that George Stevenson married a planter's daughter called Anna Watson? They met on the boat home.'

Rhona looked surprised. 'No I didn't. I remember Anna, she's a lot younger than he is. I thought she was a bit stuck up because of her very privileged life with Mummy and Daddy mixing with the Maharaja of the area. George was a widower when we knew him but I've no idea when his wife died, or for that matter, where she died.'

'What were your impressions of the managers?'

'My impressions? Well let me see. They were all older than Phillip, although J.P. wasn't as old as the rest. I thought the Pritchards were lovely but I didn't see much of the other men. The tea gardens were all at a distance from one another so we didn't run into them very often. I thought they were just old men.'

Molly took the other letter from her bag. 'Betty found this letter along with the reply from your husband. Have you any idea who sent it?'

Rhona took the scrap of paper and looked at it. 'Is this all there is?'

Molly said yes, it was. 'Do you have any of your husband's mail that he might have kept?'

Rhona got stiffly to her feet and walked over to a writing bureau under the window. She raked about in it for a moment and hobbled back again with a folder and handed it over. Molly sorted through the various letters but there didn't seem to be anything relating to the reunion. She did come across the list of names and addresses and she knew Bill had sent this along with his letter but there was no sign of it, neither was there any sign of the cryptic, unfinished one. She handed the folder back.

Molly had noticed the telephone in the hall when she came in. 'I suppose any of the men could have phoned your husband instead of writing,' she said.

Rhona said that was possible but as she was out all day she wouldn't know and Phillip hadn't mentioned anything.

Molly began to think there was nothing else she could do and as she had to work in the afternoon she thanked Rhona and left.

After she left, Rhona lit up another cigarette and thought, *Bloody India.*

40

Charlie finished his reports in the office and went looking for Andrew Williamson. He met one of the police constables who told him Andrew was having a couple of days' leave before going on nightshift.

Charlie decided to go and see the Davidsons at the hotel in Monifieth to see if they remembered anything more from the night of the robbery. The trail had gone cold and Charlie was getting desperate to solve the case. There had been no other significant robberies and Charlie hoped it would stay that way.

The early morning sun was beating down on the car as he headed to the town and he had all the windows down. As he neared the sea, a breeze was blowing and the temperature inside the car dropped slightly. When he reached the hotel there were a few cars parked in the car park and when he went inside, about twenty people were sitting in the small dining room finishing a late breakfast. The Davidsons' daughter Janet was busy serving or clearing the tables and she smiled when she saw him.

'Mum's in the kitchen and Dad's outside in the courtyard,' she said in the passing.

Charlie wanted to see Mr Davidson so he went out through the back door just in time to see the man raise his binoculars at a figure riding a bicycle up the Bergmanns' drive. He turned sharply when he heard Charlie come up behind him and he then trained his glasses on a nearby tree.

'Just catching up with a bit of bird watching,' he said with a chuckle.

Charlie wasn't going to let him get away with this lie. 'Spying on young women is against the law, Mr Davidson, and if Mrs French reports you, you could be in trouble.'

Harry Davidson spluttered. 'How dare you suggest I'm spying on women just because I like to do a bit of bird watching. You plods have to come along and accuse innocent people.'

Charlie let this statement go. 'Well take it as a warning. Now did you maybe see something with those binoculars on the night of the robbery?'

'No I didn't. I told you it was pouring with rain that night and I never went outside after ten o'clock when I put out the crate of beer bottles.'

Charlie didn't hope for anything else from this man but he had wanted to warn him about his behaviour. 'I think you would be better employed inside, Mr Davidson. Your wife and daughter are almost run off their feet cooking and serving your guests.'

Mr Davidson opened his mouth to tell this nosy cop to mind his own business but thought better of it. Instead he hurried inside the back door and banged it shut.

Charlie went to get in the car to go and see Mrs French but before he turned the key in the ignition, he saw her quickly cycle in the direction of the town. Keeping his distance he followed her, expecting her to be on her way home but she passed the row of terraced cottages and headed towards the far end of town before disappearing down a dirt track that led to a golf course.

Charlie thought she may have been visiting a friend but he was intrigued. Finding a parking spot was easy because there were a few cars in the large car park so he drew in at the end of the space and waited. He wished he had brought something cool to drink but he didn't want to get out of the car in case he was recognised by the housekeeper should she suddenly reappear.

After fifteen minutes when he was almost falling asleep in the heat, she came out of the clubhouse with a good-looking, stockily-built man. He had dark hair falling over his brow and was dressed in a patterned jumper and cream linen trousers. He carried a golf bag and Charlie saw he was wearing a very expensive-looking watch when he pushed up the sleeve of the jumper to look at the time. He couldn't catch what they were saying to one another as they stood close and spoke softly. Mrs French was smiling but the man looked unhappy as he headed off to the golf course while she got on her bike and pedalled up the track.

Charlie followed again, keeping his distance behind another car in front and once again she passed her house and headed for her work. He sat at the side of the road and watched her as she pushed her bike around the back and disappeared.

Was Harry Davidson watching all this through his glasses? he wondered.

He waited about half an hour then drove up to the house. She opened the door on his second ring and she looked calm and untroubled.

'I'm sorry to bother you, Mrs French, but I wondered if Mr Bergmann is home.'

She smiled, showing off her lovely teeth. 'Oh, he's not. He's at the shop, but do come in.' She took him to the kitchen where she was in the process of making coffee. 'Would you like a cup?'

Charlie said no, he wouldn't wait, but would come back another time to see her boss.

She said, 'I've just stopped for coffee as I've been busy spring cleaning some of the rooms.'

Charlie smiled. 'I bet you've been working all morning.'

'Yes I have. I got here about seven-thirty and I'll not get finished until late this afternoon.'

He didn't stay much longer, and as he drove away he wondered why she had lied. Surely she was allowed to meet a friend or acquaintance at the local golf club without her boss bothering about it, especially when he wasn't there.

'Then why lie about it?' he said out loud.

41

Sonia said airily, 'I'm just going out for a couple of hours, James.'

James muttered something that she didn't catch and she walked quickly down the street to the empty shop that she had hoped he would buy to turn into an up-market art gallery. Leonard was waiting for her.

He greeted her warmly. She was a good-looking woman, he thought. Just the kind of woman who could run his art gallery in Edinburgh and lend it some class and also make money, which was an important part of Leonard's life. He had hoped to sell this place for an art gallery but he had had a firm offer from the owner of a ladies' dress shop so he was happy about that.

'Are you sure James won't mind losing you to another business, Sonia?' he asked her.

'I think he'll be devastated, Leonard, but I have to think about my own life. He had his chance to buy this place and he turned it down and I have to move on.'

'Right then, I want to open within the next two weeks so can you move to Edinburgh and oversee the grand opening?' he said.

Sonia didn't have to hesitate. 'I'll have to look for somewhere to stay first and then I'll be ready for this new chapter in my life.'

'Well let's go and celebrate with a drink.'

They both left the shop and headed for the big hotel on the seafront where Leonard was staying while overseeing the sale of his empty business. They were the only two people in the lounge bar but Leonard ordered a bottle of champagne.

For a brief moment, Sonia thought about James and how he had been good to her but when she sipped her drink she felt so happy. Leonard and she would make a great team, she was sure of that.

42

Molly was back at the Stevenson house. Anna had said a quick hello when she arrived but she was rushing out to go to another meeting. 'I've got the book finished and left the new pages on the desk,' she had said as she got into her car.

The house was very quiet as Molly settled down to type up the loose pages and she reckoned that George must be off to play golf. Anna's story had reached the year of independence and some of the scenes made her feel sick.

Anna had seen a lot of the mayhem and massacres that had happened and one scene described the awful slaughter of a couple of her parents' servants. Her father had chased the rebels away with his shotgun but the family realised then that they had to make plans to leave the country they loved.

She was so immersed in her work that she didn't hear the door opening. George was standing behind her and when he spoke Molly got such a fright that she dropped the page she was holding. 'Oh! I thought you were out,' she said.

'No, I was going to play a game of golf but it's too hot outside to lug a golf bag around the course.' He looked over her shoulder. 'I heard my wife tell you she had finished her story. How long will it take you to finish typing it up?'

Molly thought another day's work would clear it up and she said so.

As he seemed to be in the mood for a chat, she said, 'I went to see Rhona Thorne. Bill Reid had been in touch with Phillip about the reunion.'

George looked surprised. 'How did you find that out?'

'Betty, his sister, came across some letters he'd written and one was to Phillip regarding the reunion and enclosing all your names and addresses. It's a wonder you didn't hear from him.'

George said, 'Well I certainly didn't. Maybe he planned to write to us all but he had his car accident.'

Molly began to type and he wandered out of the room. The golden Bhudda seemed to watch her and she had to give herself a shake to stop this stupid nonsense. It was only a statue, for goodness' sake.

Then Molly found she was at the part of the story that covered the deaths of Susie and Naomi Pritchard. Anna had a dramatic style of writing which made the event seem so clear, as if it had happened yesterday instead of years ago.

There was a rumour that a car was seen in the vicinity of the house but the police never found out whose car it was. It seems unlikely that the bandits had access to a vehicle but perhaps they had stolen it from one of the villages.

Another story going around was that Michael, the son, had witnessed the shooting and that was why he was in a state of shock and unable to speak. Whatever happened will maybe never be known but I think the truth will come out one day. J.P. Pritchard's life ended that day, and who knows for sure if he left India that week, or did he take his own life and now lies somewhere amongst the tea gardens of Darjeeling?

Molly had to take a deep breath at these passages. Anna had been a witness to the event just like the managers but none of them had even hinted at a car being seen or that the boy had been in the house when the killings took place. And they hadn't mentioned the likelihood of suicide. She made up her mind to go and see the men again and ask them for their views on this new information.

George came in with the usual pot of coffee and biscuits. She stopped typing and said, 'George, did any of you hear that a car was seen at the scene of the murders?'

George was about to eat a biscuit but stopped. 'No, I don't remember that story.'

'Or that Michael was in the house when the shootings took place and J.P. maybe took his own life through grief?'

He shook his head. 'No I never heard that either. The police said it was bandits. The gun was never found but the bullets came from an old army gun that had been issued to the British Army soldiers. They reckoned the bandits had either found it or stolen it.' He looked at her. 'Where did you get these ideas?'

Molly pointed to the book. 'Your wife has written it down.'

He shook his head in dismay. 'My wife's parents moved in higher circles in those days so no doubt there was a lot of gossip and untruths bandied about. I'll have a word with Anna about this. She can't write down anything that can't be proven or could be untrue.'

Molly saw he was agitated and quite red about the face.

Then Anna arrived back. George immediately pounced on her and told her she couldn't write about things that she wasn't sure about.

Molly thought Anna would be annoyed but she said quite simply, 'I heard those stories from my father, who was very friendly with the chief of police, and that's what they suspected.'

'Then why say it was bandits?'

Anna gave him a rueful look. 'The country was on the verge of anarchy with deaths happening every hour of the day. The police investigated it all right but they had no strong evidence to arrest anyone so they wrote it off as bandits.'

George said, 'But you can't prove it. What you've written is hearsay and your parents and maybe even the chief of police are all dead so you will have to scrap that bit in the book.'

Anna looked bullish. 'No, I'll keep it in and say it is just a theory.'

George shook his head in annoyance but said no more. He went outside and the two women saw him walk away down the drive.

Molly was embarrassed by the scene so she put the cover on the typewriter and said she would finish for the day. 'I'll come on Friday and that should be your book all ready.'

Anna seemed to be distracted. 'What . . . Oh yes, Molly, I'll see you then.'

As Molly walked away to catch the bus, Anna stood by the window with a thoughtful look on her face.

All the way home, Molly thought about this new turn of events and she made up her mind to visit the managers again to see if they remembered these rumours.

That evening after tea she decided to go to see Alex McGregor. She reached the flat on the Perth Road just as the shops were closing. The street was busy with last-minute shoppers and workers on their way home.

Alex opened the door and he didn't seem very pleased at seeing her but was too polite to say so.

'I'm going out soon,' he said. 'So I can't let you stay long.'

Molly wasn't sure if this was an excuse but she said it would only take a short while. She explained the new events to him and asked him if he had heard these rumours.

'No, I didn't,' he said. 'But at the time I did wonder about Michael. The shock he got was severe and I asked myself, "Had he witnessed it?", but J.P. ushered him away and even the police couldn't get him to speak. Did I mention he was found by the side of the river by some Indian women who were doing the family washing?'

Molly said he hadn't but did he think there was any truth in the theory that a local man had done it?

He said no, he hadn't thought anybody he knew was responsible. The police were wrong. It was bandits who had carried out the crime.

He looked at his watch. 'Now I'm sorry but I have to go.'

Molly thanked him and set off for the Hawkhill to see Edmond Lamb.

* * *

202

The man was as cautious as ever. 'Who is it?'

Molly said could she have a word with him, it wouldn't take long.

He opened the door but, like Alex, he didn't look pleased. 'I've just finished my tea. Can you come back another time?'

Molly said it would only take a few moments and he grudgingly let her in. He had been listening to the wireless and the tea things were still on the table. He turned the wireless off and sat down. 'Well why do you want to see me again?'

Molly explained the passages in Anna's book and asked him if he had heard anything of the rumours.

'No, I didn't and have you asked yourself why she is writing about this now?'

'She's hoping to get her book published.'

'Exactly, and don't you think she wants some juicy story to spice it up?'

'So you don't know anything other than what you said when I first came to see you?'

'No, I don't.'

Molly sighed. It was like trying to hold a piece of slippery jelly in her hand. Nothing about this case was solid. Rumours, stories and unhappy times, all seemed to shift and change with each telling and she knew she wouldn't get anything new from Edmond.

43

Charlie was unhappy when he got back to his office. Why had Laura French lied about meeting the man at the golf course? He had looked quite prosperous and yet she was worried about losing her job. There may be a simple reason for it, he thought, but he wanted to know more.

Leaving the police station, he walked quickly up to Bruce Street where he knew Andrew Williamson stayed with his parents. The police constable looked surprised when he answered the door.

'Can I have a word with you?' asked Charlie.

'Certainly, sir.' The young man moved into the hall and ushered Charlie into a well-furnished and very tidy living room. 'Dad's out at work and Mum is away to the shops so we won't be disturbed.'

Charlie said, 'I want to ask a favour from you. I know you're on two days off but I wondered if you would like to play a game of golf with me tomorrow morning at the golf course in Monifieth?'

Charlie knew that Andrew loved playing golf, and Andrew said he would enjoy a day out.

DS Johns then wasted no time in asking another, equally important, question. 'I wonder if we could use your car.'

Andrew was the proud owner of a second-hand car, a fact which most of his colleagues knew because he had mentioned it in the canteen when he had bought it. Although he seemed a bit puzzled he said that would be fine. 'What time do you want to be at the golf course?'

'Around nine o'clock. Is that okay with you?'

He nodded. 'Right then, I'll pick you up at your house about eight, sir.'

Charlie thought he had better tell the young man what he had in mind. 'It's to do with the Bergmann case.' He explained the meeting between Laura French and the stranger. 'If he appears again tomorrow I want you to try and find out his name or anything else that you can. If you book in behind him, perhaps you'll hear something that will help.'

Charlie thanked him and headed back to work. He had a lot of reports to write up today and he was hoping something would turn up tomorrow.

The next day was warm again. It was turning out to be a great summer. The sun hadn't come out yet because of the mist but when Andrew picked him up in his grey Ford car, the day held the promise of beautiful weather.

As the car headed for Monifieth, the mist grew more dense and it was impossible to see the river. Charlie was pleased about this because it meant he could stay in the car and hopefully be unobserved, a fact that Andrew had noticed when he had come out of the Dens Road flat without any golf clubs.

'As you can see, I won't be playing.'

Andrew stayed silent. No doubt all would be revealed when they reached their destination.

When they reached the golf course, the mist had risen slightly and the sun was hazy. Andrew parked the car at the far end of the car park, next to a van. Charlie was taking a chance that the man would appear again but if he didn't then Andrew could have his game and he would have to work out some other stratagem. Within ten minutes the car park filled up quite quickly and a mixture of men and women got out with their golf bags and headed for the golf club where permits were available for members and visitors.

The two men sat in the car as Charlie scrutinised every newcomer. After a quarter of an hour he began to think the man wasn't coming but then a posh car drove in and the man got out. He was wearing a different patterned jumper today and a pair of dark brown trousers. Charlie couldn't see his watch from where he was sitting but the man's face was clear. Without looking to the left or right, he made for the clubhouse.

'That's the man there, Andrew. Go and follow him in and try to catch his name or anything else. Don't try and speak to him, just act as if you're having a game of golf.'

Andrew got out and sauntered up behind him, waiting patiently while the man paid his admission money before handing over his own payment.

Charlie had brought the morning paper and a thermos flask of tea and he settled down in the warmth of the car to wait for the golf round to end. He was glad to be beside the van because he was partially hidden but he had his story all ready should any nosy steward come his way. He planned to say his brother was playing and he was merely waiting on him. As it turned out, no excuse was needed because after a couple of hours, Charlie saw the man walk towards the clubhouse. However, before he reached it, a car pulled in beside him and the driver got out.

Well, well, well, thought Charlie. *What does Benny Baxter want with Mr Mystery?* Benny was a convicted housebreaker and had served time for his crimes but he had been remarkably quiet these last two or three years.

The two men only spoke for a few minutes before Benny drove away, which was just as well because Andrew arrived just behind the man. The constable fiddled with his golf bag, putting the clubs back in and writing something in a little notebook. When he got in the car, his face was alight with good news. 'The steward knew him and called him Mr Gauld and asked if he was enjoying his holiday. He comes from Glasgow because he said the air there wasn't as good as the air at Monifieth.'

Impressed, Charlie said, 'Well done, Andrew,' and the young man's face went red with pleasure. While Andrew was telling this, Charlie saw the man get into his car. 'Can you follow him at a distance and let's see where he goes?'

Mr Gauld's car swept up along the track to the main road, with Andrew following at a slower pace. When the car reached the main road it turned right and headed towards the town, passing the cottage belonging to Laura French. Between Monifieth and Broughty Ferry, the car turned left and headed down towards a large secluded house, parking outside the front door.

Charlie said to stop a bit along the road. Getting out of the car, he walked to the end of the drive, thinking it was a hotel but it wasn't. The drive was marked 'Private' and a freshly painted sign on the gate said 'Albany House'.

He made his way back to the car. 'Drive into Broughty Ferry,' said Charlie. 'I'll treat you to a bar meal at Jolly's Hotel because you've done a grand job today.'

44

Molly finished work early on the Thursday and she decided to go and see Peter Lindsay and Douglas Kingsley. She thought it would be a waste of time but she had promised Betty that she would try and get to the bottom of the mystery of Bill's behaviour before he died.

She walked down Baxter Park Terrace and knocked on Peter's door. Once again he enquired in his reedy voice who it was.

'It's Molly McQueen, Mr Lindsay. Can I have another word with you?'

She heard him muttering as he opened the door a few inches. He had the chain on and he peered out at her. 'It's not convenient at the moment.'

'It will only take a minute.'

He shut the door and she heard the sound of the chain being unhooked. The door suddenly opened and he said, 'Well you better come in but I'm going out soon so I can't speak to you for long.'

As welcomes went, it was pretty lukewarm, but Molly realised she must seem like a pest to these men who wanted only to live in peace and leave the memories of India far behind them.

It was lovely and sunny outside and the sun was shining in the window, casting golden patches of light on the furniture which looked as if it hadn't been dusted for a long time. The cat was stretched out in front of the fire, which made the room unbearably hot. Molly came straight to the point and told him of the passages in Anna Stevenson's book. 'Did you hear anything like this when Susie and Naomi were killed, Peter?'

'I had heard it was an old army gun that had been used but no, the police never told us anything relevant except about the bandits.' He turned to look at Molly with what she thought was a sly expression. 'Although, I did tell you that it could have been any one of us, didn't I?'

Molly said he had. 'Did you have anyone in mind? Someone that you suspected?'

He gave this some thought. 'I often wondered about Bill Reid. He was very friendly with J.P. and his family. He used to visit them a lot in the course of his work and then he would socialise with them at their parties.

Molly looked sceptical. 'Bill Reid?'

'Well, you did ask and I'm just telling you what I thought at the time. I wonder what made Anna want to write a book about the awful times out there. I remember her and I thought she was a bit high-minded because her father was a rich planter, and I still can't believe old George and her got hitched.' He stood up. 'Now I have to get ready to go out so I'll have to ask you to leave.'

He walked with her to the door and she thanked him for his time. She was still talking when he closed the door in her face.

When Molly had gone, he went to the cupboard and brought out the Monopoly game. 'I'll show him upstairs how to win at the game,' he chuckled.

Molly caught the bus to the Ferry. This was definitely her last trip in regard to this case. She would write up all the extra information tonight and give it to Betty the next time she saw her.

It was another hot day and the sun beat down through the window of the bus. She wondered what Charlie was doing today and she would have been surprised to know he was roughly in same area she was. That is, if she had known his whereabouts.

As she drew level with the Kingsley house, she saw Douglas in the garden. She called out and he turned with a start. He swore softly and brought a white hankie from his pocket. He wrapped it around his left hand.

'I've stuck the fork into my hand.' He said, walking towards her. 'Come on in. My brother and his wife are away for the day.'

Molly said she wouldn't keep him long and he ushered her into the living room. 'If you don't mind, I'll just wash my hands and put a plaster on this cut. I'll not be a minute.'

Molly sat and gazed out of the window with its view of the sea. Loads of families were walking along the Esplanade on their way to the beach. It was turning out to be a glorious summer and people were going to make the best of it.

Douglas came back into the room a few moments later. His hand was covered by a large pink square of elastoplast. 'I thought I'd better clean the cut thoroughly as I don't want to end up with lockjaw. You have to be careful of getting a cut when working with soil.'

Molly said it was better to be on the safe side then.

'Now what can I do for you, Miss McQueen?'

She relayed the story she had told the other men about Anna's book. 'Did you hear anything about this after the murders of Susie and Naomi?'

He shook his head. 'No, I didn't. What did the others tell you?'

She said they had not been told anything except it had been the old army issue gun that had been used.

'There were army guns all over the place. They were left over from the soldiers fighting the Japanese army in Burma and I expect it would have been easy to get one. A lot of the bandits had weapons so that's why we accepted the story the police told us. Now Anna Watson, as she was then, tells us that the police had other ideas. Do you think she's telling the truth?'

Molly said, 'I don't know. It came as a surprise and George, her husband, wasn't very pleased about the revelations.'

Douglas scratched his ear. 'I can't say I blame him. We all knew Anna in those days. I thought she was a strange girl in many ways. She wasn't attractive and didn't seem to have many friends, boys as well as girls. I always thought she liked causing drama out of nothing, but I expect it amused her because I think she was lonely living with her parents on the tea gardens.'

'Well that's all I've come to say. I just wondered if you had remembered anything else but I'll report back to Bill's sister with my updated report and that will be the end of it. Thank you for seeing me.'

He went to see her out. 'There's one thing I remember about Anna. I think she was very jealous of Susie and Naomi, who were both very pretty women. Naomi got a lot of attention from some of the young men who were working there but they never bothered poor Anna. I used to feel a bit sorry for her, I must admit.'

As Molly made her way to the bus stop she wondered about Anna. It was clear that a woman could have done the shootings. Especially Anna, who had been photographed with a rifle in her hands at the tiger hunts.

Back in the office she typed out the updated reports and placed them in the filing cabinet.

45

Charlie went and looked out the file on Benny Baxter. He had kept his nose clean for a couple of years as the last time he was jailed for housebreaking was in 1953, but his record went right back to his teenage years. Mostly petty crime but his last two sentences had been for breaking-and-entering. On the surface it looked as if he had left his life of crime behind.

Now Charlie wondered why he was meeting up with this Mr Gauld from Glasgow. He decided to phone an old colleague who was now stationed in Glasgow and try and find out if he was known to the police there.

DS Newsome answered the phone. 'Hello Charlie, how are you?'

He said he was well. 'I'm ringing up to find out if you know a man called Gauld. About forty years old with dark hair and loves playing golf. I got the impression he might be a businessman.'

Freddy Newsome laughed. 'You don't have much to go on, do you? Glasgow's a big city.'

Charlie said he was merely fishing in the dark. 'He may be OK but the last time I saw him he was in the company of Benny Baxter. You remember him, Freddy, a small-time housebreaker here in Dundee?'

'I'll have a look around and phone you back,' he said.

Charlie made a cup of coffee and sat at his desk. He didn't know if Freddy would be able to help but it was worth a try. Whoever had committed the four robberies had been very professional and that wasn't Benny's style, who was more an opportunist thief.

The phone call came at lunchtime. 'I haven't managed to get very much, Charlie. I think the guy you mentioned is a Chuck Gauld who owns a couple of hotels, one in the city and another between here and Edinburgh. Nothing very big or grand but always well patronised, I believe. The one near Edinburgh has a golf course and quite a lot of golfers go there to stay for a holiday. There's nothing on him in the police files but he sails pretty close to the law.'

Charlie thanked him for this information and he sat and gazed out of his window, which faced a brick wall. If it was this Chuck Gauld who had committed the four robberies, how had he known the houses were empty at the time and that they had a good amount of cash and jewellery? It was time, he thought, to go and see the owners again. He decided to go to the one near Ninewells. The large detached house was situated on a small hill overlooking the river and surrounded by a well-kept garden.

The owner's wife, Mrs Wilcox, answered the door. 'My husband's at work,' she said.

Charlie said he wouldn't keep her long. She showed him into the room he had been in when the robbery was discovered. A long airy living room with a large window with its picturesque scene of the water.

'Have you found out who robbed our house, Sergeant Johns?'

Charlie said he was working on a few new leads. 'The house was empty, I believe, when the robbery took place, Mrs Wilcox? How many people knew you were to be away?'

She said she had made a statement at the time but added, 'No one as far I know. We went away for a weekend break and discovered the break-in on our return. We went to see friends in Edinburgh.'

Charlie knew all this but he had hoped she may have remembered something else. 'You didn't discover the break-in until the next day?'

'That's right. I went to put my necklace away and found my jewel box empty, then Martin found the money missing and we called the police.'

Charlie knew he wasn't going to get any new information so he thanked her and left.

It was the same at the next two houses, the ones in Broughty Ferry. Both detached houses situated on their own. The owners of the first house, 'The Gables', had also been away for a few days, but as far as they knew, they had told no one apart from their families.

Mrs Collier, a trim blonde woman who had lost her collection of gold sovereigns and money, said, 'We decided on the spur of the moment to go away for the week so I don't think we mentioned it to anyone as we have no family living near us.' She wiped her eyes as she spoke. 'I inherited the sovereigns from my grandfather and they had sentimental as well as monetary value.'

Charlie said he was doing his best to get them back and she thanked him.

As he was in the area, he made his way to Monifieth. Mrs French opened the door and again she looked as if she had been crying. 'Oh don't mind me,' she said. 'I'm busy cutting up onions and they always make me cry.'

Charlie followed her into the kitchen where she had been preparing a pot of stew. An appetising smell filled the room and made him feel hungry.

'Have you found another job, Mrs French?' he asked her.

She shook her head. 'I'm looking but I haven't seen anything suitable. I saw one at a private school. They are looking for a cook and there's accommodation with the job so I might apply for that.'

'Mr Bergmann. How is he keeping?'

'Not very well, I'm afraid. He's had a nasty shock and he still gets headaches. He is winding up his business and plans to sell this house but because it belongs to his wife he has to wait till she gets home from her cruise.'

'When is she expected to be back?'

'The week after next. In ten days' time I think. She has gone around the Mediterranean on a cultural holiday. The ship docks at all the historical places like Crete, Cyprus, Greece and Turkey.

She loves visiting ancient sites I believe, and she's lucky enough to be able to afford it.'

Charlie would have loved to mention Chuck Gauld's name but he didn't want her to warn him that he knew who he was and that she was friendly with him. He would keep that bit of information to himself in the meantime.

'Well I wish you well in your job hunting, Mrs French.'

She suddenly pulled her hankie from her apron pocket and started to cry again. 'It's those strong onions. I'm always like this when I have to handle them,' she said, moving over to the sink where she splashed cold water on her face.

As he drove away, Charlie wondered how onions could cause another bout of crying. Mrs French was suffering about something and it could only be because of the robbery, he thought.

46

George Stevenson was in a strange mood when Molly turned up for her last day. Anna was nowhere to be seen but he said that all the manuscript was in place for typing. Molly started work right away because she knew this would be her final day and that Anna wanted it finished.

She was busy when Anna came in. Bustling as usual, she looked extra-smart in a blue suit and high-heeled shoes. 'Right then, George, are you ready?'

Molly looked up from her typewriter. Anna saw this and explained, 'We're both going out today to a wedding but we should be home before you leave, Molly.'

Molly said, 'Should I wait till you get home or do you want me to lock the door when I've finished?'

'No, that won't be necessary as we'll be home in the early afternoon.' She turned to her husband. 'You haven't forgotten the flower buttonholes have you, George?'

He muttered something and went into the kitchen, coming out with two sprays of carnations. Anna fitted one to her suit jacket while he stood there holding the other one. 'Well put it on,' she said, quite sharply.

With a final goodbye the pair of them departed and Molly saw them get into his car and drive away down the drive.

She had to laugh as they disappeared. What a busy woman Anna was. If she wasn't running off to meetings she was hustling her husband out to a wedding he obviously didn't want to go to. He would think it was a waste of good lazing-around time.

Still, she quite enjoyed her own company and she got on with finishing Anna's story. The house was quiet, with just the ticking from the grandfather clock and the typewriter keys clacking to break the silence.

Anna's book was coming to an end. She had made no more reference to the murders of the Pritchards but described the carnage and futility of the break up of a beautiful country that had once been referred as the Jewel in Queen Victoria's Crown.

When the time came for us to move, I remember I cried. We were leaving this wonderful place behind. A magical land of riches and poverty now degenerating into a bloodbath. In spite of that, I will always remember it as a golden, exotic place where I grew up and which I was now leaving behind.

Molly typed the last page and in spite of herself she felt quite moved by the sentiments of the writer. Anyone reading the book, should it be published, would think of Anna as a gazelle-like creature instead of a hearty, tweed-wearing and organised woman, but that was where its magic lay.

Molly glanced at the clock just as it struck midday and she went into the kitchen to put the kettle on for a cup of tea to eat with her sandwiches. The kitchen was large with two white sinks and a wooden draining board. An Aga cooker and a kitchen table and chairs filled the space. A jug filled with wild flowers sat on the table and Molly thought this feminine touch was so out of character with the owner.

When the kettle boiled, she carried the cup through to the living room, making sure she didn't drop any crumbs on the carpet. The Bhudda's eyes seemed to watch her and the sun glinted off the large brass gong with its wooden hammer. These items must have been shipped back to Scotland and Molly thought they must have been family treasures.

After washing her cup and putting it back in the cupboard, Molly tidied the desk and placed the typewritten pages into a leather-bound folder, with the book's title on the front. It was called 'An Indian Childhood'. Molly wondered if it would ever be published but she had to admit, it was a good story. She would look out for it in the bookshops.

At two o'clock the door opened and Anna rushed in. 'George is putting the car away and he wants something to eat. We didn't wait for the wedding breakfast as it isn't going to be until five o'clock.'

With that statement she hurried into the kitchen and came out twenty minutes later with a plate of cheese sandwiches. Molly said she had already eaten so if Anna didn't want anything else done, she would go back to the agency.

'I'll post my invoice next week,' she said as she picked up her handbag.

Anna was saying thank you for a job well done when George came in. His face fell when he saw the sandwiches. 'I was hoping for something cooked,' he said.

Anna looked like he had asked for a trip to the moon. 'Something cooked. You'll be getting a cooked meal for dinner as usual at seven o'clock.'

Molly tried not to look amused because it was only two-thirty.

47

He was in the middle of another nightmare. The rain was heavy and swelling the river so that it rushed past his feet and threatened to pull him away, down into its foaming depths. The bank was muddy and when he looked down he saw he was running in his bare feet. The mud sucked and tugged at his feet and he knew he was sinking into the boggy ground.

With an almighty struggle he managed to get free and was now running on a leaf-strewn path. His heart felt like it would burst and he was sweating. He rubbed his face and the salty sweat stung his eyes. He felt like he was slowly dying.

Then he woke up, puzzled by the dimness of his room. The moon was out and he saw the clock hands were at two o'clock. He was tangled up with the blankets, and his pyjamas were wet with perspiration.

He got up quietly and went to the sink where he ran the cold tap over his face and neck. Why had that woman come back again with the news of Susie and Naomi? Wasn't he tormented enough?

He went back to bed but sleep wouldn't come. He was surrounded by the noises and smells of India and it was almost like being back. He just had to keep his head and it would all blow over, he told himself before finally falling asleep at six o'clock.

48

Alice and Maisie turned up for work on the Monday morning. Irene, Mary, and Edna greeted Alice with smiles and asked her how she was keeping.

'I'm a lot better, thank you,' she said, hoping that no one knew what was wrong with her.

Molly and Jean arrived and after the rest of the workers had gone, Molly asked Alice how she was feeling. 'Now remember, Alice, I don't want you taking on too much hard work,' she said when Jean went to put her coat away.

Alice promised she wouldn't and she set off for her morning stint. She wasn't feeling a hundred percent well but she knew she had to keep her job going as her wage was needed even more than before.

Grace and June came in together and Molly was struck by how pale Grace looked compared to June, who was almost bouncing with good health. Molly thought how great it must be to be eighteen again and full of life.

Grace looked like she hadn't slept. Not that she was untidy. In fact, she was smartly dressed in her navy suit and pink blouse, but her face seemed to be drawn and grey and she had dark shadows under her eyes. Molly hoped she wasn't coming down with some illness as the work schedules were stretched to the limit.

It was the holiday season and a lot of small businesses needed temporary workers to cover for the permanent staff, which was good business for the agency. Now that the job was finished at the Stevenson house, Molly headed off to a solicitor's office in Reform Street to replace the head typist who had gone to Blackpool for two weeks' holiday.

The sun was shining and it promised to be another glorious day. The papers had been warning its readers that a water shortage was imminent and that everyone had to try and use less water in their daily lives. The headlines had been 'Conserve Your Water'.

Molly hadn't been to see her parents for over a week and she wondered how their plans were going for their move. She made a mental note to try and see them this evening. That was the beauty of the long summer nights. It was possible to do so much after work.

She had to climb a flight of stairs to reach the office which was a series of four rooms and the one that was the main reception office was small and airless, with a desk, a filing cabinet and a chair. If this was the main typist's domain then she was glad she wasn't filling in for the office junior. No wonder the woman had escaped to Blackpool for fresh air and the sight of the sea. Still, the rest of the staff were friendly and Mr Miller, the solicitor, was grateful that she could come and 'hold the fort', as he said.

At lunchtime she headed for a bench in the City Square with her sandwich and small bottle of lemonade. The Square was packed with people all enjoying the sun's warmth and the pigeons strutted around, scavenging for any crumbs that were lying on the ground.

At five-thirty she made her way back to the agency before heading for Craig Pier. Her mother had just laid the tea on the table when she appeared and she went back into the kitchen for an extra portion of shepherd's pie, even though Molly had said not to bother.

'It's no bother,' her mother insisted. 'Now sit down and eat up.'

Molly was hungry and she didn't need a second telling. As she looked at her parents she suddenly realised how much she would miss them when they left to go to the other side of the world. Her father had finished his meal and was now sitting with his cup of tea, reading the paper and listening to the wireless while her mother took the dishes into the kitchen.

'Just leave them, Mum. I'll do the washing up.'

Nancy popped her head out of the door. 'No, you go and keep your dad company. I won't be long.'

She was back in the living room within ten minutes. 'Have you had a hard day, Molly?' she asked.

Molly sighed and let her head rest against the back of the comfy armchair. 'It was pretty busy but the office was stuffy which made it more tiring.' She thought she should mention the move. 'Have you heard any more from Australia House?'

Her dad said they hadn't but added, 'The fact that we're being sponsored by the boat-building yard should help.'

Nancy said, 'We've decided not to sell the house yet. We thought you might like to come and live here if you ever give up the agency, and we're leaving the car with you as well.'

Molly was touched by their concern. 'I could always come over at the weekends and keep an eye on the house.'

Then it was time to go back to Dundee. There was a glorious sunset as she crossed the water, turning the river into a ribbon of gold. Molly thought to herself that there was no place like Scotland when the weather was good and it beat all the fancy foreign resorts.

Alice was tired when she finished work and as she set off for home with Maisie she felt she couldn't bear to cook her evening meal. Her plan was to go to bed right away. As if she sensed this, Maisie asked her to join her for her tea.

'I made a pot of mince this morning and the tatties won't take long.'

Alice didn't want to hurt her friend's feelings but the last thing she wanted was a plate of mince. 'Maybe another night, Maisie, if you don't mind.'

Maisie said that was all right.

When they reached the landing, Alice got her key from her pocket but before they parted company, a figure appeared at the top of the stairs. It was Sandy and he was carrying a bunch of flowers.

Alice said, 'Come in with me, Maisie,' but before she could answer, Sandy said he wanted to see Alice on her own.

Maisie had no option but go into her own house while an unhappy Alice led the way into hers.

Sandy sat down and placed the flowers on the table. Alice made a great fuss of looking for a vase to put them in but he took hold of her hand.

'I don't know what's gone wrong with us, but I thought I would come round and tell you that Victor has moved to Govan this week.'

Alice said that was great.

'I know you don't want a relationship but can we still be friends like we used to be?' he said.

He gave her a pleading look and she was suddenly very sorry for the way she had treated him. 'Yes we can, Sandy.'

'I've missed you terribly, Alice.'

Without thinking she rushed into his arms. 'Oh and I've missed you. It's been terrible.'

'Right then I want to take you out for your tea and we can go to the pictures if you want to,' he said.

She knew she had to tell him about the baby but what if that sent him away, never to see her again? Getting her courage together she looked at him. 'I've got something I must tell you before we do anything, Sandy.'

He sat at the table, twisting his hands together and she realised he was as nervous as she was.

'I'm going to have a baby.'

He looked stunned.

'I should have said we're going to have a baby.'

Suddenly his face lit up and he hugged her tight. Then he asked, 'When?'

'The doctor says about January next year.'

He became serious. 'Let's get married right away.'

Alice thought you couldn't do it right away. 'Won't we have to wait till the banns are read and plans made?'

'Well let's get the plans started tomorrow.' He drew a small box from his pocket. 'I've been carrying this around for weeks.' It was an engagement ring.

He put it on her finger and she burst into tears. 'I've never had an engagement ring before, Sandy.'

'Well, the future Mrs Morgan has one now.'

'We must tell Maisie.'

Maisie was delighted when they both went to her door. Afterward Sandy took Alice out for her tea then on to the pictures.

When they were gone, Maisie sat down to her mince and tatties and said to the cat, 'Well what a lovely surprise, isn't it, Bobby?'

Bobby was washing his face after eating his fish-flavoured cat food and let the good news go over his head.

The next morning, Alice was like a woman transformed. She showed her ring to Mary and said, 'Snap.'

Within a couple of minutes the entire staff was surrounding her and admiring her solitaire diamond. Even Grace and June, who didn't really know her that well, seemed to be delighted. But the person who was the best pleased was Molly. 'Congratulations, Alice. You deserve loads of happiness.'

'The wedding is being planned right now and we hope to be married as soon as possible.'

She caught Molly's eye and smiled shyly.

49

Charlie was re-reading the robbery victims' statements. If Chuck Gauld from Glasgow had committed the crimes, how had he managed to pick out houses where a lot of good quality jewellery and money were kept?

There had to be a link. Benny Baxter hadn't been noted for his housebreaking antennae. The only thing he was good at was his method of breaking-and-entering. He never made a mess of any of the rooms and in fact, it was often a few days afterwards before the victims knew they had been burgled.

But how had he managed to team up with Gauld? His record sheet said he hadn't committed any crime for almost two years but that didn't mean much. It could be that he hadn't been caught.

Charlie noted that the Wilcoxes had been in Edinburgh for a short break when the robbery took place, while the two others had been away in Glasgow. He checked the rest of the statements to see where they had all stayed but there were no addresses mentioned.

Then there was the first robbery at the Bergmann house. If Benny Baxter had committed it then he had changed his methods. Charlie recalled the drawers lying on the carpet floor and why steal some paintings? No, he thought, this crime didn't tie in with the first three, plus the assault on Eric Bergmann. It was too much of a coincidence that jewellery and money was stolen in four of the cases and paintings in this one. It looked as if a different hand had committed it.

Andrew Williamson passed the door and Charlie called out to him, 'Bring the car around.'

When he was reversing out of the police station, the constable asked him, 'Where are we going, sir?'

'I want to see the victims of the robberies. We'll start with the Wilcoxes at Ninewells.'

When they drove up the drive, the front door was opened by Mrs Wilcox. She was dressed in a very stylish dark blue cotton dress with navy sandals and handbag. Charlie wondered if she had been on the verge of going out or did she normally dress like this every day.

'My husband's at work and I have to be at a meeting.'

Charlie knew his suit was a bit rumpled and although his shirt was clean he still felt at a disadvantage next to this cool lady.

As Andrew followed him out of the car, Charlie said, 'I promise I won't keep you long, Mrs Wilcox.'

She shrugged her slim shoulders and went back into the house and led them into the living room. Once again he was overwhelmed by the magnificent view, especially on a sunny day like today. Dragging his eyes away from the window, he asked her, 'When your robbery took place, you said you were both away to stay with friends in Edinburgh. Can I have their address please?'

She shook her head. 'No, we didn't stay with them. They arrived from London and we went through to see them for a couple of days. We all stayed at the Briar Hotel on the outskirts of Edinburgh. It has a good golf course and both our husbands love playing the game.'

'But you didn't want to take your jewellery with you?'

'No, it wasn't like one of my husband's work weekends when we really have to dress up. This was just a couple of days spent with old friends and we were all casually dressed.'

Charlie looked over to see if Andrew had written it all down and, like the good boy scout that he had been, he had.

Charlie thanked the woman and they both left.

'Right then, let's try the Colliers'.'

Andrew loved driving and he made good time on the road to the Ferry. When they reached the house they found Mrs Collier sitting out in the garden in the sunshine. She was wearing a pair of shorts, a cotton top and dark sunglasses. A book and a tall glass of lemonade were placed on a small table by her side. She was surprised when the two men appeared at the gate. She didn't look too happy but she stood up. Before she could speak, Charlie said once again that they would only keep her a minute.

She went inside and Charlie was grateful to be out of the hot sunshine. She didn't ask them to sit down but went straight into the kitchen. Everything was neat and clean. Even the saucepans were shining and didn't look as if they had ever graced a hot stove.

She leant against the worktop. 'Well what do you want to ask me now?'

'You and your husband were away when the house was broken into, Mrs Collier. Can you tell me where you were?'

She looked annoyed. 'I explained all this to the police at the time. We were on business in Glasgow.'

Charlie looked at his notes. 'Your husband was at a conference and you went with him for a break?'

'Yes, I wanted to do some shopping and also visit an old friend.'

'Did you both stay with the friend?'

'Look,' she said. She sounded exasperated. 'What's all this got to do with us losing all my jewellery and money?'

'It's just a new lead, Mrs Collier, and I would be grateful if you could just answer the question.'

'No, we didn't stay with my friend. We booked into Hunter's Hotel. It's a hotel we've stayed at before as we like the old fashioned atmosphere of the place.'

Charlie said he was grateful for letting him take up her time.

Back in the car, Andrew Williamson said, 'She didn't like being bothered by us again.'

Charlie laughed. 'No, I suspect we interrupted an exciting part of her book and made her go indoors out of the sun.'

The next port of call was a large detached house overlooking the sea. This was the home of Mr and Mrs Walters. This time, both the occupants were at home. They were both out in the garden working. She was kneeling on a thick rubber mat and digging into the earth while he was pushing a mower over the pristine grass lawn.

Unlike Mrs Collier, Mrs Walters was dressed in an old pair of brown slacks and a sun hat shaded her eyes. They both stopped working and asked the two men if they wanted a cup of tea.

Andrew's eyes lit up but Charlie said no. 'I just want to ask you where you stayed when you were away at the time when the house was broken into.'

Mr Walters looked at him with shrewd eyes. 'Is it relevant?'

Charlie said he didn't know yet but was tying up loose ends.

'We stayed a week at the Briar Hotel. It's near Edinburgh and is convenient for the shops, the museum and art gallery. Places that we like to visit.'

'Well I won't keep you away from your gardening,' said Charlie.

'Is there any news on our robbery?' asked Mrs Walters.

'I'm following some new leads and I'll keep in touch.'

As they drove away from the pleasant streets and the smell of the sea, Charlie was excited.

Andrew Williamson said, 'It's funny how two of them stayed at the same hotel at different times.'

Charlie said it was.

Back at the station, Charlie looked at the notes he had made when he phoned Freddy in Glasgow. The two hotels owned by Chuck Gauld were the Briar in Edinburgh and Hunter's Hotel in Glasgow.

He felt a tingle at the back of his head and he realised he had found the common link to the three crimes, but how did the Bergmann robbery fit into the pattern? Eric Bergmann hadn't been on any holiday, so how did the criminal brain behind it know he would be carrying a briefcase full of expensive jewellery? Did he, or she, just land lucky with this? He thought not. They must have known about his shop and the two safes and knew he owned a large amount of jewellery.

He left his desk and went to see his superior officer. Inspector Alexander was in his office. Charlie explained his theory and

Inspector Alexander said, 'Have you any firm evidence that this Chuck Gauld is the culprit?'

Charlie said no, he didn't. 'I just found it strange that the three couples all stayed at hotels owned by him when the robberies happened.'

'Yes, it's a good theory but try and get some evidence against him and get this case solved,' said the Inspector.

Charlie said he would.

50

Sonia had her bags packed and was waiting for James to come home. She had rehearsed her speech over and over again. She was sorry to be leaving James but he wasn't as ambitious as she was and even although he would be devastated by her news, she planned to stay firm.

He arrived home at lunch time and by then she had almost forgotten what she wanted to say. He saw the three suitcases by the front door but said nothing.

'James, there's something I have to say.' She was surprised that her mouth had gone dry. 'Do you remember Leonard Matthews, the owner of the empty shop I was hoping you would buy for an art gallery?'

James said he did but he hadn't changed his mind about it.

'No, I know you haven't. It's just that he's offered me a job in is art gallery in Edinburgh and I've said I would take it.'

James stared at her. 'In Edinburgh?'

'Yes I know you'll be upset at me leaving but it's a great chance for me. I mean I could always come back here from time to time to see you so it's not as if we won't see one another again.'

He sat in silence and she went on. 'I won't take the job if you don't want me to.'

'Oh no, Sonia, you must take it and good luck with it.'

'Thank you, James. I'll always think of you and, as I've said, I'll get back as often as I can.'

He stood up. 'Let me help you with your suitcases. Is he coming to pick you up?'

'No, I thought it would be better if I got a taxi and met him at the railway station.' She turned at the door. 'I expect you're devastated and I'm sorry about that.'

He was busy stashing the cases into the taxi's boot. 'Don't worry about me. I'll be fine.'

She frowned as she got into the taxi. He was taking it remarkably well, she thought as the car drove away and turned the corner of the street.

Leonard was waiting for her at the station and he helped her to load her luggage into the train compartment.

'Well here's to a happy partnership,' he said.

Sonia settled back in her seat and once again thought of the look on James's face. He hadn't looked as brokenhearted as she thought he would. If she had known at that moment he was on his way to see his brother John she would have been very unhappy. When he reached the house, John answered the door. 'James, how lovely to see you. Where's Sonia?'

'She's gone. She's been offered a job by Leonard Matthews, who has an art gallery in Edinburgh.'

John didn't know what to say to his brother. He knew he always had a soft spot for her.

'This Leonard, he wanted me to buy an empty shop he owned and Sonia wanted me to take it on. To open a "high-class gallery", she said, but I didn't want to change my way of doing things. I like the paintings I do.'

John said, 'I have to pick up Billy from the school but will you wait here until Edna comes home and have your tea with us?'

James said he would. When Edna arrived home, she heard the story. 'I'm so sorry to hear what's happened, James,' she said. 'Are you very hurt the way she's treated you?'

'A little bit. She said I was a second-rate artist and that hurt me even more.'

John was annoyed. 'You're not a second-rate artist. You're quite famous and you sell nearly all your paintings.'

James said that Sonia promised to come back and see him as often as she could.

Edna and John looked at one another. 'Don't let her ruin your life, James, now that she's gone. She'll just use you when it suits her.'

'I know,' he said.

'Does she still have a key for your house?'

He nodded.

'You should have asked her to give it back,' said John 'Write to her and ask her to send it through the post.'

James turned to look at him and he was smiling. 'Oh don't worry, John and Edna. As soon as she was out the door I phoned the locksmith and he's changing the locks tomorrow. I may be soft but I'm not daft.'

John and Edna burst out laughing and James joined in, much to Billy's puzzlement when he came down from his room for his tea.

5 1

There had been another break-in at a house in Blackness Road. Charlie and Andrew Williamson went to speak with the owners. The house, although not isolated, was situated at the end of a cul-de-sac and sat back from its neighbours. A large garden with trees successfully screened it from the road.

Mr Bell, the owner, was waiting. He ushered the two men in to a glassed conservatory where a tearful Mrs Bell was sitting.

The fingerprint team had been and Charlie tried not to upset the woman any more than he had to.

He spoke to the husband. 'Can you give us a list of what was stolen, Mr Bell?'

The man handed over a pencilled list. 'All my wife's jewellery, plus three hundred pounds in cash which I was hoping to put into the bank today.'

Charlie glanced at the list and it contained quite a large amount of items. 'Did you have the jewellery insured?'

'Yes we did but most of it has sentimental value to my wife. It was left to her by her late grandmother and is very valuable.'

'I believe you were away from home when the robbery happened.'

'Yes, we were. We had to go through to Edinburgh to help my parents get away safely on their holiday. They needed help with luggage, although they were at the railway station when we arrived. I suppose they could have managed on their own but I didn't think about it.'

'Did you stay in Edinburgh overnight?'

'No, we stayed with friends who live in Fife. We stopped with them on our way back.'

'Did your parents stay anywhere in Edinburgh?'

'They didn't say they had. They arrived from Inverness and I assumed they had just changed platforms. To be honest, we didn't have much time with them as we were late in arriving due to the car having a puncture.'

'So the Briar Hotel doesn't mean anything to you?'

The man shook his head. 'No, I've never heard of it.'

So, his pet theory was a lost cause, he thought, but he said, 'Where are your parents going on holiday?'

'They're going on a five-day cruise to the south coast of France. I tried to tell them about the Bay of Biscay and how rough it can be but my father wanted them to go so he wouldn't listen.'

Charlie thought he had been annoyed at his father and now this robbery was the final straw. Especially when Mrs Bell started crying again.

As they were driving away, Andrew said. 'What was that about the Briar Hotel, sir?'

Charlie said it was just an idea he had but now it seemed he had been wrong.

'Do you want to go back to the station?'

'Yes.' Then he thought about it. 'No, wait a minute. Take me to Parker Street as I want to look someone up.'

Benny Baxter lived in Parker Street with his mother and Charlie planned to see him. He had seen inside the Bell house and it was immaculate. Almost as if the invisible man had stolen the items.

Andrew parked the car and they set off for the top flat in the close nearest the steps that led up to Dudhope Park. There were four doors on the top landing but none of the nameplates said 'Baxter'. Instead there was a new name on the door where Benny used to stay.

However, he knocked at the door. It was opened by a young woman holding a baby.

Charlie smiled. 'I'm looking for Benny Baxter. Does he still live here?'

'I've heard the name but I think he must have moved because we've lived here for six months.'

As the two men headed off downstairs, the woman turned and her husband said, 'I wonder why the police are looking for the last tenant.'

His wife looked alarmed. 'Was that the police?' she gasped.

'Aye, it was,' said the man, picking up the paper and resuming his interest in the horse racing page.

They were almost out of the close when they stood back to let an old woman past with her message bag.

Charlie stopped and looked at the woman. 'Excuse me, have you lived here for long?' he asked.

She looked up at him. 'Aye, I have.'

'Do you know where Benny Baxter and his mother have gone to live?'

'Oh, the poor soul's in the Royal Infirmary. Been in there for a few months. Benny moved to a good job in Glasgow and I believe he's doing well for himself.'

When they were on their way back to the station, Charlie thought, *I bet he's doing well for himself. Helping Chuck Gauld with robberies.*

The problem was Charlie had no proof.

52

Alice and Sandy were busy planning their wedding. It was to be at the registrar's office with a small reception in St Mary's Hall on the Hilltown where Sandy lived with his parents. Mr and Mrs Morgan had made Alice very welcome when she first met them and she was grateful for their help with the arrangements.

Alice had asked Maisie to be a witness at the wedding but Maisie said, 'You want someone younger, Alice. Just think what your wedding photos will look like with an old hen like me standing beside you two young people.'

Alice said that she was her best friend and neighbour and that's why she wanted her to be at her side on her big day.

Maisie had taken her hand as she said, 'I'm very grateful you think that but I still think you should look for someone else.'

'Who can I ask?'

Maisie gave this some thought. 'What about Mary or Edna or Molly?'

Alice said that was a great idea. 'I'll ask Molly.' She looked at her friend. 'Do you think she'll do it?'

'Well, you can always ask her.'

Alice said she would.

Maisie felt so happy for her. In the space of a few weeks, Alice had gone from despair to joy and now with a new husband and baby on the horizon, her life would be transformed. She thought back to the terrible life Alice had suffered under the brutal hands of her ex-husband Victor and said a little prayer of thanks.

Alice turned up for work early the next morning as she wanted to catch Molly before the rest of the staff turned up for work. When

Molly came downstairs, she was sitting in the chair by the window.

Molly's heart sank when she saw her and she hoped there was nothing wrong with her.

Alice stood up when she saw her. 'Molly, I wondered if you would like to be my witness at the wedding. Sandy has one of his best mates from the shipyard to be the best man.'

Molly was so touched that she felt tears threatening to spill. 'Oh Alice, I'd love to be your witness.' She stopped and looked at her. 'I thought Maisie was to do that?'

Alice was always brought up to tell the truth so she said. 'I did ask her, Molly, but she called herself an old hen and said she would spoil the wedding photos so I thought I would ask you as you've always been so good to me.'

Molly didn't know whether to laugh or cry but then she had a fit of the giggles at Maisie's description of herself. Alice was taken aback by this but Molly said, 'I'm laughing at Maisie's description of herself.'

Alice burst out laughing as well and when Jean arrived, the two women were wiping tears from their eyes.

Stan always came round for his tea at Mary's house on Monday nights as he went to an evening class to learn French. This saved him going all the way home to Barnhill. Mary's mum would make a special tea on those nights but tonight her father was late coming back from the foundry and the tea was sitting in the oven, slowly getting burned.

She bustled out of the kitchen into the living room where Mary, Stan and Mary's brother Colin were sitting.

'We had better start without your dad as I'm not sure what time he'll get in.' She wiped her hands on her apron and said to Stan, 'I don't want you being late for the night school.'

Stan and Colin sat at the dining table while Mary and her mum carried the hot plates from the oven. Her mum had bought a large steak pie from the butcher and there were mashed potatoes and peas to go with it.

They had barely started when the doorbell rang. Mary said she would get it and went to answer the door. She came back in with a stranger.

'I'm sorry to interrupt your meal,' he said, 'but Mr Watt has had an accident at work and he's at the casualty department of the Royal Infirmary.'

Janet Watt leapt up to her feet and cried out, 'Is he badly hurt?'

The man said he didn't know. 'I've been sent by the foreman to tell you and to drive you to the infirmary.'

Mary and her mum went to get their coats. 'Colin, you can stay here till we get back,' his mum said. 'Stan, just you finish your tea and we'll see you later.'

Stan said he was going with them.

Mary said, 'But what about your studies?'

'They can wait. I'm not letting you both go on your own.'

The man's car was sitting at the entrance to the close. It was a small car but they managed to squeeze inside, Mary and Stan in the back and Mrs Watt in the front.

At the infirmary, they headed for the casualty department with Janet Watt on the verge of tears by this time. They sat on the hard chairs in the room which was unusually quiet given that the casualty was often the first call for any injured people and could be very busy.

The nurse told them Mr Watt was in with the doctor. Mary's face was white with anxiety and Stan took her hand and squeezed it tightly. 'He'll be fine, Mary.'

Janet Watt said to the man who had brought them here, 'If you want to go home, we'll be all right here, and thank you for coming to tell us and for the lift.'

He hesitated but Stan said, 'I'll phone for a taxi when Mr Watt comes out.'

'Are you sure? I can easily wait with you,' said the man.

Mrs Watt said no, they would be fine and after saying goodbye, he left.

Half an hour later the doctor appeared. A young, fresh-faced man wearing a white coat with a stethoscope around his neck. He sat down beside them. 'Your husband has had an accident at work. A heavy steel pipe fell on his arm and I'm afraid his arm is broken. He's been taken to get it set with plaster and we're keeping him in overnight for observation.'

Stan felt Mary relax beside him as she let out a deep sigh. Although she didn't want to say anything in front of her mum, he knew that she thought her dad had died. A broken arm was serious enough but not as serious as it could have been.

Stan said he would phone for a taxi to take them back to the house and he set off to look for a coin-operated box. He was back in fifteen minutes and the taxi turned up a little while later.

Back in the house, Colin jumped up when they came in. His mum said, 'Dad's broken his arm but he'll probably get home tomorrow.' Then she burst into tears.

Mary was making a pot of tea when the bell went again. Stan opened the door and the Watts' neighbour, Mrs Duffy, was standing on the doorstep.

'I saw the taxi and wondered if everything was all right?' She sounded anxious.

Stan ushered her into the house and went to help Mary in the kitchen. She was washing the dishes and had put the remains of the pie back in the oven.

'Dad can have that for his tea tomorrow,' she said.

Stan smiled at her. 'He'll be starving by then so he'll enjoy it.'

They then went and joined Mrs Duffy and the family. Janet Watt had just told her all about the accident and Mrs Duffy was saying how dangerous some workplaces could be. 'I mean to say, I remember when my man worked down at the docks and a crate fell on his foot. He hobbled around for weeks.'

Mary said, 'If you want to go home, Stan, we'll be fine.'

Stan said he wanted to stay the night with them. 'I'll go and phone my parents and tell them what's happened.' He eyed up the settee where Mrs Duffy was holding forth on accidents suffered by various members of her family. It sounded like a gothic horror story. 'I'll sleep on the settee.'

Mary was unsure. 'It's not very comfortable, Stan.'

He said, 'Come with me to the phone box.'

It was a lovely night as they set off and on their return they passed Massari's Chip Shop in Strathmartine Road.

'Do you think your mum and Colin would like some fish and chips?' asked Stan. 'They didn't eat much at tea time.'

Mary said they could all do with something to eat so they returned with two fish suppers and two white pudding suppers.

Mrs Duffy had left a few minutes before they arrived and Mrs Watt said the fish was a lovely surprise.

She said to Colin, 'Wasn't that good of Stan to bring us back something to eat?'

Colin looked up with his mouth full and nodded.

Mary said that Stan had offered to sleep on the settee.

'It isn't very comfortable but if you want to, we'll be grateful,' said her mum.

'I can easily stay off work tomorrow and help you when Bob gets home.'

Janet Watt said that wouldn't be necessary as the doctor had said he might get brought back by an ambulance. 'I know Mary can't stay off work as the agency needs her and just you go to work as well, Stan. I'll manage.' She added, 'And thanks for all your help.'

It was a bit of a queue in the morning as they all waited on their turn for the bathroom but as Mary and Stan headed off to catch the tram into the town centre and Colin went off to school, Janet went back to bed for an extra couple of hours. She hadn't slept last night because of storm and the accident. It kept replaying in her head but it could have been so much worse. So very much worse.

53

The good weather had finally disappeared and a thunderstorm through the night kept people awake with its ominous rumblings and vivid flashes of lightning. By morning the streets looked like a war zone with rainwater that ran down the steep streets like a river. Piles of discarded litter and broken branches from trees were scattered across the pavements and the early morning rush hour traffic had to slow down in order to splash through deep puddles. Some cars and lorries carried on without slowing down and the passing pedestrians were treated to a cold shock of water on their legs.

In the agency, Jean was puzzled. Some of the files in the cabinet were not in alphabetical order. Mary had come in and was telling Molly about her father's accident.

'Stan had to stay the night with us and sleep on the settee. I wish Mum and Dad would let me get married before he goes away as I'm sure he'll forget all about me.' She looked anxiously at Molly. 'Do you think that will happen?'

Molly said it wouldn't. 'You know he loves you, Mary, and he doesn't seem the type of man who would let you down like that.'

Jean muttered to herself but her voice cut across Molly's words. 'Some of the files are wrong and I'm sure I put them away all right.'

Molly turned in Jean's direction. 'What's wrong?'

'The file for the initial "J" is in front of the one for "I", instead of the other way around.'

Molly was worried. This was the second time there was something wrong with her filing system. She said, 'Perhaps it's just a mistake, Jean.'

Jean shook her head. 'No, I checked Mrs Jennings' account the day before yesterday and I remember I put my hand over the "I" file as I put it back.'

Molly said no more as she handed Mary the work sheet. 'Now don't you worry about Stan. It'll all turn out all right.'

Mary didn't look reassured as she went out.

Molly went over to the filing cabinet. 'Have you seen anyone looking through the files, Jean?'

'No, I keep my key in the desk drawer but I can't see any of the staff wanting to look through the invoices, can you?'

Molly said she couldn't but added, 'I think we should keep our keys in our pockets, Jean. Just to be on the safe side.'

Jean nodded and placed the files in the right order.

Although she had spoken lightly, Molly was worried. There was nothing confidential in the files but why should anyone want to look at them? It was a mystery and Molly was getting tired of mysteries.

She hadn't seen Charlie for a couple of days and she wondered how he was getting on with solving the robberies. It was certainly taking its toll on him because she couldn't remember when she had seen him looking so tired. No doubt there would be an enormous amount of pressure on the police to solve these crimes and she was glad she wasn't in his shoes.

Lately, Molly had been feeling the pressure of running her business, along with her worries over her parents' imminent departure to Australia. She had always thought they would be here for her but she also realised that Nell could be feeling the very same thing. No doubt she would love to have her children's grandparents near them.

Molly thought, *Am I being selfish?* Unfortunately there was no one to answer that thorny question and she would just have to cope with whatever lay ahead.

With that thought in mind, Molly decided to concentrate on her work and when the inevitable departure of her parents drew nearer, then she would deal with that when the time came.

There was no use in worrying over the future.

54

The storm woke him up. The strengthening wind and battering rain against the window and the flashes of lightning once again brought on the panic. For a brief moment he thought he was back in India.

He looked down at the two bodies and saw the gun in his hand. It was like a scene from a film, and he was the onlooker, not the perpetrator. He fell to his knees and cried, but when he came to his senses and realised he wasn't back in Darjeeling, he stuffed his fist in his mouth to stifle the noise.

The storm raged outside while the panic within him slowly subsided. He had to keep calm, he realised that, but the nightmares were getting worse. It was all the fault of that woman poking into the dark recesses of his mind. That was where all his terrors lay, in his darkest memories.

He breathed deeply and tried to calm his fears. This was something he had learned in India, to be able to control himself and show a normal face to the world.

Another white flash lit up the room and he saw the ring was still on his finger. The golden, twisted band and the deep red eye of the Indian ruby. It was all he had left of Susie. The only tangible memory.

Except for the nightmares.

55

While Molly thought the ground was shifting under her feet, Charlie was at his desk, surrounded with paperwork. The police constables, who had done all the house to house enquiries they could, searching for possible witnesses, had put all their reports on his desk but there was little to go on. No one seemed to have heard or seen anything while their neighbours' houses were ransacked.

He still thought Chuck Gauld had something to do with them but he couldn't prove it. Quite a lot of the known criminals who regularly broke into houses had been interviewed but they either had cast-iron alibis or Charlie didn't think they were smart enough to rob on such a large scale.

He hadn't been able to trace where Benny Baxter was staying in Glasgow. He had gone to see Mrs Baxter in Victoria Hospital but she couldn't help. The woman was seriously ill and not expected to live for very much longer. Charlie reckoned she was in her early fifties but she looked old and wizened and lay like a ghost against the white sheets on the bed. She had opened her eyes when he sat by her side but she hadn't spoken.

Charlie was grateful that the heat had gone and was now replaced by a fresh wind that made it more comfortable to work in. He was feeling tired this morning because he hadn't slept well through the night, mainly because of the storm's lightning that had lit up his room with white intermittent flashes and the rain that beat a loud tattoo on the window. The fresh air would help waken him.

He stood up and went to look for PC Williamson, who he

eventually found in the staff room. 'Williamson,' he said, 'I want to go and see the golf club again.'

The constable was eager to be out of the station and he brought the car around to the front. The sun had come out but although it was mild, the heat of the past few days had gone and it was more like a normal Scottish summer day. The streets had a clean, washed look and the air felt invigorating and so different from the cloying heat that had settled over the city before the storm. The beach at the Ferry was deserted, quite unlike the previous visit when it was crammed full of families enjoying a day out.

Andrew Williamson was intrigued by Charlie's request. He knew Charlie had no proof of Gauld's guilt but he also knew that instinct was a good tool in policing. He loved watching how Charlie's mind worked and he hoped when he was promoted he would do the same and use his gut reaction.

They reached the golf club shortly after, and Williamson parked at the far end of a row of cars.

Charlie said, 'Is it still possible to play golf after heavy rain? I would have thought the green would be waterlogged.'

Andrew grinned. 'It's obvious you don't know golfers, sir.'

There was no sign of Chuck Gauld's car. Charlie didn't want to draw attention to them so he told the constable to drive away.

On the way back, he said to drive to the Bergmann house. Mr Davidson was working in the courtyard of his hotel and scowled at the car as they passed. Charlie thought how wonderful it would be if he was the thief because he didn't like the man. But it didn't work like that. Often the culprit was charming with a fresh-faced manner.

To Charlie's surprise, the door was opened by Mr Bergmann. He had aged considerably since his ordeal and Charlie felt a great deal of sympathy for the man. Allowing them in, he took them to the kitchen where a pot of coffee sat on the stove. He brought down a couple of cups and filled them then turned his attention to his own drink. A tin of biscuits stood on the table and he said to help themselves, an invitation that Andrew took advantage of instantly.

Charlie got straight to the point 'We still haven't found out who assaulted and robbed you, Mr Bergmann, but we are working hard to solve it.'

The man nodded. 'I'm just waiting for my wife to get back then we can sell this house and maybe buy something much smaller.'

There was no sign of Mrs French.

As if reading his mind, Eric Bergmann said, 'I'm afraid poor Mrs French is not well. She hasn't been well since the incident and I think she is afraid to be in this house. I've told her that I have nothing left to steal and the robber won't be back but I don't think I convinced her.'

Charlie said that she had told him she was working her notice.

The man sighed. 'Yes, I'm afraid that's true. If we do move to somewhere smaller we won't need a housekeeper. Anyway, I can't afford to keep her on but I hope she gets something else soon.'

Charlie was curious. 'Has she any friends who come and visit?'

He shook his head. 'I don't think anyone has come to the house, but of course I don't know what kind of social life she has in the town.'

'Does she ever mention her husband?'

He shook his head again. 'In her references she said she was a widow and I've no reason to doubt her. I like her and she's a super worker and a great cook.'

Charlie noted that the liking was all his and not his wife's opinion, but maybe it was just a slip of the tongue.

'We'll keep in touch, Mr Bergmann, to let you know how the investigation is going.'

When they got into the car Charlie said, 'Out of all the victims of these robberies, he's the one I feel so sorry for. His livelihood has gone and soon it'll be his home.' He sighed then said to Andrew, 'Drive past Albany House and stop.'

The constable drew into a small lay-by that overlooked the river and Charlie got out, sauntering causally, as if looking at the scenery. The gate was open and he saw the car parked in the drive. Just then Chuck Gauld appeared from a small shed in the garden and went back into the house.

So our Mr Gauld is still here, he thought as he walked back to the car. He had just closed the door when he saw a cyclist appear round the corner and turn into the drive.

Andrew turned to him and said, 'Isn't that Mrs French on the bike, sir?'

'Yes it is.' Charlie wondered if she had seen him and if she had, would she report this to Chuck Gauld? He hoped not as he didn't want the man to go to ground before he had any evidence to either charge him or eliminate him.

Andrew was curious. 'Did you see Mr Gauld?'

Charlie said he had but he added, 'I wonder why Mrs French is going to see him. This case becomes more baffling by the minute. What connection do Benny Baxter and Laura French have with Albany House and Chuck Gauld?'

Andrew tried to look as if he might come up with the answer but after a minute's silence, he said. 'I've no idea.'

56

Molly was worried about the mixed-up files. It might not be anything but a mistake but she recalled the same state of her folder on her investigation of Bill Reid's death. She didn't think anyone in the office had been secretly reading the folder but if they had, who could it be? She immediately dismissed Edna, Mary, Alice and Maisie from the list and that left Irene, June and Grace.

She mentally scored Irene out as she had known Edna's mum ever since the agency opened. So it was down to June and Grace. June was a young lass waiting to go to university in the autumn and Molly couldn't see what she would want with her folder. Grace, on the other hand . . . What did she really know about the woman except what she had told her and she had no references? But why would someone just back from Cape Town be interested in an eight-year-old mystery?

She decided to keep her eyes open and the two keys to the cabinet firmly hidden from anyone except Jean and herself. She also would have a word with Grace tomorrow morning.

Before going upstairs that evening she checked the cabinet and everything was under control and filed properly. She made a mental note to do that every morning and evening until she got to the bottom of it.

The next morning, Mary was in first. She looked anxious. 'Molly,' she said 'Can I have this afternoon off work as my dad is getting home from the hospital? I need to be there to help Mum when he comes home.'

Molly had a quick look at the work sheets. 'If you want to go away now, Mary, I'll cover for you. Your mother will need you to be there when he gets out.'

Mary was grateful. 'I'll be back in to work tomorrow, and thank you.'

Because she had to set off right away for an eight o'clock start at Mary's office, Molly didn't have time to wait on Grace. However, she warned Jean to make sure the files were locked up at all times and the key hidden in her pocket.

Bob Watt came home at lunchtime in an ambulance. His arm was encased in plaster and he wore a huge white cotton sling to support it. He seemed grey and drawn and looked as if he had aged ten years.

Janet made a huge fuss of getting him comfortable in his chair while Mary had made something to eat. It wasn't the steak pie from yesterday because it had dried up into an unpalatable mound.

'I've done some scrambled eggs, Dad. Would you like some?'

Bob shook his head. 'Not for me, Mary. I'll just have a cup of tea.'

Janet immediately made a fuss. 'You have to eat to keep up your strength, Bob. Did you have any breakfast in the hospital?'

He said he hadn't felt hungry but added, 'I'll maybe have something at teatime.'

Janet wanted to know what had happened at the foundry but he said it had been an unfortunate accident. He said, 'I think I'll go and have a lie down. I didn't sleep last night in the ward as there were two admissions and although the nurses were as quiet as they could be, I still couldn't get to sleep.'

Mary was miserable. 'How long do you think he'll be before he gets better, Mum?'

Janet said she didn't know. 'It all depends on how quick the broken bone heals.'

He was still asleep at teatime and Mary, Colin and Janet ate their meal in silence.

★ ★ ★

Stan arrived at six o'clock to see how the patient was getting on.

'He's in bed because he's very tired, Stan,' said Janet. 'But he hasn't eaten anything since he came home.'

Stan thought getting a good sleep was more important than food and he was proved right. At eight o'clock, Bob woke up and he had more colour in his face. Even better was the fact he was feeling hungry. 'I wouldn't mind those scrambled eggs now, Mary,' he said.

Mary jumped up from her chair and hurried into the kitchen, with Stan following her. She turned to him and began to cry softly.

Stan held her close and said, 'Your dad's going to be all right so don't worry.'

Mary wiped her eyes and brought the pan down from the shelf. She cracked three eggs and added milk and butter. Stan said he would make the toast and she said through her tears, 'You'll make a wonderful husband, Stan.'

He smiled at her. 'If only we could be married before I go away.'

She nodded but said, 'Not now, I can't bring this up when my dad's not well.'

Stan knew that it was her dad's worry about her age that had been the stumbling block. Her mum was worried as well but not on the same scale as him. Still he understood the situation because his parents were the same. They loved Mary as much as he did but they said she was too young to get married, even more so when it meant going to live on the other side of the world in a strange and unfamiliar place.

57

Charlie was on his way to see Freddy Newsome in Glasgow. He had phoned his old colleague and asked if they could meet up. Freddy had suggested meeting on his day off, at the Red Lion pub in the city centre.

Charlie had taken the train because he wasn't sure of the parking in the city and when he reached Queen Street Station he had to look at his map to find where the pub was. It was down a small side street and when he went in, Freddy was sitting at a table with a half-finished pint of beer in front of him.

Charlie bought him another one, along with his.

Freddy said, 'You're looking well, Charlie. It's ages since I saw you. So how's the job in Dundee?'

'It would be much better if I could solve these jewel robberies. We had another one last week.'

'Was there a connection with Chuck Gauld with that one as well?'

Charlie shook his head. 'Not as far as I know. Anyway, how are you keeping? Still working hard?'

Freddy said it was all go. 'I really liked working in Dundee but Glasgow is my part of the world. I was born just a few streets away from here,' he said as he pulled a couple sheets of paper from a rucksack that lay at his feet. 'As I said on the phone, Chuck Gauld is, on the surface, an entrepreneur but we think he has dealings with some dodgy customers.'

'I think he's linked to Benny Baxter,' said Charlie. 'You'll maybe remember him, Freddy? He's been in trouble since his schooldays.'

Freddy nodded. 'He's a bit small-time for cleverly organised jewel raids, is he not?'

'I would have thought so but I saw them both together and I added up two and two and came up with four. I went to his address but seemingly he's moved to Glasgow. His mother is dying from cancer and is in the Royal Infirmary so I couldn't get any information from her.'

Freddy smoothed the sheets of paper on the table. 'According to the grapevine, our man owns the Briar Hotel in Edinburgh, the Hunter's Hotel here in Glasgow and is on the verge of opening another one in Dundee.'

Charlie was surprised until he remembered Albany House. *Was this to be his latest purchase?* he wondered. He mentioned this and Freddy said it was possible but no names had been forthcoming with the information he had.

'I would like to look at the Hunter's Hotel, is it far?'

Freddy said it wasn't and they could easily walk there.

They set off and Charlie was soon lost as Freddy went down various streets and lanes, finally emerging onto a busy road with shops and the hotel fronting the street. It had a homely look that Charlie could imagine would be popular with people.

A glass door stood at the top of four steps with its panes shining in the sunlight. Charlie went inside. A square lobby with a patterned carpet and good quality prints on the wall. A receptionist's desk stood against the left-hand wall and a wooden flight of stairs swept upwards.

A grandfather's clock chimed eleven o'clock and it was a pleasing sound. As if hearing this, a well-dressed young woman came out from one of the doors and smiled at him. 'Good morning. Can I help you?'

Charlie had his spiel all ready. 'My parents are hoping to spend some time here in Glasgow and I said I would check out accommodation for them. Do you have a brochure I can show them?'

She smiled again, showing white, even teeth. 'Certainly.' She went over to a rack that stood on a small table and chose a leaflet that had a picture of the hotel on its cover. 'This shows the kind of accommodation we have, plus the restaurant and our small bar,' she explained.

She turned the brochure around. 'And on the back it lists the prices and our telephone number. We get lots of guests staying with us and they all say how much they enjoyed their visit.'

Charlie made a big thing of looking at it. He gave her one of his smiles, although his teeth weren't as white as hers. 'Thank you so much, you've been very helpful. I'll take this with me and show it to them.'

He thanked her and went back down the steps. Freddy was waiting for him on the corner of the street.

'Well, how did it go?' he asked.

Charlie said it all looked well run and above suspicion. 'This hotel is definitely owned by Chuck Gauld?'

Freddy nodded. 'It was actually run by his wife before she divorced him but he was so inflamed by the divorce that he left her almost penniless.'

Charlie said he didn't know he was married.

'Oh yes, but it didn't last long. She was a lovely-looking woman but the rumour was she didn't know about his other activities, the ones we can't prove.'

Charlie asked where she was living now but Freddy said, 'I've no idea where Laura went after the divorce.'

Charlie gave him a sharp look. 'Laura?'

Freddy was surprised. 'Do you know her?'

Charlie said he thought he did. 'Mr Bergmann, one of the victims of the robberies who lives in Monifieth, has a housekeeper called Laura French.'

Freddy stopped walking. 'French was her maiden name. So she's living in Monifieth? I wonder if her ex-husband knows that.'

Charlie said he did. 'She's spoken to him on two occasions at least.'

'Well, what a coincidence,' said Freddy.

Charlie, who didn't believe in coincidences, said, 'Isn't it.'

58

Molly was sitting with Marigold in her garden. She had finished the day's work and had headed over the river but not before double-checking the files again. The evening was still warm, even though the sun was dipping towards the western horizon and the perfume from Marigold's roses was heady.

'What I can't understand is why anyone would want to see how the business was doing,' Molly said.

'You still think it is Grace who's doing it?'

Molly said she was the only one she could think of. 'It's not as if there's lots of business secrets but I do like to keep my accounts and clients confidential.'

'What do you know about her, apart from arriving here from Cape Town?'

'I don't know anything other than what she's told me about her fiancé coming here later. She didn't have any references, which I now think is a bit shady. What do you think, Marigold?'

Marigold finished drinking her tea before answering. 'I don't know what to think, except she may be thinking of starting her own agency and wants to have details of your customers and what you charge. That way she can maybe undercut your prices to get started.'

This made sense to Molly and she felt betrayed by it. If Grace did want to start her own business then she would have given her any help she needed. Grace didn't have to turn to underhand tactics like this.

Marigold looked serious. 'One thing, Molly. Are you sure someone has tampered with the files? I mean, maybe it's been a simple mistake by both of you.'

Molly recalled the pages of her report to Betty Holden. How they had been mixed up. Could she have done this herself? Had Jean been rushed and was to blame for her mix-up?

Molly was suddenly tired of the entire episode. 'Oh, I don't know. Maybe we both made mistakes.'

But even as she said it, she didn't believe it. Molly couldn't put into words this feeling she had. It was just her intuition that something wasn't right. Was this a reaction to her parents' decision to move, this undercurrent of tension?

She placed her empty cup on the tray and stood. 'Thanks for listening to me, Marigold. I do trust your judgement.' She stretched her arms above her head. 'I better go in and say cheerio to Mum and Dad before I catch the next ferry.'

Marigold wanted to know about Betty. 'Have you heard from her again?'

Molly nodded. 'She wrote and thanked me for the reports on Bill's colleagues but she said she would have to accept that her brother's death was an accident. As for the murders of the two women in India, the police closed the case years ago with the verdict on the bandits, even though Anna Stevenson says otherwise. I guess we will never know the entire truth.'

Marigold said that sometimes the truth had a habit of popping out when it was least expected. 'I think you should speak to Grace about this and get it sorted out, Molly.'

As the ferry crossed the river, everything was calm and peaceful. There was hardly a ripple on the water and Molly wondered why she had this cold feeling of doubt and upheaval. It was as if she was heading towards something but she didn't know what.

59

Charlie had the hotel brochure on his desk and he had read it through a couple of times. It was well presented and he could see why people would want to book into a hotel near the city centre. The brochure gave the impression it was a family-run business and perhaps it had been in the past but if Chuck Gauld was now the owner then those days were long gone. According to Freddy Newsome, he had his mark on quite a lot of enterprises but no one knew just what they were or how many. He was the original sleeping partner.

Charlie wasn't sure if his hunch about the hotels in Glasgow and Edinburgh were the link with the robberies but it was a link and at the moment he had no other suspects in sight. The fact that Laura French was also Gauld's ex-wife made the connection even more believable.

Charlie decided to pay another visit to Eric Bergmann and Laura French.

He first went in search of Andrew Williamson and found him typing out a report about a couple of broken shop windows that were obviously the result of some drunken act. After Charlie told him of his plan and his intention to take Andrew with him, Williamson got to his feet, glad to finish the report and drive the car.

Mr Bergmann and Mrs French were both in the house when they arrived but Laura went into the kitchen after opening the door to them. She still looked awful, although she had made the effort to put on some make-up and tie her hair back with a neat band. In spite of this, there was still a tightness around her mouth and tension in her eyes.

Eric Bergmann was sitting in the living room with a tray of coffee on the table. He was reading the morning paper which he put down when the men were shown in to the room. When he first saw them, a spark of hope showed in his face but it soon died away when Charlie said he had no news yet. There was no sign of Mrs Bergmann but her husband said she was on her way home and would arrive in a couple of days.

Charlie said, 'I wonder if you can now remember anything about the night you were robbed? Has anything become clearer now?'

The man sat for a moment in deep thought then shook his head. 'I get a flashback of seeing a light but I'm not sure if it was at the front door. I do know that Mrs French was on holiday and I think I was surprised.' He shook his head again. 'Then I sometimes think it was a dream. I'm sorry not to be able to help you.' He looked distressed.

Charlie said it didn't matter. 'It's just that sometimes with a head injury a memory comes back later.' He stood up. 'We'll let you finish your coffee and we'll be in touch. But before we go, I would like a quick word with Mrs French if that's all right?'

He nodded. 'She'll be in the kitchen. I hate to have to pay her off but I've no option.'

Laura French was where Mr Bergmann said she'd be. She was rolling out pastry on a marble slab. A couple of pie dishes stood beside her, both filled with apples. She deftly put the pastry on top and put them in the oven.

There was a pot of coffee on the stove and she filled three cups and handed them over with a plate of scones, butter and jam. Andrew Williamson's eyes lit up like beacons when she said to help themselves.

Charlie said, 'I don't think you'll find it hard to get another job, Mrs French, as you're an excellent cook and housekeeper.'

She nodded but didn't look at him.

'You would do well in a job in a catering firm or some hotel,' he said deliberately, wondering what her reaction would be.

She stared at him and almost dropped her cup. 'No, I never

thought of that,' she said but Charlie didn't believe her. In a sudden blinding flash it came to him that this was where she had met her ex-husband. She had worked in one of the hotels when he bought them over.

'You said you were divorced. Have you had any contact with your husband?'

By now the panic was clear to see and even the constable noticed it. He stopped eating his scone and brought out his notebook.

'No, and I don't want to ever see him again. Ever.' She sounded angry and two red spots appeared on her cheeks. As if she was aware of this, she turned her back to the sink and began to wash her cup.

'Mr Bergmann gave you a holiday a few days before the incident. Can you tell me why?'

She turned and looked furious. 'Why! I was entitled to a few days off and we both never imagined this happening.'

'You said you went to a stay with a friend. Can you give me his or her address?'

'It's a her. I didn't actually stay with her but just visited and stayed at my own house. She lives in Dundee.' She gave him the name and address and Charlie was surprised to see it was a hotel.

'Was she staying there on holiday?'

'No, she's the housekeeper but she's also an old friend.'

She seemed to be on the verge of tears so Charlie thought it was time to leave.

Driving back, he told Williamson to stop at the Royal Hotel in Union Street. He managed to park the car a few yards from the entrance and they both went inside. The woman at the reception looked at them brightly. 'Can I help you?'

She was well made up and wore a smart suit with a badge that said 'Meryl Cole'.

'I wonder if I could see your housekeeper, a Miss Barbara Metcalfe? I won't keep her for long.'

The receptionist was clearly intrigued but she used the

telephone on her desk and a few minutes later a very smart woman dressed in a navy overall joined them.

Charlie introduced himself. 'Can we go somewhere and have a chat?' he asked.

The woman looked at Meryl who nodded and said to use the dining room as it was now empty.

They sat at one of the tables which had a snowy white tablecloth, silver cutlery and sparkling glasses. Charlie made a mental note to come here one day with Molly. 'You have a friend called Laura French, Barbara?' he asked.

She nodded. 'Yes I do.'

'She told us she met up with you when she was on holiday a few weeks ago?'

'Yes, we met up in the town and had a meal together then we went to the pictures. Is something wrong?'

Charlie explained about the robbery that happened on the same day.

Barbara nodded. 'Yes, Laura told me about it when we met up later.'

'Have you known one another long?'

'Yes, we both met in a hotel in Glasgow. Laura ran the hotel and I was the housekeeper.'

'Was she married at that time?'

'Yes she was but she was getting a divorce. He was the owner of the hotel but the marriage wasn't happy so she left him. There was a big stink about it at the time as he was furious.'

'What is his name?'

'Charles Gauld. A real charmer, but obviously Laura didn't think so and she left. She wrote to me later to say she had got this job with Mr Bergmann and she was very happy.'

Charlie looked to see if Williamson was getting everything written down.

'Just one last question, Barbara. Did her husband Charles ever find out where she went?'

Barbara's face went bright red. 'Laura doesn't know this but I mentioned to the receptionist at the hotel and she told him. I was mortified as I had told her to keep quiet about it. You won't mention it, will you?'

Charlie said, 'Did you leave the hotel in Glasgow the same time as Mrs French?'

'No, I wanted a change of scene and saw this job advertised and I got it.'

Back in the office, it was all beginning to make sense. He had wondered at the time how Chuck Gauld had known about the Bergmanns' jewellery business but he had been told by the receptionist he had met at Hunter's Hotel the day he met up with Freddy Newsome.

It was time to have another talk with Laura French.

60

Molly had made up her mind to tackle Grace but she didn't get the chance because most mornings were a rush as the staff arrived and left together. She didn't want to ask her outright to stay behind as this would cause some talk so she decided to be patient and wait for the right moment.

She still didn't know what she was going to say to her and wondered if she was making a drama out of a couple of files but her instinct told her there was something going on and it was better to get it out in the open.

When the staff started to filter in there was always a lot of chatter as they took up their work sheets. Maisie and June were usually the liveliest while Alice was the quietest. She looked around for Grace but there was no sign of her.

As they all departed for work, Jean was still holding Grace's card. 'It's not like her to be late,' she said. 'But it doesn't matter because she's not due to start until nine-thirty this morning in the council office.'

By nine o'clock it became clear that Grace wasn't coming in to work and Molly had to get herself ready to take over the assignment.

Jean was worried. 'Maybe she's ill. Do you want me to go round to see her?'

Molly said she would go on her way to the office as it wouldn't take more than a few minutes to go to the address in Commercial Street, which was just around the corner from St Paul's Church. It was raining as she walked along the High Street and when she found the entrance leading to Grace's flat she hurried inside, glancing at her watch as she made her way up the stairs. She didn't want to be late for her job.

There was three flights of stairs with two doors on each landing. Most of the doors had cheap nameplates, except two. Molly decided to knock on the first one. It was opened by a sleepy-looking young man who had been in the process of getting dressed. He was in his bare feet but didn't look in the least embarrassed by it. Molly thought he must be a student at the university or technical college.

She said, 'I'm sorry to bother you but I'm looking for Grace Carson who lives at this address.'

The young lad looked mystified. 'I know everybody who lives in this close but I've never heard of a Grace Carson. But try one of the other doors, they might know her.'

Molly saw she had only fifteen minutes to get to work but just as she had made up her mind to leave, a young woman came out of door on the first landing. She gave Molly a smile and went to pass her.

Molly said, 'Excuse me but I'm looking for a Grace Carson who lives at this address. Do you know which flat she's in?'

The woman stopped and said, 'There's nobody here called Grace Carson. We all know one another here as we are all students.' She stopped. 'Not unless she lives here with one of the students. There are a couple of flats let out to girls so maybe she's a friend and is visiting.'

Molly didn't think so but she said, 'If I come back tonight can you ask around and see if she's here? I employ her but she didn't show up for work. I hope she's not ill.'

The woman said she would ask everyone later after her courses at the university.

'I'll come back later tonight and speak to you and thank you,' Molly said. Then she hurried off to the council office and got to her desk with a couple of minutes to spare. There was a lot of work to get through but all day she couldn't stop thinking about Grace.

She didn't know what time the woman would be home as she

forgot to ask her but she went back to the agency after work and decided she would go to back to Commercial Street about seven o'clock. That should give the woman time to chat to all the occupants of the other flats.

Jean was as mystified as she was. 'Why give us a fictitious address?'

Molly said she didn't know but something was wrong. Of that she was sure.

She went upstairs and made something to eat and tidied the flat but her mind wasn't on what she was doing. With Grace not turning up like this it put her under pressure to keep all the bookings filled but maybe she would show up tomorrow full of apologies.

At seven o'clock Molly was back at Commercial Street and the woman opened the door on her first knock. 'Come in,' she said and led Molly through a large hall to a room with a high ceiling and period features still in place, like the wonderful elaborate plaster coving and the solid wooden doors. An electric heater stood in front of a lovely marble fireplace and although the furniture had all seen better days, it looked comfortable.

Molly had left her card with the woman this morning but she didn't know the woman's name; this was soon remedied.

'Hi,' she said. 'I'm Constance.'

Molly thanked her for all her trouble and Constance said it was no bother. 'I've asked everyone if they know a Grace Carson but no one does. She certainly doesn't live here, I'm sorry.'

Molly said she had maybe got the number of the street wrong and she would check the other closes.

'There's quite a high number of students that live around here so maybe she's found other accommodation. It happens all the time.'

That was probably true, thought Molly, but Grace wasn't a student. However, she didn't have time to check out the other addresses at the moment but she would if Grace didn't show up for work tomorrow.

Later, she had spent ages in the office rearranging all the work cards before going to bed with a slight headache. She couldn't sleep and got up to take an aspirin and a glass of water at two o'clock.

It was raining heavily and she heard it beating against the window. She pulled the curtain to look out at the wet pavement below and even in this weather there was still the odd pedestrian hurrying up the street.

Her head was full of unanswered questions but she had no answer to the mystery of Grace's disappearance.

61

The rain was still heavy when Charlie set off for work and his raincoat was soaked by the time he reached the police station. Every morning he hoped this would be the day when the case would get a breakthrough, but there was no new information coming in.

He had many other cases on his workload but these robberies still bugged him and he thought, if only he could get some proof . . . He had gone to see the Bell family yesterday but they had had no word from the parents who were on holiday and he couldn't see the connection to Chuck Gauld.

That meant there was no connection to the hotels owned by Gauld but he read over the reports again, hoping to see something he had missed.

But if there was something, he couldn't see it. In fact, he could probably recite the reports from memory as he had read them so often. Freddy Newsome had said that Chuck Gauld sailed pretty near the wind but the Glasgow police hadn't been able to pin anything on him, not even as a suspect in various crimes. Charlie thought he was just the right kind of mastermind to organise robberies like these. Then there was Laura French, his ex-wife. Where did she fit in? In a matter of days she would be away from her job with the Bergmanns and she would probably move away. Freddy had said that Gauld had been so incensed by the divorce that he had left her without any means of support, so why was she still seeing him and, more importantly, did she know why he was in Monifieth?

He decided to have a cup of coffee before heading off to check on an assault case that had happened the night before. It was the usual fight that happened after the pubs had closed but the victim had ended up in the casualty department of the infirmary, though thankfully he was now nursing his wounds back at home. The young man lived in Byron Street and Charlie set off with PC Lawson because Williamson wasn't available as his shift started later. When they reached the house, the victim was sitting at the fire and listening to the wireless. He had the makings of a black eye and a cut above his lip but otherwise he looked fine.

Charlie asked him for the name of his assailant but he said, 'Och it was just a wee argument and because he's my pal I don't want to press charges.'

Charlie tried to persuade him to press charges but the lad was adamant so they had no option but to return to the station.

'What a waste of police time,' he said to Lawson, but the constable stayed quiet because he was a new recruit and he wasn't sure if he should voice an opinion.

At lunchtime, Charlie debated about going out for something to eat but as it was still raining he decided to get a sandwich and a hot drink from a small shop in Bell Street and have it at his desk. His coat had got wet again on his trip to Byron Street so he hung it on the back of a chair beside the radiator. Then his phone rang.

To his surprise it was Laura French and she sounded upset. 'DS Johns, I wonder if you can come to see me today?'

Charlie said, 'Are you in the Bergmann house?'

'No, I'm in my own house. Can you come here?'

'What is it, Mrs French?'

'I can't say over the phone but I'll explain when I see you.'

He spotted Williamson who had just come on duty and he called him over. 'Mrs French wants to see me and you can drive me there.'

The rain was still pouring down and the sky had heavy grey clouds which forecasted more rotten weather. When they got nearer to the river the wind had picked up and it was choppy. There were no families on the beach today, not a soul on the street and even the shops had a desolate air about them.

Charlie said, 'It looks like the summer's over.'

Williamson nodded. He had got soaked as well on his way to work and now had to sit in the car with his wet overcoat which made the windows mist up.

When they got to Monifieth, Charlie said to park the car away from Mrs French's house. 'There's a small car park across the street.'

She must have been waiting at the window because the minute they crossed the street, she opened the door. Before closing it, she glanced up and down as if checking no one was watching. Williamson thought it was all very cloak-and-dagger drama.

Her house was small and the living room tiny with just enough room for a settee and chair, a bookcase and a coffee table. A small fire was burning in the tiled fireplace which had a homemade rag rug in front of it. It was cosy and homely and nothing like Charlie's flat in Dens Road, which was functional but certainly not cosy.

She had made a pot of tea and there was a plate of biscuits on the table. Charlie noticed she still looked ill. When they were settled and she had hung their coats on a hook in the tiny lobby, he asked her what it was she wanted.

She fiddled with the edge of a cushion, not looking at him. Then she suddenly straightened up in her chair as if she had made up her mind about something. 'I know who robbed and attacked Mr Bergmann.'

Charlie heard Williamson splutter as he choked on his biscuit but he asked her how she knew.

'Because it's my ex-husband.'

He didn't want to say too much and waited until she explained further.

'His name is Chuck Gauld and he's a criminal, although he's never been caught.'

Charlie asked her if she had proof he was the culprit.

She nodded. 'He had great pleasure in telling me when I begged him to return Mr Bergmann's jewellery. He laughed in my face.' She blushed a deep red. 'He said it was because Mr

Bergmann was my boyfriend that I was asking him to hand it over. Mr Bergmann is a right gentleman and he's been good to me and there has never been anything improper between us.

'I never knew he was into crime when I married him but when I did find out I left and got a divorce. I saw this job advertised and I ended up here where I've been very happy. I thought my life in Glasgow was over but Chuck traced me to here and when he knew about Mr Bergmann's business then he decided to rob him.'

'Is he also responsible for the other jewel robberies in Dundee, Mrs French?'

She looked shocked and her face turned white. 'What other robberies?'

'There's been four that we know of and we think his pal Benny Baxter is also involved.'

She screwed up her face. 'Oh, that Benny. I'm not surprised if he's involved. I've never liked him nor his other two pals in Glasgow, Bert and Alex Chandler.'

Charlie looked at her. 'The problem we have with your ex-husband is a lack of proof. We can't jump in and arrest either him or his pals without evidence. Now if we knew where the proceeds of the robberies were, then that would be different.'

'I know he has Mr Bergmann's things at his house in Broughty Ferry. It's called Albany House and he's planning on turning it into a hotel like the other two that he owns.'

Charlie couldn't believe his luck but he was still unsure of her motives for this confession.

'I need you to come with us to the police station to make a statement, Mrs French, and then we can decide what we'll do.'

She looked horrified. 'I'm not sure. He'll kill me if he finds out I told you.'

'We'll keep your name out of it if we can,' he said.

She was still not convinced but she knew she had no option. They hurried quickly to the car and Charlie was pleased that the heavy rain had kept the street clear.

Back in the station he put her into one of the interview rooms and went to see Inspector Alexander to bring him up to date with the developments.

'She says he has the jewellery and money at Albany House and if we can organise a warrant and a police presence we can get this case solved. I also think Benny Baxter might be there but she mentioned two other pals and if we can get the Glasgow police to check on them, plus the Hunter's Hotel and the Briar Hotel.'

Inspector Alexander said to leave it with him but Charlie said the sooner the house was searched, the better. 'If he's planning on going back to Glasgow then we'll never trace the jewellery and money.'

Charlie then went back to the interview room.

62

It was very early the next morning when the police arrived at Albany House. It had rained overnight but was now dry with a mist rising from the river. It was very picturesque but Charlie had no time or inclination to admire the view.

If Laura French had been telling the truth then the case would be solved soon and the culprits arrested. Charlie's stomach was churning. He knew what a fine line there was in situations like this and if the stolen items weren't in the house then Chuck Gauld could sue them for wrongful arrest or police harassment. Either way, Charlie would be left with the cases unsolved and worse, his career at an end.

PCs Williamson and Lawson, plus four other officers, were stationed around the house as Charlie knocked on the door. No one answered and he called out, 'Police, open up.'

A ground floor window opened suddenly and a figure tried to escape but was soon apprehended by two of the constables. Then the door was opened by a woman with untidy hair and deep circles under her eyes; it was clear she had just awoken. It was the receptionist at the hotel and she recognised him right away. She tried to slam the door but Charlie was too quick for her. Even so, he got his foot caught in the door and the pain shot up his leg. Seething from the injury but quickly collecting his thoughts, he brought out his search warrant and Williamson escorted her to one of the waiting cars.

There was no sign of Chuck Gauld but when Charlie went upstairs, he was met by Benny Baxter. Charlie read him his rights and, to his amazement, he came downstairs quietly. Then a door opened and Chuck Gauld stood in the threshold. He was dressed in a pair of blue paisley-patterned pyjamas, and he was furious.

'What's the meaning of this?' he asked. 'I'm a reputable business man.'

Charlie also read him his rights and said, 'I believe you are responsible for various robberies in Dundee and I have a warrant to search this house.' Lawson appeared and took his arm to lead him downstairs. Chuck Gauld took exception to this and pushed the constable before darting towards the open door.

He almost made it but a big burly constable called Bedford caught him and Charlie put a pair of handcuffs on his wrists. All the while Gauld was swearing at the police, saying he would get them all sacked for treating an innocent man like this.

When the occupants were all on their way to the police cells, the fingerprint team arrived. Charlie hoped and prayed that the stolen goods were still on the premises but it took less than half an hour for them to find some of the jewellery in a strongbox under the bed. Along with this was a briefcase that Charlie hoped had belonged to Eric Bergmann. It was clear from the suitcases that lay packed in the living room that they had just arrived in time.

Charlie left the team to check out the house and headed back to the station. His foot felt like it was on fire but he tried to ignore it as he had to wrap up this case as soon as possible. He knew he couldn't keep Chuck Gauld for questioning for long so he had to move quickly.

Back at the station, Chuck Gauld was still protesting loudly and demanding to see his lawyer. The suspects were all put into separate interview rooms and Charlie decided to start with Benny, who also protested his innocence.

'I just work as a barman for Mr Gauld in his hotel in Glasgow.'

Charlie asked him what he was doing in Albany House. 'How does the bar run without you then, Benny?'

Benny scowled. 'I came here with the car because Mr Gauld was leaving. He's been on holiday and now it's over. He phoned the hotel yesterday and I drove here last night.'

'And what about the receptionist and Alex Chandler, the one who tried to escape through the window?'

'They came with me and we were all leaving today.'

'It must be a very big car if you're all travelling together, Benny. I would have thought a big businessman like Mr Gauld would want the car to himself and not have to crush in beside all the staff.'

Benny said, 'Well that's the way he wanted it.'

'Well the way I see it,' said Charlie, 'is these robberies have your trademark all over them.'

Benny shrugged. 'I'm not the only criminal in Dundee.'

Charlie ended the interview and Benny was taken back to the cells.

Inspector Alexander was going to interview Chuck Gauld, who had phoned for his lawyer, so Charlie went to see Alex Chandler and then the receptionist who turned out to be his wife, Pat.

They pleaded ignorance of any robberies and said they were just here for the trip. 'Benny had to come to pick Mr Gauld up and we came with him.' They both said the very same words, as if they were memorised and easily repeated, like a pair of parrots.

Charlie again said, this time to Pat Chandler, that Mr Gauld must like his staff very much in order to travel with them after a holiday.

She gave him a defiant stare.

Later, back in Inspector Alexander's office, there was good news. 'We've got Benny Baxter's prints on the jewellery and Mr Gauld's on the briefcase which means he must have been at the Bergmann house. He's got a top-notch lawyer with him and he's trying to implicate Baxter and the Chandlers in the robberies, saying he didn't have a clue about any of it, as he was just here on business and holiday.'

Charlie asked if there was any news from Glasgow but Inspector Alexander said not yet. He added, 'Well done, DS Johns. Let's hope we can convict them all.'

With the accused all now resting in the comfort of their cells,

Charlie decided to call it a day and headed for the agency to see Molly.

Molly had just gone upstairs when he arrived. She could see by his face that he had good news.

'We've got the gang who committed the jewel robberies.'

'Oh, well done, Charlie,' she said. 'Did they confess?'

Charlie said no but it was just a matter of time. 'The main guy, he's a well-known businessman, and he's hired a top lawyer so no doubt we'll have to get concrete evidence if we're to convict him. He's well known for being slippery.'

Molly said if anyone could solve the case then it was Charlie. She noticed he was limping and asked him what was wrong.

'I got my foot caught in a door but the doctor said it's just bruised with nothing broken.' Suddenly he became aware of how hungry he was. 'Let's go out to get something to eat as I'm starving,' he said.

Molly went to get her coat as it was still misty and wet outside, then the two walked together into the rain.

63

Molly overslept the next morning as Charlie had insisted on celebrating with a drink after their meal in Wilson's Restaurant. They both had a glass of whisky in the Old Bank Bar before going home.

She had to get dressed quickly because she wasn't sure if Grace would show up today. She didn't expect she would so she had phoned Sandra, her friend, to see if she could do a few days' work until Molly could advertise for someone new. The mystery of Grace's disappearance still lay heavily on her mind. Molly had thought she was an excellent worker and she hoped nothing had happened to her. However, with Grace giving a fictitious address there was nothing she could do.

She had been checking out the addresses in Commercial Street, starting at the side of the close where Grace said she lived but there was no one by the name of Carson. At first Molly thought Grace had got mixed up with the number but it now looked as if she had deliberately told a lie. And what did she want with the files? That was another mystery.

Swallowing a quick cup of tea and a slice of toast, she then went downstairs.

Catching sight of her, Alice came up and said, 'I'm going to look for my dress on Saturday, Molly. Do you want to come with me?'

Molly said they could maybe go in the morning as she had to go and see her parents in the afternoon and Alice said that was fine.

It wouldn't be long now till Alice's wedding day and Molly thought it was nice to have this to think about instead of all the investigation of the Indian managers, Bill Reid's death and Grace's disappearance.

She didn't have time to worry any more about Grace as she had to go to her job at a solicitor's office in the Nethergate. It had just come in yesterday afternoon. The person on the phone had said one of the typists had to go home because she was ill. Molly had told Jean that she would take on the job as there was no one else available from the agency.

She quickly combed her hair and checked the seams of her nylon stockings were straight before she put on her new raincoat which had a hood.

The rain had come on again and it was pretty heavy so Molly decided to catch the tramcar at the Wellgate steps and get off in Tay Street. That way she would stay reasonably dry. Luckily one tram was coming to the stop when she reached the top of the steps so she ran to catch it. When she got off at the stop in Tay Street she was pleased to see the office was just around the corner.

She was welcomed with relief by an elderly, grey-haired solicitor called Mr Walls who didn't actually give her a hug but gave her a huge smile.

'Thank goodness you could come,' he said, moving into his office. 'I've a huge backlog of work waiting to be typed up.'

He wasn't joking as he handed her a large pile of papers. He said apologetically, 'I'll need these by the early afternoon. Do you think you can manage that?'

Molly thought it would be cutting it fine but she said she would do her best.

He showed her into the typist's office and she was pleased to see the desk was by a large window – not that she wanted to look out all the time, but it did make the room airy and a lot lighter. There was another desk at which sat a young woman with dark curly hair and a face like a doll. She was very pretty and Molly put her age at about seventeen.

She looked up and smiled. 'Hello, I'm Marilyn Jones. I'm glad you could come and help out as Jane had to go home yesterday with pains in her stomach. Mr Walls is hoping it's not appendicitis.'

Molly introduced herself and said she hoped it wasn't anything serious.

By eleven o'clock she had managed to wade through more than a third of the papers when Marilyn left her desk and said it was time for a quick break.

'We normally have a cup of tea or coffee at this time in the staff room,' she said.

The staff room, although quite tiny, had a small cooker with a boiling kettle on the top, and to one side a window overlooked the Nethergate.

Molly said she would love a cup of tea and Marilyn quickly produced three cups, sugar, milk and a tin of biscuits. She sat down on one of the two folding chairs.

While Marilyn was taking a cup of coffee to Mr Walls, Molly glanced out of the window at people hurrying past. It was still raining. Suddenly a woman came in sight and Molly almost dropped her cup. It looked like Grace and Molly watched in amazement as she hurried towards a door across the street and pushed the bell. The door opened and Grace, if it was Grace, went inside.

Marilyn came back and sat down. 'Gosh you've gone all white, Molly. I hope you're not going down with what Jane had.'

Molly smiled. 'No, it's just that I've seen someone I know.'

When she got back to her desk she had made up her mind it couldn't be Grace. It must have been someone who looked like her but then Molly remembered the distinctive coat Grace had worn and this woman had one identical to it. There was nothing she could do at the moment but she planned to have a look at that door before she went home tonight. She inserted a new sheet of paper in the typewriter and began to wade through the pile still sitting in the tray.

At five-thirty, Marilyn put the cover on her typewriter and stood up. Molly had finished her work at about three o'clock, much to Mr Walls' delight. He had produced some more but said it wasn't urgent.

Before leaving, Mr Walls said, 'I haven't heard from Jane today but if I need you tomorrow can you come in?'

Molly said to phone the agency if he needed her and she said cheerio to him and Marilyn.

Marilyn hurried after her. 'I live in Princes Street and normally get the tramcar. Will we wait on one together?'

Molly said she would have loved that but she thought she would drop in and see the friend she had spotted in the morning. Marilyn waved goodbye and Molly pulled up the hood of her coat in an effort to hide her face. Thankfully it was still raining so she didn't look odd.

She walked slowly across the street at an angle so she could walk down the pavement beside the house. She almost burst out laughing at her antics. *I feel like a spy*, she thought.

The building had lots of windows but just the one door. A typed list of the occupants, protected by a sheet of plastic, was fixed to the door jamb. Molly quickly scanned the list and halfway down she saw the name Carson. It looked like a joint occupancy because there was another name beside it.

When she saw this name, she felt light-headed because she recognised it.

64

Charlie had Freddy Newsome on the phone. 'It's bad news,' he said. 'There's no trace of any money or jewellery at the Gauld house or in either of the two hotels.'

Charlie felt a sinking feeling in his stomach. 'We didn't find any money in Albany House or in the car and only a fraction of the jewellery so it must be somewhere. Do you think he has a lock-up or something where he has stashed it?' He added, 'What about Bert Chandler who works in the hotel? Has he been searched?'

Freddy said he had. 'He's known to us. Another petty crook but we've had nothing on him for a year or two.'

Charlie asked if a photograph of the man could be sent to him. He had a hunch about him but didn't want to say too much yet.

Freddy said a photo was on its way and they would still be searching. 'We'll keep in touch,' he said.

Charlie was due to interview Chuck Gauld again but he would have to wait till his lawyer arrived. At one o'clock, the man came walking in like he owned the station. Dressed in his expensive suit, pristine blue shirt and deep-blue silk tie, he gave off an aura of competence. In his mind it was only a matter of time before his client was free.

When the lawyer and Mr Gauld were seated in the interview room, Charlie went though the robberies. 'In the Bergmann case, a briefcase full of jewellery was stolen. Do you know anything about that, Mr Gauld?'

'No I don't.'

'What would you say if I told you your fingerprints were on this briefcase?'

Gauld looked shocked. 'I've no idea what you're talking about. I came here to have a holiday and to look for new premises for another hotel.'

Charlie produced the briefcase. 'This is it. Do you remember it now?'

Gauld opened his mouth to deny it then stopped. 'That briefcase was in my bedroom. Of course I handled it. I didn't know it was this one you were talking about. I picked it up and asked Benny where it had come from but he didn't know.'

Charlie changed the subject. 'I believe you've been seeing your ex-wife while you've been here. Did you know she was living and working in Monifieth?'

Gauld turned a red, furious face to his lawyer. 'No I did not. I was totally amazed when she came to see me at the golf club last week. Benny will tell you, he was there.'

'I've heard you were pretty upset when she left you and got a divorce. Did you decide to teach her lesson and rob her employer and get her the sack? Especially when she was left with nothing after the divorce.'

He shook his head and Mr Nesbitt, the lawyer, looked sharply at Charlie.

Gauld leant his arms on the table. 'Can I make one thing clear? Laura didn't divorce me. It was the other way round and if you ask my lawyer you'll find she ended up with a hefty lump sum.'

Mr Nesbitt nodded. 'Yes I can confirm that. I drew up the agreement and Mrs Gauld was fully compensated for her input in the marriage.'

'Why did you divorce her?'

Gauld's face took on a bullish look. 'It's personal and has no bearing on this.'

'So why did she come to see you at the golf club?'

Mr Nesbitt whispered to his client and Gauld nodded. 'She wanted a reconciliation but I said no.'

Charlie thanked them for their time and the constable took Gauld back to the cells. As he went out the door, Gauld turned and said, 'I haven't done anything.'

Benny Baxter entered the interview room next. He had been a handsome lad when young and now in his early thirties he had retained his good looks. His hair was cut in the latest style and Charlie could understand why he was a popular barman at the hotel.

Charlie said, 'I'm sorry to hear about your mum's illness.'

Benny looked away and muttered his thanks.

'I know you work in Glasgow in Mr Gauld's hotel but do you manage through to Dundee to visit your mum?'

Benny nodded. 'I try and come through on my days off.'

'Can you give me a list of your days off over,' Charlie gave the impression he was thinking, 'over the last two months?'

Benny said he couldn't.

'If I asked the hotel, they would be able to tell me.'

Benny shrugged. 'I also come through to run Mr Gauld about.'

'Does he not drive?'

'Yes he does but he likes me to do the driving between Glasgow or Edinburgh and Dundee. It's just because he is buying that new hotel here. He keeps his car at Albany House and he phones when he wants me.'

'So how do you get here?'

'I usually get the train but this week Pat and Alex had to come here to look at the hotel,' he explained. 'When it's up and running they will be managing it. Pat will be the receptionist and Alex will be the manager.'

Charlie then asked for Benny's thoughts on why Alex had jumped out of the window.

'He doesn't like the police.'

'Why's that?'

'His brother Bert, who is a waiter at the Briar, was in trouble years ago and the police picked up both brothers, even though Alex was innocent. He's disliked them ever since.'

'Does Bert have a wife or girlfriend?'

'Yes, a girlfriend. She's a housemaid at Hunter's Hotel.'

Charlie said he was impressed by all the family connections at both hotels. 'Mr Gauld must like you all.'

'I wouldn't say that. It's probably because we're all good workers and trying to leave our pasts behind.'

'Very commendable,' said Charlie. 'Did you know Laura Gauld and the housekeeper Barbara Metcalfe?'

Benny pulled his handkerchief from his pocket and wiped his nose. 'Sorry, I've got a bit of a cold. Yes I knew both the women but I haven't seen either of them since they left.'

Charlie felt elated. He knew this was a lie. He leant on the table, looked Benny squarely in the eye and said, 'The thing is, Benny, we've found your fingerprints on some of the jewellery and the box under your bed. How do you explain that?'

He shrugged. 'I thought they belonged to Mr Gauld?'

'But the briefcase has only his fingerprints on it. Why do you think that is?'

'Probably because it belongs to him.'

'It doesn't. It belongs to one of the victims of a robbery.'

'Well he must be the culprit. Stands to reason.'

'Then why do we not have the victim's prints on it as well?'

Benny said he didn't know.

'It looks like it was wiped clean and left in Mr Gauld's bedroom, like he says, and he picked it up.'

Benny shrugged. 'I don't know anything about a robbery or a briefcase. I just work for Mr Gauld.'

Charlie mentioned the other robberies. 'Do you know what I think, Benny? I think you're the one who broke into all these houses and that you assaulted Mr Bergmann and stole his keys. Those are very serious offences, and if he had died then that would have been murder. What do you say to that?'

Benny's face took on a stubborn look. 'I didn't have anything to do with any this.'

Charlie realised he wasn't going to get a confession so he decided to terminate the interview.

When he got back to his desk the photo he had requested from Glasgow had arrived. He asked his colleagues who had delivered it so quickly. 'It was a PC from Glasgow who's due to give evidence in the court today,' was the response.

Charlie went in search of Williamson, taking the photo which he had put in a folder with him. Finding Andrew, he asked the constable to drive to see Eric Bergmann. He was amused when the man shot off like an eager beaver and within five minutes they were on their way.

It was a better day, although the sun was reluctant to come out. However there were more families and pedestrians on the beach and the streets when they reached Monifieth.

Mrs French opened the door. 'Mr Bergmann's just finishing his meal,' she said.

Charlie said it wouldn't take a minute so she showed them into the dining room. She said she was sorry to interrupt but the police had wanted a quick word.

He said, 'That's all right, Mrs French.' He stood up. 'How can I help you?'

Charlie waited until the woman had left before taking the photo out and showing it to him.

'Do you recognise this man, Mr Bergmann?'

Eric stared at it. 'Yes I do, it's the man who sold me his grandmother's jewellery. Have you got the robbers?'

Charlie said he had.

65

Molly was in a quandary. She didn't know whether to go to see Grace or forget all about it. If she had spent another day at Mr Walls' solicitors office then she might have done but he had phoned the agency first thing in the morning to say Jane was coming in.

Jean had laughed when she told Molly this. 'He said what a pity she hadn't stayed off for a few weeks as he was most impressed by the woman who had stepped in for her. I told him you were the owner and he said you were a great help.'

Molly said that was nice to get a good recommendation.

As it turned out, it was just as well that Mr Walls hadn't needed her because there was an urgent job needing done, and so Molly set off.

She had so much to do this week. Alice wanted her to come with her to choose her wedding dress on Saturday and Molly wanted to visit her parents over the weekend. She wondered if Charlie had managed to wrap up his case and hoped he had as it meant they could maybe spend more time together. Then she thought again about the strange behaviour of Grace and what it all meant.

When she returned to the agency later, Jean said there had been a phone message from Anna Stevenson.

Molly wondered if she needed any more help with her book but when she called her back, Anna was annoyed. 'I've had someone from your agency asking questions about our time in India.'

Molly said she knew nothing about it but when Anna described the woman she realised it was Grace.

She said she would sort it out, which meant she would have to go and see Grace and find out what was behind all this strange behaviour.

66

Charlie was experiencing some unease about the case. Things weren't adding up in his mind and he read through all the statements again in case there was something he had missed. He knew he couldn't keep the suspects much longer without charging them with the robberies but a small, niggling worry had developed in his head and he couldn't shift it.

He marched out of the office and got hold of Williamson. 'I know we've just visited the Bergmann house but I want to go back and see Mrs French.'

Williamson kept his face straight but he was wondering if DS Johns maybe fancied the woman. She was certainly a good looker in his books, although a bit old for him personally.

As they drove along the coast road, Charlie said, 'Given the time, I'm guessing she'll be in her own house so we'll try there.'

As it turned out she was opening her front door as the car went past so he was in luck. She didn't look pleased when she opened the door but Charlie said he just wanted a few words with her.

Williamson got the impression she would have kept them standing on the pavement but Charlie said, 'Can we come in inside?'

When they entered the small lobby they nearly tripped over a couple of suitcases. She saw the two men look at them. 'I'm getting ready to leave,' she explained. 'I've finished working with Mr Bergmann and I'll be gone tomorrow morning.

Remaining quiet, they made their way to the living room. Once seated, Charlie said, 'I think you should stay until we charge Mr Gauld with the robberies.'

'No I don't want to hang around as he'll know who told you about him.'

Charlie leant forward and placed his hands on his knees. 'There's something I'm not sure about, Mrs French. I can see Benny Baxter committing all the break-ins because it has his stamp on them but I can't see him assaulting Mr Bergmann or stealing the paintings in the first robbery.'

She gave him a defiant stare. 'Well maybe it was Chuck who did the assaulting. He's certainly capable of it.'

Charlie said that was possible but Chuck Gauld's statement didn't tie up with hers. 'You told us that you divorced him and he left you without any means of support.'

She nodded. 'That's right.'

'Yet he says that he divorced you and you got a good settlement when you left.'

She tried to laugh but couldn't. 'And you believe him?'

Charlie said no, he didn't but he did believe Mr Nesbitt, the lawyer.

She said, 'He's as big a crook as Chuck is.'

'Yes well maybe but it will be easy to check it out so do you want to change your story?'

Once again she glared at him. 'No I don't. I've told you the truth and don't forget you wouldn't have known about him if I hadn't told you.'

Charlie said that wasn't true because he knew all about him long before she had volunteered the information.

She looked shocked and glanced at Williamson for confirmation but the young man sat with his notebook and didn't look at her.

'When you were running Hunter's Hotel before your divorce, did you know Bert Chandler and his girlfriend who worked at the Briar Hotel in Edinburgh?'

'Yes, I knew them slightly. It was Chuck who hired him, and Lorna, his girlfriend, was already working there when he started. She is a housemaid and he's a waiter.'

'And your friend Barbara Metcalfe was a housekeeper at Hunter's Hotel before she left?'

Laura nodded. 'Yes she was. She was also the relief housekeeper at the Briar. She worked between the two hotels.'

Charlie stood up and Williamson clambered to his feet.

'Well that's all for the moment, Mrs French.'

They were barely out of the house when the front door slammed on their backs.

When they got to the car, Charlie said to drive away as if they were leaving then find a parking place near at hand and try and keep her under surveillance.

'I'll catch a bus back to Dundee. Watch and see what she does then come back with the car. If you think she's leaving, then try and follow her and see where she goes.'

Charlie was in luck as a bus appeared at the stop the minute he reached it. It seemed to take ages before it reached the city but he was soon back in the station and sitting across from Benny Baxter.

Benny wanted a cigarette but because he didn't smoke, Charlie had to borrow a packet of cigarettes from one of the constables.

Once Benny had lit up and was blowing blue smoke towards the ceiling on the interview room, Charlie leant on the table as if about to have an amiable conversation with the man.

'I've got a problem, Benny,' he said. 'I've just been to see Mrs French and she's all packed up and ready to leave.'

Benny tried to keep his face straight but Charlie was gratified to see a flicker of alarm in his eyes. However, attempting to act composed, he blew more smoke from the side of his mouth and said, 'What's the problem with that?'

'The problem, Benny, is that you'll be going to jail for a long time over the attempted murder and robbery of Mr Bergmann, plus the other four crimes. You and Bert Chandler.'

Benny said, 'You've left out Mr Gauld.'

Charlie leaned nearer him. 'The thing is, Benny. I don't think he did any of it.'

Benny snorted. 'Well you're daft.'

'So what you're telling me is that Mr Gauld, yourself and Bert Chandler did all the robberies?'

'No, I didn't say that. They were all committed by Chuck Gauld. He's the one who did them all.'

'So if I get him in here, that's what I'll be able to tell him?'

Benny went white. 'I don't want to be the one who narks on him.'

Charlie looked at papers he had brought in with him. 'I've checked with the hotel and they've been able to give me a list of all your days off during the past two months and I've also checked with the hospital and they have a record of all your visits to your mother, and do you know what's very surprising, Benny? All the crimes were committed when you were here in Dundee and you already know we found some of the jewellery under your bed.'

Benny stayed silent and stubbed his cigarette out in the bashed tin ashtray that sat on the table. 'I'm not saying another word until I get my laywer here.'

Charlie said that could be arranged, then added, 'When your lawyer arrives, you'll be charged with aggravated burglary plus the other four robberies unless you tell us the truth.'

Benny said he had nothing else to say but Charlie was gratified to see a spark of fear in his eyes.

Charlie didn't think Benny had committed the Bergmann robbery but he was sure he had been the housebreaker in the other crimes. He knew once again he wouldn't get a confession so, calling the interview to another close, he went to see Inspector Alexander to tell him how things were progressing. Then he returned to his desk.

Two hours later, Williamson appeared at Charlie's side.

'Well, what happened?' Charlie was impatient.

'She stayed in the house for about an hour and then came out and got on her bicycle. I let her get a bit ahead and followed slowly. She stopped at the foot of the drive.'

'Where did she go?'

Williamson looked puzzled. 'She left her bike and got into Mr Davidson's van.'

Charlie nodded as if his hunch had been correct and went back to see Inspector Alexander.

'I'm going to bring John Davidson and Laura French in for questioning over the robbery at the Bergmann house,' he told. 'I firmly believe the proceeds of that robbery will be with the two of them.'

67

Molly couldn't concentrate on her work, too lost in thought, wondering what Grace was up to. She didn't want to confront the woman but she didn't like the idea of her impersonating her position at the agency with Anna Stevenson.

By six o'clock that evening Molly decided to go and see the occupant of the flat in the Nethergate. It was another wet, dismal evening which suited her as it meant she could approach the door with her raincoat hood up. That way if Grace happened to look out of the window then she wouldn't be able to see Molly's face. At least that was the idea, but as she walked along the Murraygate she suddenly felt like some kind of spy, a feeling she had grown used to recently since Bill Reid's death had catapulted her into this drama.

Her heart was beating as she stood on the small flight of steps that led to the door of the flats. Taking a deep breath she pushed the small bell that lay alongside Grace's name. After what seemed an eternity, the door opened and Molly stared in amazement, an emotion that was mirrored on the face of the person standing by the open door.

68

Charlie told the duty sergeant to put the suspects into separate interview rooms. Williamson was in one room with one of them while another young constable was in with the other.

He decided to see Davidson first. 'You're under arrest for the attempted murder and robbery of Mr Eric Bergmann of High Haven, Monifieth.'

John Davidson sneered at him. 'So you said but that's a lie, I've never robbed anyone or anything.'

Charlie looked at his notes. 'When we searched your hotel, jewellery and money was found in one of the cupboards. Can you explain why that is?'

Charlie could see the sweat starting to form on the man's forehead. 'I got them from her.'

'Her?'

'Aye, you know. That Mrs French.'

'Now why would someone who says she hates you give you expensive jewellery and money?'

'She didn't say she hated me the last time we were together.' He smirked.

'When was this?'

'I've been seeing her since Easter and the last time we were together was last week.'

'Do you understand the seriousness of the attempted murder charge and the thefts at the home and shop of Mr Bergmann? Mrs French is blaming you, said it was your idea.'

By now Davidson was sweating heavily. 'All right, I'll tell you the truth.'

★ ★ ★

When he was taken back to the cells, Charlie went to interview Laura French. 'We've found a large amount of money and a collection of gold sovereigns, plus all of the jewellery from the robbery of Mr Bergmann in one of your suitcases, plus jewellery from the four other robberies in Dundee. Not only that but we've recovered the stolen paintings from the back of John Davidson's van. What do you say about that?'

She glared in fury at him. 'I don't know anything about all that.'

'How did all the money and jewellery get inside your suitcase?'

She leant forward. 'I think Chuck Gauld put it there.'

'Chuck Gauld? But he's still being held here in the cells. How could he put it in?'

'Don't be stupid. He has friends all over the place. Some of them must have done it.'

'Mrs French, I have to tell you that we arrested Barbara Metcalfe on conspiracy to commit a crime. She also says you both had a meal at lunchtime and went to the matinee at the picture house – not at night when you said that was when you both went. Mr Bert Chandler has confessed to the Glasgow police for his part in the crimes and we have the whole story. Do you think Mr Gauld planned all that?'

She shrugged. 'I suppose so.'

'Well, Mr Gauld has been released with no charges, along with Alex Chandler and his wife. Pat Chandler told me that you were stealing from the hotel, along with your friend Barbara, even while you were married to your husband. He verified this and said it was the reason for the divorce.'

She stood up. Her face twisted in anger. Williamson looked disgusted and for a brief moment Charlie was amused. The young man had now seen his idol toppled from her perch.

'You've no proof I stole anything then or now.'

'Oh, I think you'll find I have.' He turned to the constable. 'Please take Mrs French back to her cell.'

Once again Charlie was amused by the expression on Williamson's face.

Benny Baxter was next. Charlie said that Mrs French was planning on getting away with over two thousand pounds and a small fortune in jewellery.

'She was planning on leaving you all with the charges of attempting to murder Mr Bergmann and the robberies. Do you still want to stay silent on these very serious charges or do you want to confess to the break-ins?' He stopped and offered Benny a cigarette he had scrounged from one of the constables. 'I'm afraid your lawyer hasn't arrived yet but if you want to wait till he does, then we will talk later.'

Benny's face was white. 'I didn't know anything about the robbery at the Bergmann house and shop. I admit I did the break-ins at the four houses but I handed over everything to her. Laura said we would be together afterwards and I believed her.' Tears ran down his face.

Charlie said, 'Well that's what some women are like, Benny. They string you along because it suits them.'

Barbara Metcalfe was a tougher nut to crack but when she was told of Chuck Gauld's and Alex and Pat Chandler's release, plus the fact that Benny Baxter and John Davidson had told them everything, she realised she had no option.

'Who did all the planning of the robberies?' asked Charlie.

Barbara said, 'It was Laura. We had a great scheme going for ages. When visitors came to the hotel we had their home addresses and in the course of the conversation they would tell us all about themselves. I used to see items of jewellery and money in the rooms so it was easy to keep a note and if they came back then the robbery would take place. The same thing happened at the Briar Hotel. Bert Chandler was a charmer and he chatted easily to the guests and got to know who had money and something worth robbing.' She added, 'But I knew nothing about the Bergmann robbery or assault. You must believe me.'

Charlie said, 'And what about Bert Chandler's girlfriend Lorna, was she part of the scheme?'

Barbara said no, she was too young and empty-headed to keep a secret.

'Why did you leave the hotel in Glasgow and come to work in Dundee?

Barbara clasped her hands together as if she was praying. 'Mr Gauld had offered me a job in his new hotel in Dundee when it was up and running, but to tell the truth, I was getting a little bit scared of Laura and I wanted out. I told her that on the afternoon we met.' She didn't mention how badly her friend had acted, calling her a coward and telling her to keep her mouth shut about everything. However, that had been before the attack on Mr Bergmann and she wasn't going to keep quiet any longer, even though it meant a jail sentence.

After Barbara Metcalfe was taken back to her cell, Charlie saw Laura French again. 'Well, Mrs French, everyone's confessed and your friend John Davidson says it was you who hit Mr Bergmann and stole all the jewellery.'

She sat silent for a moment then said, 'He's lying. It was him who did it.'

Charlie said it didn't matter who did what as they were both being charged for attempted murder in the pursuit of a robbery. She didn't like that at all and all the prettiness of his first meetings with her had vanished to be replaced by a hardened expression.

Later Charlie sat in the office with Inspector Alexander and gave him the whole story. 'Benny Baxter, Barbara Metcalfe and Bert Chandler are charged with robbery; John Davidson and Laura French for the attempted murder and robbery of Mr Bergmann. They are all blaming each other but my money's on Laura French. I thought she liked her employer but it seems she loved money more.'

The inspector asked him. 'What made you suspicious about the housekeeper?'

'It was when Mr Gauld's lawyer verified the details of her divorce settlement. I knew then she had lied and it made me wonder how many other lies she was telling me. Then when she came to tell me about her ex-husband's involvement in the robberies, it didn't ring true. I think she's been planning her revenge for some time and when he came to Dundee to buy the hotel, she saw her chance'

Inspector Alexander said, 'Congratulations, Charlie, on a case well done.'

Charlie was putting his jacket on when Williamson appeared at his desk. He looked tired. 'I can't imagine Mrs French being the culprit. She made such a wonderful Victoria sponge.'

Charlie laughed. 'Well there you go, my young lad. Never let your stomach override your head.'

69

At first, Molly thought she wasn't going to be invited into the building but the door was finally held open and she entered a long narrow hall with a staircase at the end. There was a mixture of cooking smells and she thought it was the typical student accommodation. She was shown into a first floor flat that had all the hallmarks of a furnished let. A battered table and chairs were situated by the window and a sagging sofa and chair sat beside the gas fire.

She sat on one of the dining chairs because she didn't want to disappear into the depths of the sofa. She glanced at the young man. A man that she had last seen on the footpath at the Soldier's Leap at Killicrankie.

He was a tall, very slender lad with a pale face and a thick mop of light brown hair. He was also extremely nervous. He looked embarrassed as she gave him an appraising look. 'I expect you're wondering about me?' he said.

Molly said she was. 'Where does Grace Carson fit in here?' she asked him.

He sat opposite her. 'Grace is my sister. I'm Michael Pritchard, the son of J.P. Pritchard.'

Molly said that Grace had told her she had arrived here with her mother from Cape Town. 'But that must be a lie because your mother was killed in India.'

Michael's face went pale and Molly was annoyed at herself for being so blunt. 'I didn't mean to come out with it like that, Michael. I'm sorry.'

'No I'm the one who's sorry that Grace lied to you but she

had to find out about the whereabouts of the managers after they left India.'

Molly held up her hand. 'I think you should start at the beginning.'

'I came to Edinburgh last year from Cape Town, along with my step-mother as I had enrolled in the university there. I'm studying medicine. In April this year one of my flatmates came to Dundee to visit a friend and he saw the newspaper cutting. He recognised my father because of the name and also saw a photograph of him in my room. I wrote to Phillip Thorne to get information on the men and he was so pleased that I had got in contact with him. He told me that Bill Reid was the only other person to write and he gave me his address.' He stopped. 'Do you mind if I get a glass of water? Would you like one?'

Molly shook her head. He left the room, and she could hear the tap running.

He came back and sat down. 'I wrote to Bill and he said he wanted to see me, asked if we could we meet up in Pitlochry, and I said I would travel there to see him. He said to meet him on the path at the Soldier's Leap and he would give me the list of names so that I could contact Dad's colleagues. Well, I went there but I got a bit lost and then I met you and saw that Bill was either dead or very badly injured. I thought he had missed his footing and hit his head on a rock. I'm afraid I panicked and didn't stay around. I'm sorry.'

Molly was puzzled. 'How did Grace know where to find me?'

Michael's face went bright red. 'That was me. I overheard you and your friend give your names and addresses to the ambulance men.'

'Was that why you searched Bill's pockets?'

'Yes it was. I know I should have said who I was and ask if you knew where they were but I don't like getting involved with the police.'

'Why does Grace want to get in touch with these men so desperately?'

'Oh she isn't desperate. We both want to try and understand

what happened to Mum and Naomi and we thought they could tell us.'

'Was that why she went through my files?'

Again there was that deep red flush. 'Oh you knew that, did you?' When Molly nodded he went on. 'She wanted to get the addresses as I said but then you wrote such good accounts of your visits to them that she was able to get the feel of the terrible situation that happened. I think she always felt guilty for not being in India when it happened. We both enjoyed reading about the past.'

'Where is Grace now?'

'She's gone to visit our step-mother. She lives in Berwick on Tweed. That was where she was born and although she has spent most of her life in South Africa that is where she wanted to retire to.'

'Is Grace planning on coming back to work at the agency?'

He said he didn't know. 'She's away for a week or two to see Lily, our step-mother, and I'll mention it to her when she gets back.'

Molly was far from happy about this but there was nothing she could do. She could hardly frog march Grace to the agency. 'I have to advertise the job as soon as possible so if she can let me know . . .'

He seemed keen to get rid of her and she was glad to be out in the street after the musty stuffiness of the flat. She stopped at the steps and looked up at the windows. Michael was standing at a small one to the left of the living room. It must be the scullery, she thought.

His face was a pale blur before he stepped back out of view.

As Molly walked away she had a sudden thought. Had Grace come back from somewhere and had Michael made a sign from the window to warn her?

Molly shook her head at her stupid thoughts. She was playing the game of spies again.

70

Alice and Maisie were waiting for Molly in the City Square. Alice had a small list of shops that she wanted to visit to buy her wedding dress. As it was to be a registrar's office ceremony, she wanted something simple and she hoped that both the women would be able to help her choose.

Molly arrived with a few minutes to spare. The first shop they tried was AC Little at the top of Crighton Street. Maisie, who admitted to not having any fashion sense, sensibly stayed out of the choosing.

There were a couple of dresses that Alice liked in Little's but next on the list was Paige's Fashions in the High Street. Alice spotted the one she liked as soon as she walked in the door. It was a sleeveless cream dress with a slim-fitting skirt in a heavy brocade. A small bolero with beads around the neck and front went with it and when Alice came out of the fitting room, both women said she looked beautiful in it.

Maisie breathed a sigh of relief. She had hoped that this shopping trip wouldn't take long but she was prepared for a long haul. Alice got a pair of high-heeled cream sandals and a handbag in the shoe shop next door then it was back to the milliner's shop in the Wellgate. Alice said she didn't really like hats but the owner produced a tiny cream hat that clung to the head like a claw and she was enchanted.

Molly said that she had bought a summer dress but hadn't worn it yet and she also had white sandals. Would that do for the bridesmaid's outfit?

Alice said it would and Molly said she was treating them to lunch at Franchi's Restaurant in the Overgate. Alice said she had never been in a restaurant in her life and Molly hoped that her marriage would be a very happy one with Sandy and the new baby. She knew the rotten life Alice had suffered at the hands of her first husband Victor and if anyone deserved happiness then it was her.

When they had ordered their meal, Alice said she was planning to have a show of wedding presents later in the week. 'People have been so kind to us. You should see what we've got, Molly. They almost fill the bedroom.'

Molly said she was delighted to hear it and she meant it.

Maisie said she had heard a rumour that Mary and Stan were also on the verge of getting married. Mary's parents had been against it because of her age but her mum and dad had been very impressed by his help and behaviour when her dad had broken his arm.

Molly had heard this from Mary but she hadn't said a word about it, as Mary wanted Alice's wedding not to be overshadowed by hers. Not that her ceremony would be any grander but one wedding a month was enough for the staff at the agency to cope with.

Alice said, 'I'll keep on working for another six weeks or so, but if you haven't got a replacement then I'll stay until you do, Molly.'

Molly said thank you. 'I'm hoping to place adverts in the papers next week. If Mary does get married then she'll be leaving for Hong Kong and I don't think Grace will be back. I'll have June until the end of August so that will be a few vacancies coming up. I hope I get results.'

Maisie said she would. 'Word gets around about jobs and we all know what a great place the agency is to work in. I mean, where else would you find Mrs Jankowski and her brown curtains?'

They all laughed and once again Molly was pleased to see how happy Alice was.

Later, when the two women caught the tramcar to go home, Molly hurried to Craig Pier to catch the Fifie. She had promised her parents she would visit them this afternoon and she also wanted to see Marigold. It had turned out a lovely sunny day and Molly enjoyed the refreshing breeze as the ferry set sail out onto the river.

Marigold was in her garden when Molly arrived and she called to her over the garden fence. Molly said she would pop in later to see her after she saw her parents. As she walked towards her parents' gate, she missed the worried look Marigold had on her face.

Her mother was in the kitchen when she opened the door and her father was out in the back garden mowing the grass. Molly felt like she was ten years old again and coming home from school instead of being grown up and having her own business.

Nancy saw her and hurried over. 'Great news, Molly. We've got our leaving date for Australia. We leave at the end of August.'

Molly felt a cold hand clutch her heart. She had been so happy this morning with Alice and Maisie and the wedding plans but now the reality of life was rearing up and slapping her in the face.

Nancy's face was beaming and Molly managed to smile. 'That's great news, Mum. What does Dad say about it?'

'Oh he's as thrilled as I am.'

Molly said she would go and see Marigold and when she appeared in the garden, her friend said, 'Well you've heard the news then?'

Molly said she had and when she looked up at the sky she noticed the sun had gone behind a big black cloud.

She spoke to the sun, 'That's both of us with our own black cloud.'

71

Charlie was in the car with Benny Baxter and PC Williamson. They were on their way to the infirmary as Mrs Baxter wasn't expected to live through the night. Benny sat with his head bowed and didn't say a word. Charlie didn't know what to say so he stayed silent as well. When they reached the Royal Infirmary, a porter took Benny and Charlie along to the ward while Williamson stayed in the car.

Mrs Baxter was in a small side room and when the two men entered, a nurse who was attending to her left the room. Charlie saw there was a window in the room and he said that he had to stay but would sit by the open door.

Benny sat beside his mother and took her hand. She opened her eyes and recognised him, 'Benny, you've managed to come and see me?'

'I've been here lots of times, Mum, but you've been sleeping,' he said quietly.

'I'm so glad you've found a good job and settled down and stopped all your bad behaviour.'

Benny nodded.

'Are you married yet to your girlfriend Laura? You must bring her here to see me.'

Benny said he would. 'I'll bring her in when you're feeling better, Mum.'

Mrs Baxter smiled and gave a big sigh before falling asleep again. The nurse came back in and said it was time for her medication and Benny stood up.

Charlie said Benny could wait longer if he wanted to but he shook his head. 'I don't think I want to see her die.'

Charlie rarely felt sorry for any of the criminals he arrested but he felt so sorry for Benny. He had overheard the remark about Laura and Benny had been a fool for listening to her promises of marriage.

Back in the car, Benny started to cry silently.

Charlie had finished writing his report and statement out and was once again back in Inspector Alexander's office.

'That's all the culprits charged and in remand, sir.'

Inspector Alexander looked at the report and nodded his head. 'You've done a first-class job, Charlie. Now, give me a quick overview of the case and I'll read the report later.'

'As I said before, it was the behaviour of Laura French. Whenever I visited to speak to Mr Bergmann she was there, teary-eyed but putting up a good front. Still, something about the way she acted didn't quite sit with me. Also, the first break-in didn't tie up with the other robberies and I thought at first it was someone else who had done it. Then when Mr Bergmann was robbed and assaulted I wondered what was behind it. When Chuck Gauld and Benny Baxter came on the scene, I thought they must be the ones behind it, given their criminal backgrounds and their presence in the area, but then things didn't seem to add up. The briefcase in Chuck Gauld's room with his fingerprints on it, for instance. I asked myself why a successful businessman with his background would leave incriminating evidence behind. Benny has confirmed that Mrs French came to Albany House one day when Chuck Gauld was playing golf. She had a rucksack on her back and asked if she could use the bathroom. Benny thinks that's when she put the briefcase in Chuck's room. Then there were the strange crying fits I mentioned. I thought that was because she was fond of her employer but then she let slip how onions always made her cry and I wondered if that was her trick to always have weepy eyes when I called.

'Mrs French, Barbara, Benny and Bert had been working this successful scam for ages, getting the staff at the hotel to chat away to the customers about their way of life and, of course, they had the names and addresses in the hotel register. It was the perfect set-up.

'Then Chuck Gauld came to Dundee to check out a potential hotel and have a golfing holiday and Mrs French knew she had the perfect scapegoat for her plan to rob the Bergmanns. She would kill two birds at once. She would have all the jewellery and money and he would get the blame.

'Benny and the other two said they didn't know anything about the Bergmann robberies and I believe them. Benny said Laura had asked him to point the finger at Chuck Gauld because he had been bad to her during the marriage and had left her penniless. Of course, being in love with her, he believed it.

'Then she pointed the finger at Davidson, saying he was spying on her and I had another hunch. She had needed help with the robbery because she knew she couldn't do the job on her own. That is why she made Davidson believe that she was interested in him. I don't know who hit Bergmann but they were both in the plan to drive the car and van away and then go on to rob the shop and house. If Mr Bergmann had regained conciousness during the trip to Dundee, she would have told him she was taking him to the hospital but of course he didn't.

'She got the safe and shop keys from his keyring and put the rest of the keys back in the car. Then when it went off the road, that was a bit of bad luck because she had originally planned to drive it back to Dundee and make it look as if the crime had been committed there. She was driving too fast when it skidded on the pavement and when the door jammed she had to make her exit through the window. But because the weather was wild and wet, no one saw her. John Davidson was right behind her in the van and he was able to help her. Then they had to get to the shop and commit the theft and it was the same at the house. She used to go around the town on her bike all the time, giving people the impression she couldn't drive a car, but of course she could.

'My witness on the night said he saw the car drive away, with a van quickly following, and I had noticed a van matching the description in the courtyard of the hotel. I chatted to Mrs

Davidson, who initially told me her husband had only been outside for a few minutes at ten-thirty that night but she later confessed that it was a lie. Her husband told her he was going to his late-night card game in Dundee, something he had been doing for a few weeks, but I suspect he was meeting up with Mrs French.'

Intrigued, the Inspector said, 'And was she going to share the proceeds with him?'

Charlie shook his head. 'She tried to say it was all his doing and she knew nothing about it. First it's Chuck Gauld then it's John Davidson. We found over two thousand pounds and most of the stolen jewellery in her suitcase, along with her passport and the gold sovereigns. It was these sovereigns that tied her to the robberies. My hunch is she was going to run and leave everyone else in the mire.'

'Why did she commit the first crime? Wasn't that a stupid thing to do to get the police involved?'

'I would have thought so,' said Charlie, 'but she was so eager to get her ex-husband jailed that her cool and careful planning of the great scam they all had going went out the window. It's like we always say: The cleverest criminal often makes the biggest mistakes.'

The Inspector shook Charlie's hand. 'Well done, Charlie. You've done an excellent job. Now let's leave the courts to hand out the justice.'

72

It was Alice and Sandy's wedding the next day and Molly was trying to get all the work finished at the agency as all the staff had been invited to the reception. She was busy typing out the week's invoices when Charlie came in. He looked tired.

'I won't be long, Charlie. Do you want to go upstairs and wait?'

He said no. 'I'll head back to my flat and get changed. I'll see you in an hour. Is that all right?'

Molly said it was.

He was as good as his word and was back by eight o'clock. They headed off to get something to eat but Molly was surprised when he ushered her into the reception foyer of the Royal Hotel.

Before she could say a word, he said, 'I thought we would have a special meal tonight to celebrate the end of my case.'

'Have you managed to prove they are all guilty?'

'Well I have done all I can and it'll now be the turn of the justice courts.'

They followed a waiter into the very posh dining room. It was three-quarters full with smartly dressed couples, Molly noticed as they were guided to a table by the window that overlooked the High Street. Friday night was a busy night on the street and crowds of people walked or hurried to the Green's Picture House or one of the dance halls.

Molly was quite overwhelmed by all the finery and the sparkling cutlery and glasses and the smart waiter hovering at her side, but once they had ordered she began to relax. However she couldn't help noticing the lines of tension around Charlie's eyes and knew this case had been a hard slog for him, but he had got there in the end.

The food was delicious and by the time they were sitting in the comfortable lounge with their drinks, Charlie with a beer while Molly had a Pimms No. 1, he also became more at ease. 'I seem to be a jinx at my job,' he said. 'This is the third time I've had a woman for the suspect in a serious crime. I'm beginning to wonder if women are taking over men's roles in the crime world.'

Molly knew he couldn't tell her much but she could understand his dismay at his perception of the fairer sex. She wanted to lighten the conversation and mentioned the wedding. 'I hope you can be there, Charlie. Even if it's just at the reception.'

He said he would. 'I might even manage to stand outside the registrar's office and throw some confetti on the bride and her attendant.'

She laughed. 'This will be my third time as a bridesmaid but never the bride.'

He looked at her and said, 'Then I'll have to do something about that.'

Molly felt herself go red, a deep flush that annoyed her. To cover her embarrassment she said, 'My parents are going to Australia at the end of August.'

'Oh, and how do you feel about that, Molly?'

She sat for moment. 'I feel abandoned but I know that's stupid.'

Charlie asked her if she wanted another drink but she said no. 'I have a busy day tomorrow so I better not risk a headache but it's been lovely tonight.'

Charlie paid the bill, trying not to look shocked when he saw the amount, and they walked back through the town. It was a beautiful night and was just beginning to get dark.

When they reached the agency, she asked him if he wanted a cup of coffee but he said he better not. 'I might take advantage of a three-times bridesmaid and elope with her.'

Molly was grateful the growing darkness hid her crimson face.

The next day was lovely and sunny. Even the breeze was warm. Molly padded around the flat in her dressing gown until it was time to get dressed. She had ordered a taxi to take her to the City

Square where she planned to meet up with the bridal couple and the best man, who was Sandy's pal at the shipyard. She had bought a small hat to go with her dress and took the spray of carnations from the vase. She decided not to pin them on her dress but instead sellotaped them to her handbag.

The taxi was on time and it only took a few minutes to reach the Square. She was first to arrive but within a few minutes Maisie and Sandy's parents, along with the groom and the best man, were waiting in the sunshine.

Because it was a lovely day, the City Square was busy with people and quite a few spectators had gathered to see the bride. All of the staff were there and Irene held a large cardboard tube of confetti in her hand which she handed over to Billy with a whispered word.

When Alice arrived, Molly couldn't get over the transformation. She recalled the plain-looking, downtrodden woman who had started at the agency a year ago and now here she was, looking beautiful in her cream dress.

The ceremony was the same as it had been for Edna and John's wedding but once again Molly felt choked up with emotion.

When the couple were pronounced man and wife, they all trooped outside where Sandy had hired a photographer. Molly felt self-conscious as the man asked them to pose in various formations but it was Alice and Sandy's special day so she gladly moved around and smiled.

When the photos were finished, Billy gleefully emptied his box of confetti over the happy pair and then, to Molly's surprise, Charlie showed up and did the same thing, with Molly getting the lion's share.

'I told you I'd come with the confetti,' he said. 'I'd better get back to work but I'll see you tonight.'

Maisie laughed. 'That's what I like about your man, Molly. Now you see him, now you don't.'

Molly had to laugh at Maisie's insight.

St Mary's Hall, which lay up a pend on the Hilltown, was all set out for the reception with the catering staff from Andrew G.

Kidd's bakery business all waiting on the guests. Long trestle tables with white cloths were set out around the floor. Molly was at the top table along with the bridal party. Sandy's parents, Mr and Mrs Morgan, were sitting beside the groom but because Alice had no parents, Molly and the best man, Harry, were together.

All the staff at the agency with their partners were there except Deanna who that night would be on stage at the theatre. There were also a few of Sandy's aunts and uncles, plus their children and Billy.

Sitting all together were some of Sandy's workmates and young apprentices from the Caledon shipyard. They were a cheery lot and greeted Sandy's speech opening of 'On behalf of my wife and I' with whistles and cheers.

It had been a long time since Molly had been in such a happy and cheery crowd and she was enjoying every minute of it. It had been a hectic couple of weeks, with everyone taking on extra work to cover for Grace.

Then there had been the hilarious evening at Alice's house when she had the show of presents and Molly still had to laugh at all fun they had had. Especially with Maisie who had entertained them with her song 'Auld Maid in the Garret'. Molly smiled when she recalled the event.

At five o'clock, a three-piece band trooped in and set out their instruments. At this point Molly was sitting with Mary and Stan.

'It'll be our wedding next,' said Stan. He turned to Molly. 'Mary's mum and dad have said we can get married before I go to Hong Kong. Isn't that great, Mary?'

Mary said it was. 'The banns are being read next Sunday for the first time and Mum and Dad are organising everything. Well, I have to say it's Mum because Dad still has his plaster on his arm.' Her face grew serious. 'It means I'll be leaving the agency, Molly, and I know you're really short-handed with Grace leaving. Still, it won't be for a few weeks yet but I'm so sorry.'

Molly said not to worry. 'It's been a pleasure to have you for the past two years, Mary, but now you both have your future to think about.'

Then the band began with a loud drumbeat and Alice and Sandy went on the floor for their first dance as a married couple, followed by Harry and Molly. When the dance finished, Molly was pleased to see Charlie had arrived, carrying a large wrapped wedding gift. 'It's a picture, I hope they'll like it,' he said.

Molly laughed. 'I thought it was a table.'

He gave her look, which said, 'That isn't funny.'

The noise and fun grew as the evening went on. Then the band began to play 'Rock Around the Clock' and a couple of young men took June and Maggie on the floor and everyone clapped as they jived to the music.

Charlie said when the dance ended, 'June and Maggie are enjoying themselves with that young crowd.' No sooner were the words out of his mouth than Maggie came over and asked him to dance. 'It's a lady's choice,' she said, which was untrue but he gallantly got up. It was another rock tune and Molly was sore laughing at his antics. He was a super detective, she thought, but would never put Gene Kelly out of a job.

When he sat down she was still laughing. He gave her a pained look. 'What?'

Molly looked serious. 'Nothing.' Then she burst out laughing again.

Alice came over. 'Sandy and I will be leaving in a few minutes, Molly. Thanks for everything.' She leaned over to whisper to her. 'We're going to Oban for our honeymoon but don't say a word.'

Molly smiled. 'I've had a wonderful day, Alice, and I hope you both have a long and happy life.'

Alice went over to speak to the Morgans. 'Thank you, Mr and Mrs Morgan, for this lovely reception. It's been a magical day.'

Mrs Morgan said, 'It's not Mr and Mrs Morgan, Alice, it's Mum and Dad.'

Alice almost burst into tears. It had been a long time since her own mother has died. 'Thank you for that, Mum and Dad.'

After the newlyweds left, the band played a few more dances

then it was time to go home. The young people all gave a groan and said, 'Play some more,' but the small man who was the leader of the trio said that the hall had to close soon but wished everyone goodnight.

There was a great deal of putting on of coats and picking up handbags and the crowd all dispersed into the night with noisy chatter and laughter. Molly was amused to see Maggie and June making arrangements to meet two of the young apprentices the following Saturday to go to the pictures. *Oh to be young and carefree again*, she thought.

Charlie walked with her to the agency and they bid each other goodnight at the door. Charlie said he was working tomorrow but he would come and see her in the evening.

As she watched him walk in the direction of the tram stop in Victoria Road, she almost called him back. Molly had enjoyed her day so much that it would have been lovely to have Charlie's company for a bit longer, and Charlie had looked like he would have loved to stay . . . but in the end she decided to let him be.

As she climbed the stair she realised she hadn't given a thought to her parents' imminent departure all day but now she was in her room she suddenly felt so alone.

73

It was the phone ringing that woke her. She had been in a deep sleep and looked at the alarm clock. It was almost ten o'clock and a sliver of sunlight hit the wall beside the bed. Molly had never stayed in bed so late as this before and hurried through to take the call. To start with she couldn't understand what the person was saying because they were agitated and talking so quickly.

She asked who was calling and said, 'Can you slow down please?'

The caller hesitated then said quite clearly, 'Miss McQueen, it's Michael Pritchard. Is Grace with you?'

Molly was confused. 'Grace? No she's not. Is she coming here?'

'Look, it's something serious, can I come and see you?'

Molly said yes and told him she was at the agency. Dressing quickly and making a cup of tea, she wondered what this was all about. Why would Grace be coming to see her, especially as she had left with no prior warning?

Twenty minutes later Molly heard what sounded like a motorbike roaring through the quiet of a Sunday morning. This was followed by a loud knock at the agency door. Michael Pritchard stood on the doorstep and he looked terrible. A silver and blue motorcycle was parked at the kerb.

Molly expected people from the houses opposite to be peering through their curtains but the street was quiet and devoid of pedestrians. She asked him to come in, saying, 'Do you want anything to drink?'

He shook his head but didn't sit down.

Molly asked him why he thought Grace would be here.

'She said she was coming to see you because she wanted some advice but then I stupidly let something slip out and I think she's gone to tackle him.'

Molly didn't understand a thing. 'Tackle who?'

He finally sat down. 'It's a long story and you know some of it but I didn't tell you the whole truth when you came to see Grace.' He gazed down at his hands, which were in two tight fists in his lap. 'The day Mum and Naomi were killed it was assumed I wasn't in the house, but I was. I was in my bedroom reading *The Boy's Own Adventure Stories*. Then I heard angry voices coming from the lounge. It was Mum and Naomi and a man. I could only see a small part of him because he was behind the door but when Mum saw me she shouted for me to run. Of course I didn't but she shouted at me again and that's when I saw the man's arm and the gun. I still didn't know what to do when Naomi leapt forward and tried to take the gun away. I stood there as she was shot and then Mum launched herself at him and he shot her.'

Michael stopped as he began to cry. His voice was trembling as he continued, 'My first thought was to run to see how Mum and my sister were but I remembered her telling me to run so I did. I ran for ages until I collapsed at the river and was rescued by some Indian women. Afterwards, I couldn't remember anything but slowly over the years with the help of my step-mum Lily I've managed to remember most of it and come to terms with the guilt I've felt all these years over leaving Mum and Naomi to die.'

Molly said, 'But you were only a ten-year-old boy. If you hadn't ran away then you would have been shot as well.'

'I know, that's what I tell myself in the middle of the night when I wake up with a nightmare.'

'So why are you so worried about Grace?'

'It's what I suddenly remembered a few months ago. To begin with, I thought it was part of one of the nightmares but the vision was so clear after all these years that I'm sure it must be real.'

Molly asked him what it was.

He hesitated again then said. 'When the man raised his hand to shoot Naomi I saw something.'

'What?'

He told her and Molly felt faint. 'Oh my God, Michael. And you think Grace has gone to tackle him?'

He nodded. 'When I let slip about it last night, Grace went to read over your reports again and she found what she was looking for.'

'He's a killer, Michael. We have to let the police know and they will arrest him.'

'They maybe won't act on someone's hunch. I mean, we don't know if she's gone there.' He didn't sound too hopeful. 'I can't stand by and see my only remaining sister killed so I have to go and see him.'

Molly was torn between phoning Charlie and not letting this vulnerable lad away on his own.

'Can I ride on the pillion of your bike?' she asked.

He said she could so they hurried downstairs and soon they were travelling through the streets, which were now busy with people. Heads turned as they rode along but Molly was so worried that she barely noticed them.

Before reaching the house, she shouted at Michael to stop. She had seen the phone box and she wanted to call Charlie. This was too dangerous for the two of them. Michael didn't want to stop but she said they couldn't drive up to the man's house and alarm him. If Grace was there then he might do something stupid.

She hurried into the phone box and put her pennies in the box. When she heard the voice at the other end she pushed button A. 'Can I speak to DS Johns please, it's urgent.'

The voice asked her what it was she was calling about. 'Look, I don't have time to explain as someone's life could be in danger, please put me through to DS Johns.'

After what seemed like a lifetime, a voice answered. 'PC Williamson, can I help you?'

Molly said a small prayer of relief. 'It's Molly McQueen, Constable Williamson, I need to speak to DS Johns urgently.'

'He's out of the office at the moment but I'll give him a message.'

Molly told him the situation and gave the address. 'He's dangerous and might be armed, we're not sure.'

When she came out of the phone box, Molly said to park the bike in a small car park across the road. It was only about fifty yards from the house. They walked up the road together.

The house looked just as it did on her last visit with its neat garden overlooking the sea. She stopped Michael before they reached it.

'We can't just walk up to the front door and knock.'

'Well what do you suggest?

The trouble was Molly couldn't think of a thing. There was no way they could reach the door without being seen. Then they heard the scream.

Michael sprinted up to the door and knocked loudly. Molly tried to stop him but he was too quick. Seeing her chance, she hurried to the back door and it was unlocked. She was sure she would bump into Bunty or Douglas's brother but there was no sign of them. She could hear the shouting going on in the hall as Michael pushed his way into the lounge.

Molly was in the kitchen and the door was open. She quietly made her way around the formica-topped table and edged nearer the hall. She heard Grace's voice. She was practically screaming.

'You killed my mother and sister. Look Michael, he's wearing mum's ring.'

Michael sounded angry. 'Take it off, Doug King.'

Molly stopped dead. *Doug King, of course!* She gave her head a slap and wondered if she was losing her brain cells. Bill hadn't said 'digging' but a shortened version of this man's name.

He was talking now. 'I didn't mean to kill them, it was an accident. I loved your mother but she wouldn't leave your father and go away with me. I thought if I produced the gun she would. Then Naomi lurched at me and before I knew what I was doing, the gun had gone off.'

Michael said, 'But you didn't have the guts to own up, did you? You left us all in limbo.'

Douglas stayed silent.

Grace said, 'You let Michael suffer years of torment and guilt, you pathetic little man.'

Douglas's voice took on a hard angry tone. 'You watch your lip, Grace. You were always an aggressive child. Now we are going to go outside into the car and if either of you make a noise then I'll have to use this gun.

Molly gasped. *Where was Charlie?* she thought desperately. She looked around the hall but it was a typical lobby with a row of hooks for the coats and a small hall table. She tried to think about her next move but as she took a step forward, she hit the side of the table and it made a noise.

Douglas's voice shouted out, 'Whoever you are you better get in here.'

Molly stayed silent, she was barely breathing. She quietly edged her way back to the kitchen and stood behind the open door. Grace shouted, 'Watch out!'

Molly could hear the distant sound of sirens and hoped that the police would get here soon. She saw the door move slightly and then he came into view. He was walking behind Grace and he had the gun pointed at her back.

'You had better come out here where I can see you,' he said, glancing around the kitchen.

Molly couldn't decide what to do next but before she could think of something, Doug pulled the door closed and when he saw her, he told her to join Grace.

Molly moved towards him as instructed but just before reaching Grace's side, she tripped over a chair, almost falling on the floor in front of them. Grace screamed.

Suddenly, Michael came running in and brought him down with a rugby tackle. The gun shot across the tiled floor. Douglas managed to get to his feet but the sirens were louder now. For a second or two he stood transfixed but then rushed out the door. He ran across the road and disappeared over the sand dunes towards the sea.

At that moment Bunty and her husband arrived back and they stood with looks of shock on their faces. Then the police arrived in various squad cars and Molly had to sit down. Her legs felt like jelly. Beside her Grace was crying and Michael had hurt his leg in the tackle.

Charlie came in with a dozen policemen and, finding her, he glared at Molly. Everyone began to talk at once, with Bunty's voice the loudest.

'What's the meaning of this?' she asked the nearest policeman. 'We go off to church and come back to this. Are these people burglars?'

Charlie said they were all being taken to the police station. Molly, Grace and Michael were put in the car driven by PC Williamson while Bunty and her husband were placed in another one.

Neighbours and people passing by were all standing in the street wondering what the commotion was but the police were telling them to get back in their houses and moving the other pedestrians away from the area where Douglas was last seen. Soon more cars arrived and a stream of police spread out across the road in search of him. Molly had managed to tell Charlie the gun was lying on the floor so they knew he was no longer armed.

As the car drew away toward the station, Molly was conscious that the young constable was looking at her in his mirror. She drew her coat tightly around her and wished she could disappear into some large hole.

Grace and Michael were quiet but every now and again Grace wiped her eyes with the back of her hand. Back in the station they were put into a bleak room with a chipped table and grey walls. Molly had no idea where Bunty and her husband were. Williamson brought them large cups of tea then went to stand beside the door.

Much later Charlie arrived. He looked tired and grim. He asked Grace to accompany him to another room and she got up reluctantly and glanced at her brother. Another detective came for Michael and Molly was left alone with her thoughts. She could see it all now. Douglas Kingsley had been the one who had met up with Bill Reid, but how had Bill known he was the killer?

Did Douglas push him from the path or had that also been an accident?

Then Charlie entered the room and he didn't look pleased. 'Are you some kind of Kamikaze person? Why do you always seem to be in danger? Is running your agency not enough for you, Molly, that you have to be involved in some sort of mystery?'

Molly stayed silent. She had nothing left to say in her defence. She didn't know why she was always getting into these dangerous waters but she reckoned they weren't really her fault.

Charlie said, 'We've got the story from the Pritchards and we'll get Kingsley's version when we catch him. I'll get Williamson to run you all home.'

He marched out of the room and Molly thought that was the end of their beautiful friendship.

Before Grace and Michael left the car, she said, 'Can we come round to see you tomorrow night, Molly?'

Molly, who couldn't have cared if the devil himself had planned a visit, said, 'All right, Grace.'

74

Charlie finally sat down to write out his report at seven o'clock. The witnesses had all written out their statements and a search party was still out looking for Douglas Kingsley. The team that had initially been drafted in for the emergency had gone home and it was now the case of finding the missing man. Thinking back on the day's events, Charlie still couldn't believe how close Molly had come to either being killed or badly injured.

By half-past eight he was ready to go home. He stood up and stretched his back. He still felt some sore muscles after the dancing last night and he couldn't believe it had been less than twenty-four hours since they both had such a super evening. Now, with this incident, it meant more man-hours and more paperwork.

He put on his jacket as it had turned cooler and was almost out the door when the search team phoned in. Douglas Kingsley had been found dead on the beach. He had been seen entering the sea this afternoon and had apparently drowned. However the post mortem would discover how he had died.

Charlie was ready for his bed but first he wanted to drop in and see Molly. He still felt guilty for shouting at her this afternoon. As he reached the agency he wondered if she was in bed or if she had gone to stay with her parents. He saw the light on in the flat and rang the bell. After a minute or so Molly came to the door and said, 'Who's there?'

'It's Charlie,' he answered.

She opened the door a fraction and peered out. She looked as if she had been crying. 'If you don't mind, Charlie, I'm not in the mood for being questioned again.' She closed the door firmly and after a few minutes the light went out.

He went to ring the bell again but decided against it. He hadn't been going to question her again but merely wanted to be there for her, though he realised she could be prickly when it came to her independence.

He was walking away when the window opened. 'Do you want to come up?' Molly called.

He hurried back and the door was open. Without a thought, he gathered her in his arms and held her while she cried softly.

'I can still see the gun in his hand and I'm afraid to be here alone.' Molly's voice was weak and trembled.

He half-carried her upstairs and made her go to bed. 'I'll stay here tonight, so don't worry about being on your own.'

She fell asleep almost at once and he scrutinised the studio couch. It looked quite comfy so he settled down and although it took longer to go to sleep, he slept well all night.

When she woke up in the morning, Molly seemed to be embarrassed by her need for companionship but Charlie said he would get away home to have a wash and get changed for his shift.

Before he left she said, 'Grace and Michael want to come here tonight. I'd like you to be here if you can make it.'

He said he would, then added, 'I'd better clear off before your staff arrives. You won't want them to gossip.'

'Quite honestly, I don't care,' she said, and she meant it.

Molly had to make a big effort to get going but once she was downstairs she managed to get all the assignments out. Fortunately she didn't have to go out herself until the afternoon so she decided to go see her parents. She caught the Fifie with a few minutes to spare and the sharp wind from the river helped her shake off the sleepiness.

Her mother had just finished making breakfast when she arrived and although she was surprised to see her, she didn't comment on it. Instead she placed a plate of bacon and eggs in front of her and Molly realised then how hungry she was. She hadn't eaten since yesterday morning, just after Michael's call.

Molly didn't want to alarm her mother with the story. She knew they were worried about going to Australia without her and this would be a huge worry for them both.

After exchanging light conversation, Molly excused herself from the table. 'I'll pop in and see Marigold.'

Marigold was out in the garden, Sabby the cat sitting on a basket chair. When she saw her friend Marigold took one look at Molly's face and asked her what was wrong. Without need for further questioning, Molly told her the entire story.

'So that's why Grace took your reports. How did she know it was this Douglas Kingsley who was the killer?'

'It was the snake tattoo on his upper arm. Michael remembered it a few months ago but only told his sister on Saturday night. They are coming around tonight and I'll get all the facts. I was hoping to give the reports to Betty and wondered if you wanted to come with me to Pitlochry this Saturday.'

Marigold said she would be delighted. 'I'll book us into the Bay Guest House but I don't suppose you'll want to go to the theatre. Not after all this drama.'

Molly said to go ahead and book two seats to see Deanna again. Changing the topic, she said, 'It won't be long now till Mum and Dad leave.'

Marigold said to remember they weren't selling the house. 'Maybe they are keeping it in case they don't like all that sunshine and when the grandchildren start growing up, who knows, they might want to come back.'

Molly smiled. 'Yes, who knows.' But she wasn't convinced.

75

The whole police station was abuzz with the events of the previous day. And first thing that morning, Charlie spent over an hour with Inspector Alexander, telling him the whole sorry saga.

'It all began in 1947 in India,' he said, and went on to fill him in on the course of events leading to yesterday.

When he came to the part about Bill Reid's death, the Inspector stopped him and said, 'I believe your friend Molly McQueen was one of the witnesses to it all?'

Charlie said she was. 'And on the request of his sister, she was asked to find out about the reunion that never happened. Mr Reid's sister and Miss McQueen had no idea it would turn out like this.'

The Inspector nodded. It had been a busy few weeks with the jewel robberies, and now this.

'You've done another great job here, Johns.'

Charlie wanted Andrew Williamson's contribution acknowledged as well. 'He helped a great deal in the robbery enquiries and also this case, sir, and I think he would make a good addition to the team.'

The Inspector nodded. 'I was just thinking that myself.'

After Charlie left, Inspector Alexander pulled out the folders with all the evidence of the robberies and the death of Douglas Kingsley.

Yes, he thought. *DS Johns and his team have done a wonderful job.* It was always the gut instinct of a good detective that solved the crimes and he was lucky to have people like that working for the police force.

He put the folders away and lit a cigarette. He knew he should really give up the habit but it was difficult. Still, maybe he would stop smoking next week when things had died down considerably.

Grace and Michael arrived at the flat at seven-thirty. They had a woman with them.

'This is Lily, our step-mother,' Michael said.

Lily was a petite woman with short white hair and deep blue eyes that seemed to reach into one's soul. She smiled and shook Molly's hand. 'It's good to meet you at last,' she said.

Molly was surprised to hear she still had her Scottish accent after years of living in South Africa. When she commented on this, Lily said she had only been in Africa for fifteen years. 'I applied for a job as a psychiatrist in Cape Town in 1940 but now that I've retired I wanted to come back home.'

This amused Molly because she knew of several people who had emigrated to the USA and had developed American accents overnight.

Grace said, 'I'm sorry I lied to you, Molly, but some of it is the truth. I came over with Lily and Michael to get him started at the university. I don't have a fiancé in Cape Town but I do have a husband, James Carson. He's in the South African navy.'

Michael explained, 'Our father and grandparents went to South Africa after Dad came back from India. He got a job there and said it was to be a new beginning for us all. Personally I was a mess. I couldn't remember anything about the incident but then I would get flashbacks and images would appear. Dad got me to see Lily who had experience dealing with people who had witnessed traumatic events and slowly over the years I got better.'

Lily laughed. 'Then J.P. married me and I always said it was to save him my fee.'

Michael and Grace shook their heads. 'No, Lily, you helped – Dad as well – to recover from the awful deaths of Mum and Naomi.' Grace brought out a tiny hankie and wiped her eyes. 'We were getting on just fine when Michael's flatmate came here to Dundee and brought back the cutting from the paper. Of course he wrote to Phillip Thorne and was put onto Bill.'

There was something puzzling Molly. 'Why did Bill contact Douglas? All the men knew was that the killers were bandits.'

Michael blushed, his thin face turning red. 'It was me. I told Bill about the snake tattoo and he said he knew someone who had one. It wasn't common knowledge because he always kept it hidden under his shirtsleeves. Bill told me to come and see him and the rest you know.'

'If it was hidden under his sleeves, how did you manage to see it, Michael?'

Michael shook his head. 'I don't know. I don't think he had his shirt on that afternoon and that's why I was able to see his arm. It had been a terrible day of rain. It was the monsoon season, that was why I was in my bedroom because I couldn't go outside and I think it was the same for Naomi. Before you came in the house, Douglas did say he thought Mum was alone that day. I always called him Doug King. It was my own special nickname for him.'

Grace said bitterly, 'He was wearing Mum's ruby ring and I don't think we'll ever get it back.'

Lily said the police would hand it over when the case was closed.

Molly suddenly remembered. 'I think he was wearing it on the day I visited him. I surprised him in the garden and he put his hankie over his hand saying he had cut himself. He came back through with a large plaster on his hand.'

Suddenly, the memory of that last visit became clear. Molly wondered if she had been in any danger then. But thankfully none of that mattered as the worst was over and she had survived. Along with Grace and Michael who, sadly, had to live with the deaths of their mother and sister Naomi.

They were sitting on the couch with Lily and Molly hoped their lives would be a bit happier now that the truth had come out.

Molly asked them what their plans for the future were.

Grace said she was going back to Cape Town but added, 'I'll come back if the police need me to give evidence at any inquiry.'

Michael said he would be living in Edinburgh and doing his

medical degree and Lily would be back in Berwick where she grew up.

They all said goodbye but Lily said as she walked down the stairs to the street, 'It may not seem like it just now but I think Grace and Michael are pleased to have seen justice done over these terrible killings. The police told us before we left that Douglas is dead. He seemingly swam out to sea and drowned. Perhaps he was glad to finish it like this, who knows.'

Molly wasn't so sure but then she remembered the cheery man she had met. He hadn't looked like a killer, she thought, but then she wondered out loud, 'What does a killer look like?'

An hour after they had left, Charlie arrived. Molly repeated the story again. 'I have to go to see Betty Holden this Saturday and give her an update then it's over, thank goodness.'

Charlie said it had been a strange case, and although it had taken years to solve, the perpetrator had been caught.

'What I can't figure out, though,' said Molly, 'is this. Douglas said he was with his brother and his sister-in-law at a family wedding then they went off for a holiday. This was at the same time as Bill's death.'

Charlie said no. 'Bunty told us that they had all gone to the wedding but it was held on a Saturday, the day before Bill died. Douglas made an excuse that he had to visit an old friend on the Sunday but that he would be back that night. Then they all left for the holiday.'

'How are Bunty and her husband?' Molly remembered the warm welcome she had received on her visit and how much she had liked Douglas.

Charlie said they were both very shocked and that they might have to move. The entire street had seen what had happened and Bunty said she could never hold her head up to their neighbours again.

Molly was shocked. 'Surely people will understand it wasn't their fault.'

'That's what I told them but I don't think they believed me.'

Charlie looked really worn out and Molly felt guilty at bringing all this trouble to his door, just like the previous times when he had saved her from disaster.

She stood up. 'I've got some beer in the cupboard. Put your feet up and I'll bring you a glass.'

76

Molly picked Marigold up in the car. She had asked to borrow it for the weekend as it would save time travelling by train. She had written a letter to Deanna to tell her they were coming to see her in the play *Arms and the Man*. It was misty when they set out but by the time they reached Pitlochry the sun was shining. Bess Smith was pleased to see them and she had their rooms ready. Molly said she wanted to see Betty right away to give her the news. Marigold asked her if she wanted her to come along for support and Molly said yes.

Betty was waiting for them with the usual tea, scones and shortbread. Molly's throat felt dry so she didn't want to eat anything. When they were sitting in the cosy living room, Betty said, 'I got your letter, Molly.'

Molly had brought with her all the reports, newly updated, and she handed them over. 'There's a good chance that Douglas was responsible for Bill's death but I've no evidence of it. Whether he fell by accident or as a result of being pushed, I can't say.'

She went on to tell Betty the story and the tragic end. Betty sat in silence all through this but when Molly stopped talking, she said, 'Bill was so pleased to see the cutting and get in touch with Phillip Thorne again. He said that it would be good to meet up with all his old friends again. He never thought it would kill him.'

Molly and Marigold didn't know what to say. As they were leaving, Betty said thanks for getting to the bottom of the mystery and at least Grace and Michael Pritchard were safe. 'I know Bill and Annie were very fond of the Pritchard children when they were growing up but it's a great pity he didn't take his suspicions to the police and they might have got involved instead of him.'

Molly said she would keep in touch and both she and Marigold stood to leave.

Once outside, Marigold suggested another trip to see the Salmon Ladder at the dam. They retraced their steps from the previous fateful walk months ago, over the imposing concrete walkway and down the stairs to the pools. Salmon were jumping that day and Molly had the foolish notion that they were trying to escape from the river and go somewhere else. She felt the same way. She would have loved to escape from all the worries and tragedy of the past week but like the salmon she was tied to home and work.

After their walk the women had a high tea in the Tower Restaurant before going to the theatre, and by the time they were seated in the auditorium, she began to relax. The play by George Bernard Shaw was a bit over Molly's head but she enjoyed it, especially seeing Deanna again.

At the end of the performance, Deanna appeared and said she would see them in the morning so they left the theatre and walked down the hill to the guest house. In spite of having a head full of thoughts spinning around in her brain, Molly slept really well and both she and Marigold enjoyed a hearty breakfast.

Deanna appeared at ten-thirty on her own. Marigold asked her where Brian was.

'He has to work this morning but we're going out this afternoon.'

Molly gave her all the news of the agency and Deanna was full of all that had happened to her over the summer. 'I'm going on to the Rep in Dundee for the winter and the theatre here has asked me back for next year's season.'

Marigold and Molly said that was wonderful and it was no more than she deserved.

'I've had an invitation to Mary and Stan's wedding and I'm hoping I can manage it. I was sorry to miss Alice's wedding but I was working that day,' she said.

Molly said that was another one leaving and she was interviewing some more candidates for both the secretarial and domestic work during the coming week. Although she didn't voice it, she also thought the next few weeks would see her parents leave for Australia. It was something she didn't want to dwell on. However, she was glad the Pritchards had seen some closure in their lives and she hoped they would try and put it all behind them, if that was possible. There would always be mourning for a well-loved mother and sister, especially by Michael who had witnessed it, but with luck and time, the memories would grow a bit dimmer and they would remember their family with love and joy.

The journey back to Dundee was uneventful and Molly knew she had another busy week coming up. There were also the interviews to get through but thankfully she had four people who were interested in joining the agency.

77

On Monday morning Charlie went to see Mr Bergmann. The hotel at the foot of the drive was closed, with a 'For Sale' sign at its entrance and he wondered where Mrs Davidson and her daughter Janet had gone. They hadn't hung around for long and this reinforced Charlie's idea that the marriage hadn't been very happy.

Eric Bergmann opened the door and he looked much older since Charlie's last visit. He still walked straight and tall but his face held a grey tinge that, combined with his white hair, made him look ill.

Mrs Bergmann was sitting in a chair in the lounge, reading the morning paper. She stood up when Charlie entered the room and he saw that she was an imposing figure. Almost as tall as her husband, she was dressed in a fashionable navy and white woollen dress and her hair, which was as white as her husband's, was set in a fashionable style. She was an extremely handsome woman.

When she shook his hand, she said, 'I'm Magda Bergmann.' Charlie saw the three expensive-looking rings on her wedding finger and he was pleased that these were things that Laura French and her cohort hadn't been able to steal.

Her voice was low and deep when she asked Charlie to sit down. 'I hear you have arrested the thieves and Eric's jewellery has all been recovered.'

Charlie said it had but it was still needed as evidence but would be returned after the trial.

'That will be too late for us,' she said. 'But never mind, we still have each other. That's the important thing.' She sat beside her husband and clasped his hand.

He gave her a grateful look but still seemed sad. 'I couldn't believe it was Mrs French who stole everything from us. I thought she enjoyed working here, and although I say it myself, we were good to her.'

Magda Bergmann said, 'I did warn you about her, didn't I, Eric?'

He nodded dumbly.

She turned to Charlie. 'I never liked her one little bit. There was something not quite right about her and her story. It's as you say, there was something fishy about her references.' She gave a deep sigh. 'However, Eric was taken in by her big eyes and pretty face.'

Charlie thought he wasn't the only one. He himself had thought she was very attractive while PC Williamson had positevly drooled in her presence.

'Will you both have to sell up?' he asked.

'No,' said Eric. 'The house is all paid for, and Magda has her own money which we will live on, but I will still have to sell the shop. I'm getting on a bit now, so retirement will be a bit of a novelty which we hope we both will enjoy.'

Charlie said he was glad, and he meant it.

The next call was to the Colliers' and Mrs Collier was pleased to hear all the items had been recovered, especially her collection of gold sovereigns The other two families said the same.

That just left the Bells. They were sitting in the lounge enjoying the view with their breakfast coffee. Seeing Charlie, Mr Bell said, 'You've just caught me before I go to the office. I was going to get in touch with you. Do you remember you asked me if any of us had any dealings with two hotels?'

Charlie said he did remember.

'Well it now turns out that my parents stayed at the Briar Hotel in Edinburgh overnight before catching their train in the morning. We didn't know this until they came back from their holiday. Dad says my mother was telling some of the staff about how successful I was with my own business and the waitress asked where we lived and she told her. The girl said it was a small world because she herself came from Dundee, as did her boyfriend who also worked here.' He stopped and folded his newspaper. 'Is that important?'

Charlie said it was and thanked the man for mentioning it.

When he got back to the station, he updated this information in his report.

78

One of the first women to be interviewed for a domestic job was one of Maisie and Alice's neighbours. Mrs Young was forty years old with two grown-up children. A small, jolly woman with dark hair set in a tight perm and a ready smile, she was ideal for the job and Molly hired her at once.

When she left, Molly hoped the other three would be as easy to hire. The second person that day was for the secretarial side. Lorna Hammond was in her early thirties. Tall and very thin, she was well dressed and had a great reference from her first and only job in the accounts office of DM Brown's where she had worked after she left Morgan's Academy.

'I've been there since leaving school,' she explained. 'I've recently got married and feel I need to experience different companies and new people.' She smiled. 'I suppose you can say I feel a bit stifled there and I thought this post would offer a variety of jobs.'

Molly almost said she would certainly have that. 'I feel I have to warn you about giving up a steady and reliable job, Mrs Hammond. I try and keep everyone employed but there are some times when the work might not be an eight-hour day or even a five-day week.' She added quickly, 'So far that hasn't happened but I do like to warn potential staff.'

Lorna said that would suit her very well. That is, if Miss McQueen wanted her.

Molly said she did.

The third person turned out to be a sixteen-year-old girl who had not long left school. She arrived clutching her school leaving certificate which gave good passes in shorthand, typing and bookkeeping. For a brief moment Molly thought she was back in 1953 and interviewing Mary again. Evelyn Carter was keen and very pretty. Molly was unsure of hiring her, though, as she felt she needed someone more mature. She was losing Mary who had grown into a proficient worker but she had Maggie who was doing well but was still learning. Molly didn't know if she could have two such learners on the team.

Then she had a sudden recall of her own very first job and how the interviewer had thought she was too young. She made up her mind and told Lorna she had got the job. Lorna didn't do a somersault but she jumped up with glee and Molly thought for a panic-stricken moment she was going to give her a hug.

It was almost six o'clock when the final interview took place. Thankfully the last woman, Miss Clark, was quieter. Middle-aged, she had just come from her job as a spinner in the Manhattan jute mill. She explained she wanted out of the stoury mill and, as she had always enjoyed housework, she wondered if she could maybe take it up professionally.

Molly had never met anyone who said they enjoyed housework so she was a first. She reviewed the staff list. Alice would be leaving at some point to have her baby and June would be going to university, which left Maisie, Irene and Mrs Young.

By now Molly was getting tired by all the questions so she made a snap decision and said she could start work the following week. One plus in her favour was her address at the foot of the Hilltown, which was just yards away from the agency. Miss Clark thanked her politely and went home, no doubt to have her tea.

Molly sat for another hour, thinking how far she had come with the agency. In the beginning she had only Edna, Mary and a few of her friends who helped out. Now she was running a payroll for four more workers, as well as her permanent staff. The agency was certainly on the Dundee map and she should have been proud of her achievements. Why then was she feeling so insecure, as if she was walking on ice and afraid she would fall through it?

79

Mary and Stan's wedding day was at the beginning of August. It was a typical summer day with rain in the morning then some sunshine in the afternoon. The ceremony was in Clepington Church with the reception next door in the church hall. Everyone at the agency had been invited but the office had to stay open on a Saturday in case there were customers. Molly had told Jean she would stay behind and let her go to the church with her husband but Jean had said they would just like to go later in the day to the reception. Charlie couldn't manage to the church but he had promised to come later after his shift finished.

Molly sat in one of the pews along with Edna, John, Irene and Billy. Behind them were Alice, Sandy, Maisie, Maggie and June. Molly wondered if Deanna would manage to come but she thought probably not as there were two performances at the theatre on the Saturday. That was why she was surprised when Deanna came in with Brian. She looked stunning in a blue suit with a large matching hat. Heads turned round in the church as they managed to squeeze in beside Molly. She whispered that she wasn't needed that afternoon but would have to be back for the evening performance. Everyone was so pleased to see her and her very handsome boyfriend.

Stan came in with his best man, Phil. Another great-looking guy. Stan seemed nervous but it was always the waiting for the bride that was the problem.

Then Mary's mother, brother and various other members of the family sat down in the front pews and the organist played various hymns. The church was beautifully decorated with flowers and once again the solemnity of the occasion gave her a spiritual uplift.

Then the organist stopped playing for a brief moment and the church went quiet until he played the 'Bridal March', the notes of the organ soaring and filling the church. Mary appeared with her father and two bridesmaids. She looked ethereal in her white dress and veil, carrying a bouquet of white roses and small lilac flowers. Molly felt a lump in her throat when she saw her. She looked at Edna and saw she was the same.

The bridesmaids were dressed in lilac chiffon dresses. Molly recognised the older girl as Rita, Mary's friend, but she didn't know the other one. Mary's dad had his plaster off; his broken arm must have healed.

The wedding service was lovely but like all good things it was over too soon. Then they were all outside in the sunshine as the photographer took his pictures. Edna stood beside Molly and said, 'She hardly looks like the wee lassie that started work two years ago.'

Molly said that was right, and although she didn't put her thoughts into words, she wondered if she was getting old. It was the fault of all these weddings this year. It made someone who wasn't married feel like Methuselah.

Inside the hall everything was set out for the wedding meal and the agency staff all stood together with their glasses of sherry. Deanna was the centre of their attention. Maisie, Alice, Irene and Edna all wanted to hear her news because they hadn't seen her since she left. Maggie was listening to her and Molly could see that she was mesmerised by her.

'It must be great being an actress, Molly,' Maggie said.

Molly said it was probably like any other kind of job. 'I would think it'd be hard work learning your lines and having to remember them in front of crowds of people.'

Maggie said she hadn't thought of that. 'Anyway, I prefer my job to anything else.' She turned when the best man walked past. 'I wonder who that super-looking man is?'

Molly said it was Stan's best friend who was on leave from his

National Service in Germany. 'He got married to Linda last weekend.' She pointed to a very pretty girl in a blue and white frock and high-heeled white sandals. Molly had got all this information from Mary, that was why she was so knowledgeable.

When the photos were all taken, the guests sat down at the tables that lined the walls. There was a small table with a three-tier wedding cake. There was soup for starters with steak pie, potatoes and vegetables, followed by ice cream with fruit jelly and a cup of tea.

Afterwards, when everyone was sitting waiting for the band to arrive, Mrs Watt came and sat beside Molly. 'Mary is a lovely bride, isn't she?' said Mrs Watt.

Molly agreed wholeheartedly. 'Edna and I were just saying how quickly time has gone. We still remember her as a schoolgirl with her hair in plaits.'

Mrs Watt said they hadn't been happy about her getting married so young. 'Stan has promised us that if she doesn't like Hong Kong or if it become a dangerous place to live then he'll bring her home and we trust him.'

Molly said he was a very trustworthy young man and perhaps Mary would love living in another country.

Mrs Watt wasn't a hundred percent sure about that, but you had to let your children go when the time came, she said.

The dancing had begun and after the first waltz, Mary and Stan came over to speak to Molly. Molly said Mary was looking radiant and wished them both good luck in their new country.

Mary smiled then said, 'I'm so pleased Deanna could make it. Didn't she look fabulous? She's had to leave now but it was great meeting up with her again. Stan and I told her if she ever wants to work in the theatre in Hong Kong then we'll put her up.'

As the evening wore on there was no sign of Charlie but at eight o'clock he suddenly put in an appearance. He had obviously gone home to change because he had a small cut on his chin where he had shaved. He sat down beside her. 'There must be something about weddings that brings on a spate of criminal activity in the town,' he said.

'So you've had a hard day?'

'I've had a hectic day and it'll probably be worse tomorrow.'

'Well I'm ready to go home soon as I have to see my parents tomorrow,' said Molly. 'They will be leaving in a couple of weeks and I said I would help them pack what they want to take with them and take the car over to the flat. Dad has a job with a man who owns a boat-building firm and he's offered them a furnished house to live in. He's told them they can stay in it for as long as they like or if they want to get something else it'll be up to them.'

'So that's why they're not selling their house at the moment,' said Charlie.

'No. Marigold will look after it and also keep Sabby the cat. She reckons they may want to come home after a wee while but I'm not sure.'

An hour later the happy couple said goodbye to all their guests and left on their honeymoon. There were a few dances afterwards but most people started to get ready to leave soon after Stan and Mary had gone. Molly, too, put on her coat and said cheerio to everyone.

As they walked down the hill to Dens Road, Charlie said his flat was just across the street. 'You've never been in my flat, Molly. Do you want to see it?'

Molly said she did so they climbed the two flights of stairs and he unlocked one of the doors on the landing. It was clear that he had been in a rush to get to the wedding because his clothes were piled up on one of the living room chairs. He deftly gathered them up in one quick move and went through into the other room.

When he came back he said, 'It's not as cosy as your place but it suits me.'

Molly thought it was all right. 'You've painted it a nice colour and I like your paintings.' She studied the three pen-and-ink drawings of Dundee streets from the last century. She then said it was time to go home. 'I'll catch the bus at the bottom of the road so just you stay here.'

'No, wait till I put on my jacket and I'll walk down to the stop with you.'

As they stood at the bus stop, Charlie said, 'Well that's another wedding over.'

Molly agreed with him. 'Yes it's certainly been a year for getting married.'

Charlie went to say something but the bus arrived, so he said, 'I'll see you tomorrow.'

80

Molly was busy helping her mother pack for leaving. They had already boxed up sentimental items that her parents had earmarked for shipping out to their new home. Things like their wedding china and photos and other objects that Nancy wanted around her in her Australian house.

As Molly went around the house, she became more depressed. Seeing her parents' belongings packed into boxes for the journey made the fact that her parents were leaving truly sink in. She didn't know what she would do once they had gone.

Nancy said, 'I do wish you were coming with us, Molly. It would be a big worry from our minds.'

Molly laughed and said she was a big girl now and capable of looking after herself.

Nancy said she knew that. 'It's just that we were hoping you and Charlie might be married by now and you could be living here.'

'Mum, Charlie hasn't asked me to marry him.'

Nancy looked unabashed. 'Well he should have, after all the time you've known him.'

Molly very sensibly stayed silent.

'Your dad and I have left money with our solicitor and Marigold will be able to draw on it to pay any bills as they arrive. I also hope you will stay here and look after the place for us.'

'Mum, why didn't you sell it before going away?'

'It was your dad's doing. He wanted you to have somewhere to live if the agency ever closed. But if we still like Australia after a couple of years then we will consider selling it.'

Molly thought Marigold had been right when she said her

parents wanted their new lives to succeed but they weren't altogether sure. This was their back-up plan in case the move didn't work out.

This revelation cheered her up.

Betty Holden had gathered all her brother's things together and placed them in a trunk which she put up in the loft. She felt sad at shutting away her memories of him but his death had left a big hole in her life. Especially the brutal way he died, which could have been avoided if that blasted cutting hadn't appeared in the paper.

How strange it was, she thought, how old sins had a nasty way of resurfacing and causing havoc in the present.

The last item she had put away was his diary for 1947. She had read and re-read it and felt morose at all the sad things that had happened, not only to the Pritchard family but to everyone else who worked in the tea gardens of India.

She knew she was now the only one of her Reid family left, but she took some comfort from the fact that she had lots of friends. *I'm really very lucky*, she thought.

Maisie was in Mrs Jankowski's house. She had arrived to find the woman looking at her photo album again. She had the page opened to the photos of her niece with her mother and father, all of them looking happy and carefree.

Maisie said, 'You must miss your family.'

Mrs Jankowski said she did, very much so. 'My husband and I come here years ago and we leave my sister Bertha, her husband Boris and little Maria. They are all well. Then Maria she dies with diphtheria and they are inconsolable. We say to them, come here and live with us but Bertha says she can't leave little Maria behind in the cemetery. I tell her that Maria isn't there any more, that she lives on in the hearts of her parents but Bertha doesn't want to leave her.'

Maisie said that was sad. 'Did they come over later?'

Mrs Jankowski shook her head. 'No, they leave it too late.

Because Boris was Jewish and they had been married in the synagogue, when Hitler marched into Poland they are taken away to the concentration camp. We never see or hear from them ever again.'

Maisie said how sorry she was to hear that.

'You know something, Maisie. Life is very fragile and we don't know how breakable it is until it's broken. We think we can control our lives but we cannot. Other people and events shape them, sometimes for good and other times for evil. If we realised how fragile our lives were then we could maybe look after ourselves a bit better.' She closed the album and put it on the bookshelf.

Maisie stayed silent for minute or two then said, 'Aye, you're right, Mrs Jankowski.'

Edna and John weren't expecting James on the Sunday afternoon but he arrived looking cheerful. He carried a brown paper package under his arm.

Edna said it was lovely to see him.

'I've brought some good news,' he said. 'I had a letter from Sonia yesterday to say she has recently married Leonard.'

John asked him if he was unhappy about that but James said it was the best news he had had for ages.

'I brought this painting for you both to look at. I thought of giving it to Sonia as a wedding present. What do you think?'

They both thought it was excellent.

'It's a view of Arbroath harbour and Sonia always hated my "seaside postcard paintings" as she called them so I just wondered if this would go down a treat.'

John laughed. 'You've always had a mischievous streak, James. I bet she'll hate it.'

81

At the end of August, Molly, Charlie and Marigold stood on the railway platform at Wormit Station. Molly had driven the car from the house to help Archie and Nancy with their luggage on their way to a new life.

Molly had promised herself not to cry but when the time came, she burst into tears. Hating herself for making her parents look more worried than ever, she tried to smile. 'Write soon, Mum and Dad, and give us all your news.'

One good thing about saying goodbye at the station was that once the train arrived there was little time for prolonged farewells. The train drew into the little station with a huge puff of steam and once Nancy and Archie were seated, Charlie got the four large suitcases into their compartment. Then the guard blew his whistle and they were off.

Nancy opened the window and she was also crying. 'I don't know if we've made the right decision,' she said as the wind whipped her words away with the steam.

Molly shouted back, 'Yes you have, Mum and Dad. Enjoy your new lives, both of you.'

Archie appeared at his wife's side. 'Keep your chin up, Molly.' Then the train set off across the Tay Bridge and they were lost to her sight.

When her parents were gone and they were heading toward the car, Molly said, 'Dad always used to say that to Nell and me when we were small, especially if we fell or had an argument with our friends.'

They drove Marigold back to her house then caught the morning Fifie to Dundee. Charlie would be a little late for work but he had explained the situation and he had got some time off.

'I'll be round tonight, Molly, and remember what your dad told you.'

She nodded.

Then instead of going into the office she headed towards the High Street to a travel shop situated beside Green's Picture House.

Charlie arrived after teatime. He seemed excited and out of breath. 'I've got something I want to say, Molly.'

Molly said she also had something important to tell him.

Charlie said, 'Well, you go first.'

She hesitated. 'I made up my mind this morning, Charlie, that I'm going to Australia as well.'

He looked shocked. 'What, for good?'

'No, only for a holiday. I leave at the beginning of October and I'll be able to see how Mum and Dad settle in then be there for the new baby. I haven't seen Nell and Terry since 1953 and I've never seen little Molly.'

'What about your agency?' he asked.

'I've thought it all out. Jean and Edna will run the office side and Maisie and Irene will be in charge of the domestic set-up.' She looked at him. 'What did you want to tell me?'

He was on the verge of saying it was nothing but she wouldn't have believed him. He produced the small box from his pocket. 'I was going to ask you to marry me,' he said, holding out the engagement ring.

Molly was overcome with emotion. 'Oh, Charlie, it's gorgeous! Of course I'll marry you.'

'But you're going away to the other side of the world.'

'So why don't you come with me?'

He smiled as he put the ring on her finger. 'I think I will. Maybe not as long as you'll be there, but once we get this robbery trial and the Douglas Kingsley affair over with, then I'll ask for an extended holiday.'

Molly said, 'Good. Well that's settled then. In fact, why don't we get married while we're there?'

Charlie smiled. 'Do you know something, Molly. That's a brilliant idea.'